LIVING THE GOOD LIFE

CELIA ANDERSON

B

Boldwood

First published in Great Britain in 2025 by Boldwood Books Ltd.

Copyright © Celia Anderson, 2025

Cover Design by Rachel Lawston

Cover Images: Rachel Lawston

A CIP catalogue record for this book is available from the British Library.

Paperback ISBN 978-1-83617-155-3

Large Print ISBN 978-1-83617-156-0

Hardback ISBN 978-1-83617-154-6

Ebook ISBN 978-1-83617-157-7

Kindle ISBN 978-1-83617-158-4

Audio CD ISBN 978-1-83617-149-2

MP3 CD ISBN 978-1-83617-150-8

Digital audio download ISBN 978-1-83617-152-2

This book is printed on certified sustainable paper. Boldwood Books is dedicated to putting sustainability at the heart of our business. For more information please visit https://www.boldwoodbooks.com/about-us/sustainability/

Boldwood Books Ltd, 23 Bowerdean Street, London, SW6 3TN

www.boldwoodbooks.com

For Peggy Joy Laycock; my sunshine after the rain.

Happiness resides not in possessions and not in gold, happiness dwells in the soul.

— DEMOCRITUS

Some cause happiness wherever they go; others whenever they go.

— OSCAR WILDE

PROLOGUE

The three ladies sat in a row on the cottage garden wall sucking humbugs.

'We're like those wise monkeys, that's what we are,' said Beryl, shrugging off her cardigan with what she felt was gay abandon. After all, it was only the beginning of June, and there had been a nasty run of chilly weeks before today. The cold wasn't good for arthritic bones, which was why the three friends took as many holidays together as they could afford and was one of the reasons that locally they were known as the Saga Louts.

Winnie, distracted by her efforts to find the property that they were sitting in front of on Rightmove, raised her head. 'There's a bad signal down this lane. What are you talking about now?'

'*See no evil, hear no evil, speak no evil.* I bet that's been said before about us.'

'So which monkey are you, Beryl?' said the third of the trio, whose name was Anthea. She was more elegant than the others, dressed in layers of linen in various shades of earthy green and brown. No woolly cardigan could be seen in Anthea's wardrobe, unless it had a designer label and called itself a shrug. 'I want to be *speak no evil*, because I'm not so likely to blab what I'm thinking as you two.'

'Ha! That's a matter of opinion. I'll be *see no evil*, because I like to see the best in people,' said Beryl. 'Winnie can be *hear no evil* because she's deafer than the rest of us.'

'What's that? What did you say?' said Winnie, peering at her phone and giving it a shake. 'This new handset the shop in town sold me is totally rubbish. They must have seen me coming. I just wanted to see how much this place has sold for. It's not much to ask.'

They all twisted round to look at the cottage behind them. It wasn't a pretty sight at the moment. All the window frames needed a coat of paint and so did the front door, which had once been red. The garden was badly overgrown with bramble bushes everywhere and the roof had a thick layer of yellowy-green moss.

'I like a house to look a bit weathered, but this one is going to take some sorting. Do you remember when Hollyhocks was one of the nicest properties in the village?' said Beryl. 'Poor old Edwin really let it go. Mind you, he wasn't well, and that daughter of his...' She sniffed, and the others nodded in agreement.

'Anyway, it's going to have new people in it next week, or so I've heard,' said Anthea. 'They're from somewhere up north. Sheffield, I'm told. Three of them, apparently.'

The other two looked interested. Beryl nudged her friend, almost toppling her off the wall. 'Where did you get that info from? You made it up, didn't you?'

'I most certainly did not. Kate at the café told me yesterday, and she had it from Joel, and he had it from the butcher, and *he* had it straight from the vicar.'

That appeared to settle the matter. The Rev Bev could definitely be trusted. She'd probably be struck by a thunderbolt if she lied, Beryl thought. Their young vicar might look a bit skittish with her spiky auburn hair (renewed to full glory every six weeks) and her many piercings, but she'd proved herself to be just what the sleepy parish of Willowbrook needed.

'I hope the new people are going to fit in,' she said. 'They'll not be used to village life, coming from a big place like Sheffield. Ingrid got on all right though when she moved down here from York, didn't she? I wonder if they'll bring as much stuff with them as she did.'

'That's hardly likely, is it?' Anthea smiled at the memory. 'Ingrid had a whole shop full of tat.'

Beryl thought back to the previous spring, when Ingrid Copperfield had landed in Willowbrook. The Saga Louts were not only renowned for their fondness for adventures but were also generous hosts and more than happy to share their prosecco. Ingrid, although a little wary to begin with and much younger than the three, had become an occasional member of the group and was now one of their best friends.

'Ingrid soon shifted all her stuff though, didn't she? Who'd have thought people would buy so much junk?' Winnie said. 'It was a nice change to have The Treasure Trove at the end of your road for a little while, Beryl, but it's even better to get a proper village store back now Ingrid's moved across to the country park. I miss her being handy, but Mr and Mrs Habeeb in the shop seem nice. They're stocking our favourite teabags now and they've got a whole range of my Caribbean spices on the shelves. I only had to ask once.'

The three sat in silence for a while, thinking back to recent times when they'd plunged headfirst into helping Ingrid to set up her emporium to get rid of all those accumulated and inherited belongings. It had been fun.

'Maybe the new people at Hollyhocks will end up being our friends too?' suggested Winnie, giving up on her phone with a sigh. 'They might be interesting. I wish it was still like the old days when the gentry called with their cards after a decent interval to suss out new arrivals, don't you, Beryl? Like in *Downton Abbey*? We need a carriage.'

'You think we're the gentry?'

'Well, Anthea's quite posh. We could send her to set the tone.'

Anthea smiled. 'If we're going to visit the newcomers, we'll do what we always do – stick together. We don't want to scare them though. Anyway, they're bound to want to make friends. Everyone likes to fit in when they move to a new place, don't they?'

Beryl looked doubtful, and she was right to be so. Two of the incoming Willowbrook residents would turn out to be very keen to immerse themselves in village life. The third... well, not so much.

1

THE PREVIOUS JANUARY

Nell watched the man in the front garden hammering a For Sale sign into the hedge and cursed him, deep inside her heart. It wasn't that she was against the move. Not totally, anyway. Well, fairly against it, if she was being honest. The man looked up and caught her eye as she stood in the doorway, arms folded. He stepped back a pace and visibly flinched.

'Erm... you okay, love? This is the right house, ain't it? You *are* Mrs Appledore?' he said, scratching his head.

Nell made her face smile. It must have looked like a rictus grin, she realised, because it didn't seem to help. 'Yes, yes – this is the one for sale,' she said. 'I just...'

'Oh, I get it. Forced move?' he said sympathetically. 'We get a lot of those. It'll be fine, mark my words. Going somewhere a lot smaller on your tod, are you?'

With a shock, Nell realised he was assuming she was in the process of a divorce, or similar, instead of relocating to an idyllic village with her husband Barney and his not so idyllic father. You couldn't blame Frank for his moods though, she told herself hastily. Ever since his beloved wife had died, he'd lived a kind of shadow life, with only his dog, Anton, for company. Perhaps the move was just what they all needed. Perhaps.

The man from the sign company was clearly tired of waiting for a response. He picked up his toolbox and raised a hand in farewell as he sauntered back to his van. Nell contemplated shouting after him that she wasn't a dejected, deserted wife, but decided against it because it was none of his business. Anyway, she did feel quite dejected today, even if she wasn't being deserted.

The familiar *thunk, shuffle, thunk* sound of someone approaching from beyond the thick yew hedge was a welcome distraction. 'Hello, Frank,' Nell said. 'Is it teatime already?'

'No, but I was hungry,' said her father-in-law. 'Have you got any cake?'

'I think there's a piece of Victoria sandwich left,' Nell said doubtfully. 'But it might be a bit dry.'

'Didn't you make any more? Why not?'

Nell viewed Frank with mingled irritation and affection. It was true that she usually made sure he was never without his homemade cake fix, but today had been completely taken up with beginning the epic task of sorting many overflowing cupboards, drawers and chests, not to mention the garage and the loft. This family certainly knew how to hoard. Nell wondered if it was too late to try and get on one of those TV shows where they drag all your possessions out onto the back lawn and then hurl most of them into a skip. She shuddered at the thought. The trouble was, she wanted to keep almost everything.

'So, are you putting the kettle on, or what?' Frank was skirting round her now and making his way into the house and down the hall, almost toppling when his walking stick caught on the first of the bags that were heading for the charity shop.

Nell followed him as he entered the kitchen and flopped down into his usual chair by the Aga. The day had begun with a shower of rain and Nell was glad of the warmth too. She filled the kettle and set it on the hob to boil, waiting for the comforting whistle as she assembled cups, saucers, milk jug and sugar bowl. Frank had always been a stickler for doing things properly, even more so since Lottie was no longer there to keep an eye on him in the kitchen. Nell had tried to convert him to her way because the delicate china cups and saucers didn't seem to last long, especially when Frank was doing his own washing up. He would let the tap run until the steam rose, fill a bowl with hot, soapy water and then shoot the whole lot in, china or not. Nell had even bought Frank a substantial mug with his initial on and a picture of a cricket bat, but the disgusted *humph* sound he'd made when she'd first produced it meant it was now languishing at the back of the cupboard.

'Where's Anton today?' Nell asked. It was unusual to see Frank without his faithful sidekick.

'He's having a nap. I took him right round the park this morning. He's not as young as he was. Someone I was chatting to thought he had a bit of terrier in him,' Frank said proudly. 'Or possibly beagle.'

Privately, Nell and Barney had always thought that Anton had a bit of most kinds of dog in his background. He'd been found as a small, unkempt puppy abandoned on a rubbish tip some years previously but in Frank's eyes, Anton was as beautiful as any pedigree hound. He had a definite smile when he was in the right mood, hence his name. Frank's wife had been a big fan of *Strictly Come Dancing*.

Usually, Frank would be more than happy to extol the

virtues of his pet for some time when Anton's name was mentioned but he seemed preoccupied today. 'Are you feeling a bit under the weather, Nellie?' he asked, as Nell handed him his tea.

Nell was so surprised she almost dropped the cup and saucer in his lap. She couldn't remember any other time when Frank had noticed her mood or asked about her health, at least not in the last few years, when Lottie's slowly worsening dementia had overtaken all other concerns.

'I'm fine,' she said, not meeting his eyes. It was one thing being fed up, but another matter taking someone else down with you. Nell knew that Frank was even less enthusiastic about the move to Willowbrook than she was, but Barney had his heart set on downsizing and living life at a different pace. So far, he'd breezed through any objections of theirs as he waxed lyrical about the peaceful village with every facility you could wish for. In Barney's opinion, the change couldn't come soon enough.

'I wouldn't worry,' Frank said. 'We've got to sell my house and yours before we can go anywhere. It could take months. It might never happen. And then there's always the chance that the place our Barney's set his heart on will sell before we get to the point of being able to make a firm offer.'

Nell viewed him over the rim of her own teacup. It was tempting to think Frank was right. She knew how hard he was finding every single day without Lottie in his life, and in Nell's opinion uprooting Frank from the home he'd shared with her beautiful, gentle mother-in-law was nothing short of cruel. If both their houses weren't snapped up fairly quickly, it was likely that the cottage in Willowbrook would be bought by a developer. Looking at the details online, Nell could see that it was clearly in need of a lot of TLC, but it was oozing bucolic charm and was at the end of a quiet lane, only minutes from the village amenities.

It would take a lot of luck for Barney to get all his ducks in a row in time to seal a deal, Nell thought to herself. There was probably no need to worry. But as it happened, those treacherous ducks had ideas of their own, and even as Nell and Frank shared the last piece of Victoria sponge, Barney's dream was beginning to look very much like a reality.

2

JUNE

'It ought to be raining.'

Barney looked across at his wife as she stood by the bedroom window, gazing out over the sunlit garden. He frowned. Had Nell flipped? Her short, snowy-white hair looked wilder than usual, as if she'd been running her fingers through it in agitation. Nell had had an abundance of flowing auburn locks when she and Barney had first met. The combination of the hair and Nell's startlingly gentian-blue eyes completely bowled him over and he was instantly smitten. However, just like her mother before her, Nell's hair had turned white well before she was forty years old, much to her disgust. Barney loved her unusual but very stylish look but when the hair stood on end it was normally a sign for the family to beware. There was no secret as to why she was stressed right now. He knew full well that his wife had been under a lot of pressure with all the sorting and packing and charity shop trips. He'd not expected it to be easy for her, giving up years of much-loved possessions and mementos, but this was their long-awaited Moving Day, and the last thing they needed was to arrive at the new cottage in the rain and find a sea of mud.

When Barney didn't reply, Nell turned to him, her face streaked with tears.

'Look at you, standing there as if you haven't a care in the world. We're leaving our home, Barney. We brought our children up here. It's been such a happy place for years and years. Aren't you even a little bit sad?' Barney looked away. Nell paused and rubbed her eyes. 'Anyway, at the very least the weather should have the decency to pour with rain instead of all this... this bloody sunshine.'

With that, she turned on her heel and marched out of the empty room, almost knocking over Frank who was on his way in, leaning heavily on his walking stick. Behind him trailed Anton, looking almost as dejected as his master. The dog's tail drooped, and his trademark grin was absent.

'Sorry, Frank,' Nell muttered as she shouldered past him. 'Just going to check the men have finished loading. Have you packed your medication somewhere we can get hold of it if we need to?'

Frank shrugged. 'I thought you were organising all that kind of thing,' he said. 'I've had my work cut out making sure Anton isn't traumatised by it all.'

Nell opened her mouth to reply, but obviously thought better of whatever retort she'd been going to fire at her father-in-law. Barney breathed a sigh of relief as she clattered down the stairs. All the rooms were echoing emptily now. It was true that a rainy day would have matched Nell and his father's mood better, but for himself, he was riding high on a wave of excitement. A new start in a peaceful country village with more time on his hands to explore the place and to maybe have a few hobbies for a change. Total bliss.

'Look at you,' said Frank, coming over to stand beside his son. 'Like the cat that's got the cream, that's what you are. It's sickening. Why do we all have to uproot ourselves just because you've been watching too many of those stupid TV shows about living near cows and sheep and weaving your own underpants?'

He sniffed, and Barney was alarmed to see that his cantankerous father was closer to tears than he'd ever seen him in his whole life. He put a tentative arm around the old man's shoulders, but it was shaken off before he could turn the gesture into a proper hug. Frank had never been one for demonstrations of affection and today wasn't shaping up to be the best time to start.

'I thought you were starting to be okay with the idea of moving,' Barney began, but Frank held up a hand.

'You wanted to think I was okay, but you haven't listened to anything I've said. You were too busy trying to get your own way with poor Nell. What about me missing my old mates, eh? The domino nights at the pub, the bowls club, the trips to the seaside on the coach with a few cans and a bag of sausage rolls apiece. How am I going to find anyone to talk to, buried in the back of beyond? They're all going to be too posh for me. I bet they all have "sappah" instead of their tea. I want to stay here.'

Barney could hear an ominous series of crashes and clangs coming from downstairs, suggesting it was almost time to leave. Their old piano was coming with them after much discussion, and the removal men wanted to leave it until last. Nell had wanted to have a specialised removal firm to transport it, but the possible cost of doing that alarmed them both. The piano had sentimental value, having belonged to Nell's mother, but nobody played it these days and it needed tuning so badly that no amount of shaking it around could make it sound any worse, Barney reflected sadly.

He turned his attention back to Frank, who was now blowing his nose and doing a lot of blinking. This was awful. It was true that he'd put in hours of effort persuading Nell that the radical move was a good plan but he had given a lot less time and thought to his father. He'd assumed that Nell would have talked to Frank while he was at work and smoothed out any ruffled feathers and reservations, playing up the advantages of them all living under one roof instead of Frank being half a mile down the road in a house that was too big for him and was showing signs of needing thousands spent on it before too long. It looked very much as if this wasn't the case.

Remorse washed over Barney. Frank had clung grimly to his independence since his wife had died, but the onset of rheumatism was making life very hard for his father these days and Nell had shouldered the extra care he'd needed even though so much of her time lately had still been taken up volunteering at the homeless centre in town.

'I think someone's calling us,' Barney hedged. 'The men must have finished loading the piano. Let's get this show on the road, Dad, and we can talk later. I'm sure you'll find lots of new friends in Willowbrook. There's a great pub. It's called The Fox and Fiddle. They do food and there was a darts match going on when Nell and I called in to recce. The locals play cricket on the village green most weekends too,' he added, clutching at a window of hope.

'Hmm. Cricket, eh? You didn't tell me that before.' Frank was following Barney out of the room now and making steady progress down the stairs with Anton at his heels. 'Well, I just hope you haven't made the biggest mistake of your life, son. Reducing your hours at the office, working from home... it's not going to be a picnic, you mark my words.'

Barney watched as the door of the second van slammed behind the piano. Nell was looking anywhere but at him as she wiped her eyes and he could feel the waves of antagonism still emanating from Frank, even after the mention of cricket and the pub.

He turned to look at the house that had been home for so long. The windows were still curtained because Nell had decided to start afresh, with curtains at least, but the place had a forlorn look about it already. He felt like a deserter, leaving the sanctuary that had sheltered the family almost from the moment they'd known Elliot was on the way. Their twin daughters had been born only a couple of years later, and before very long he'd been erecting a swing, building a tree house and playing football on the long, rather scrubby lawn at weekends.

'Are you both ready to go?' Nell asked, pushing a crumpled tissue into the pocket of her jeans and squaring her shoulders.

Barney nodded and held out an arm to help Frank into the car. Was it true that they were making the biggest mistake of their lives? Well, there was only one way to find out.

'We're ready, aren't we, Dad?' he said.

Frank didn't answer. His bushy eyebrows were pulled close together and the set of his mouth was mutinous under the grey moustache. Even Frank's beard looked angry. Barney recognised the glower. It had been a familiar sight over recent months. Sadness had always translated into crossness with his father, and it was hard to know how to help him.

'Right, follow that van,' Barney said brightly, as they pulled out of the drive. 'And let's hope Anton holds on to his breakfast. In an hour or two we'll be on the brink of our brand-new life. I can't wait, can you?'

There was no reply, either from Frank beside him in the passenger seat or Nell in the back. Anton, safe behind the dog guard, let out a small whimper. Barney heaved a sigh. It looked as if he was in sole charge of jollity today. Ah well, that was no more than he'd expected. They'd all be fine once they got used to living in Willowbrook. Fresh air, pub lunches with local beer, long walks around the nearby country park, time to spend together instead of trying to fit too much into every day. What could possibly go wrong?

3

Nell finished unpacking the box containing the contents of her desk and put the last piece of bubble-wrap in a bin bag by her side. She'd already polished the treasured piece of furniture, making the walnut and leather surface gleam. It was good to be able to make at least one small corner of the house feel normal. Nell belatedly tore the top page off her desk calendar and frowned at the sickeningly cute picture of a puppy sitting in the middle of a bed of petunias. Really? Whoever dreamed up these ridiculous scenarios? She supposed because it was June, everyone was supposed to still feel full of the joys of spring, with summer just around the corner and the prospect of barbecues with friends in the garden.

The garden at Hollyhocks Cottage was full of weeds and overgrown shrubs, with a creaking plum tree that looked as if it badly needed pruning. It was in no way barbecue ready and anyway, she and Barney didn't know anyone to invite round. All their old friends and neighbours were safely ensconced in their comfortable Sheffield homes, enjoying the benefits of a bustling northern city. Nell ached for her previous life. Yes, the village was pretty and the lane where they now lived was tranquil compared to the old house on the edge of town, but she desperately missed the camaraderie of the homeless centre and even the roar of the traffic past her bedroom window when she woke every morning.

As she slid further and further into melancholy, Nell heard Frank approaching the room that was going to be a shared study for herself and Barney. At the moment, their two desks jostled for space due to all the boxes piled up around them, but Nell had made sure there was a high-backed chair in here for her father-in-law in case he wanted company, and a soft blanket for Anton to doze on. Going by the noise downstairs, Barney was busy unpacking the various pieces of a new cupboard and she knew that Frank had always had a talent for standing wherever his son wanted space. Nell was uncomfortably aware that she should really be helping her husband because flat-pack assembly wasn't one of his life skills, but she'd suddenly craved solitude.

'Hello, love,' Frank said as he entered the small room, his stick clattering on the bare floorboards. 'Am I disturbing you? Are you writing? I was going to offer to give Barney a hand, but he seems a bit tetchy today, for some reason. He's trodden on poor Anton twice already.'

Nell smiled up at her father-in-law and gestured to the chair. She felt a wave of respect for the bravery with which he'd embraced this big move once the long day of departure was over. She'd heard from Barney that Frank was still much less than happy with the changes around him, but with her, he'd dropped his reservations and only been positive since they'd arrived at the cottage. Perhaps it was because he was aware that Nell had similar misgivings about living in a small village after the buzz of Sheffield.

'Are you okay, Frank?' she asked, as Anton subsided onto his blanket with a sigh of relief. It was a pointless question. Frank clearly wasn't okay. 'Is your bedroom cosy enough?'

'It's fine. I'm glad I brought my old double divan with me. It's seen a lot of life, has that bed. Our Barney was born in it and my Lottie died there. Mind you, in between times, we had some fun there, did me and Lottie. We broke the headboard twice. I don't know why there weren't more kids, after...' He paused and blinked hard. 'Well, anyway, we tried hard enough.'

The words hung in the air, and Nell found herself blushing. Even if you tried not to, it was quite possible to imagine Frank as a young man, leaping into bed with his pretty young wife and throwing caution to the winds as they joyfully tried to expand their family. It wasn't a welcome thought. He still had a maverick air about him and a twinkle in his eye when he'd had a drink.

'You won't be in the other spare bedroom forever. We'll have your annexe fixed up before too long, and then you and Anton will have your own space,' Nell promised, with more conviction than she felt. The two rooms plus a rudimentary bathroom tacked on to the back of the cottage were basic in the extreme at the moment. Barney was full of schemes to make them into a dream refuge for Frank, but with the best will in the world, Nell's husband could never have been described as the handy type. The only renovations he'd completed at their old house had been an airing cupboard with collapsing shelves and a louvred summerhouse which looked great from a distance but had been put together with all its panels upside down so that instead of rainwater running off the walls, it had seeped in, causing the electrics to fuse and mould to take over. There had been a fine crop of mushrooms growing in there when they'd left. Hopefully the new owners would demolish it before it collapsed on them.

'Cheer up, Frank. It's all going to work out in the end, I promise. Barney's so excited about the move,' Nell said, trying hard to sound enthusiastic. 'He says this is going to be a very good life for us all.'

'A good life? Oh dear. Is he imagining us all in that old TV sit com where the couple were busting a gut to have some sort of self-sufficient idyllic existence? The best thing about it was Felicity Whatsit with her lovely...'

'Lovely what? I don't remember that programme,' said Nell, totally confused now.

'Never mind that. He's going to have us growing all our own vegetables and living off the land before we know it. I bet before we know where we are he'll be buying a goat, you mark my words. Anton's not going to like that one bit.'

Frank settled himself in his chair and stretched out his long legs, wincing as his knees creaked. He rested a hand on Anton's silky head. 'I've been meaning to ask,' he said, not looking at Nell, 'whyever do you and our Barney sleep in separate bedrooms? I didn't realise that was a thing till we came here.'

Nell made an effort to switch to this brand new and definitely unwelcome topic of conversation. Sometimes Frank's thought processes were hard to follow these days. She bit her lip and wondered how to answer his question. The truth was that after Barney had had his near-death brush with cancer a couple of years previously, he'd stayed in their biggest spare bedroom, having removed himself from the shared one when he'd felt so ill and restless. Nell assumed he would come back when he was better, but it hadn't happened. She'd suggested it several times, but Barney always made excuses. It was hurtful, and she missed him dreadfully in the night. Whispered pillow talk had been a big feature of their marriage up until that point, and they'd often made each other giggle so much that their three children had needed to bang on the walls to make them stop.

'I... erm... we seem to sleep better if we have our own space,' Nell said eventually. 'Barney nods off as soon as his head hits the pillow these days and I like to read in bed. It's just what we do.'

Frank shook his head in disbelief. 'It doesn't seem right to me, but I suppose it's your choice. Anyway, that's beside the point. I've got something to ask you. It's about your writing. Is this your big moment, now that we've moved, and you've got a change of scene?' he said. 'More time on your hands too. Are you planning something epic?'

Nell, preoccupied with arranging her laptop and favourite pen pots on her desk, didn't register the question at first. Frank prodded her with his foot. 'I'm just saying, are you ready to write your book? I've always thought that all that volunteering stuff was stopping you from being creative. Now's your chance.'

Nell wasn't sure how to reply to this. For one thing, looking after Frank had been taking up at least as much of her time as the homeless centre. Not only that, although she'd had the burning desire to start a novel for years, now the opportunity had reared its head she had absolutely no idea where to begin. It was one thing getting a few short stories and letters to newspapers published, but a completely different ball game planning and writing a whole book.

'I'm still thinking about the plot,' she prevaricated. 'I need to get this place straight first.'

'Excuses,' said Frank. 'You can't play at houses and paint walls all day long. Give yourself a couple of hours a day just to cogitate and make some notes, that's my tip.'

This advice, from a man who had seldom written more than *best wishes* on a birthday card or his signature on a cheque, was galling to say the least. Nell gritted her teeth. 'I'll start when I'm ready,' she said. 'You can't rush the creative muse.'

Frank snorted loudly. 'Creative muse? Ha! Listen to yourself.

Just get on with it and write. You can tighten it up and sort the full stops and all that malarkey afterwards.'

Nell debated losing her temper in a very big way. She didn't do it often, but it would be so good to scream at Frank that she'd been busy. *Busy!* How did he think this move had happened? Okay, Barney had done the financial organising, but Nell had packed boxes, sorted removal vans, sent out numerous change-of-address cards and booked redirection of post. In the months before that she'd been helping with her mother-in-law's final care, trying to keep Frank from being submerged by grief, cleaning his house, cooking for him, making sure her daughters were packed off safely to their university in Edinburgh and bailing Elliot out when his overdraft became too big for even her impractical son to ignore.

'Have I upset you?' Frank asked mildly, looking at Nell's bright red face with some concern. 'I didn't mean to do that, it's just that I know you've put yourself on the back burner for a long time now. It's time for *you* to be happy, Nellie, not just our Barney.'

Nell stood up and went over to the window. She looked down at the jungle of the garden, took several deep breaths and counted to ten. Then ten more. The anger began to subside and after a minute or two she was able to turn and face Frank.

'I'm going to start my book, I really am,' she said, with as much confidence as she could muster. 'It's not as easy as you make it sound, you know.'

'Hmmm.' Frank's overgrown eyebrows were drawn close together. He placed his elbows on his knees and joined his fingertips together as he pondered. 'Well, I don't claim to know much about being an author...'

'You could've fooled me,' Nell muttered. He ignored her and carried on.

'I did read somewhere that you should write what you know. I'm not sure how that works if you want to start a murder mystery though. You can't really go out and biff someone over the head with a brick to see what it feels like.'

Nell didn't answer. She had no idea where this train of thought was going, and her mind was already wandering to what they might have for dinner. Frank clapped his hands together.

'I've got it. Write about a woman like you.' He sat back with a satisfied smile.

'A woman like me? And what sort of person is *she*, exactly?' Nell wasn't sure if she wanted to hear his answer. She waited, her heart beginning to race uncomfortably. She and Frank never had conversations like this. He treated her with absent-minded affection as a rule, and they definitely didn't go in for deep and meaningfuls.

'Well, someone who's always been a bit... stunted,' Frank said. When Nell didn't comment, mainly because she was so taken aback, he carried on. 'A woman who has dreams, but she's been too caught up with looking after everyone else to follow them. You could tell the story of how she learns how to be happy.'

Nell stared at her father-in-law, and he dropped his gaze first. 'That's hit the nail on the head, hasn't it?' he said gruffly. 'You're not very happy right now, are you?'

There was a long silence. Eventually Nell came back to sit at her desk.

'It's an interesting idea,' she said. 'But I'm fine really, Frank. It's just been a bit of a mad few weeks. Months...' she added.

'More like years,' said Frank. 'It's different for me. I'm seventy-six. I don't know how long I've got left to be a grumpy old bugger, but you've got lots more years. Lots of reasons to be happy. Plenty of new people still to meet and make friends with.'

Nell was still formulating her answer, horrified to think that not only did Frank think he might not have long to live but that he was also insinuating that she was sad and grumpy, when her husband's voice could be heard bellowing from downstairs.

'Nell! We're out of milk. Could you go to the shop and fetch some? I need a cup of tea.'

Frank and Nell exchanged glances. 'I don't know about being happy, but it looks as if I'm about to meet some new people,' she said, deciding now wasn't the time to tell Barney to get some milk himself. If she stopped him at this crucial stage of putting together an Ikea cupboard it could well stay in its flat state for months.

Nell ran downstairs two at a time, suddenly full of enthusiasm for getting away from Frank's barbed comments and the chaos of the house. She grabbed her purse and set off at a fast pace up the lane that led to Fiddler's Row with Frank's words still echoing around her head as she walked. Her own dad had been a big fan of Ian Drury and the Blockheads in the late seventies, and she remembered him playing his record of 'Reasons to be Cheerful, Part 3' until it was too scratched to function properly, but surely finding true happiness was a different matter from just being upbeat. Maybe cheerful would be a start though. She plastered a wide grin on her face as she entered the corner shop at the end of the road. After all, there was no point in giving the villagers the wrong impression.

4

———————

The shop bell clanged as Nell made her way inside, weaving her way around metal stands that contained a variety of items on offer. She picked up a basket and made her way to the back of the shop. There was a gaggle of customers at the counter waiting to be served and their heads had all turned as she walked in. It was unnerving to be the centre of so much attention, but Nell supposed that would be the norm for a while.

She ambled around the shelves, picking up milk as she passed the big fridge in the corner and adding a few random items that would do for lunch. When she finally reached the till, unable to delay the moment any longer, she let out a gasp. Arrayed to one side of it in glorious splendour were three shelves of crusty bread, currant buns, croissants and all sorts of other delicious-looking goods. The scent of freshly baked bread mingling with the sweet, buttery almond and cinnamon aromas of the pastries caused Nell's stomach to rumble loudly, a sound that, owing to a sudden lull in conversation, carried to the woman standing behind the till.

'That's exactly the effect I'm after,' she said, laughing. 'It gets most people. The baker I'm ordering from in Meadowthorpe knows his stuff, doesn't he? I'm Maryam. I don't think I've seen you in here before, have I? In fact, I know I haven't, because I'd have remembered your lovely hair.'

Nell automatically put a hand up to check her short mop and tried to tidy it. 'Hello, I'm Nell,' she said. 'I must look a right state. It's a bit breezy out there today. No, I haven't been anywhere much yet. We've just moved into Hollyhocks Cottage on Tinderbox Lane.'

'What an amazing address,' said Maryam. 'Welcome to Willowbrook, Nell. I'm a newcomer too but Rashid and me are beginning to find our feet now, thanks to these friendly residents.'

Maryam gestured to the small group still standing near the till. They were all gazing at Nell with interest. She felt her face flushing scarlet and cursed the fair complexion that always let her down at times like this.

'Hello there, duck. I'm Beryl and this is my friend Winnie,' said a small, bright-eyed lady who was clutching a bottle of prosecco and a bag of Danish pastries. 'We were going to call on you and introduce ourselves, but Winnie thought you might need a bit of time to settle in first.'

'Yes, we didn't want to crowd you, but it's nice to have new faces in Willowbrook,' said her friend, beaming at Nell. 'You're very welcome, isn't she, Maryam?'

The shopkeeper nodded and the other two people in the queue chipped in with their own comments. Soon Nell was in the middle of the group, being questioned from all sides about her new home, the work that would be needed to fix everything and who would do it.

'And what brings you to our little village, Nell?' Beryl asked, when the subject of the state of Hollyhocks Cottage had been

exhausted. 'We heard you were from up north? I expect everything's a bit different there. City life... and all that...' she finished
vaguely.

'Don't make Sheffield sound like another planet,' said
Maryam, laughing. 'There is life beyond Watford Gap, you
know.'

'So I've heard,' said Beryl. 'But you'll probably find things
very quiet in this neck of the woods, dear. Although, to be fair,
we do know how to enjoy ourselves. We like a good knees-up
when we get the chance, don't we, Winnie?'

'Oh, yes, we sure do, honey,' said her friend. 'There's the
bingo and the church groups and quiz nights at the pub and so
on, but if we get bored, we just go on holiday with our buddy
Anthea and paint the town red somewhere else.'

Beryl chuckled. 'Remember that time we went to Alicante,
Winnie? I tried topless sunbathing and got my bosoms burnt. It
was a hoot. Then there was you and that club singer? His name
was Dick, and it suited him because he *was* a bit of a—'

'Let's get everybody sorted, shall we? It's getting a bit
crowded in here,' said Maryam, taking pity on the newcomer
and beginning to serve the others which gradually eased them
all towards the door, still chattering. As the last one exited, she
turned to Nell.

'That was all pretty full-on for your first visit to our shop,
wasn't it? I hope it hasn't put you off for good. They mean well
and they're all very kind-hearted, but they do like to know everything. I felt as if I'd been turned inside out when Rashid and I
took over this place.'

'It's fine,' said Nell faintly, putting her basket on the counter.
She felt her head begin to spin and she reached out a hand to
steady herself.

'Are you okay? Come and sit down and I'll get you a drink of water,' said Maryam, pushing a wooden chair forward and reaching into a nearby fridge for a bottle. 'Are you feeling poorly?'

Nell sipped the water gratefully. 'I think I might have forgotten to have breakfast,' she said. 'It's not like me to starve myself. I guess I was busy when the others were ready to eat, and my husband sorted food out for himself and his dad. I was going to have something later...'

Her voice tailed away, and she sat back, relaxing for the first time that day. The shop was blissfully quiet now the customers had departed. Maryam seemed to sense that Nell needed some space. She busied herself ringing up Nell's milk and other purchases and put them into a cloth bag.

'I'm providing these bags for regulars,' Maryam said. 'Then they can bring them each time. We've had them printed with the shop's name. I'll give you one as you're a local now.'

Nell blinked and tried to focus on the words which stood out clearly in green on a cream background. The Treasure Trove. There was also a small outline of a treasure chest with a string of beads pouring out of it.

'I thought this was a food shop,' she said.

'It's that, yes, but it's a lot more. Have another look around next time you're here. The previous tenant had a plan to sell everything she didn't need and make her life simpler. When Ingrid left, there were just a couple of boxes of her treasures... and white elephants, frankly... that had been missed.'

Nell was interested now, and the woozy sensation was clearing. Maryam handed her a golden pastry from the shelf by the till. It was covered with toasted almonds. 'If you're anything like me you've been too busy to eat properly for a few days with all this moving house business? Yeah? So have this one on us.'

Almost on autopilot, Nell bit into the crumbly pastry. The

sugar hit was instant, and the intense flavour of almonds made her senses sing. In the centre of the croissant was soft, fragrant marzipan. Nell almost moaned with pleasure. When she could speak again, she mumbled through flakes of pastry, 'This is amazing. Thank you so much, it was just what I needed. Anyway, go on. Tell me more.'

Maryam laughed. 'That was all you needed to bring you back to life, wasn't it? So, Ingrid had got the attention of the villagers and people beyond Willowbrook with her idea and when we took over, although they were mostly pleased to have a traditional store back, they missed the excitement of not knowing what random pre-loved items might appear on the shelves. We decided to keep a corner just for treasures, and people bring their unwanted belongings here. We sell them and the money goes to the village hall fund to give the kids of Willowbrook a party every now and again.'

'That's wonderful.' Nell swallowed the last of the almond croissant and stood up. 'I must go and organise some lunch for the blokes now, but thanks so much for... for everything. I'll be back soon to look at the treasures.'

Maryam handed over the shopping bag and Nell looked at the other woman properly for the first time. She was stunning. Probably in her forties, her long, shining hair flowed down her back and her sari in shades of turquoise and gold reached right to her sequin-encrusted ballet slippers.

Catching her looking, Maryam smiled. 'My mother always wanted me to dress traditionally but I rebelled when we lived in Leicester. It's ironic, isn't it? Now she's gone, here I am wearing the full works. Rashid's the same. He's gone back to being traditional in his clothes since we came here. It's as if we're flying the flag for our heritage now that we're more out in the sticks, you know?'

'You look amazing,' said Nell. 'I'll be back in the shop soon. Most likely tomorrow because I don't seem to have got my act together with food yet.'

They said goodbye and Maryam was instantly distracted by a couple of young mums with prams who had entered the shop. As she walked home, Nell reflected on the shop and its unexplored treasure corner. She was sure this would be a place to visit and revisit often. Maybe she could sneak some of their own unwanted treasures in there. This shop was definitely a find.

5

The now-balmy month of June progressed quickly, and Nell began to enjoy the wild garden that wound its way right round Hollyhocks Cottage. Most days she tried to do a bit of tidying out there, slashing away at the bushes with her shears and revelling in the earthy, woody scents that she stirred up. Anton often kept her company, finding a new lease of life here too. He frolicked in the long grass, his ears bobbing up and down as he hopped over fallen branches and tussocks of rough grass. Frank had weeded a space around an ancient wrought-iron bench and liked to sit and watch, laughing at his dog's antics.

Not only was the garden proving an ideal place to clear her head, but Nell was finding a daily walk helped. Barney didn't come with her. He was gradually working his way around the house, 'putting the place to rights', but as far as Nell could see, that meant messing up one job after another and moving on to the next with nothing properly fixed. She wondered what she could do to stop this trail of destruction without sending Barney into a downward spiral of feeling inadequate. Not only that, all of her efforts to make the master bedroom a haven of tranquillity and comfort hadn't managed to lure him back to her yet. It was disheartening to say the least.

To distract herself, Nell had begun to explore further and further afield on her walks, often taking Anton along as Frank snoozed in the sunshine. The various routes usually took her past the corner shop at some point. There was always a bowl of water left outside and a hook for anyone who didn't feel their animal was shop-friendly, but dogs were allowed in there on a lead because the Habeebs were keen to accommodate all the villagers' needs. Each time Nell visited the shop, she felt less conspicuous as a newcomer. The locals, when she met them around the village, were already starting to get used to seeing her and had even started chatting to her now and again.

The fourth time Nell visited the village stores, she saw that Maryam was behind the counter as usual. Maryam smiled a welcome but was obviously too busy to talk, so Nell began to browse the shelves looking for something for lunch. Since the move, Frank and Barney seemed to think Nell was responsible for providing three interesting meals every day, which was getting tiresome. Previously, Barney had eaten lunch at work and Frank had made his own arrangements, although Nell had often invited him round for dinner or made sure he had something home-cooked to microwave. Now, they both appeared on the dot of 12.30 wherever Nell happened to be, smiling hopefully.

There were going to have to be changes, but for now, Nell had decided to go with the flow to keep everyone happy. Left to herself she'd have raided the fridge for a yoghurt and a chunk of cheese and then eaten an apple or a banana if she was still hungry. Now, apparently, that wasn't good enough.

As Nell wandered around the shop she could hear the women at the till chatting. The one who'd introduced herself as Beryl, who seemed to be pretty much in charge of her two friends, was holding forth about something that was happening at the village church.

'You've got to hand it to our lovely vicar, she throws herself into everything good and proper. Last week she had us knitting and nattering. Winnie made a right pig's ear of hers, didn't you?'

Beryl turned to the friend nearest to her, the more flamboyant of the three women. She was dressed in a floor-length robe of vibrant purple and blue with a matching headwrap and was holding an overflowing basket full of what looked to Nell like curry ingredients. Winnie shrugged.

'Knitting's not my scene, is it though? Never has been. I can't see the point when you can get a perfectly good jumper at M&S without all the hassle. If we'd been doing a cookery demo, I'd have been right up there. I might suggest that for the next lot of stuff she organises. She loves her groups, does the Rev Bev. Caribbean soul food, I could do that for her, like my ma used to make. What do you reckon, Anthea?'

The third woman, who Nell realised she hadn't met before, nodded. 'I'd be up for something even more spicy than one of your curries, personally. I'd like a bit of belly-dancing,' she said. 'Use it or lose it, don't they say? We can still wiggle.'

'Only now it makes us widdle,' said Beryl, winking at Maryam, who looked as if she wasn't quite sure how to take all this frivolity. The three women paid for their various shopping and greeted Nell as she joined them at the counter.

'Settling in okay, dear?' asked Beryl. 'It's nice for you and Maryam to be new girls together, isn't it? Oh, look, here's the vicar now. Have you met our Bev yet? We'll leave you to it. Don't let her try and convert you though. We just go round to hers for the weekday groups and the tea and biscuits. We like a good hymn, but we can't be doing with all that praying. See you.'

With that, the three friends left, waving merrily. Maryam breathed a sigh of relief. 'They're lovely, but they're a bit...' She hesitated.

'Overwhelming,' finished the newcomer, who was partly identifiable as a vicar due to her crimson shirt with a dog collar attached, but in contrast had three large piercings in each ear, a tiny diamond stud in the shape of a cross in her left nostril and a pair of tartan Dr Marten boots worn with ripped jeans. Her cropped hair was dyed a glorious burnished copper colour, standing up in proud spikes. Nell guessed her to be around thirty at the very most and thought Bev looked amazing. She suddenly felt very dull in her own much tidier Levi's and checked shirt.

'Don't get me wrong. The Saga Louts have hearts of gold. They add a lot of spice to our groups. I've been meaning to talk to you on that subject, Maryam, and now I can kill two birds with one stone.' Bev smiled at Nell. 'So you're Nell? Pleased to meet you, I'll call round sometime and introduce myself properly, but I was wondering...'

She broke off as Maryam turned to serve a new customer and focused on Nell properly. 'How are you doing?' she asked, her voice warm with sympathy. 'It can't be easy starting all over again in a place you don't know.'

Nell tried to answer but the unexpected kindness prevented her from speaking for a moment. Eventually, she managed to croak, 'It's hard sometimes.'

Bev patted her arm. 'I felt just the same when I first landed here. I lived in Bristol before this, so it was a big culture shock. Oh, look, Maryam's free now, so we can all talk. I wanted to see if you'd be interested in helping me start up a brand-new kind of group.'

'I don't think belly-dancing's for me, if that's what you were going to suggest,' said Maryam.

Nell laughed, and some of the tension left her tired body. 'Me neither.'

Maryam folded her arms and settled herself against the counter. 'I thought you'd got enough groups going already, Bev. What were you proposing this time, if it's not exotic dancing?'

'That's a good question. Maybe we can come up with a few ideas between us. I've been thinking about the sense of community we've got here. It's growing, I know it is, although I can't help feeling that there are still people in the village who are hiding their loneliness or their worries or... or just are generally not as contented as they could be.'

'But that's life, surely,' said Maryam. 'We can't all be hopping and skipping and singing Abba songs around the place from dawn to dusk.'

'No, but my gut feeling is that there could be more done to help everyone to live their best lives.'

Nell started to wonder if she should escape home while she could. This was getting heavy. Maryam seemed to agree.

'Your idea sounds great when you put it like that but isn't it something of an impossible dream?' she said. 'I don't want to be a glass-half-empty kind of person, I'm just saying...'

'Yes, yes, I suppose it does seem too much to hope for, but you've got to start somewhere if your aim is to give people the tools to find what they need for themselves,' interrupted Bev. 'I want to make a safe, comfortable place for people to share their thoughts more. The longer I live in Willowbrook, the more I think the locals all live in their own little bubbles. Oh, they meet up at the pub, and my other groups are ticking over nicely now, but they're all places to *do* things rather than learn about each other. I want to try something different next.'

'I'm still not quite sure what you mean,' said Nell, trying desperately to keep up. 'Kind of like Alcoholics Anonymous, only without the booze problem? Sharing why you're unhappy?'

Bev pulled a face. 'Not quite that. I'm thinking aloud here. It's one of my many weaknesses. But yes, a sharing of ideas and experiences, and a way to move forwards if something's not right. Maybe you don't even realise it, but you're not feeling quite as okay as you'd like to. I mean... not you personally, ladies, I'm sure you're both fine.'

Maryam's face was thoughtful, but she didn't comment. Nell's mind was a complete blank for a couple of minutes and then the spark of an idea began to flicker and then burn more brightly.

'How about basing the new group around the quest for happiness?' said Nell, coming to life as Frank's words came back to her. 'We're all searching for that elusive something, aren't we? Or so my father-in-law says. He says it about me,' she added, wondering why she'd let this thought out. Maryam and Bev would think she was a proper misery.

Neither of the other women answered so Nell soldiered on, desperate not to come across as one of those depressing glass-half-empty people.

'I mean, I think a lot of us have things holding us back from being long-term happy. Or... maybe not happy exactly, because what is true happiness anyway? Maybe it's more about finding... contentment. A balance.'

Nell bit her lip. What was she thinking of, sharing such personal thoughts with two almost-strangers? She hadn't even properly digested Frank's remarks herself yet, preferring to push them away until life was more settled.

'Tell me more,' said Bev. 'Don't stop now, this is great.'

'Well... okay...' Nell frowned as she struggled to get her ideas in order. 'I guess it often comes down to regrets... and memories. Not always bad memories, although a lot of the time they might be about people who we've lost in one way or another, or...' She bit her lip, trying to put the scraps of thoughts into words. 'Or memories of people who've been important in our lives and had an influence, or things we've done and wished we hadn't, or haven't done and wished we had...'

A couple with a baby came into the shop at that point and Nell and Bev stood back from the counter while Maryam dealt with their shopping. When they'd gone, Bev turned back to Nell.

'I like your thinking,' she said slowly. 'Where did it spring from? Were you focusing on anyone in particular in your own memories? Or is that too personal a question? Tell me to mind my own business if you like. Curiosity comes with the job. Well, that and the praying, obviously.'

Nell considered this question carefully. Who had she been wanting to remember? Was anyone or anything in her own past holding her back?

'I think I was probably coming at this more from my father-in-law, Frank's, point of view,' she said. 'He misses his late wife terribly. If he could talk about all the good things about her to a new set of people, I'm sure it would help him. A new audience. He doesn't speak to Barney and me in that way. I think he's afraid of upsetting us because we loved her so much too.'

'Keeping the memories alive,' Bev said, nodding. 'And at the same time thinking about what happiness really is. This is just the kind of thing I had in mind. We could have a general natter first – and tea and cake, of course – and then each week we could home in on a different way to find...'

'That elusive something,' finished Maryam. 'No praying though, right? I'm up for the cake but not the Christian stuff. I haven't got a problem with anything that you do, or what any other religion gets up to for that matter, of course I haven't, but my mum would turn in her grave.'

Bev laughed. 'I promise. You're quite safe with me. I might sneak in a bit of non-religious reflection though.'

Nell looked at Maryam and they both smiled. 'Let's do it,' said Maryam. 'I'm in.'

Bev took out her phone and prepared to make a firm arrangement to discuss the idea at the vicarage over coffee. When they'd agreed on a date in two days' time, because Bev said she wanted to get on with the meeting plans right away, the vicar put her phone away and said, 'So, in other news, how are you both settling in? I know Maryam's been here a bit longer but you're still both new to the village, aren't you?'

Maryam looked over her shoulder to check that Rashid was out of earshot. He could just be heard stacking boxes in the storeroom. 'It's been better since I discovered Rick,' she whispered.

'Oh, Rick,' said Bev, with a grin. 'Yes, he's a definite asset. I've used him myself on occasion, and he's well worth the money.'

Nell's mind was starting to boggle. Was Rick some kind of communal village gigolo?

'Er... who is Rick?' she asked tentatively.

'You should see your face, Nell,' said Maryam. 'I reckon she thinks we're part of some sleazy rent-a-man scheme, Bev. Well, we are, sort of, but it's all above board. Rick's the local handyman. He's handy, he's definitely a man and he's fit. Fit in the healthy sense,' she added. 'He's done a few jobs for us in the shop, with the okay from our landlady. Sylvia's agreed to whatever improvements we do here, it'll make it easier for her to sell the shop eventually if that's what she decides to do. We're only renting at the moment, to find out if it takes off, you see.'

'Ah.' Nell's mind was whirring now. 'And... this wonderful

Rick... is he very busy at the moment, do you know? Only, I might have a few things he could help with.'

She thought of all the partly finished jobs that Barney had attempted since their arrival. Frank couldn't really help with most of them and Barney was becoming more and more dejected as his few DIY skills proved hopelessly inadequate. Nell had offered several times to have a go herself or just to work alongside him, only to be met by outrage and a huff. It would be wonderful to find someone who could step in and get the house and annexe into shape.

'Why don't you give him a ring? I'll jot his number down for you,' said Maryam, reaching under the counter for a scrap of paper. 'Or if he calls in here later, I'll pass the message on. He's worth his weight in gold, that man, eh, Bev?'

As she walked home, Nell could feel the paper rustling in her pocket, bringing hope of finished work at last and the cosy house of their dreams. Surely Barney wouldn't object to her paying for a bit of extra muscle and skill? Her nerve failed at the thought of the argument this suggestion would trigger. Nell decided to phone this marvellous Rick as soon as she had time to walk further into the village to get a decent signal. If it was a done deal, her husband couldn't really say no, and Rick might just be free to start soon. It had to be worth a try.

6

Meanwhile, back at the cottage and completely unaware of his wife's new acquaintances and plans, Barney was finding life in Willowbrook a lot less satisfying than he'd expected.

Frank ambled into the kitchen and eyed his son balefully. 'Have you got any further with my annexe?' he asked Barney again, as he did most days. Barney, as usual, had to admit that no, he hadn't. When Frank and Anton had returned to the bench in the sunshine with Frank clutching the biscuit tin and Anton following him, dribbling, Barney mooched around the house, clocking the various disastrous and unfinished projects. He'd been so keen to start them when they first arrived but now, as he wandered around on his tour of gloom, he couldn't see his way clear to ever getting them done. He emerged into the garden and was overcome with envy to see his father happily snoozing on the bench with his old Panama hat tilted over his face. Anton looked up and wagged his tail as Barney approached.

'It's all right for some, isn't it?' said Barney bitterly.

Frank stirred himself and opened his eyes. 'Are you feeling a bit liverish, son?' he asked. 'Maybe it was that red wine last night. I thought you were hitting it hard. Nell and I only had one glass apiece and you necked the rest and opened another.'

'Oh, what are you now, the wine police?' Barney snapped, and then regretted his bad temper when he saw the hurt in Frank's eyes. 'Sorry, Dad. I guess I'm just grumpy because I'm not getting on very well with all the work I've got to do. I think I'll go for a walk. Shall I take Anton?'

The dog was on his feet before Barney had finished speaking, loping off toward the hook in the hall where his lead was kept.

'I'll take that as a yes,' Barney said. 'When Nell gets back, tell her not to wait for me for lunch. I'll get a sandwich or something while I'm out.'

'You're not going to the pub, are you? Can I come?' Frank said, sitting up straighter.

'Not this time. I want to go down that lane the other side of the green. I haven't explored the country park yet. It'll be too far for you with your dodgy hip, but Anton needs the exercise. We'll go to the pub tomorrow if you like.'

Mollified, Frank settled back into nap mode and Barney went into the hallway to clip the lead on Anton, who was bouncing up and down and whirling round in circles in excitement.

'Come on, smiler,' he said to the dog, who grinned up at him, tail wagging frantically. 'Let's go and see what other delights this place has to offer.'

They set off across the green, with Anton tugging hard. Barney knew he'd need to do a lot more than the occasional walk with the dog if he was going to get properly fit. He really wanted to get in shape, for all sorts of reasons. Being tall and well-built meant that his gradual weight gain since his teens hadn't been noticeable to most people, he supposed, but in his mind, he felt clumsy and not particularly agile. Barney had actually been quite thin for a while after his cancer treatment, but it had left him with a less than wonderful body image and he'd gone in for some serious comfort eating to compensate. Now his dark, curly hair had fully grown back and he was shaving again. His last appointment at the hospital before they moved had been a positive one, but Barney still felt out of sorts with himself, in mind and body.

It was good to be outdoors on this warm, sunny morning and as he walked, some of Barney's gloom left him. There was nobody about apart from a couple of teenagers lounging under the biggest willow tree lobbing stones into the stream, so Barney risked letting Anton off the lead. They progressed slowly, with the dog finding an assortment of fascinating smells to investigate, but when they reached the pub on the far side, Barney put the dog's lead back on.

'We're going across the road and then down this little lane,' he told Anton, feeling faintly ridiculous for giving an update to a dog but continuing all the same. 'I want to see what those lakes are like. No chasing ducks and so on though, okay? Is it a deal?'

Anton gave a reassuring woof, and Barney patted his head. At least the dog seemed to be pleased with him, which was more than Nell or Frank were right now. Was it his fault if he wasn't a natural born handyman? He'd never claimed to be good at DIY. At least he'd had a try, though he'd got no thanks for it.

Barney stomped on, giving Anton another run off the lead as soon as they reached an open field. Soon they were at the edge of the park, and he looked around in satisfaction. This was more like it. Two lakes stretched out, one either side of him, and paths led off enticingly in various directions. Far away in the distance he could see a car park and a cluster of buildings. A warm breeze lifted the fur on Anton's back and Barney experienced a wave of relief at being away from the house that was the main source of his irritation and better still, away from the two people who seemed to be constantly irritated with him at the moment.

'Let's go and explore,' he said to Anton, and the two of them set off along a path that skirted the largest lake. 'Life's too short to worry about building shelves, my friend. It's time for you and me to have a day off. I'm done with apologising for not being the husband Nell wants.' Anton jauntily wagged his tail in agreement and cocked a leg against a handy tree.

With that, they forged ahead, man and beast in perfect accord. Today was for an adventure, even if it was quite a small one in the grand scheme of things. Who cared? The sun was shining, and as they drew nearer, Barney was almost sure one of the buildings looked like a café. Coffee and a sticky bun. That's what he needed, and that's what he would have. Dieting could wait. He clipped Anton's lead back on, to the dog's obvious disgust, and set off in search of sustenance.

The path around the lake was edged with various memorial benches. As he passed, Barney read dedications to several people who had apparently loved to sit here. He would have liked to do that himself, but keeping Anton from tugging him into the water after the wildfowl was a full-time job, so he pressed on until he reached the nearest building which was indeed a café, and which had the unusual name of Golden Brown. Checking that dogs were allowed inside and relieved to find they were welcome, Barney opened the door and stopped in his tracks, stunned by the delicious aroma of hot buttered toast that met him. Anton whimpered in sympathy.

'Hello there, do come in,' said the woman behind the counter. 'Don't worry about your furry mate, if that's why you're stalling. We like dogs here. Mine's upstairs snoring, but he often pops down to see if there's anyone interesting to sniff.'

Barney led Anton inside and sat down at the nearest table to the door, just in case they had to make a sharp exit. 'I'm Barney Appledore, and this is Anton,' he said. 'I'm new to Willowbrook and it's the first time I've explored this far. We've just moved into Hollyhocks Cottage down at the end of Tinderbox Lane.'

'Ah, you're the new resident, great to meet you, and Anton too, of course. I'm Kate. I run this place with my partner, Milo.' The woman beamed at Barney, and he smiled back, encouraged by her friendliness.

'Hi, it's good to meet you too. Another local? You said your own dog's upstairs. You live over the café?'

'Milo does, with the dog and cat. I'm in Fiddler's Row, so we're almost neighbours. What can I get you? I'm expecting a small party of ladies in soon, so make the most of the quiet. Maurice here won't disturb you.'

The elderly man in the corner raised his head and waved as Barney chose a double espresso and a toasted currant bun and settled Anton under the table with a dog chew. They watched as Kate bustled around behind the counter, making strong coffee with a very noisy machine and setting the toaster working. It was an immensely comforting sight. Kate's shining brown hair was cut into a bob that framed her heart-shaped face and rosy cheeks perfectly and she was wearing a yellow and white gingham overall. She hummed to herself as she worked and when she turned to tell Barney his order was ready, her eyes were bright with interest.

He went over to the counter to collect it, and Kate said, 'Tell me to leave you in peace if you want to because I know this is going to maybe sound a bit premature, but are you interested in becoming a Friend of Willowbrook Country Park? We're recruiting local residents to volunteer to help with all sorts of activities and I wondered... of course if you're still busy settling in... just ignore me if it's too soon...'

Kate's face was flushed now, and Barney rushed to put her at her ease. 'No, don't be silly, no problem at all. Tell me more. I have to tell you that I'm rubbish at DIY if you're needing practical work doing though.'

Maurice overheard Barney's answer, and chuckled. 'You don't need to worry about that. Kate's got a small army of locals all desperate to wield saws and axes and build things. I'm guessing you're thinking he might be useful in other ways though, eh, dear?'

Kate nodded. 'Oh, yes, it's not the practical stuff I'm short of. Shall I put you on my list?'

'Sure. But what kind of things are we talking about?'

Kate leaned on the counter and pointed out towards the nearest lake. 'I'm finding it very frustrating that we're not taking advantage of golden opportunities to show people how great this place is. The bottom line is that I really need people who can lead guided walks around the park. I don't suppose... look, don't take this the wrong way, but have you got any experience in talking to people?'

Barney grinned. 'Oh, yes, I do that all the time, try and stop me, but I'm guessing you mean in a more organised way than just babbling to random strangers in cafés?'

Kate blushed. 'That didn't come out how I meant it to. Have you ever led groups? Are you familiar with giving talks?'

'Oh... I see. Well, I lead a team at work, mostly on Zoom now but it always used to be in real life, before the pandemic changed everything. I gave training lectures too, in those days. Why do you ask?'

Kate was on a roll now. 'That's brilliant. You must like walking if you've got a dog, that goes without saying. Are you interested in nature? I really, really need somebody to take on a few guided walks around the park. Would you be interested? Please tell me to leave you alone if this is too sudden.'

Maurice leaned forward, his eyes twinkling. 'That's our Kate all over. She doesn't let the grass grow under her feet. Look how she took over the café when there was a chance it might have closed.' He waved an arm around the room to illustrate his point and knocked over a milk jug, which fortunately was empty. Righting it, with an apologetic glance to Kate, he added, 'She's a human dynamo, this woman.'

By now, Barney was so entranced by the beauty of Kate's long-lashed eyes and her warm smile that he'd thought he'd probably have agreed to run a skydiving course for her. 'Anton's not actually mine. He belongs to my dad, but I do like being outdoors with him,' he said. 'To be honest, I'm so sick of being cooped up inside trying to fix the unfixable that guided walks sound fantastic, but I don't know anything at all about the area.'

'That's nothing to worry about. I'd give full training,' Kate said. 'I tell you what, leave me your number and I'll text you to see when we can have a trial run. I need to get moving now because I can see the troops approaching. Action stations, Maurice, unless you and Anthea have made friends since I last saw you?'

At this, Maurice got to his feet, collected his newspaper and coat and hurried towards the counter, whereupon Kate lifted the flap for him to go through. He was in the kitchen and out of sight in seconds. Barney heard the back door slam at the same moment as the front door opened. In came three ladies of a certain age, talking loudly as they made their way to the biggest table in the café.

'I thought Maurice might be here, Anthea,' said the one leading the way, who was dressed in a flowing, colourful robe with a matching headwrap and was carrying a bundle of holiday brochures. She put them down on a nearby table and several cascaded onto the floor, one landing right at Barney's feet. He reached to pick it up and passed it to the lady. On the cover was a photograph of a bunch of older ladies and gentlemen sitting on camels, clearly having a whale of a time.

'Thanks, dear,' she said to Barney. 'Oh, you've got Egypt. I don't really fancy spitting camels and all that sand. I don't know why I brought that one. We're overdue a holiday and I think I just got a bit excited.'

'Story of your life, Winnie,' said the smaller one. 'Hang on, that *is* funny about Maurice. He's usually around at this time of day, isn't he? Anthea, have you seen him lately?'

The lady addressed as Anthea rolled her eyes. 'No. I'm not surprised he's keeping a low profile, if I'm honest. I think I scared him off after we went out for dinner last week when I asked him back for a brandy and showed him my collection of wedding rings. He was asking about my relationship history... so I told him. I think he might be avoiding me now. I say, you're new round here, aren't you?'

This last was directed at Barney who had just taken a large mouthful of toasted bun. He struggled to swallow and managed to choke on a crumb, bringing on a violent coughing fit that instantly set Anton off barking and had all three ladies and Kate gathered round him, proffering water, patting him on the back and generally flapping. Eventually he got control of his breathing and gulped down some water, eyes still streaming.

'Ladies, this is Barney,' said Kate. 'He's moved into Hollyhocks Cottage, and he's just agreed to help to lead our guided walks, or at least to have a bash at learning more about the place first.'

'Goodness me, you didn't waste much time signing him up,

darling,' said Anthea. 'He's hardly had time to unpack his boxes, poor chap.'

'I... I don't mind, honestly. I want to find out more about Willowbrook,' said Barney, cringing slightly as he was fixed with three inquisitive gazes.

Kate took pity on him. 'Barney, let me introduce you to Beryl, Winnie and Anthea. We call them the Saga Louts. I expect you'll find out why they're known as Louts in your own good time, so I'll leave that one hanging and make the coffee. The Saga bit's more obvious, now you've seen their brochure addiction in action.'

'We favour holidays for the more discerning older customer, you see,' said the tallest lady. 'We like to shake them all up a bit, don't we, Winnie?'

'We definitely did that when we went on the river cruise in Portugal,' said her friend. 'My samba was the talk of the boat and when Beryl did the twist at the disco on the last night, she nearly gave that nice waiter a hernia.'

'He couldn't keep up with me,' said the third lady, with satisfaction. 'He ripped his trousers in the end. They *were* a bit tight though. It's not good for a man to have his—'

'Anyway,' interrupted Kate, 'I think Barney's got the idea. Let's not frighten him at this early stage, eh?'

Barney reached for a paper napkin, wiped his eyes and then stood up to shake hands with the newcomers. Saga Louts? He had the strangest feeling that he'd stepped into some sort of surreal parallel universe, or a reality TV show.

'Ah, you're Nell's bloke, aren't you?' said the smallest of the three. 'We've already met her in the shop. I'm Beryl. I'm very glad to see someone in that old cottage. It's been a wreck for much too long, but you'll soon have it shipshape.'

Barney couldn't think of a reply to this hopeful sentiment. If

Kate's tempting invitation worked out, he'd be more likely to be striding around the park in his walking boots and shorts than knocking together shelves and making the annexe habitable for Frank.

'Stand up, dear,' said Beryl. 'Let's have a proper look at you. Have you got what it takes to lead a walk? I've heard you're from up north. Sheffield, isn't it? Mind you, it's hilly there, isn't it? You might be up to it, in that case. How much stamina have you got?' She reached out, squeezed one of Barney's biceps and sniffed.

'Beryl, you're awful! Leave the poor man alone,' said Kate, but Barney, bemused, was already on his feet. The ladies stood round him in a semi-circle, looking him up and down. He felt as exposed as he had the time he'd entered the knobbly knees contest at Elliot's school summer fair. He tried to smile and style it out, but their piercing gazes were deeply embarrassing.

After a moment, the three exchanged looks and nodded. 'You'll do, darling,' said the tallest one. 'You're nice and sturdy with good strong calves. I like a man who wouldn't blow over in a gale. I'm Anthea, by the way.' She held out a hand to Barney and he was impressed by the strength of the warm handshake.

Kate, looking mortified, was now serving another customer. She shot Barney a look that said *I'm so sorry* but by now he'd recovered his equilibrium and was struggling not to laugh.

The third lady, who by default must be Winnie, Barney concluded, smiled at him. 'Well, I for one am very glad to see some good, strong new blood about the place. Welcome to Willowbrook, Barney. You're going to be a very useful addition to our little community, I can see that already. A nice bit of beef-cake. Do people say that any more? I expect it's not PC, or whatever, but you know what I mean.'

The idea was heartening. All Barney had to do now was explain to Nell why they should urgently make an effort to find someone to pay to do the jobs he couldn't finish. It was awful to imagine her disappointment when he'd been so adamant he could do everything himself. Barney resolved to take some of Kate's fine selection of cakes home for the others as a sweetener. One way or another, he had to persuade Nell to release him from yet more household disasters before the whole place crumbled around their ears. It wouldn't be easy, but he'd have to try, and soon.

7

Nell didn't go straight home from the shop. Her mind was full of the prospect of almost having someone lined up to finish Barney's botched projects, but she felt much too edgy to tackle the subject with him yet. It would take a while to think of the right words to sell the idea to her husband. Taking a slight diversion, she wandered across the village green, following the path of the stream that gurgled and frothed over rocks and stones. She wondered idly where it was going. Maybe to the river. Nell had heard there was one running alongside the nearby country park. One day she'd go and find it, but today, a sudden weariness came over her and she sank down onto the grass under the willow trees to rest.

Disturbed sleep had been a problem for months for Nell. Ever since Barney had been diagnosed with cancer, she had struggled to get through the night without the need to get up and pace the floor downstairs and make a cup of tea. The situation had become even worse when he'd decided that it was his fault that she was so restless and had moved into the spare bedroom, allegedly on a temporary basis to give Nell a break.

Then, once his chemo had started, Barney announced that he would stay put in there for the time being as the nausea he was suffering made his sleep pattern so erratic.

Nell sighed. It was a while now since Barney had been given the good news that his cancer was in remission but understandably, his anxiety refused to completely go away. Nell was deeply sad that he was still in a separate room now they'd moved house, even though she'd played down the situation when Frank had commented on it. She could feel the gap between them widening as the days passed. She knew her husband was furious with himself for not being able to do the DIY jobs properly and now that Frank was living so closely with them while his annexe was still unfinished, they never seemed to have time to talk alone. The conversation about bringing in extra help was bound to be a touchy one but there was no point in putting it off.

She stood up and brushed dried grass from her jeans, wondering if their old lawn mower would be up to the job of tackling the overgrown lawn at the back of the cottage. It was time she got to work on either that or some more serious weeding and pruning.

Nell had only just rejoined Fiddler's Row when she heard someone calling her name. She turned, not recognising the voice and stopped dead in her tracks. Loping towards her was the most attractive man she'd seen in a very long time. Muscular and tanned, he had short blond hair and was wearing work boots, denim cut-offs and a tight black T-shirt with the slogan 'Born to be Wild' on the front.

'You *are* Nell Appledore, aren't you?' the vision said, coming to a halt in front of her. He wasn't even breathless after his run, Nell thought, although actually, she was finding it quite hard to breathe herself as she looked into those blue, blue eyes. What a cliché. Could a man *be* any more gorgeous? Nell thought, paraphrasing Chandler Bing. But how on earth did he know her name?

'Yes, that's me... but...?' Nell gazed at him, lost for words.

'I'm Rick. I do most of the odd jobs around here. Maryam gave me your name?'

The man finished his sentence with an unnecessary questioning lilt which Nell usually found irritating, but for some reason sounded quite appealing today.

'Oh, I see. I was going to call you later. Does this mean you might be free to do some work for us?' Nell said, pulling herself together with an effort. 'There's a right hotchpotch of jobs to do, if I'm honest. My husband...' She ran out of words again, unwilling to badmouth Barney. Rick grinned.

'Say no more, doll. I get it. Shall I come and take a look now?'

Doll? Nell wanted to cringe, but Rick was smiling at her so beguilingly that she couldn't bring herself to mind the silly name. It would be hugely tactless just to turn up with a handyman before she and Barney had had the chance to discuss it, but on the other hand if she put Rick off, he might be too busy to come round another time. Nell made a snap decision.

'Yes, that'd be great if you've got time,' she said. 'You can maybe give us a rough quote. I haven't actually talked to my husband about getting some help yet though.'

'Don't worry, babe. I'll be tactful,' Rick said. 'Some blokes get a bit iffy about letting someone else do the dirty work, but his loss is my gain, if you get my drift. Let's go.'

Nell couldn't make her mind up if *babe* was better or worse than *doll,* but this was too good an opportunity to miss. She led the way down Tinderbox Lane until they reached her new home, with Rick giving her a running commentary of all the houses in the village he'd worked in and how much everyone had appreciated him. Nell was barely listening, preoccupied with how to broach the subject of Rick with Barney, but to her intense relief, only Frank was in evidence when she ushered Rick into the cottage, and he was busy in the kitchen foraging for lunch.

'I thought you were never coming back. I'm starving,' Frank said. 'Oh, I didn't realise we had a visitor.'

'This is Rick... erm...' said Nell, realising belatedly that she didn't know his surname. 'He's just popped round to see if there's any handyman-type work he can help us with. The annexe... and so on...'

Frank clapped his hands together. 'Thank heavens for small mercies, I was beginning to think I'd be in that poky spare bedroom for the rest of my days. Pleased to meet you, young man. My son's not in at the moment, he's taken the dog for a walk, but don't let that stop you having a look round.'

Nell and Frank exchanged glances, and she could tell they were in perfect accord. With Barney out of the way, they could get this sewn up before Nell had to justify the expense of letting someone else tackle the work, let alone deal with the issue of Barney's hurt pride. She began to show Rick around the house as Frank brewed a large pot of tea for them all and muttered about sandwiches.

'Jeez, I can see why you need me,' said Rick, as they returned to the kitchen from the annexe. 'Your old man doesn't specialise in DIY then?' He laughed, and Nell looked towards the door nervously, hoping against hope that Barney would stay away a bit longer.

'When can you start?' she said, even before Rick had finished scribbling figures on a scrap of paper he'd found in his back pocket.

'As it happens, I'm all finished at the shop now, so I can get stuck in tomorrow if you like, sweetheart. Here's the damage, just a ballpark figure for now, okay? See you at around eight o'clock? Oh, and I'm a tea with two sugars guy before you ask. I always start work with a brew, but I won't stop now, thanks.'

This last was to Frank who was waving the teapot in Rick's general direction. Nell watched him go. *Sweetheart* was a marginal improvement, she supposed, but he could call her what he liked if he was going to finish the work. She turned to face Frank.

'So, will you tell our Barney, or shall I?' he said.

The question hung in the air for a few seconds. 'Leave it to me,' Nell said, mentally girding her loins. 'We can't live in this mess any longer. I'm sure he'll agree when he's had time to think about it.'

'Of course he will,' said Frank. 'Chin up. You're a good lass, and that was a grand thing you did there. Remember what I said about being happy? This is a fine start and you're on the right track, my girl.'

8

Barney pushed the ancient mower around the lawn, reflecting on how surprisingly yesterday had turned out. He'd started out feeling gloomier than he'd been for years but then his walk had woken him up to the beautiful area that he could now call home and on top of that he'd met lovely Kate, who seemed to need him to do something useful at last.

Then, when he and Anton had eventually reached the cottage, he'd found both his wife and his father sitting waiting for him at the kitchen table looking sheepish. The upshot had been that Barney had somehow managed to give the impression that he was sad to be denied the chance to improve their new home but after some thought, would magnanimously agree to this Rick character taking over the work. Everyone had been in celebration mode after that. They'd abandoned the idea of cooking that evening and headed for the pub, where they had eaten most satisfactory curries and tried several of the local beers.

This morning, Barney had woken feeling distinctly fragile, but still pleased with the idea of jettisoning the jobs. However, when Rick banged on the door at the unearthly hour of eight o'clock, his mood became a lot less amiable, and after a quick shower and a mumbled greeting to the new arrival, he'd made tracks to the garden to get out of the way. It was embarrassing to see someone else wading in with such gusto, and faintly sickening the way Nell and Frank fawned round the man, providing tea *and* bacon sandwiches.

Barney could see his own sandwich sitting there on a covered plate on the garden bench, but he was determined to finish the lawn before he sat down. He didn't want to look like a lightweight, but he was already itching to go back over to the country park café and find out more about his possible new volunteering role. He paused for a moment and leaned on the mower, wondering how soon he could escape.

'Are you going to eat this sandwich, or not, lad?' said Frank, coming out of the house. 'Because if you don't want it, I'll take it off your hands.'

'I've got work to do first,' said Barney virtuously. 'We can't all just down tools whenever we feel like it.'

'Could've fooled me,' muttered Frank, going over to sit on the bench. Anton was nowhere to be seen this morning. *Probably gazing at the wonderful Rick*, thought Barney. *Seems like everyone but me loves the man.*

From inside the house, he heard the sound of his wife's laughter and gritted his teeth. This was sickening. Barney finished the mowing in record time and came to sit on the bench with his father, who was already dozing. He ate the bacon sandwich without his usual enjoyment and got to his feet, brushing away crumbs. He'd dressed with unaccustomed care this morning. The faded khaki cargo shorts were his favourites, and the T-shirt was a *Game of Thrones* one that Elliot had left behind. It was an old burgundy Lannister shirt. Kate was bound to think it was cool, surely? Teamed with his battered hiking boots, Barney reckoned he looked exactly like someone who enjoyed tramping country paths but also had an awareness of popular culture.

'You off somewhere?' asked Frank, opening one eye. 'Aren't you going to see if Nell wants any help first?'

Barney made a sound that was a cross between *Humph!* and *Ha!* 'They don't need me in there,' he said. 'I'm going for a walk.'

'Are you taking Anton again?'

Barney shook his head, but then, feeling mean, gave a whistle, hoping that the dog would be too fascinated with his new builder friend to come out. Rick had a pocket full of dog treats, being the proud owner of an elegant Borzoi named Bathsheba, as he'd lost no time in telling them all. Even so, Anton must have got bored with watching the action indoors because at the sound of Barney's whistle, he dashed outside, ears flapping.

Resigned, Barney fetched the lead and they set off together, with Anton looking up at him so joyfully that Barney's heart melted. The dog's tongue was lolling out of the side of his mouth and as Barney bent to pat him, he gave his trademark grin. 'You and me are going to do good works for our new community, mate,' said Barney. 'Don't let me down, now. None of your silent and deadly attacks of wind when we're in the café. Okay? And no excitable piddling on the floor. We've got standards, us two, and don't you forget it.'

A teenage girl walking towards him across the green sniggered and rolled her eyes, but Barney ignored her and carried on walking. Once again, he reached the edge of the park and skirted the biggest lake, hearing the excited cries of windsurfers on the smaller one. It was a gusty day, warm and sunny. Barney's spirits lifted as he and Anton made their way past the memorial benches. A man on a ride-on mower gave them a wave as he trundled up and down the gentle slopes by the water, just as the scent of newly mown grass reached Barney, making his senses sing. Summer was here, and he was in a great place to enjoy it. Birds wheeled and swooped up above him, and Anton barked at them joyfully.

Entering the café, Barney was disappointed to see that Kate wasn't behind the counter today. Instead, a tall, stunningly handsome boy... or possibly man was busy making coffee for a group of ramblers. He had long, wavy blond hair tied back in a ponytail and sparkling brown eyes full of mischief. He grinned at Barney.

'Great dog,' he said. 'What breed?'

'Who knows? Even he's not sure,' said Barney, finding a seat over by the wall out of the way of the group, who were loudly discussing their next walk.

When all the customers were served, the man behind the counter called over to Barney, 'Coffee, mate?'

Barney told Anton to *sit*, as firmly as he could, and got up to look at the cake selection. He was well aware that his waistline was still expanding, and that walking with Anton often involved more of a wander these days but maybe living in a more rural area with handy walks would help him to get back into shape. All the more reason to see if the volunteering job was really going to happen.

'Is Kate not around?' Barney asked, having chosen a large square of millionaire's shortbread.

'The boss is just finishing making the lunchtime cobs and so on, did you want her? I'm Sam, by the way. And you are?'

'Barney Appledore. Moved into the village recently and Kate was asking if I'd be interested in leading some guided walks. It's okay, I'll wait.'

Barney shuffled his feet and looked at the floor. He didn't want to seem too eager, but Sam was already shouting for Kate, who emerged from the kitchen drying her hands on a tea towel.

'Oh, hi, Barney,' she said, giving him a shining smile that immediately warmed his heart. 'I hoped you'd be back. Give me ten minutes to get this job done and I'll come and have a cuppa with you to talk about the walks. That is, if you're still interested in finding out more?'

'No rush, and yes, I am,' Barney replied. He took his drink and cake and went to rejoin Anton, who was having his head scratched by a couple of the ramblers, an ecstatic expression on his face.

'He's so sweet. I've never seen a dog with such an adorable smile,' said the woman. 'Amazing teeth. He reminds me of...'

'I know. His name's Anton,' said Barney, and the dog's new friend nodded understandingly.

'Of course it is,' she said.

Barney ate his cake, unknowingly adopting a similar look of bliss to Anton's, who was still gaining fans and a lot of fuss. Soon, Kate came out of the kitchen again and poured herself a large mug of tea. She came over to Barney's table and sat down, rotating her shoulders as she relaxed.

'I've been on the go since seven o'clock this morning,' she said. 'Milo's had to take our dog to the vet's in Meadowthorpe for booster injections so he couldn't help today. I'm free now for a little while though, unless we get another rush.'

The walkers were now all in the process of gathering their bags and visiting the cloakroom, but soon the place was almost empty. Barney sat back in his chair and sighed happily.

'That was fabulous,' he said, pointing to his empty plate. 'Do you do the baking here?'

'We all do our specialities,' Kate said. 'The shortbread's Sam's signature dish.'

Sam heard his name mentioned and beamed at Kate. 'My daughter Elsie loved being the tester for that one,' he said to Barney. 'Do you want to try one of my lemon cookies next? They're our newest invention.'

Barney knew he should resist but it was impossible. The cosy atmosphere of the café and the tempting scents of baking in the air were too much for him.

'This is a taste of heaven,' he mumbled, trying not to spray Kate with biscuit crumbs. He finished his coffee and attempted to focus on the matter in hand. 'I'm going to have to cut back on the calories living here, but more walking should help. Tell me more about what you need me to do.'

Kate needed no further bidding. She began to outline her plans for the revamped guided walk programme, waving her hands excitedly to illustrate her ideas. 'I used to do most of them myself before I started work here,' she said. 'The previous owner, Pat, was great at giving people opportunities to try new schemes, but I haven't got the spare time now. I'd obviously train you up with a few of my favourite routes. Can you really help us? I guess you're still quite busy settling in at the moment. All new homes need a shedload of TLC, don't they?'

Barney thought about the man who was at this very moment taking charge of the TLC at Hollyhocks Cottage. He shook his head. 'I've recently dropped my working hours and most of those are from home.' He tried not to pull a face as he added '... and the DIY suddenly seems to be under control. I can start anytime.'

'In that case, let's go for tomorrow morning – 10.30 a.m., after the breakfast rush would suit me. Is that too soon?'

'Perfect. I'd better get back now and put a couple of office hours in this afternoon, but I can definitely be here for 10.30. See you soon.'

Barney called goodbye to Sam, and he and Anton left the café. The stroll home was punctuated with constant glances up the paths that led off the main route round the lake and Kate was on Barney's mind all the way home as he wondered where they'd go tomorrow. He was already looking forward to his training. Kate's enthusiasm was infectious, and she had the kind of personality and natural good looks that must make her a popular feature of the café. So many people never achieved that welcoming aura, in Barney's experience, but this was someone who had it in spades. He couldn't wait to start his new project, and the thought of having Kate as his instructor was a bonus he couldn't ignore.

Stuff you, Rick the Builder, Barney said to himself as he crossed the green. I'm going to find my own place in Willowbrook. Who needs to be able to knock down walls and plaster ceilings? Not me, that's for sure.

With his new positive attitude at the ready, Barney wasn't too disconcerted to find that Rick was still making a lot of noise inside the cottage and that Nell and Frank were in the garden animatedly discussing his progress. He decided that this afternoon he would bring his laptop outside to work. That way he'd be away from the din and the constant reminder that someone else was making his new home more habitable. What was that saying his mum had liked? *Horses for courses*, that was it. Barney was never going to be the right horse for Nell and Frank's DIY course, but he was well on the way to finding his own steeplechase. And that was just fine by him.

9

Later that evening, Nell was trying not to let herself scream as she watched Barney meticulously loading the dishwasher in his usual way when the doorbell rang.

'I'll get it,' she said, before Frank had the chance to stir himself from his post-dinner nap in front of the TV.

At the front door stood Reverend Bev, looking apologetic. 'I hate calling on people unannounced in the evening,' she said. 'Only, I forgot to ask you for your number and Maryam just called me to see if we could pull in a quick meeting about ideas for our new group tonight. I know it's a bit last minute but apparently Rashid's in the shop later so we could get together in their lounge upstairs and she'd still be on hand in case he needs her. How are you fixed?'

Nell had grabbed her bag and keys almost before Bev had finished speaking. 'I'm popping round to the shop for a chat with Maryam!' she called, loudly enough for Frank and Barney to both hear. 'Won't be too long. There's a cheesecake in the fridge if you're still hungry.'

'Wow, that didn't take long to make your escape,' Bev said as they walked up the lane. 'If that'd been my ex-husband, I'd have had to have a reason for going out in writing and in triplicate. And he'd still have made a fuss.'

'Oh, I didn't realise you'd been married. Well, I don't know anything about you at all, actually. There's no reason why I should, of course, as we've only just met.'

Nell could hear herself babbling, but the expression on Bev's face as she'd made the statement put her on edge. Bev's mouth had set in a straight line as soon as she finished speaking and Nell had the uncomfortable feeling that the vicar had said more than she'd meant to.

After a moment, Bev said, 'It all seems like a long time ago now. We married when I was barely twenty. It was a big mistake as it happens, and it took me five years to extricate myself. I'll tell you about it sometime, but not now. It isn't a pretty story.' She smiled, but there was sadness in her eyes. 'Anyway, I'm glad you could get away a lot more quickly than that tonight.'

'I was happy to have an excuse to get out, to be honest,' Nell continued. 'Barney with his perfect dishwasher-loading technique always sets my teeth on edge. One plate out of place or a knife the wrong way up and you'd think the world was ending.'

They were in Fiddler's Row now, and in the silence that followed, Nell admired the terrace of cosy-looking houses and wondered how to change the subject to a safer one. Luckily, they were soon outside the shop on the corner, and Bev pushed the door open without further comment.

'Hello, ladies, good to see you,' said the man behind the counter. 'Maryam's upstairs. She's just getting a few samosas and so on out of the oven, in case you're peckish.'

'Hi, Rashid. I didn't realise I was hungry, but I didn't have dinner tonight because I was doing a funeral visit. They smell wonderful. Have you met Nell?'

Nell smiled at the man. He was traditionally dressed, and Nell, having lived near one of the best Indian clothes shops in Sheffield, recognised a stylish Kurta set with a printed cotton jacket and black trousers. Rashid was very handsome, with short, dark hair lightly touched with grey at the temples and mischievous dark brown eyes. 'Hello,' Nell said. 'I've already been in here a few times, but I think you were either at the Cash and Carry or busy in the storeroom. I love your shop.'

'It's coming together a bit now,' Rashid said, looking around proudly at the well-stocked shelves. 'Maryam wants to start producing her own snacks too but there are all sorts of hygiene regulations regarding cooking food to sell on the premises, so we'll have to work on that one. Anyway, go up to the flat. I'll only shout if a coachload drops by.'

Rashid waved them towards the door, and Nell followed Bev up the stairs, with the delicious spicy smell getting ever more enticing as they climbed.

Maryam turned from the flat's open-plan kitchen area as they emerged into the living room. 'Great, you made it,' she said, wiping her hands on her apron and coming forward to give them both a hug. 'Sorry it's a rush job, but it seemed like too good a chance to miss, with Rashid free at last. Our daughter's coming here tomorrow for a week. She's at uni in Leicester and she mostly stays with a friend or one of the family, but she's got study leave. When Uma gets here, we'll be busy. She wants to help Rashid to decorate what she says is going to be her bedroom. And then there's the boys.'

The worried look on Maryam's face belied her light-hearted tone. Nell was intrigued.

'You've got sons too? Where are they?' she asked.

'Well, they changed schools when we moved here but luckily their old place honoured the booking we made for a residential trip. It's a two-week tour around European cities and we saved up for it for ages so it was a big relief that they could still go. Mind you, when they come back, they're going to have to try harder to settle in here.'

Maryam turned away to sort out the food and Bev mouthed, 'Don't ask.' Nell was even more curious now as to why the mysterious sons and their new lives in the village shouldn't be discussed but she swallowed any possible questions and made herself comfortable with Bev on the sofa. They accepted plates, each containing two crisp, golden-brown samosas and a yoghurt-based dip. Maryam produced a tall jug beaded with condensation.

'My homemade lemonade,' she said.

'If only all meetings were like this.' Bev bit into her first samosa and moaned with pleasure. 'Oh, this is heavenly.'

'That's a great recommendation from a woman of the cloth,' said Nell, tucking into her own plate of snacks. It was a while before she and Bev could speak again. Maryam poured lemonade into delicate goblets, and they all raised their glasses.

'To our fledgling project, and also to our latest friend,' said Bev. 'Welcome, Nell. You're going to be an asset to the village, I can tell. That is unless you insist on hogging the delectable Rick for weeks on end. I need my guttering fixed.'

Maryam made herself comfortable in an armchair and got out a large notepad. 'I'll take notes,' she said. 'I mustn't forget to get the onion bhajis out of the oven in ten minutes though. It's my mother's recipe. I do miss her. She was an excellent cook. A bit of a tartar in some ways with an iron will, but a lovely mum.'

Nell and Bev exchanged awed glances. 'I hope when it's my turn to host you're not too disappointed if I only provide biscuits,' said Bev. 'My mum's signature dish was tough mutton stew with added gristle. I don't think that'd inspire us much. I do dinners but not snacks.'

It wasn't long before Maryam was on her feet again producing more food, and they hadn't even begun to think of a name for the group. For the next few minutes, the bhajis and mango chutney took precedence but soon, Bev was ready to get moving on her plan.

'Right, first things first. We need a kind of mission statement or tagline that will make people want to join us,' she said. 'Come on, Nell. I met your father-in-law the other day when he was walking his dog, and he told me you're a writer so you must be good with words.'

Nell could feel her face burning. What had Frank been thinking of to tell Bev such a thing? 'An aspiring writer, that's all,' she said. 'And not getting very far, what with the move... and everything...'

'Even so – have a bash. What are we aiming for?'

This was tricky. Nell had only a vague idea of what they were planning and why, but Bev was looking at her so trustingly and with such hope that she couldn't bear to let her down.

'Can I borrow the notepad?' she asked Maryam. When the book and pen was passed across, Nell scribbled for a minute or two, crossed a few words out, rewrote them and sat up straighter to give herself confidence.

'How about this? "Have you found that elusive key to happiness in your life? If not, why not? Join us on our weekly quest for contentment. Even if you don't discover your Holy Grail, the cake and biscuits will be sure to make the effort worthwhile."'

'Brilliant!' Bev clapped her hands together and Maryam cheered. 'It's not too serious but it puts the message across. I think this is something we all need to investigate,' said Bev. 'I know I do... I mean... this isn't about me, not at all... I'm hoping it'll be useful for everyone. Now all we need to do is plan how we're going to tackle the subject, week by week. I think we should go in with a gentle type of opener that doesn't seem scary or too deep.'

The three women fell silent, each one lost in her own thoughts. Maryam was the first to speak.

'If this is going to work like a course, we'll be giving people the next week's topic to prepare for and think about, I guess,' she said slowly. 'That means the first session has to be something that we can start from scratch. What's the simplest thing that makes you happy?'

Bev glanced at Nell. 'I don't want to act like I'm in charge here...'

'Which you are,' Maryam said. 'It's your baby. We're just your sidekicks. Go on.'

'You're *so* not,' Bev answered, smiling. 'But if I had to choose something, I'd say we start with a topic that most people can relate to, and that's music. It brings back memories, it generates new ones, and everyone would have a favourite piece that makes them feel relaxed and happy.'

'That's a great idea,' said Nell. 'But wouldn't we need to have their song picks beforehand to get a soundtrack ready?'

'Nope. I've got a great Wi-Fi signal in the church and the meeting room. It was one of the things I insisted on when I came. We can use Spotify and make up a playlist on the hoof. If we listen to each other's choices as we go along, we can think about why certain music can lift our spirits and make us feel better about everything.'

Maryam was writing notes at speed on her pad now. 'Excellent. Do we need to make a plan for the whole lot of sessions, Bev?'

'Maybe a loose one, but we can go with the flow when we see

where it takes us each time. Now all we're looking for are people to come along. Leave the next part to me, I'm on it. Thank goodness most of my older regulars are in the Silver Surfers' group so I can get hold of them instantly. This is fantastic. We're going to make a great team.'

Nell gazed at her two new friends. Both had shining eyes and were bursting with enthusiasm. If Frank was right and she needed to find some happiness of her own, perhaps this was the perfect place to begin. If only she didn't feel so apprehensive. Nell had a feeling that this whole scheme sounded far, far too simple.

_____

10

When Barney reached the café in Willowbrook Country Park the next day, his mind was already whirling with suggestions for making the guided walks his own. Maybe he could incorporate a treasure trail for children in the holidays? Elliot and the twins had always loved the ones he made up for them around the town when they were smaller. Or how about a walk that focused on the memorial benches dotted around the country park? Each one must have its own story.

By the time he'd pushed the café door open and inhaled the mouth-watering aroma of freshly baked pasties, Barney was buzzing with a whole bunch of different ideas. Kate was busy serving a customer but looked up and gave him a beaming smile.

'No Anton?' she said. 'This man has the dog with the best smile in the world.'

The last comment was directed at the lady she was serving. Barney recognised Beryl, the ringleader of the ladies Kate had introduced as the Saga Louts.

'I know, I remember thinking the same when we saw you in here before,' Beryl said. 'Why did you leave him at home today?'

The guilt that Barney had felt when he'd crept out of the house while Anton was busy trying to beg some of Frank's toast overwhelmed him again. 'I thought I should be here without any distractions if I was going to be useful,' he said lamely.

'Barney's here to work,' Kate explained, as Beryl joined her two friends at a corner table. 'This is his introduction to starting the walks I was telling you about. That is if I don't take him too far today and wear him out. Sam's taking over shortly for me, Barney. Coffee first?'

Barney accepted a mug of black coffee but refused the offer of cake. It was time he got into shape again. The horrifying brush with cancer had seriously damaged his general fitness and it had taken a while to get his energy back. Since then, getting regular exercise hadn't been at the top of his list, when getting back up to speed with work had seemed more important. Now perhaps it was time to start to feel good about himself again.

The Saga Louts had paused in their booming conversation and when Barney turned to look their way to see what had stalled them momentarily, he realised he was being closely observed.

'Erm... can I help you?' he asked, automatically checking to see if his flies were undone.

'We were just wondering what this new group with our Bev was all about,' said Beryl. 'Can you fill us in? Only, we saw that your wife's involved in setting it up.'

Barney shook his head, thinking he must have misheard. 'I'm really sorry but I don't know what you're talking about,' he said.

The taller one of the trio, who Barney remembered was called Anthea, rolled her eyes at him. 'I bet you weren't listening when she told you about it. They never do, do they, Winnie?'

'No, and Anthea's had enough husbands to be able to speak with authority on that subject, haven't you, love?' The large Black lady by her side laughed uproariously and poked her friend in the ribs. She was a vision in a yellow and green tropical print robe with a headwrap in the same material. 'Give him a clue, Beryl. He looks lost, bless the lamb.'

Beryl turned her chair slightly to address Barney more easily. She was almost as colourfully dressed as Winnie, favouring a fuchsia tracksuit teamed with white pumps.

'We've all three had an email this morning to tell us about a new group the Rev Bev's setting up in the church meeting room. Your missus and Maryam from the shop are in it with her. Are you sure she didn't tell you? It's about the quest for happiness, or some such nonsense.'

'You've... had an email?' Barney was struggling to keep up. He felt as if he'd slipped into a parallel universe where elderly ladies flitted around on the internet exploring quests, while dressed in wildly clashing outfits. At least Anthea was less flamboyant, wearing a selection of draped linen garments in muted shades of mushroom and chocolate brown.

'Ha! I bet he thinks we're too old for all that computer malarkey,' said Winnie.

Barney blushed. 'No, not at all, it's just that I haven't a clue what this group thing is all about. Are you sure Nell's involved?'

'That's what was in the email,' said Anthea. 'I say, Kate, did you get the message from Bev too?'

'I haven't had time to check my emails today, I'll have a look later,' said Kate. 'But I do know Bev's been looking to set up something completely different.'

A husky voice from over by the doorway chipped in at this point. Barney turned. Maurice must have decided to be brave and face up to the Saga Louts today. 'I heard what you were saying. I got a message too,' Maurice said proudly. 'I'm going to go along. There'll be cake,' he added.

Still flummoxed, Barney was about to ask for more details about this mysterious group when Sam emerged from the kitchen and Kate wasted no time in getting ready to leave. Soon, she and Barney were striding along the water's edge, with the June sunshine bringing out all the bright colours of their surroundings.

'I have absolutely no idea what they were talking about in there,' said Barney. 'Is it always this confusing, living in Willowbrook?'

Kate laughed. 'It can get a bit like the Mad Hatter's Tea Party in the café. Don't worry, I'm sure your wife will be able to clear it all up when you get home. I found I'd got an email too, as it happens. I just checked my phone. But that's not important now. Let's just enjoy this gorgeous day, shall we? The park's looking at its best.'

'Fine by me. This must be a stunning place to work,' Barney said, thinking Kate was pretty stunning in an understated way, and admiring the way her hair caught the glints of sunlight as they walked. Like him, she was wearing shorts and a T-shirt today, with well-worn hiking boots that looked as if they'd covered many miles in their time. Her arms and legs were lightly tanned and as she walked, he caught the exotic scent of coconut from the sun cream she'd just applied.

'I love it here,' said Kate. 'I was a teaching assistant at the local primary school for years, and that was great too, but I was ready for a change. Pat, the previous owner, gave me a job and eventually when she left, Milo and I took over. Let's sit down for a minute and I'll show you the map of the park that we give to visitors.'

The bench that Kate had chosen faced the lake, and was

surrounded by lush grass, with tall oak trees giving shade. Barney paused for a moment to take in the plaque attached to the back of the bench. He read it aloud.

In memory of Frances (Frankie) Clifford, our sunshine girl
10 February 1987 – 1 December 2022
Four Seasons in One Day

'Did you know this girl?' he asked Kate, both intrigued and saddened.

Kate sat down. 'Not personally, but Frankie was Milo's sister. She died before I met him. The family commissioned the bench from our local carpenter, Joel. He makes a lot of the benches for the park. Each one's different. Frankie left a big gap in the family, Milo said. I've often wished I'd known her. Some people leave more ripples behind them than others, don't they?'

Barney thought about this as he joined Kate on the bench. The death of his mother had left them all reeling and had indeed left many ripples. Her passing wasn't unexpected and in some ways, he'd had to agree with the numerous people who'd told him it was a blessing that she wasn't suffering any more, but the reality was that his gentle mum had been fairly happy in her bubble of confusion for many months. It was only latterly that the crippling anxiety had gripped her, and towards the end, uncharacteristic anger had made her hard to care for. His other loss, however... no, that one was too painful to think about on this beautiful day.

'So, let's see this map of yours,' Barney said, keen to get away from the troubling thoughts and unwilling to share them with Kate when they'd only recently met. 'Did your walks all start and end at the café?'

'Yes, with hot or cold drinks included, according to the

season. Pat insisted on that. What times of the day are you most likely to be free?'

With the map and notebook in his hand, Barney began to outline his ideas. He ran through the plan for providing treasure hunts in the holidays or weekends and also for using the benches as a trail starter, then, inspired by Kate's bright-eyed interest, began to think aloud about the possibility of early-evening walks for working people, or mid-morning ones with a packed lunch provided from the café for halfway round.

'My working hours are pretty flexible,' Barney told Kate. 'I can be free whenever it works best for you.'

'That's great. Let's have a walk now and I'll show you a couple of the basic routes and you can mark on your map a few useful pausing places. I can give you pointers about what you'd need to tell a group each time you stop, but I know you'll develop your own patter as you go along. Then after that you can explore by yourself if you've got time. I'll need to get back to help Sam with the lunchtime rush.'

Barney and Kate ambled along various paths, under leafy archways of branches, over wooden bridges across fast-flowing streams and an inlet of the river and finally back to the café. Barney made copious notes as they went along, scribbling furiously so as not to miss any of Kate's information. They said their goodbyes, and Kate promised to show Barney a rough copy of her new timetable of walks for his approval when he was happy with the park layout and was sure how many he could commit to.

'Give me a few days to get sorted,' Kate said, opening the café door. 'I'll message you when I'm properly organised and we'll make a final plan.'

Barney watched her go inside and smiled to himself. He couldn't remember when he'd last felt so peaceful and at one with the world. It had been a tough couple of years all in all and the run-up to the move had become more and more stressful as the date approached. Nell and Frank had been alternately morose and ratty, and Barney had almost begun to wish he'd never pushed for the change of scene.

Now, with a soft breeze ruffling his hair and a contented hour just spent with a companion who had no axe to grind, Barney rejoiced in his new surroundings. The others would surely settle down soon. If what the Saga Louts reported was correct, Nell seemed already to be getting involved in village life, although for the life of him he couldn't see how that had happened. Then he remembered her coming home the night before just as he'd been off to bed. She'd started to tell him something, but he'd been too tired to listen, and with them still being in their separate bedrooms, there had been no chance for any more chatting.

With a pang, Barney thought back to the days before his illness when the two of them had shared a bed and had talked and talked, snorting with laughter at silly things that had happened during the day, propped up on a mountain of pillows, drinking tea in the mornings and sometimes wine at night, eating random snacks when both were wakeful or cuddling up together to go to sleep. He knew Nell would like them to be in the same room again, but Barney still felt a sense of panic at the idea. He knew why this was, of course he did, but he couldn't talk to Nell about it. Not yet. To begin with, it had been a purely practical decision to withdraw to the spare bedroom when they'd both been so anxious and restless and then it seemed essential to shield Nell from his night sweats and accompanying nausea even though she'd insisted that she'd rather be awake with him than in another room worrying about how awful he was feeling.

Deciding to have another good look around the paths he hadn't explored with Kate, Barney resolutely pushed the mournful thoughts away and set off again with his map. There would be time for soul-searching when the sun wasn't shining so brightly. The prospect of being needed again was ahead of him. It was time for a whole new chapter.

11

Over the next few days, Nell found herself missing her old life a little bit less. Several things lifted her mood. She'd heard from Elliot, and he hadn't asked for any money, which was a huge bonus. The twins, Ginny and Alice, also seemed to be fairly stable, and having all three offspring on a relatively even keel was also a boost, even if they didn't appear to be particularly bursting with fun at the moment. At the best of times, they tended to be up and down like the needle on a barometer, all emotional and easily disconcerted.

This shared trait had been more obvious since Lottie's death, which had thrown the three younger Appledores off balance more than Nell had expected. They'd loved their grandmother deeply and always made an effort to see her as often as possible, but Nell hadn't realised how much her three children had relied on the security of Lottie's gentle, undemanding love, even latterly when dementia had taken away great chunks of her memories. Now, all three seemed to feel the need to check in more regularly with their parents and also with Frank. Thinking about what her father-in-law had said about happiness, Nell couldn't help thinking that missing Lottie was draining an awful lot of her family's zest for living. It was only natural that they should all feel battered by their loss but there must be a way to help at least those closest at hand, namely Barney and Frank, to recover some of it.

Belatedly, Nell was also beginning to accept that her offspring's unfortunate tendency for fluctuating moods probably came from her side of the family. It might be time to try harder to look on the positive side of life. Her own volatile nature had caused problems between herself and Barney at times, sometimes serious ones. She'd always had a tendency to fly off the handle and say things she'd regret afterwards, whereas Barney was much more measured if they argued. On the other hand, Nell never sulked after a row. Barney could brood about things for days on end.

The uncomfortable train of thought brought her quickly round to wondering if Bev's new group would take off. The vicar hadn't wasted any time in pinging emails to quite a few of the people on her mailing list for other sessions currently running at the church. It was one thing sitting in a comfortable flat making plans but now the spark of an idea was looking like becoming a reality, Nell felt a flutter of nerves. She wasn't used to baring her soul to other people. Her volunteering role at the homeless centre was more about listening to the visitors' troubles and providing hot food than talking about her own insecurities.

'So, what's all this I'm hearing about a church meeting? How did you get involved, Nell?'

Barney had come into the study unnoticed, probably because Rick was making such a din downstairs with his sanding machine. Nell turned to see her husband settling himself in Frank's chair, clearly ready for a chat. They'd not had a proper talk for a while now, both busy with their own jobs. Or had they been truly preoccupied? Was the lack of conversation just another sign of the growing gap between them?

'How did you know about that? I was going to tell you, but you didn't seem interested.' Nell could hear the undercurrent of bitterness in her own voice and saw Barney wince. This new thinking-positive resolution wasn't going well so far. She tried again.

'I met the local vicar in the shop on the corner of Fiddler's Row. She's a livewire, you'd like her, Barney. She looks like a rebellious teenager, but she must be in her thirties, I guess. She's older than I first thought. Anyway, Bev... that's the vicar... and Maryam from the shop want me to help to set up a new group to...'

Nell ran out of words. It was difficult to pinpoint what their aim was without sounding what Barney might class as 'airy fairy'. He had a horror of anything unspecific, preferring facts and figures to more nebulous schemes.

'Go on, I'm listening.' Barney crossed his legs and made himself more comfortable. It was good to have her husband's full attention for once. Nell tried to gather her thoughts.

'They asked me to make a kind of blurb for the group. Hang on, I'll read it to you.'

Nell rummaged for her notebook, where she'd copied down the final draft of the mission statement. She put on her best speaking voice, imagining she was making a radio announcement.

'Have *you* found that elusive key to happiness in your life? If not, why not? Join us on our weekly quest for contentment. Even if you don't find your Holy Grail, the cake and biscuits will be sure to make the effort worthwhile.'

'Really? The key to happiness? You don't set yourself small

goals, do you? Who's going to join this? Is it just for OAPs? The Saga Louts have all had emails.'

'Oh, so you've met them too? I wondered how long it would be before they found you. I get the impression that they like to keep tabs on all the residents of the village.'

Nell and Barney fell silent. It was as if they were recalibrating, Nell thought. They'd only been in this place for a short while but instead of finding their feet here together, it seemed they'd made headway separately. Barney was the first to speak.

'I bumped into them at the café in Willowbrook Country Park. It's called Golden Brown. A woman called Kate runs it and she's asked me to be a volunteer.'

'In the café?' Nell couldn't believe what she was hearing. Barney surely wasn't going to be helping with serving food and washing up? He hardly ever did any cooking, having only a handful of tried-and-tested dishes, and although his dishwasher-loading skills were of Olympic standards, he was hardly an ideal candidate for general kitchen work.

Barney laughed at Nell's horrified face. 'No, I don't think that's quite my forte. Kate wants me to lead guided walks around the park. I've already had a bit of training. She's just planning the whole thing in more detail before she puts the offer out there to the public.'

'Wow.'

'Yes, wow. We've both got a new interest, and we didn't even realise what each other was up to. What's next? Maybe Frank has set up an online gambling forum. Or Anton is running a dog yoga course.'

Nell giggled. This wasn't so bad after all. At least they were talking.

'Do you want me to come to the country park with you and

do some practice walks?' she said tentatively. 'We could bring Anton... that is if he's not too busy with his own hobbies.'

There was another silence. This one was definitely uncomfortable. Barney looked out of the window as he spoke. 'No, it's okay,' he said. 'I guess I need to find my way round by myself to begin with. You know... explore all the options. Erm... do you need me to help to plan your group?'

Stung at this rejection, Nell shook her head. 'This is between me and the other two, thanks,' she said. 'I'm off round to the vicarage this evening, as it happens. Bev's making a lasagne. Can you rustle up something for you and your dad?'

Barney looked nonplussed and Nell's resolve hardened. She'd been planning to make the other two a cottage pie but her husband's flat refusal to involve her in his walks made her feel as if cooking for him was the last thing she wanted to do.

'There's mince in the fridge. You can do your special bolognese,' she said. 'Frank'll like that. Everything else is there. I'm going out at six, okay?'

Barney nodded and got to his feet. 'I'll go and make it now,' he said. 'The sauce is always best made earlier, so the flavours can mingle.'

He left the study and Nell seethed quietly. Flavours can mingle? He was making it sound as if he was an experienced chef now, instead of a man who had, since the move, avoided anything to do with buying for or preparing their meals. Well, let him find his way around the unfamiliar kitchen by himself. In previous, happier times, when Barney had said he'd make the dinner that night, Nell had always got all the ingredients and utensils out ready for him, as if he was a contestant on *Ready, Steady, Cook*. Let him fly solo and see how much longer it took.

Nell swung her chair round and faced the computer. There were dozens of emails waiting for her attention. Most could be deleted but her attention homed in on one from Bev, entitled 'Food for Thought'. Maryam was copied in too but hadn't replied yet. Nell put on her reading glasses and scanned the text.

Hi Both,

I've been pondering prior to our get-together later (make sure you're hungry, by the way, I always cook too much) and thought I'd send you a few brief notes.

- I've already had replies from a few folk saying they want to join us, so we need to fix a day and time for the first meeting asap. I know I seem to be rushing this along, but I don't want to lose momentum. Any suggestions? When can you most easily get away from the shop, Maryam?
- Should we limit the number and have a waiting list, if it seems as if we've got too many people? I want everyone to get the chance to speak each week so it can't be too big. How about 12, including us 3? I guess we'll want to have our say too, to help it along.
- Name for the group? How about Reasons to be Cheerful, like the song? Or shall we go for Reasons to be Happy? I'm open to ideas but we need to decide on this quickly so I can make some programmes.
- With that in mind, how many weeks should we plan for? I'm suggesting 6 to begin with, but we can always add more if it takes off.

Anyway, looking forward to seeing you later, I'm off to do a christening visit. Wish me luck, small babies aren't really my thing. They always scream at me.

Bev xx

Nell's head was reeling by the time she'd taken all the notes in. It was really happening, and she was going to be expected to join in with the soul-searching. She realised that she'd kind of expected her role to be more like that at the homeless centre, welcoming people in and providing the tea and cake. This sounded much more hands on. As she bit her lip, alarmed at the thought, she heard the clunk of a walking stick on the varnished floorboards of the landing and Frank came shuffling into the study followed by Anton.

'I think it's lunchtime, Nell,' he said hopefully. 'Are you doing some writing?'

Nell looked up at her father-in-law, suddenly longing to tell someone about the new project and have an unbiased opinion.

'I'll come and make some sandwiches in a minute,' she said. 'Sit down, Frank. There's something I want to run past you. It's about a new group I'm helping to start over at the church, and actually...' An interesting thought occurred to her as he settled himself in his chair with an 'Ooof' noise. '...Actually, it might be right up your street too.'

12

As Nell made her way up Tinderbox Lane to join Fiddler's Row, she felt a wild urge to break into a run. It had been a long time since she'd left Barney and Frank completely to their own devices in the evening, and the jolt of freedom was exhilarating. They had both looked at her with lugubrious reproach in their eyes as she'd left, and even Anton had whimpered.

'Bye, blokes,' Nell had said cheerily, but only muttered replies had sent her on her way. Hey ho. They'd be absolutely fine together, and Barney's bolognese smelt delicious, filling the whole house with aromas of garlic, herbs and tomatoes. Rick had sniffed appreciatively and had looked as if he was hoping for an invitation to stay, but Nell knew there was no chance of that. Barney would probably sooner ask Attila the Hun for dinner than their helpful, friendly builder. The animosity on her husband's side crackled every time he and Rick were in a room together. Luckily, Rick had either not noticed or sensibly decided to ignore it.

Nell had reached the turning that would take her further into the village and eventually to the church when she heard her name being called, and a battered van pulled up alongside her. She turned to see Rick with one elbow propped on the open window of the driver's side.

'You shoulda said you were leaving, babe,' he said. 'I can give you a lift. Where are you off to?'

'Only to the church, and I needed the fresh air,' said Nell, admiring the way dimples appeared in both Rick's cheeks as he grinned at her. In fact, she was painfully aware that she'd been admiring quite a lot of Rick's various attributes since he began working at Hollyhocks Cottage. Just seeing him with his tanned and muscular legs and arms on show was enough to set her senses swimming. It was getting ridiculous. No wonder Barney seemed to have picked up on it, knowing her so well. Nell had caught herself watching their builder out of the corner of her eye whenever she was far enough away for it not to be too obvious. Had Rick noticed? Her face flamed as he gestured for her to get in the van.

'Hop in, I'm going that way,' he said, and Nell obeyed without further ado, unable to resist. A faint hint of sawdust and new wood hung around the interior of the van, mixed with the heady scent of Rick himself. How could he manage to smell so good when he'd been working hard in a warm atmosphere all day?

'So, you're off to see the Rev Bev?' Rick asked as they set off again. 'What's that all about? Is it one of them religious meetings?'

Nell laughed. 'No, we're setting up a new kind of thing. I'll tell you more about it tomorrow if you're interested.'

'Oh, yes, babe... I wanted to talk to you about that.' Rick seemed to be avoiding looking at Nell, although granted he was driving, so he had good reason to keep his eyes on the road. 'It's a bit awkward. You see, Bev's asked me to fix the dodgy lock on the church door tomorrow and do a few more little jobs while I'm there. You don't mind, do you?'

They were already at the vicarage, and Rick slowed down to let Nell get out. She opened the passenger door, lost for words. The disappointment at not having the prospect of Rick around to liven up her day hit her sharply. Also, was it right for Bev to poach her only helper like this, especially when the work was so important? Frank must be given his own space as soon as possible. She swallowed her annoyance and did her best to smile. 'Of course that's fine. You'll be back the day after though, won't you? Only, Frank's desperate to get into his annexe as soon as he can.'

'Yeah, yeah, no worries. I'll get done here by nightfall. See ya.'

Rick drove away with a somewhat unnecessary screech of his wheels and Nell watched him go. She shook herself and tried not to be so churlish. Bev had a church to look after as well as a large and draughty-looking vicarage and she was on her own. Surely Nell could get over herself and stop being petty.

'Hiya, come on in,' Bev said, as she opened the door. 'You're very welcome. It's not a comfortable house in the winter but on a warm night like this with the French doors open into the garden, it's lovely. We're eating on the terrace and then we'll move inside before the midges and gnats start eating us. Maryam's running a bit late, but she'll be here soon.'

Nell followed Bev down the long corridor, through a large living room and out into the garden, where a table with benches attached had been covered with a bright plastic cloth.

Bev was looking just as colourful as her table, in yellow dungarees with a cornflower-blue striped top underneath. Her feet were bare, and her hair looked even spikier than usual.

'I've been looking forward to this all day,' Bev said. 'You girls are the best. I can't wait to get going on our group. We can all do with a dollop of happiness. Here, have a glass of fizz. The parents of the baby I'm christening gave me some prosecco. I earned it. The little treasure threw up all over me as soon as I got there and then its nappy leaked on my jeans.'

Bev handed Nell a champagne flute and opened the bottle with a flourish.

'You've done that before,' Nell said, sipping her drink.

'A bit too often, I suppose. It's hard not to reach for the bottle after a day like the one I've had. I was called out to visit a dying man an hour or two ago. I was just in time to be with him and his family. It's my job and I'm glad to be doing it but...'

Nell could see that Bev was exhausted. There were shadows under her eyes and her shoulders were drooping. 'You should have put us off, we could have come another night.'

'You're kidding. This is just what I need. Oh, that's the doorbell, I'll go and let Maryam in.'

Soon the three women were sitting round the table, eating the best lasagne Nell had ever tasted and listening to the sound of Bev's neighbours' children protesting as they were hustled off to bed.

'You're wasted in the church, you should open a bistro,' said Maryam, reaching for another chunk of garlic bread.

'It might be easier, but I think I'm in the right place now. Actually, that brings me on to our first session. You two need to think of a favourite song that means a lot to you. If we three start the ball rolling, the others will soon get the idea. That's one of my favourite songs.'

'What is?' Nell was confused. The prosecco had gone straight to her head and the warm evening, combined with the friendliness of the other two, had put all grumpy thoughts about Rick defecting to help Bev out of her mind.

'"The Right Place". It's by Eddi Reader. I might pick a

different one for the group though. Go on, think about it now
and when we go inside, we'll make a proper list.'

'I'd choose something with a beat. Something you can dance
to,' said Maryam. 'We probably don't strike you as disco divas
but Rashid and me can sizzle on the dancefloor if we get the
chance. How about one from *Dirty Dancing*? Or an old Bee Gees
hit? Yes, that's it – "Stayin' Alive". I choose that one.'

Nell wasn't sure what to settle for. There were so many songs
that brought back happy memories or that triggered more
melancholy, nostalgic ones. 'I'll think about it,' she said
eventually.

When Maryam was the first to be bitten by a ferocious
evening bug, they all retreated to the living room and settled
round a large oak table at one end.

'This house is enormous,' said Nell, half envious and half
daunted at the thought of the upkeep. 'I bet you rattle round in it
on your own.'

As soon as she'd said the words, Nell was mortified at her
own tactlessness, but Bev just smiled. 'It's better to be by yourself and your own boss than to share a home with someone who
doesn't fit into your life,' she said. 'I'll tell you about the fiasco
of my marriage sometime, but not tonight. We've got work
to do.'

Bev reached for her iPad which was ready on the table. She
gestured to a stack of paper and coloured pens. Nell and
Maryam both took a sheet of paper and selected a colour.

'Now we're ready to roll,' said Bev, switching on the iPad.
'This is the fun part. I want you both to write down as many
different themes as we could explore on a weekly basis with our
group. I'm aiming for a mixed age range and topics that'll set
discussions going. I'll open a new file on here called *Reasons to be
Happy* because I think that's the best title for us, and we can add

the shortlist when we've narrowed it down. I've done my list already. Off you go!'

Bev got up to light a few candles, and even though it was only twilight outside, the atmosphere in the room was enhanced by their flickering glow. Nell and Maryam stared into space for a minute or two before beginning to scribble frantically. Nell had chosen a purple felt tip and her words flowed quickly. Her fingers tingled as she wrote, and a fleeting thought struck her that she might be more productive with her embryonic novel if she took a pack of coloured gel pens and a new notebook out onto the green and let the ideas spill out instead of torturing herself in front of her laptop.

After five minutes, Bev called a halt. 'Next I'd like you to read through your ideas and circle the five best ones, okay?' she said. 'Then we'll share what we've got.'

This was trickier. Nell chewed her thumbnail and viewed the bright purple words on the page in front of her. Maryam was circling away already but Nell was reluctant to ditch any of her suggestions. In the end, a stern look from Bev nudged her into making her choices.

'Shall I go first?' the vicar said. The others nodded, reprieved for a moment.

'Bearing in mind the first week will be all about the effects of music in our lives, my final five are...' Bev left a pause worthy of *Strictly Come Dancing*. '...how to sleep more peacefully, mindfulness, the importance of good food, friendships and coming to terms with your memories. Over to you, Nell.'

Nell's eyes were wide with amazement. 'How did you do that?' she asked. 'Did you peep at my paper?'

'No, I absolutely did not. Why, have you got some similar ones?'

'Here are mine. Living in the moment – that's pretty much

the same as mindfulness. How to get a good night's sleep to set yourself up for a better day. You are what you eat – which foods make your life better? How to build strong friendships, and why our memories are so important, going forward.'

'That's uncanny,' said Bev. 'We literally *are* on the same page. How about you, Maryam? Don't tell me you wrote the same things, that would be too weird.'

Maryam held out her sheet of paper. 'Look for yourself.'

Bev looked down and read, '"Why a bad night's sleep can stand in the way of a happy day. How to concentrate on the *now*, not the *then*. Nurturing yourself and others with good food. Toxic friends – how to avoid them and find better ones. Looking back on our lives, at who has been influential and why."'

The three women looked at each other without speaking for a long moment. Bev nodded slowly. 'Well, if that isn't a sign that we're on the right track, I don't know what is,' she said. 'All we need now is to put them in a logical order and we're away. Any thoughts?'

'How about we just pick the second week's theme so we can give people an idea of where we're going next?' said Maryam. 'By the time we're ready for week three we'll have more of an idea how it's going. I reckon we might be best to keep it low key and go for the foodie week. There's a lot of mileage in that and everyone will have stories to tell and favourite comfort foods. They might even want to bring samples, if we're lucky.'

'Great suggestion, Maryam,' said Bev. 'Also, if we give everyone our entire programme, they could be tempted to skip weeks they don't fancy. We want everyone to get the full effect. I think the memories one would be best left until last though. By that time everyone should be feeling more comfortable sharing their more personal thoughts.'

Nell shivered. The more she thought about this whole

concept, the less confident she felt in being a part of the action rather than just a helpful assistant to Bev. She was an organiser at heart. A listener, always ready with sympathy and a mug of tea or some comfort food. It looked as if there was no way of avoiding joining in with a whole lot of soul-searching. The prospect was quite, quite terrifying.

13

The next fortnight seemed to fly by. Summer was well under way now and Barney escaped to the country park as often as possible. Day by day he was looking much happier, with a slowly deepening tan on his face, arms and legs. Even Frank commented on the changes.

'I don't know what you've been doing over at that place, but it's put a sparkle in your eye, lad,' he said to his son when he found Barney once again sitting on the bench lacing up his boots ready to check out more walks.

Barney opened his mouth to speak but seemed to think better of it and whistled for Anton. The dog's lead was already by his side. Nell, watching from the kitchen doorway, was intrigued and vaguely unsettled. She knew what was going on with the guided walk planning, but she hadn't expected this new project to have such a dramatic effect. It was only now that Barney was looking fitter and walking with a spring in his step that Nell realised how much less than contented he'd been feeling lately, even with the decision for the move going his way.

She came out into the garden just in time to see him heading down the path.

'Have a good morning!' she shouted after Barney. 'Will you be home for lunch?'

'Probably not, I'll get something at the café,' he called back over his shoulder.

'Don't forget tonight's the first one of the group meetings that we're starting. I'll be going out around six to help set up!' said Nell, raising her voice a few more decibels. It was too late. Barney and Anton had gone.

'He's spending more time at that park than he is with us these days,' grumbled Frank. 'I was hoping he'd come over to the pub with me for a game of darts at lunchtime. I never get to go anywhere.'

Nell glanced at her father-in-law and saw that his shoulders were drooping and even his bristly grey moustache looked sad. He lowered himself onto the garden bench with his customary wince of pain.

'Why don't you come round to the church room with me tonight?' Nell said. 'I think you'd like the people who've signed up. I've already met some of them and there's still a couple of places going spare if you want to give it a go?'

'What, spend the evening whingeing about how miserable I am? I think you're expecting to wave some sort of magic wand and have everyone floating around like hippies at a festival. Not likely!'

'So, what will you do instead? The alternatives aren't that inspiring. There's *Eastenders*, or a documentary about the state of the nation's prisons. Or you could watch Barney trawling the internet for background information about his new stamping ground.'

Frank huffed to himself and didn't answer so Nell decided to go and see if Rick was ready for more tea and biscuits. At least *he* always smiled at her.

In the annexe, Rick was putting the finishing touches to the new shower and wet room he'd been working on for Frank. He looked up as Nell came in bearing a tray with two mugs of tea and a plate of chocolate chip cookies.

'My favourites,' he said appreciatively, downing tools. 'You're spoiling me. The Rev Bev only has the plain kind. I've dropped enough hints, but she never gets it. Craftsmen like me need quality biscuits. Those pathetic Rich Tea ones just go slimy when you dunk them.'

Nell sat down on the floor cross-legged, glad she was wearing shorts and a baggy T-shirt that didn't matter if they got dusty. Rick joined her and she handed him the tea with the added sugars.

'It's looking great in here,' Nell said, looking around. 'You've finished all the painting in the living room too. I think Frank should be able to move in soon.'

'And then I'll be out of your hair. You'll be glad to get your space back,' suggested Rick, dunking a cookie in his tea.

Nell's mood plummeted even more. With Rick off the premises, Barney always out and Frank often lost in his own world of grief and loss, who was she going to talk to? She'd loved these chats with Rick and having him working around the house, not least because it meant she could admire his rippling biceps and strongly muscled legs. She couldn't help wondering what it would feel like if he suddenly turned to her and pulled her into a passionate clinch. Would she protest violently and run out of the room, or would she kiss him back and lose herself in his arms?

Rick appeared to have asked Nell a question, but she'd missed it completely, lost in her fantasy. It was dangerous, this lack of physical contact in her life. It had been a long time since she and Barney had done any more than peck each other on the cheek as they headed for their respective bedrooms.

'Sorry, I was... erm... thinking about something else. What did you say?' Nell asked, hot embarrassment reddening her face and making her tingle all over.

'Oh, nothing much. Just wondering about this meeting thing you and the other two are organising. Bev told me about it the other day. I might come along, if that's okay. Do I have to book?'

Nell was dumbfounded. Rick was the last person she'd have expected to want to join in the quest for happiness, but maybe that was just her snobbish preconceptions. He might be just the same as the rest of them, wanting to know if there was more to life than plodding from day to day trying to make sense of everything and not having much success.

'Of course you can,' Nell said. 'That'd be lovely. It starts at seven o'clock. I'll put your name on the list. Frank might come too, if the thought of the alternatives is bad enough, and that'll make it the full twelve.'

'Ace. I could pick him up in the van if you like? I guess you'll be going early to get sorted.'

Nell was touched by this thoughtful gesture. Her eyes met Rick's and for a moment neither of them spoke. Nell wondered if she was imagining the sudden electricity flowing between them. It was probably just wishful thinking. Before she could say anything, he got to his feet.

'Right, this shower room won't finish itself. Thanks for the brew. I'd better get on. See you tonight, yeah?'

Partly relieved but somewhat deflated, Nell nodded and stood up, bending to retrieve the tray. She'd need to stop this foolish dreaming. Rick wasn't in the least interested in her as a woman, she was just someone who paid his wages. And if he had been, what would she have done? Barney didn't deserve an unfaithful wife, even if it was only in her mind. But a small, bitter voice in Nell's head said, 'He's spending all his spare time with another woman and it's not fair. There's nothing left for me.'

As she washed the mugs and put them away, Nell reflected that at least tonight she'd get to meet the mystery lady who was enticing her husband away on such a regular basis. She dried her hands and sat down at the kitchen table, reaching for the notebook where she'd been jotting down more details and ideas for future group meetings. The list of potential attendees for tonight's session was a few pages in. Nell ran a finger down the names and then added Rick and Frank at the bottom. She tried to imagine how the evening would pan out as she looked at the list.

1, 2 and 3. Bev, Nell and Maryam (group leaders)

4, 5 and 6. Beryl, Winnie and Anthea (Saga Louts)

7. Maurice (friend of the SL)

8. Kate Brown (café)

9. Ingrid Copperfield (ran The Treasure Trove corner shop before Maryam)

10. Harry Henderson (apparently the nearest thing to gentry that Willowbrook possesses)

11. Rick

12. Frank?

If Frank came, that completed the total that Bev had antici-pated being the ideal benchmark. If they all turned up, there would be enough people to make it less stressful for everyone. Nell was thinking safety in numbers, but it would still give a chance for them all to have a turn speaking (if they chose to join in fully, of course). There were only four men to eight women which wasn't the perfect split, but at least there was a mix. Tonight was going to be exciting and alarming for Nell in equal measure. She was still nervously aware that she wouldn't be able to fade into the background and just facilitate the others contributing, and she certainly couldn't spend all evening providing hot drinks and cake.

Reminded of one of her tasks to prepare for later, Nell set about finding the ingredients to make a double batch of scones. That was one job she could do without worrying. She was rubbing the fat into the flour in her largest mixing bowl when Frank came into the kitchen.

'I think I will join you tonight,' he said, in his most off-hand tone of voice. 'Rick just had a word with me as he was leaving. If he can do it, I don't see why I shouldn't. He's picking me up at quarter to seven.'

Frank left the room before Nell could reply. She gazed after him for a long moment, lost in thought. This was shaping up to become a very interesting evening.

14

Barney strode across the green and along the track that led to Willowbrook Country Park. Had he but known it, his feelings were as mixed as Nell's about the day's forthcoming events. Kate had scheduled his first guided walk for 3.45 p.m., especially timed so it could include a handful of parents and children from the village primary school, and Barney was keen to have a practice run on his own first. He was also hoping to run a few more ideas for future expeditions past Kate when she'd finished serving lunches.

In his backpack, Barney had a series of laminated markers with numbers and pictures of wildlife on them, plus a sheaf of worksheets to make the whole walk into a treasure trail. The last time he'd made something so detailed had been when he'd organised a team-building event for his workmates. The laminator had been bought for that occasion and Barney had been itching to find another use for it ever since. Watching the hot, film-covered sheets slide out of the little machine was immensely satisfying, even though he knew Nell wouldn't have approved of all the extra plastic he was generating. Ah, well, this batch had been produced for a good cause.

As he slowly walked his planned route, trying to amble at a child-friendly pace for accurate timing, Barney stopped every now and again to attach a marker to a tree, high enough up so that any passing dogs wouldn't be tempted to leap up and grab them. He greeted everyone he passed with a smile and a cheerful hello, feeling a warm sense of shared ownership of the lovely site. In this moment, there was nowhere else in the world he'd rather be.

The weather had been cooler for a couple of days previously but today was sunny and mild again. The lake sparkled as he passed by, and even the swans seemed pleased to see Barney, waggling up to him to see if he had any food for them, but swimming away in disgust when it was clear he was empty handed. They left sunlit ripples in their wake and birds wheeled and cried as they flew ever-widening circuits over the trees and water. In the distance, Barney could see Maurice doing a circuit of the lake on his daily constitutional. They waved to each other and Barney felt an even stronger sense of belonging.

When he neared the bench that had Frankie Clifford's name on it, Barney recognised three more familiar faces. Beryl, Winnie and Anthea were sitting in a row, each with a paper bag in their hand. They were throwing torn-up crusts of bread to some very enthusiastic ducks and moorhens, with a few pigeons circling, ready to pounce on any leftovers. Barney contemplated reminding the ladies that seeds and sweetcorn and so on were considered much healthier food for the wildfowl these days, but his nerve failed him as all three turned to watch him approach.

'Hello, here's our resident hiking expert,' said Anthea. 'I was meaning to ask you if you wanted to borrow my old copy of one of Wainwright's walking books. One of my husbands left it behind. I can't remember which one. Might have been Laurence, he was a great one for going off on a ramble. At least, he said that's what he was doing...'

Her voice tailed off and Beryl laughed. 'From what you told me at the time, Laurence definitely had the wanderlust. He used to...'

'That's enough of that, Barney doesn't want a history of Anthea's exes' peccadillos,' interrupted Winnie, giving Beryl a meaningful stare. 'What are you up to with those pictures, lad?'

Barney put his bag down and began to explain about his treasure trail. All three ladies looked impressed. 'It's going to give our Kate a proper lift if all this takes off,' Winnie said. 'She's worked really hard with the local council to get the café involved with more activities in the park. We love it here, don't we, girls?'

The other two nodded. 'Years ago, it was just a load of gravel pits, you know,' said Beryl. 'I've got some old photos somewhere. It was like a lunar landscape. It's good for Willowbrook to have a place like this on the doorstep. And now you're getting the kids involved too. Good for you, son.'

Barney's heart swelled with pride. It was good to hear from other people that Kate was appreciating his efforts and now the Saga Louts were giving him their own support too. He was about to tell them more about his plans when Beryl changed the subject.

'We're all looking forward to the group tonight,' she said. 'I wonder what it'll be like. I hope the cake's as good as usual.'

For a minute, Barney couldn't think what she was talking about but then he remembered Nell calling after him as he'd left the house earlier. Slightly ashamed of himself, Barney knew he should have answered her, but he'd carried on walking and pretended not to hear. A pang of sadness hit him when he thought how little he and Nell were communicating these days.

Although he'd absorbed the basic aim of the fledgling group and Nell was aware of his walking plans, both of them were studiously avoiding getting involved in each other's activities.

'Oh, I'm sure if Nell's involved, the meeting will be a complete winner,' Barney said, but instead of his words making him seem proud of his wife's organising skills, somehow they only succeeded in sounding waspish. None of the ladies answered. For a while they all watched several swans approaching gracefully across the lake, muscling in on the crustier chunks of bread the ducks had ignored. Anthea produced another bag and shared out what looked like a stale slab of fruit cake.

'They like a treat, these big chaps,' she said. 'I always save something for them. So, will you be at the meeting tonight, Barney? Are you coming along to search for a bit of happiness, or have you already found your pot of gold?'

Barney saw the other two glance at Anthea and then at each other. He could feel a strange tension in the air as they all waited for him to reply.

'I... well, no, I don't reckon it's my thing really,' he said lamely, looking at the ground. 'I don't go in for that sort of stuff as a rule.'

'What sort of stuff?' Winnie's eyes were wide and innocent as she looked up at him. 'Talking about your feelings, and all that, you mean?'

'Maybe it's a man thing,' said Anthea. 'One of my husbands was like that. In fact, scratch that, they all were, come to think of it. It was as if they were allergic to telling you what they were thinking. Quentin was the worst. He didn't even have the guts to tell me why he was leaving. *And* he took my best silk knickers with him,' she added.

There didn't seem to be a suitable response to this, so Barney quickly said goodbye to the ladies, picked up his backpack and went on his way. Soon, the route for later was set out to his satisfaction and he headed back to the café for lunch. Sam was behind the counter today and greeted Barney warmly.

'My little girl Elsie's really looking forward to the treasure trail,' he said. 'I'm picking her up from school and meeting some of the others there. Then we're coming straight back here. She's packed a change of clothes that she says are the perfect thing to wear for an adventure. I'm not sure you'll agree but it saved an argument this morning.'

Now the time for his first official walk was approaching, Barney's nerves began to really kick in. What if the whole thing was a disaster? Kate would look at him with different eyes then. Maybe the kids would run riot. If they were bored, they'd refuse to listen to him and start moaning about wanting to go straight to the playpark instead.

'Don't worry, Barney,' said Kate, who'd clearly overheard Sam's remarks and come through from the kitchen just in time to catch Barney's agonised expression. 'I've got the clipboards and pencils ready, and there's also a pack of stickers to give out for rewards as you go along. Elsie and her gang'll do anything for a sparkly sticker. Sit down and have a sandwich while you can. I've made you a ham, cheese and pickle on seeded wholemeal.'

Immeasurably touched that Kate had remembered what his favourite lunchtime snack was, Barney accepted the mug of coffee and the sandwich on a plate that Sam was holding out and went to settle down in the only free seat, which happened to be at a table with Maurice in residence. The older man gave Barney a friendly nod, fully engaged in battling with a crusty cob, with careless disregard for his dentures. They both ate in silence while around them the comforting hubbub of the café soothed Barney's worries about the forthcoming activity. By the time he'd finished his lunch and done a final circuit of his trail, he was much calmer, and ready to face whatever the afternoon had in store.

On the dot of 3.45 p.m., Barney heard a lively burst of chattering coming from the direction of the path to the side of the village where the school could be found. Turning to welcome his guests, Barney was delighted to see that the little gang was dressed for action in shorts and T-shirts, all except for Elsie, who was rocking a purple leotard with a pink sequinned tutu and unicorn wellies.

Sam had obviously taken charge of parents and children alike, and Barney remembered Kate saying that he often helped out with school visits to various places.

'Right, everyone,' Sam said, clapping his hands. 'This is Mr Appledore, and he's got a very exciting activity for us all to do. Mind you...' he added, fixing a particularly effervescent small boy with a firm stare. 'Mind you, the only people who are going to be able to get some of Mr Appledore's very special stickers are the ones who know how to...?'

He left the question open, and six voices chorused '...behave themselves.'

'That's right,' Sam said approvingly. 'And when you do, your mummies and daddies are going to be so proud of you. Over to you, Mr A.'

Taking a deep breath, Barney launched into his introduction, keeping it brief, and then he and Sam handed out pencils and clipboards complete with treasure sheets. There was a flutter of excited chatter as the group mustered themselves ready to set off, and then Barney's inaugural walk was well and truly underway.

Afterwards, Barney couldn't bring to mind many details of

the afternoon, other than the heart-stopping moment when the noisiest boy walked straight into the shallows of the lake and then fell onto his bottom, wailing. Barney was certain that this would mean the end of his walking career before it had properly begun. He rushed forward anxiously, only to find that the boy's mother was already hauling her son out.

'George,' she said wearily. 'What did I tell you about going near the water?'

'My socks are wet!' howled George, as the others looked on in admiration and awe.

He stood on the path with pondwater running down his body from his waist to his feet as his mother quickly stripped him of his sodden clothes and replaced them with clean ones from her bag. 'Don't look so worried,' she said to Barney. 'It's fine. He always does this.' She turned to the other parents who were stifling giggles. 'Remember the pond-dipping trip?'

'George dipped himself instead of his fishing net,' chimed in Elsie. 'He did catch the most tadpoles though. In his wellies.'

The rest of the walk passed without drama. Barney's stickers seemed to fly off the page as he enthusiastically rewarded each picture the children found and talked about the different living creatures on each one. When the final photograph of an ice-cream cone was discovered, tied to the slide at the playpark, there were whoops of joy. Sam, who had slipped away moments before, returned with a box of Cornettos.

'They're all strawberry flavour, to save arguments,' he said, dishing them out. 'Kate's given me enough for your mums and dads too. No pushing though. Make sure you leave one for Mr Appledore.'

Elsie took the last ice cream and presented it to Barney, beaming up at him. 'You're a very clever man,' she told him. 'You know lots of stuff.'

'I'll have you know that's the highest praise ever from my daughter,' Sam whispered as the group settled down to eat their prizes before they melted, eager for the promised half hour on the playpark that was the final part of their tour. 'Kate's going to be chuffed to bits with you too, Barney.'

Kate was indeed chuffed with him. Her shining eyes when she'd heard how well the afternoon had gone made Barney feel as if he'd won some sort of award, something even better than a sparkly sticker. As he strolled home, the fleeting thought crossed his mind that it was a long time since Nell had looked at him like that. There was no need to go to an embarrassing meeting about looking for happiness. Barney was more contented at this moment than he'd been for years.

15

The church room looked less than welcoming when Nell arrived at six o'clock, but Bev was already bustling around putting chairs in a circle, and by the time Maryam appeared, they had added folding coffee tables here and there. A large urn was bubbling away in the adjoining kitchenette and when Nell's scones and some very fancy chocolate biscuits, courtesy of Bev, were out on covered plates and mugs were lined up by the serving hatch, Nell began to feel as if the evening was going to be a success, if only on the catering front.

'Do you think they'll all turn up?' whispered Maryam to Nell, as Bev went to station herself by the door. 'What if everyone chickens out or finds they've had a better offer?'

Nell had been having similar thoughts herself but plastered on a smile and assured Maryam this wasn't going to happen. 'Even if nobody shows, we've got a happy evening of cake eating ahead,' she said. 'And...'

But the rest of the sentence was never uttered, because now Bev was flinging the door wide to usher in the Saga Louts, closely followed by a tall, elegant blonde wearing patchwork dungarees in shades of turquoise and green and decorated with tiny mirrors.

'This is Ingrid,' said Bev to Nell. 'Ingrid ran The Treasure Trove before the Habeebs came here. She's our resident expert in decluttering your life.'

Ingrid laughed and came forward to shake Nell by the hand. This formal greeting rather floored Nell, but the cool touch of Ingrid's hand was somehow reassuring. 'I've finished all my decluttering now,' she said. 'I've hardly got anything left and it's a good feeling. This group is a great idea. I've often wondered how other people feel about the idea of chasing happiness and what it really is.'

'You and me both,' came a voice from behind Ingrid, and Nell turned to see a smaller woman with rosy cheeks and a shining bob of golden-brown hair. 'I'm Kate from the café,' she said to Nell. 'I know your husband, of course, and I've been meaning to make the effort to call and see you to say hello, but what with one thing and another, I haven't got round to it yet.'

Nell tried hard to view this newcomer dispassionately, but a sudden burst of unexpected resentment took her breath away. So this was the person who was taking up all of Barney's spare time. He'd never once asked her to come to the café with him. Perhaps this explained why he hadn't wanted her there. Kate was very attractive, in a wholesome kind of way, Nell thought. She had a comforting, nurturing air about her. Nell's own nurturing instincts had in recent months been used up in making sure her offspring were all surviving away from the nest, looking after Lottie and then, after her mother-in-law's death, in caring for Frank. Perhaps Barney had been feeling neglected in that area, but why should Nell be the only one to do the mothering? Couldn't Barney find it in his heart to fuss over *her* for a change?

Biting back these vitriolic thoughts, Nell smiled at Kate in what she hoped was a friendly manner. 'You'd be welcome to pop round anytime,' she said. 'I've been busy overseeing the building work since we came but Rick's nearly finished now. Oh, look, here he is now, with my father-in-law.'

The arrival of Rick caused a major fluttering in the group. Beryl and Winnie rushed forward to greet him, Anthea looked on with an indulgent air and Nell couldn't help a shiver of what felt suspiciously like lust as Rick shrugged off his denim shirt, revealing a pristine white vest that left his muscular shoulders bare and showed off his tan to perfection. Frank glanced across at Nell and winked, clearly amused by this show of masculine beefcake. She raised her eyebrows and grinned back but the tingling feeling lingered uncomfortably and she was forced to reach into her bag for her water bottle and take a few steadying gulps.

'Hot in here, innit?' Rick said, grinning round at them all. 'I heard on the radio that we've got better weather than they're having in the Med. Bet the guys who've booked to go to Benidorm this week are kicking themselves.'

Nell withdrew to the kitchen on the pretext of getting a drink of water. She ran her wrists under the cold tap for a few moments, a tried-and-tested tip given to her by Lottie many years ago when Nell had been pregnant with the twins during a long heatwave. Feeling cooler, she returned to the main room just as Bev was performing any remaining introductions. Nell was beginning to think nobody else was going to arrive when she heard a discreet cough and saw that Maurice had entered unnoticed. He was dressed in perfectly pressed cream linen trousers and a white shirt. As they all turned, he removed his Panama hat and gave a small bow. 'Harry's just paying our taxi driver,' he said. 'Is that the lot of us?'

Bev hurried to the door to make sure the final member of the group was safely inside, and when Nell saw the man who must be Harry Henderson, she could see why the vicar had been concerned. The old gentleman in the beige summer raincoat looked very frail and was leaning heavily on an ornate, silver-topped cane as he hobbled towards the rest of the group. With a shock, Nell belatedly realised that Frank hadn't brought his own walking stick with him. It was the first time she'd seen him without it for many months. What did it mean? Was he feeling stronger or did he not want to look feeble in front of these new people?

Bev was now guiding everyone towards the circle of chairs. 'Sit wherever you like,' she said. 'But I guess if you feel able, it'd be better to settle down next to someone you don't know well, or even at all. I know that won't be easy because most of you are familiar faces at least to each other, but let's give it a go. You'll see why later.'

Frank and Harry both looked alarmed, but the others obediently shuffled into place, with a couple of adjustments as they tried hard to do as Bev had asked. Eventually, there was just one seat left, and Bev took it, smiling around at the group reassuringly.

'Don't look so apprehensive,' she said. 'This isn't going to hurt.'

'That's what my dentist always says,' mumbled Frank, but he didn't look half as worried as Nell had thought he might. She looked around the circle and was pleased to see that the arrangement was a good balance, as far as she could tell. The line-up went as follows: Beryl, Kate, Rick, Maryam, Anthea, Harry, Nell, Winnie, Frank, Ingrid, Bev and Maurice. The only real kerfuffle had come when Anthea and Maurice had found themselves next to each other and Anthea had swiftly moved, meaning Beryl was now sitting between Maurice and Kate, but finally they all seemed reasonably settled.

'Right,' said Bev. 'My instinct tells me to start with a brief prayer but I'm worried in case not all of you would welcome that. Does anybody really mind?'

There were a couple of uncomfortable glances at Bev but to Nell's relief, nobody voiced any objections. Bev closed her eyes and bowed her head.

'Father God, bless this gathering of friends and friends-to-be. Help us to remain supportive, kind and loving as we begin to work towards knowing ourselves and each other better. Amen.'

'Well, that really *was* brief, dear,' said Beryl. 'I didn't even have time to make my shopping list in my head. The last vicar here used to ramble on forever. Winnie often had a nap during the prayers when we came to the Harvest Festival and Christmas services.'

'I wasn't the only one,' protested Winnie. 'Maurice used to snore.'

'I never did!' Maurice glared at Winnie, and Nell bit her lip to hide a smile. She hoped Bev was going to be able to handle interruptions tactfully. This group didn't look as if it was going to be a particularly peaceful one so far.

Bev held up a hand and the room fell silent.

'Back to the main business,' she said. 'As we go through the six sessions that are planned, and I hope you'll stick with us for them all, we're going to explore the things or people or places in our lives that make us feel that sense of peace and contentment.'

'I thought it was all about making us happier,' said Anthea. 'Isn't that the same thing, Bev?'

'Good question. And my answer is... sometimes, but not always. Anyway, more of that as we go along. Tonight, we're looking at something that can have a big effect on our minds, and that's music. As the bard so famously said...' She paused and waited hopefully.

'...if music be the food of love, play on,' finished Rick. Everyone's eyes were on him now, and he shrugged. 'Didn't any of you think a builder would know about Shakespeare? I do read, you know. And I did go to school.'

Nell cringed inwardly. She *had* been surprised. How snobbish. She could see Bev was a little taken aback too and was beaming.

'Great, thanks, Rick. Music can trigger a lot of emotions. Love, grief, fear, euphoria... I could go on. Now, I would like you all to talk to the person next to you about one piece of music that means something special to you and lifts your mood. I'm not going to ask everyone to introduce themselves around the circle because I think that puts a lot of unnecessary pressure on us, so let's cut straight to the chase. Off you go.'

There were a few seconds of awkwardness while people made a snap decision which way to turn and then it seemed as if everyone was speaking at once. Nell looked around the circle to check that there was nobody left on their own, then realised that there couldn't be because the group contained an even number. By her side, Harry was waiting with an eager expression on his face.

'We haven't met, my dear, but I'm Harry Henderson and I've lived in Willowbrook with my wife Penelope for many years,' he said. 'Penelope decided this idea wasn't for her. She doesn't go out in the evenings now if she can help it, but I must admit to being intrigued. You must be Nell, the new lady from Hollyhocks Cottage?'

Nell agreed that she was, and said that Frank, now deep in conversation with Winnie, was her father-in-law. 'We're only just settling in,' she said. 'But this is a great way of meeting local people. So, Harry, have you thought of a piece of music?'

'There are many I could choose,' he said. 'I'm eighty-eight this year and so my musical tastes go back a long way. Having said that, it's easy to find one that stands out particularly, and that's the wonderful love song from mine and my dear wife's favourite film. It's from *Casablanca*. Do you know the one? "As Time Goes By", it's called. How about you?'

Nell had been giving the matter some thought ever since Bev had mooted the idea for tonight. She smiled at Harry. 'Mine's not in any way a classic but it came out when I was single and had no idea what was in store for me. I thought I was an amazing dancer at the time. I wasn't, but this song always made me get up and boogie because I felt full of energy and... sassiness, I guess. It's Shania Twain. "Man, I Feel Like a Woman".'

Harry shook his head sadly. 'I'm sorry, I don't think I know that one. It sounds fun though. My Penelope has always been one heck of a woman, if you know what I mean. She's in her eighties now but we still have a little shuffle around the kitchen when the radio's playing something smoochy. Our cleaner often tunes it to a popular station. She hates Radio 3, and I forget to change it back. Or that's what I tell Penelope anyway.'

'Oh... well... that's lovely,' said Nell. The picture in her mind of this debonair man and his beloved wife dancing together in their kitchen was almost too beautiful to bear. She wondered how the others were getting on and looked across to catch Bev's eye. They nodded to each other and the vicar gave Nell a thumbs-up signal.

'I can see that Harry and Nell are ready to share their choices,' she said. 'I'm going to add all of your music to a Spotify playlist and then we'll listen to the songs while we have tea or coffee and cake. There are cold drinks too, if you're feeling the heat.'

'Do we have to tell you why we chose the music?' Maurice asked. He was looking rather downcast for someone who was supposed to have picked an uplifting tune.

'Only if you want to. The whole point is for you to identify the reason for yourself. It could be helpful to know what triggers a good feeling for you. Away you go, Nell.'

16

The others all turned to look at Nell as she told them the songs she and Harry had picked. Harry's voice cracked slightly as he explained about his kitchen dancing with Penelope and Nell wasn't the only one to blink away sudden tears. Nell's explanation was less emotional but several of the women nodded understandingly as she spoke.

'When I hear that song now, I remember how powerful I felt when I was in my early twenties,' Nell said.

'And you don't feel that way now?'

Bev's question wasn't easy to answer. Nell had known she might be put on the spot if she agreed to go first. There was always the option to say 'pass' but as one of the organisers, she thought she should probably lead the way.

'Not really very powerful,' she admitted. 'I'm a bit in limbo just now.'

'She wants to write a book, you see,' said Frank. 'I keep telling her she should just do it.'

Nell shot her father-in-law a dirty look. 'It's not just that.

Oh... I don't know what's wrong with me at the moment. I expect I'm just still settling into a new life. Let's move on.'

Winnie was next, and she'd chosen 'One Love'. 'My man loved a bit of Bob Marley. Hearing this brings him back to me,' she said. 'Ron used to play Bob and the Wailers in the car. We often nipped off to the Norfolk coast for a paddle. Cromer, Wells, Hunstanton. Ron used to say that him and me were like the song; one love and one heart. Joined at the hip, we were. He was quite the romantic at times.'

Nell could see that Bev was too moved to speak. From what she'd said, her own marriage hadn't been anything like this. It was time to move things forward. 'Go on then, Frank, what have you got up your sleeve?' Nell said. 'Surprise us.'

Nell had been joking, because she'd assumed Frank would choose a crooner of some sort, but his choice of song made her open her eyes wide.

'It's one by Marvin Gaye,' he said. 'I think it's really meant to be a love song, but I heard it when our Barney was born, and it made me realise how much he'd taken over my life and how proud I was to be his dad. It's called "Too Busy Thinking About My Baby".'

'Wow, Frank, that's so lovely. Does Barney know that you love that one, and why?' Nell asked, fascinated by this insight into the normally unsentimental Frank's past.

'No, and don't you go telling him,' Frank said. 'He'll think I'm a right soppy git. Who's next?'

Ingrid's song was 'Let Your Love Flow' by the Bellamy Brothers. 'The reason I picked it is personal. Let's just say it reminds me of when I was having a kind of *eureka* moment.'

'A positive one?' Bev asked.

'Oh, yes, the best.'

Maurice was next, and he chose Ella Fitzgerald's version of

'These Foolish Things', but like Ingrid, declined the chance to expand on the reason why. 'It's a bit of a melancholy song but it's got good memories for me,' was all he would say on the subject.

Beryl grinned at them all. 'Mine is "You Sexy Thing",' she said. 'My husband said it was my theme tune. We did have some fun.'

Winnie giggled. 'So did we. I think I've said this to Ingrid before, but the younger generations think they invented sex.'

Bev was blushing furiously now. 'Nice one, Beryl,' she said. 'How about you, Kate?'

'Mine's not a love song or a raunchy one,' Kate said. 'It's a song that celebrates meeting a person who's going to mean a lot, and who can make life better. It's about appreciating what you've got. Nick Drake, "Time Has Told Me".'

'Never heard of him, but I'm always ready to find new tunes to listen to,' said Rick. 'Mine's linked to my dad. It should have been his theme song really. He had a tough time bringing up three of us kids on his own. He always worked hard to bring the money in, but we never felt neglected after Mam died. The song's called "Life Ain't Easy". It's by Dr Hook. Does anyone know it?'

'If they don't, they soon will,' said Maryam. 'I've had a job to choose just one song. Rashid and me, we love a kitchen dance, just like Harry and his wife. I was going to go for "Stayin' Alive". But in the end, I picked a track by Kate Bush that reminds me of Rashid. He's got a sort of vulnerable look when he's worried. The song's called "The Man With the Child in His Eyes".'

Nell looked around the room. She could see by the looks on everyone's faces that they'd been enthralled and probably touched by some of the choices. Apart from Bev, there was only Anthea left.

'Well, thank goodness you've got me to lift the mood,'

Anthea said. 'There's nothing melancholy or romantic or nostalgic about my song. It's my own personal anthem and I put my Nina Simone CD on whenever I need cheering up. "Feeling Good" is my favourite track, and by the end of it, I always am. Feeling good, that is.'

Bev beamed at them all. Her eyes were bright with unshed tears. 'You are all totally amazing, and this is only the start of what we're going to achieve together,' she said. 'I haven't told you my choice yet, but I want you to listen to the words when it comes around later.'

'Is it cake time now?' Frank was peering across to the kitchen hatch with a hopeful look on his face.

'It most certainly is. I think we should all stand up and have a stretch, then collect a cuppa and a scone and maybe change places. I'm going to press play in a moment, and we can listen to each other's choices. How about that?'

Most of the group was on its feet before she'd even finished speaking, and Maryam and Nell only just made it to the kitchen before a queue formed. Nell could hear the hum of chattering as she made a giant pot of tea and Maryam spooned coffee into mugs. Soon, everyone was settled again and through the speakers came the emotive sound of Dooley Wilson singing 'As Time Goes By'. Nell's parents had loved *Casablanca* too. Her mum made no secret of what a crush she had on Humphrey Bogart and her dad had played along by pretending to be madly jealous. She went to sit in the empty seat next to Maurice and they smiled at each other.

Gradually, everyone fell silent as the music took control of the room. The choices were varied, and swung from tinkling piano through funky guitar, soul music and reggae. 'Let Your Love Flow' had nearly everyone singing along, although Maurice and Harry looked mystified. When it came to Bev's

choice, she turned up the sound slightly. Neil Diamond's voice
was familiar to most of them, but instead of the usual sing-along
sound of 'Sweet Caroline', this was a more thoughtful lyric.
'Pretty Amazing Grace' could have been a tribute to someone
special in Bev's life, but Nell had the strong feeling that it was
more about her faith journey. She clearly wasn't a person to
force her opinions on the group, but this was her way of telling
them all where she was coming from.

From there, Maurice's gentle, mournful song changed the
mood of the room yet again and Nell was mightily relieved when
'You Sexy Thing' broke the tension. Beryl was on her feet in an
instant, soon joined by Winnie and Anthea. Then came Nell's
choice and she got up to dance with them. They boogied happily
in the centre of the circle of chairs, wiggling and jiggling so hard
that by the end of the song, Bev had to pause the music while
the older ladies had what she tactfully described as a comfort
break.

When they were back again, somewhat flushed and out of
breath, Kate's choice gentled them into togetherness again, but
Rick managed to get them all on their feet for his song, and even
Harry swayed gently, arm in arm with Ingrid as Rick pushed the
chairs back and conducted a kind of impromptu hoedown.
Harry and Maurice both looked mightily relieved when they
were allowed to sit down for Maryam's selection, although Frank
was showing no sign of his usual creakiness. Nell had the shiv-
ers, as she always did when listening to Kate Bush's ethereal
tones, and then Nina Simone ended the session with panache.

Bev switched off the playlist and leaned back in her chair.
'Well, I think you're all incredible,' she said. 'Thank you so much
for doing this together. It's not my intention to pontificate about
why we made the choices we did but I'll just say that if we're
reflecting on finding happiness or, more to the point, peace and

contentment, maybe we all need to focus our minds on the moments our songs take us back to, and why they were so important.'

'Are you going to ask us to give more details about our song choices next time?' Maurice had a slightly hunted look in his eye and Bev hastened to reassure him.

'Only if you want to,' she said. 'Next week is all about food.'

'Now you're talking,' said Frank. 'Tell us more.'

Bev laughed. 'I thought that might be a popular theme. Well, we'll discuss how different foods can be a comfort at certain times and why. If you want to bring examples of your favourites for us to taste you're very welcome to do that, but please don't stress about it if you're not able to or don't want to, because we'll be providing plenty of our own things for you to try and discuss.'

'Brilliant! I've loved this,' said Kate. 'I can definitely bring some samples.'

'I wasn't sure about this idea of yours, Bev,' said Beryl. 'But I've got to admit you've got something here. We're your Happiness Gang, aren't we?'

'Love it,' said Winnie. 'A gang. I haven't been in one of those since I was at school.'

'Really?' said Bev, grinning at her. 'And what are the Saga Louts then?'

'We're a sisterhood, darling,' said Anthea loftily. 'Nothing as common as a gang. But I'm more than agreeable to be in this one,' she added hastily, when she saw Bev's face fall. 'The Happiness Gang. I like it.'

The others left a few at a time, already deep in conversation about their ideas for the following session. Rick seemed reluctant to leave but Frank nudged him so hard that he had to say goodbye, looking back over his shoulder as he went. Nell wondered if he'd been wanting to wait to offer her a lift home

too but was distracted from this intriguing thought by Bev and
Maryam enveloping her in a group hug.

'We did it, guys,' said Bev. 'We really did it. I knew we could,
but it was even better than I hoped it'd be.'

'It was amazing,' said Maryam. 'And next time we get the
bonus of food too. I'll make samosas, okay?'

'Very okay,' said Nell.

Her happy mood lasted until she and Maryam had walked
home together as far as the end of the lane. They hugged again,
and Nell walked the last part with her heart sinking. She wanted
more than anything to step back to a time when she and Barney
would have made a pot of tea or opened a bottle of wine and,
like Penelope and her beloved Harry, danced in the kitchen to
their own song choices, then gone to bed together for a cuddle
and a good catch-up on the day's events. With the best will in the
world, Nell couldn't see how she could make that happen now.

17

Barney awoke on the morning after Nell's meeting with a raging headache. He got out of bed and rummaged for painkillers, swilling a couple down with some tepid water from his bedside table. Too late, he realised that a small fly had met an untimely death in it sometime during the night. The choking fit that followed brought Nell running up the stairs and into the room, looking panicked.

'Whatever's the matter?' she gasped. 'Do you want me to pat you on the back?'

Barney regained control of his breathing with difficulty and shook his head, eyes streaming. The throbbing pain over his eyes was worse than ever now. It must have been that one extra glass of merlot he'd allowed himself while he was waiting for Nell and Frank to return. The evening had dragged unbearably with the other two out and he'd been very glad to hear the van door slam and Frank come in, although Nell wasn't with him, for some reason.

By the time she'd returned, even though she wasn't far behind his dad, Barney had checked Frank was safely up the stairs and was already in bed, feeling grumpy. He knew it was unreasonable to be cross. Nell was perfectly entitled to go out, of course she was, and he'd never minded anything like that before they moved. He supposed it was something to do with the fact that the odious Rick had been with her. Barney just could not abide the man. Wandering around with his posey vest and cut-offs, or even no shirt at all when it was particularly hot. It was unnecessary.

Barney usually gave Rick a polite but fairly curt greeting when he arrived and then avoided him like the plague, but he was no fool and he'd seen the way Nell looked at the builder. He still seethed as Frank and Nell made sure Rick was well supplied with tea, cold drinks and various treats to eat.

'Are you okay now?' Nell asked Barney as he wiped his eyes. 'What was all that about?'

She didn't sound very sympathetic now the crisis was over. Barney bet that if Rick was choking, Nell would have been on the phone to the emergency services by now. Either that or getting ready hopefully in case mouth-to-mouth resuscitation was needed.

'Swallowed a fly,' he muttered, not looking at her.

'I know a song about that,' Nell said, giggling. Barney quelled her with a glare, and she pulled a face. 'Sorry, have you lost your sense of humour this morning?'

'I've got a bad headache, if you must know,' Barney said. The sound of drilling downstairs made him wince. 'And now that... that... man is making a massive noise. I thought he'd finished in the house and was just tidying up loose ends in the annexe. When is he going away?'

Nell folded her arms and faced up to Barney. 'Your head's sore because you finished off that bottle of wine. I was hoping you might have left me just one glass as a nightcap. And you should think yourself lucky that somebody's bothering to actually *do* the building work for us, rather than swanning off enjoying themselves on lovely walks,' she spat out.

Barney stared back, speechless for a moment. Eventually he said, 'But I thought you didn't mind me helping them out at the country park. You know I'm rubbish at DIY.'

'Helping *them* out? Helping Kate, more like. I met her last night. She's very pretty, isn't she?'

Rage coursed through Barney's veins, making the headache even worse. 'I don't think you should be making that kind of insinuation,' he said, adopting a lofty air, even as an image of Kate smiling at him from behind the counter at the café flashed into his mind. '*You* spend all day drooling over Randy Rick. You can hardly talk.'

'*Randy Rick*? Where the hell did that come from?'

It was a stand-off. Barney could see that he'd hurt Nell badly, and his heart felt as if it was shrinking in his chest. How had they come to this? He was about to try and apologise, if not for his words, at least for losing his temper which he seldom if ever did, when she turned on her heel and left the room. He heard her clattering down the stairs and slumped onto the bed with a groan. Sliding back under the duvet, Barney muffled the screeching sounds from downstairs with his pillow and let himself escape into sleep.

A couple of hours later, he awoke with a hideous taste in his mouth but no more headache. Barney inched his way out of bed gingerly, uncertain if he really did feel better or if the pain was going to leap back into action as soon as he moved. Reassured that he was recovering, he headed for the bathroom, noticing that the drilling noise had stopped and the house was in silence.

After a hot shower and an intense session with his toothbrush, Barney was feeling almost human again. Vowing to lay off the red wine, at least for a while, he dressed in his usual shorts and T-shirt combo and went downstairs. There was no sign of Rick or indeed of Nell or Frank, so he put two rounds of bread in the toaster and put the kettle on. However, as soon as Barney stepped out into the garden with his belated breakfast, he realised that he'd been wrong to think he was alone. He sat down at the patio table and listened hard. He could hear a radio playing in the annexe and the sound of Frank laughing. As he turned to look at the doorway to his father's new abode, Nell emerged, carrying a tray laden with empty plates and mugs. So they'd all been enjoying elevenses together, as per usual.

Barney hated himself for feeling so bitter and resentful when it had been his idea to move to a cottage that needed work. He'd been unable to do any of the jobs properly himself, but the thought of Rick happily socialising with his wife and father was galling to say the least. It took him back to being at school, when his two best friends had briefly deserted him when a new boy arrived. The newcomer was bigger and much tougher than Barney. He was also an ace footballer, which Barney definitely wasn't. The other two had soon found out that Richard (probably another reason why Barney resented Rick, the name was too similar for comfort) was at best big-headed and at worst an egotist of the highest order.

Nell spotted Barney a couple of seconds after he saw her. She hesitated and then came towards him. 'I suppose you'll be going out soon,' she said. Her voice had lost its angry tone but sounded flat and unfeeling.

'I... I don't have to. Do you want us to... erm... do something together?'

Barney didn't recognise this sense of uncertainty when suggesting that he and Nell should go somewhere together. For years they'd been partners in all sorts of adventures. When the children were small this had involved cheap days out with lots of fresh air and exercise to wear Elliot, Ginny and Alice out. Later, they'd taken their surly brood camping to places where they could find similarly grouchy teenagers to hang around with.

When all their offspring had left home, Barney and Nell had thought they'd have plenty of time on their hands to spread their wings. Maybe they'd join a rambling club or go off on their own at weekends and explore the countryside around the edges of Sheffield. Lottie's decline into dementia had put paid to all that, because she and Frank had needed constant support, and if Nell had any free time from that commitment, she'd spent it at the homeless centre.

Now, Nell was looking at her husband in surprise, as if he'd suggested something very odd. 'Go out together? Just you and me?' she said.

'Yes, we could go exploring. Take a picnic?'

Nell seemed to be considering this idea. She looked as if her thoughts were miles away. Then Frank's voice from inside the annexe brought her back to the present. 'I can't today,' she said. 'I promised I'd go with your dad to the chiropodist. I've found one for him in the village. He doesn't want to go on his own.'

Barney didn't answer. The wave of disappointment had taken him by surprise, and he realised how much he'd suddenly wanted to have his wife all to himself, even if only for a short while.

'I could be free tomorrow morning, if you like,' Nell said tentatively.

'Yes, that'd be... oh, wait. I've got to lead a walk tomorrow. I promised...'

'You promised Kate. Of course you did. Well, the next time you have a gap in your diary, maybe you'll pencil me in,' said Nell with a thin smile that didn't reach her eyes.

There was only one thing for it. 'Would you like to come along on the walk with me?' Barney said, wincing as he saw Nell's eyes flash with anger.

'Oh, you actually thought to invite me, did you?' she said. 'Well, I've got no wish to be an afterthought. You trot along and have fun. I've got plenty to do here.'

Before Barney could make any more suggestions, Nell was on her way back to the kitchen. The set of her shoulders told him that she was not pleased, but Barney couldn't cancel a walk so soon after he'd begun leading them, could he? The six people who'd booked online would be disappointed. It'd be so unprofessional. A small voice in his head whispered, *It's Kate you don't want to let down, isn't it? And you're really looking forward to seeing her too. Go on, admit it. You didn't really want Nell to tag along.*

Ignoring the treacherous voice, Barney drank his now lukewarm tea and tore up his toast, throwing the scraps to the birds in disgust. Unfortunately, Anton, sensing a potential snack, was out of the annexe and gobbling up Barney's rejected breakfast before even the most forceful magpie had the chance to benefit.

Barney sighed. He'd be better off cutting his losses. He should probably go and map out some more walks, and to do that he'd need to go across to the park. He might as well have lunch at the café while he was there too, because with Nell in this mood, eating with her and Frank, and probably Rick too, would be no fun at all. To salve his conscience, Barney whistled for Anton and called to tell Frank he was doing the dog walk. He didn't bother letting Nell know he was going out. There didn't seem much point really.

18

The Reasons to be Happy meetings had all been planned for Monday evenings, and by Friday Nell was more than ready for the next one. The frosty atmosphere between herself and Barney hadn't abated, even though Rick had again defected to the vicarage to do some work for Bev, and Frank had been making himself busy pottering around in the garden. She and Barney could have had a day out together now, Nell thought, but he had made the excuse (which in fact was quite true) that he had an unexpectedly large workload to finish before the weekend, so Nell had had to occupy herself with giving the walk-in pantry a makeover.

As she washed the emulsion paint off her hands and admired the freshness that the coat of very pale green paint had brought to the little room, Nell's mobile rang, and Bev's name came up on the screen.

'Hello, are you okay?' she said, answering immediately. Bev was more of a fan of using WhatsApp than actual talking on the phone as a rule.

'Hi – yes, I'm fine. I've got Rick here with me and I wondered if you were free for a quick chat.'

'Do you mean now?' Nell looked down at her paint-spattered dungarees.

'If you can. I'm just making coffee, and I've got some of the good biscuits left.'

'Say no more. I'm on my way.'

Intrigued, Nell decided her dungarees, although nowhere near as cool as Ingrid's, looked quirky rather than messy. Grabbing her house keys, she went into the garden to let Frank know where she was going. In minutes, she was off up the lane and striding out towards the vicarage, delighted to be given a mission that didn't involve improving their home, for a change.

Bev greeted Nell at the door and ushered her in. 'I really wanted Maryam to be here too, but she's tied up in the shop, so I'll just have to ring her after we've talked. Come into the garden. I've made iced coffee.'

Nell followed Bev through the house and out onto the terrace, where Rick was lounging on a dilapidated swinging hammock. He waved as he saw Nell approach but didn't get up. Nell had a sudden thought that Barney would have been on his feet to greet a visitor but put the criticism out of her mind as soon as it dared to appear. She wasn't going to compare Rick unfavourably with her husband. He'd probably been working hard all day whereas Barney had been sauntering around enjoying himself in the sunshine.

'Hi, babe,' Rick said. 'Glad you could make it. We've got something we want to discuss with you.'

What was this 'we' business? Nell felt rattled. Bev and Rick were both meant to be her friends and here they were almost ganging up on her. But that was just silly, and smacked of playground childishness, so she smiled and came over to sit on a nearby deckchair. Bev poured iced coffee into a tall glass for Nell and gestured to the plate of cookies on a low table, but Nell shook her head. She didn't feel hungry after all.

'It's like this,' Bev said, sitting down next to Rick. 'We were chatting about the music meeting while Rick was fixing my shower, and he said...'

'I was just saying,' Rick interrupted. 'Just saying how brilliant I thought it was. A great night and we've ended up with a kind of soundtrack.'

Nell frowned. 'Yes, well, that was the idea, wasn't it? A soundtrack of our happy moments.'

'Right. But to Rick it seemed as if it was like one of those collections of your favourite songs you would play on a long car journey to keep you amused. We had them as kids.'

Bev stopped talking and they both looked at Nell expectantly. She gazed back, unsure what she was supposed to say to this. When she didn't reply, Bev continued. 'So Rick said to me, "Why don't we organise ourselves a good old road trip?"'

'A road trip? Do you mean for the group?'

'Yes! Who else did you think I meant?' Rick said, laughing. 'We could get everyone together and take ourselves off to the seaside and play our music on the journey. You want to talk to us about being happy? Surely that's the place where everyone feels good?'

Nell was finding it hard to take this suggestion in and at first she couldn't pinpoint why she had a strange ache in her heart. Then it clicked. She felt... excluded, yes, that was it. And how ridiculous was that? It was like being back at school when two of your friends seemed to be getting on really well without you. Nell cringed inwardly at the thought. She needed to give herself a virtual slap. Of course Bev and Rick were already good friends and she was the newcomer.

'Tell me more,' Nell said, trying to make her voice sound light and sociable.

Rick leant forward, elbows on knees, causing the seat to rock, almost catapulting Bev onto the concrete slabs. 'I've got a mate who's got a minibus,' he said. 'And he owes me a favour. I'm happy to drive us. How about if we check with the others if they could be free for the whole of Monday instead of just the evening?'

Bev's eyes were sparkling. 'I think it's a great idea. We could take our next session on the road. The food contributions could be a picnic that we'll put together and we can kill two birds with one stone.'

Nell still felt lost. 'How do you mean?' she asked.

'We'll listen to the tracks on the way there and back and see if people want to expand on why their choice made them feel good. Try to pinpoint that elusive feeling of contentment. Then when we get to the coast, we can settle down on the beach and have the meeting about why food influences your mood. What do you reckon?'

They were both looking at Nell expectantly now and she had an unreasonable urge to be churlish and tell them not to be so silly, but actually, it really was a good idea. It would be easier for people to open up to each other in the informal setting of a minibus ride and a picnic than sitting around in a church meeting room, and it might break the ice properly, ready for the session after.

'But it's such short notice,' she protested lamely. 'We can't just expect everyone to change their plans at the drop of a hat just because we fancy a trip to the seaside.'

Bev sighed. 'That's so defeatist, Nell. We can at least ask them. If not on Monday, I'm sure we can find another day when everybody can make themselves available.'

Nell took a sip of her drink, which was delicious. It didn't help her mood. She was too hot in her thick denim dungarees, whereas Bev in a floaty summer dress and Rick in his shorts and vest both looked cool and composed. As she watched, Rick stood up and peeled off his top. He stretched out his muscular, sun-browned arms and yawned, then reached for his glass and downed his drink in one. The whole thing looked so much like a commercial for suntan lotion or aftershave or something equally glamorous that Nell had to smile. Bev seemed to take this as encouragement.

'You think it's a good plan, don't you, Nell? I can tell you do. Let's at least see when the minibus is free and if that fits in with our meeting day, and check a few people out to find out who's keen. Can you do Monday?'

Nell nodded and Bev and Rick both cheered. In seconds, Rick was on the phone to his friend and had provisionally secured the bus for the whole of Monday with the only proviso that they brought it back full of fuel.

'Monday's usually my day off unless there's a crisis,' said Bev. 'Rick's almost finished here and he says he's all done at yours. That's three out of the twelve. Shall we take a few each to ask? Obviously you'll know if Frank's free but it's polite to ask him personally.'

Nell nodded again. She felt exhausted by all this enthusiasm. Sweat trickled down her back and she wondered how soon she could make her excuses and go home for a cool shower, but Bev hadn't finished yet.

'I know you're probably really busy, Nell, but do you think

you could go and see Maryam on your way home and get her to persuade Rashid to cover for her on Monday? I think their daughter should be there by now so she could always step in, and the boys might help behind the scenes after school. Would you mind? I really want to make sure everyone can join us.'

Seeing Maryam would always be a pleasure, so Nell agreed to this suggestion. It was almost on the way home, after all.

'What about me?' Rick said. 'Shall I go along to Beryl's and see how the land lies there, Bev? She'll probably ring her two mates to save us a job.'

'Yes, good idea. I've got Kate's and Maurice's details, and I can contact Harry too. Oh, that might be a problem. Could we fit his wife in if he doesn't want to leave her all day?'

'Yeah, no worries. What about that classy blonde bird – do you know her number?'

'Ingrid? Don't let her hear you calling her a bird.' Bev looked ruffled and Nell felt the need to step in.

'You sound as if you've stepped right out of a seventies sitcom, Rick,' she said, pulling a face at him. 'Even my father-in-law doesn't call women names like that and he's pretty old school.'

'Sorry, blame my dad. He called all women birds. Or chicks.'

Rick didn't look particularly sorry, but Nell could see that Bev was keen to move things on. 'I've thought of something else you might do today after the shop if you've got time and you really don't mind,' she said to Nell, smiling at her hopefully.

Nell's heart sank. She was never going to get home at this rate. 'Go on,' she said wearily.

'Only if you feel like it, of course, but maybe you could give Ingrid a ring, Nell? Or better still, pop round and see her.'

Suddenly overcome with shyness, Nell remembered the tall, elegant lady who hadn't said much at the meeting. She'd looked calm and collected, but withdrawn, as if she wasn't quite with them. 'I... I suppose so,' she said. 'Where does she live?'

'Up until recently she was renting one of the timber lodges in the country park, but she's just moved into a narrowboat moored on the river. It's easy to find, I can give you directions. You can't miss it.'

Nell thought that actually, she probably could miss it but didn't want to admit how bad her sense of direction was. Resigned now to postponing her lovely cool shower, she held out a hand for the address and phone number when Bev had finished scribbling them and a few simple directions in her notebook and had torn out the page, and with relief, stood up to go.

'I need to go home and get changed first,' she said. 'Look at the state of me.'

'You're fine. If you pop and see Ingrid first, it'll mean we can tick another one off the list. It'll only take you ten minutes to get down to the river and it's a lovely walk. Then you can do Maryam on your way back and let us know what Frank says too. Sorted. You're an angel.'

Bev and Rick high-fived each other and whooped. Nell tried to stop her shoulders drooping. She needed to channel some of their enthusiasm. All of this was for a good cause. She said goodbye and let herself out as neither of the others looked as if they were going to see her to the door. Already too hot and definitely rather grumpy, she set off through the village, across the green and down to the edge of the country park but as she walked, an unexpected feeling of contentment crept over her. It was cooler under the trees when she turned left, away from the biggest lake, and a fresh breeze was blowing now, making tiny waves on the surface of the other large pond, where windsurfers swooped around, and two small children held hands with a grey-haired lady as they paddled in the shallows.

Soon, Nell saw the track that Bev had mentioned, winding its way between ancient oak trees whose branches touched each other overhead, like a group of friends having a confidential chat. They made a shady archway, and Nell walked beneath them, marvelling at the many shades of green to be seen in their summer garb of leaves.

Bev's airy 'ten minutes' for this walk had been an underestimate and Nell had a belated thought that Ingrid might not even be in. She was thirsty again now and longed for a glass of water. She wondered if Barney came this way on any of his walks. If she bumped into him now, he might think she was checking up on him. The thought of her husband strolling down these paths with Kate as they made plans for the guided tours gave Nell a pang of fierce jealousy. Barney had never given her cause to feel anything like this before. Surely he couldn't really be interested in Kate? But she herself had been admiring Rick's fine physique far too often, it couldn't be denied. Neither of them was blameless.

By now, Nell had reached the riverbank and there in front of her was a row of brightly painted boats, moored nose to tail. She pulled out Bev's directions again and saw that Ingrid's new home was called *Galadriel*. An elderly man in a battered straw sunhat was relaxing next to the nearest boat on a rickety folding chair. He greeted Nell with a wave, and she asked him if he knew which of these floating homes might be the one named after Tolkien's beautiful elven queen.

'Third one down,' he said. 'She's just come back with her shopping, so you'll find her at home.'

Nell smiled her thanks and carried on. An all-too-familiar fluttering nervousness was beginning to make her deeply uncertain of her welcome. Nell cursed herself for being so lacking in confidence. She was aware that most people thought her to be an outgoing, self-assured individual who hardly ever worried, but this was very far from the truth. Even her three children didn't know how much Nell hated putting herself forward in new situations with strange people. In fact, the only person who understood her fears and had always given her his encouragement and unquestioning support was Barney.

Nell paused for a moment. A wave of sadness hit her as she thought of her husband. Something really depressing had happened to the warmth between them that had sustained their marriage through the years of sleepless nights with small babies, lively children and lack of funds. She wondered drearily if they could ever get it back. Maybe it was already too late. Sometimes marriages ran out of steam. She knew that in theory but had never expected it to happen to them. As she pondered, a figure emerged from a boat in front and a voice called, 'Are you looking for me?'

'Hello! Yes, I am. How did you know?'

'Bev called,' said Ingrid, jumping onto the bank and coming to meet Nell. 'She was worried her instructions weren't clear enough, so I thought I'd have a wander along the path and look for you. I bet you're dying for a drink, aren't you? How about some iced water and then a very cold beer? Let's sit on the front of the boat under the canopy and you can tell me why you want to see me. Bev was being very mysterious so I'm all agog.'

In an instant, Nell's nerves disappeared, and she beamed at Ingrid. 'That sounds wonderful,' she said. 'Excuse my messy clothes, I'd just finished decorating when Bev called me, and she insisted I dashed round to the vicarage immediately to talk to her.'

'Even more fascinating. Come on, I'll pour you some water

and get that beer out of the fridge. You can fill me in on all the gossip.'

Needing no further bidding, Nell watched Ingrid leap onto the front of the boat and took her hostess's outstretched hand as she climbed aboard. Cold lager on a boat on the river. It sounded like a recipe for bliss.

19

The interior of the boat was cool and welcoming. Nell followed Ingrid through narrow double doors and down a step into a comfortably furnished living area with a galley kitchen at one end. There were two easy chairs with wooden arms and a drop-leaved table up against one side of the small room. The carpeted floor muffled their footsteps, and Ingrid shook her head when Nell asked if she should take her shoes off.

'I don't bother unless I'm muddy,' she said. 'Have a seat for a moment and I'll get the drinks and see if I can find some peanuts and olives.' Ingrid gestured to a chair and set about preparing a tray, for all the world as if Nell had been formally invited round rather than just turning up out of the blue.

'What an amazing place to live,' Nell said, as they moved outside to the front of the boat again and settled themselves on bench seats either side. 'Is it yours?'

'I kind of wish it was,' said Ingrid. 'I'm renting it. I still haven't really decided where I want to live. I ran The Treasure Trove for a few months until I'd shifted all my goods and chattels. Then I moved to a log cabin near the café, but it didn't feel secluded enough. Too many people milling around. I was right next to the main car park. Now I'm trying out life on the water. Maybe it'll be a mud hut in the middle of a swamp next. I'm turning into a nomad.'

'But you still like being part of village affairs?'

'Oh, yes, coming to Willowbrook has been a great move. It's just that I love to be able to escape to solitude when I've had enough. Does that sound antisocial and selfish?'

Nell thought it sounded wonderful, and said so. At the moment, the thought of escape from her complicated relationship with Barney and responsibility for Frank's wellbeing seemed very tempting. They sipped their drinks and watched a pair of swans and several ducks going about their business on the water. Nell could just hear the couple on the next boat having an animated conversation about what to have for dinner, and in the distance, the chug of a tractor was the only other disturbance to the peaceful scene.

Ingrid didn't appear keen to break the tranquil mood, and Nell was grateful for this undemanding company, especially as they'd only met once before at the meeting and hadn't had the chance to chat properly or get to know each other. The cool draught of water quenched her thirst and then the icy chill of the beer calmed her frazzled nerves. The very slight rocking of the boat was soothing too.

'This is lovely,' Nell said. 'And it's a beautiful boat. How did you come to be living on it? Does it belong to someone you know? Tell me to mind my own business if you don't want to be interrogated, I've got a terrible tendency to be nosy.'

Ingrid laughed. 'Not at all,' she said. 'I've learned a lot about being neighbourly and finding out about each other since I came to the village, mainly from Beryl and co, it has to be said. The owners of the boat live in France now, and I rent it through a friend of theirs who just happened to hear I was looking for a home on the river. They don't come over to the UK very often. It looks as if they might want to sell it, but I think it'll be out of my price range.'

'I heard you downsized when you came here?'

'That's the understatement of the year. My husband died suddenly...'

'Oh, I'm so sorry.' Nell had always had a horror of treading on people's toes and here she was making Ingrid spill all the details of what must have been an awful time.

'Don't be. I'm realising more and more that Tommy and I had a friendly partnership rather than a deep relationship. I miss his company sometimes, he was great fun, but he left me with such a huge amount of his random belongings to get rid of, not to mention the horrendous debts. Is that too much information? I don't know why I slipped that one in. I don't usually...'

Nell shook her head, intrigued. Ingrid hadn't seemed like the sort of person to share private information. 'Go on, I'm all ears,' she said.

'Okay, well, the crux of the matter is that I feel as if I'm only just surfacing from all the upheaval, both mental and physical. Now, there's just me and a few basic bits and bobs. Tommy was an auctioneer, and he could never resist bringing treasures home from work. It's been a hard job getting back to owning only the things I really need.'

Nell looked at Ingrid with sympathy and understanding. She knew only too well the pain of shedding years of possessions. The two women settled back into the comfortable near-silence of the riverside. Nell thought what a relaxing person Ingrid was to be with. She'd been missing her old companions from Sheffield and putting a toe in the water of making friends from scratch was daunting. Maryam and Bev were already a welcome part of her new life, but she had a feeling that Ingrid might be someone a bit different. She was rather aloof and reserved on the surface, but today they seemed to have jumped a few stages of getting to know each other.

'I've just realised I haven't told you why I've called to see you,' said Nell. 'It's about Monday's meeting. Bev wants to make it a whole-day event. It's very short notice, I know. You probably already have plans.'

Nell explained about the prospective seaside jaunt and Ingrid listened with interest, asking the odd question here and there. 'So, in a nutshell, we're putting two aspects of being happy together – more of the music and then comfort food too?' she said eventually.

'That's it exactly. What do you think?'

'I reckon that sounds like a great plan. I'm free on Monday, as it happens. I was going to give the boat a good clean but that can happen any time. It seems unlikely that everybody'll be available though. Is it all or nothing?'

Nell wasn't sure. 'I guess so. It wouldn't be fair to leave people out, and if we did, they might struggle to get back on board with the sessions the week after. Let's see how it goes. I need to check if Maryam can get cover in the shop and if Frank is up for the idea.'

'Right. If it does happen, what food are you taking to set the mood, just out of interest? Your scones were superb last week. They reminded me of being a child and my mum making afternoon tea in the garden on summer afternoons. Scones were the only successful thing she baked so she stuck with them.'

Nell hadn't given this part of the plan much thought. 'In that case, scones it is,' she said. She drained the last of her beer in one gulp and got to her feet. 'I'd better go and see Maryam and then have a chat with Frank. It could go either way with him, he's a bit unpredictable. Wish me luck, and thank you. This has been a lovely peaceful interlude.'

Ingrid jumped lightly from the boat and held out a hand to help Nell down. 'It's great to have a chance to talk away from the hubbub,' she said. 'Come again anytime and I'll show you the rest of the accommodation. The sleeping arrangements in the tiny boatman's cabin are a work of art. You might want to escape for a night sometime, just for a change.'

'You'll wish you hadn't said that,' said Nell, smiling at her new friend. 'It sounds very tempting right now.'

She set off along the path towards the lake. When she reached a bend in the track, she turned to wave in case Ingrid was still there. The other woman was standing watching Nell go and her expression was thoughtful.

20

By the time Nell reached Hollyhocks Cottage and convinced Frank that an escapade to the seaside was just what he needed, her phone had pinged several times with messages from Bev. All the Saga Louts had said they'd be delighted to come on the trip, Maurice was currently making a call to see if he could change a dental appointment booked for Monday morning and Harry and his wife were very excited to be asked. Bev was just about to call round to the café to see Kate to find out if she could manage to get away.

Nell texted back:

> Maryam's fine too. Rashid and their daughter will cope and Ingrid's looking forward to it. Fingers crossed that Kate can be free.

Half an hour later, Bev texted again with a series of emojis including a dancing lady, a bus, a cake and five thumbs-up symbols. The rest of the message said:

> We're off! Norfolk coast here we come.

'I can't believe we're all so boring that we can make ourselves available at the drop of a hat,' said Frank.

'We're not boring. We're flexible and adaptable,' said Nell. 'Maybe we're all getting the idea that if we want to find the secret of happiness... or contentment or peace... or whatever you want to call it, we need to grab every opportunity that comes along.'

'Well, maybe. Anyway, you're making scones. What shall I contribute to the picnic?'

'You're going to have to think of something that makes you feel good. Did you have picnics when you were a child?'

Frank's bristly eyebrows, that always seemed to have a life of their own, drew together as he pondered. His grey hair was looking stragglier than usual today and he looked vaguely unkempt and unloved. Nell's heart went out to him. Lottie had kept a close eye on her husband's appearance when she'd been in good health. She'd booked him regular haircuts, trimmed his eyebrows herself and made sure his clothes were tidy and clean. All Nell had managed to do was the clean clothes part so far.

'What are you looking at?' Frank barked, sensing Nell's appraisal. 'I suppose you're thinking I look too much of a mess to take me on a bus trip. Well, I can't be bothered to be smart these days, see? Lottie isn't here and I just don't care any more.'

This outburst was the very first time that Frank had let down his guard in front of Nell since Lottie's illness and death, and she was both deeply touched and alarmed. She would need to tread very carefully.

'I know it's been awful for you, Frank,' she said. 'You must miss Lottie all the time.'

'Every moment of every day,' he answered gruffly, scrubbing at his eyes. 'And before you start pontificating, I do know how she'd have hated seeing me going to seed like this, but at least I'm getting up every day and having some sort of a life.'

Nell wondered if she dared make a suggestion. This was dangerous ground, but there was no point in holding back if she really wanted to help.

'How about I give you a quick makeover before the seaside jaunt?' she said. 'Nothing drastic. I've still got my mum's old hair-dressing scissors. I nearly threw them out, but I must have known they'd come in handy one day.'

'Do you actually know how to cut hair?' Frank asked incred-ulously. 'I don't want to look even more of a dog's breakfast than I do already.'

'Mum taught me the basics, and you only need a trim. Let's do it before Barney gets home and give him a surprise. Then we'll decide on your picnic contribution.'

Frank followed Nell up the stairs with only the faintest of hesitation. She ushered him into the front bedroom, acutely conscious that it was very much her room and not Barney's, but Frank didn't comment. He sat down in the chair by Nell's dressing table and waited while she rummaged in the bedside cabinet for her scissors.

Draping a towel around her father-in-law's shoulders, Nell set to work, hoping she looked more confident than she felt. She snipped away merrily and then stood back, rather impressed with the result. 'Now for the eyebrows,' she said. 'Dennis Healey had nothing on you.'

Frank closed his eyes tightly but bore the ordeal without comment. Nell even managed to trim his moustache and tidy his beard. 'Now, sit there for a minute while I go and fetch you some fresh clothes,' she said firmly.

Soon Frank was decked out in a pair of navy chinos bought by Nell a few Christmases ago, which he'd sworn he'd not be able to squeeze into, and she added a short-sleeved white shirt, ditto, still with the crease marks from the packet and an ancient brocade waistcoat. She guided him to stand in front of the full-length mirror on her wardrobe and he took a step back in amazement.

'Good Lord, girl,' Frank said. 'You should be on one of those TV shows making a silk purse out of a sow's ear. I don't look half bad, do I?'

Nell put her arms round him and gave him a hug, which after a moment he returned. 'Should I wear this rigout on Monday?' he said. 'It's a bit over the top. Will they all think I'm showing off?'

'Not a bit of it. You look just right for a day out at the seaside, and there are more clothes along these lines in your wardrobe that I haven't seen you wear for years. I think you've even got a Panama hat like Maurice's somewhere. Might as well totally look the part. Now, about that picnic.'

Frank stroked his moustache thoughtfully. 'Hard-boiled eggs,' he said. 'With a twist of salt each to dip them in. Simple but moreish. How about that? Our mum used to send us out for the day with a slab of bread and marge each, a couple of eggs and an apple. If she was feeling lavish, we got a bottle of cold tea. Takes me right back whenever I shell a hard-boiled egg. Revolting smell, mind you, but so good to eat.'

'Perfect. I'm going to slip down to the shop and see if Maryam and Rashid sell Dandelion and Burdock pop. That was my treat when I was a kid. This is going to be a feast like no other.'

When Barney returned from his walk, Frank made a great show of casually walking into the garden as his son took off his walking boots. He strolled across the lawn followed by Anton, bent to smell one of the roses that were going wild in the bushes and then turned to give Barney the full effect of his new look.

'Wow, Dad, what happened to you?' Barney said, standing up

to admire Frank at closer range. 'I haven't seen you look this fancy since...'

He stopped talking and the two men looked into each other's eyes. Neither seemed to be able to tear their gaze away.

'It's time I stopped wallowing,' said Frank. 'I know I'll never stop being sad. I loved your mum for years and years, but she's at peace now and I don't want to drag you and Nell down into the pit with me.'

'We don't expect you to be the life and soul of the party,' said Nell. 'We're all missing Lottie and of course you're feeling it most, but we can maybe prop each other up a bit better than we have been doing so far.'

Barney nodded but was unable to speak. He gave his dad a manly type of hug and went into the house.

'I've upset him,' said Frank. 'But we never talk about his mum properly, and I want to be able to say her name whenever it seems right.'

'Of course you do, and you will from now on. We're all coming to terms with a lot of... stuff... since we moved here. The new group's just the start of it.'

'Agreed. And on that subject, when are you going to get our Barney back where he belongs, in your bed?'

There was an awkward silence. Nell watched Anton scrabbling in the soil near the compost heap. A blackbird trilled its song above her in the oak tree.

'It's not as simple as that, Frank,' she said eventually. 'If it was, I'd have sorted it by now. Anyway, this isn't about me. You've had your makeover and you're going to knock the spots off all the other blokes on Monday.'

'Even Rick?'

Nell glanced at her father-in-law, suddenly suspicious, but he was already heading for the kitchen. 'I'm going to make a pot of tea and put my old clothes on again so I don't get these ones grubby,' he said. 'The weather's never too hot for a cuppa. Want one?'

'Go on then,' Nell said. She wondered if Barney had been with Kate when Bev called round to see her or if he'd already been on his way home. Should she ask Bev if Barney could come along on the trip? She was sure he'd jump at the chance to have even more time in Kate's company. No, she told herself. This was something just for the group. Harry's wife was only being included so that he wouldn't be worried about her all day. Barney was a grown-up. He could look after himself, and clearly did these days. This uncomfortable thought stayed with Nell as she went to fetch her tea. In fact, it hovered in her mind even as she lay in bed that night, listening to the far-off sound of the TV. If only he'd come to bed. Nell had a horrible feeling that nothing was going to be right in this house until that problem was unravelled. How to solve it was completely another matter.

21

With Kate having given the green light to join the party on Monday, it was all systems go. Sam had been only too delighted to have an extra shift and Kate's new part-time assistant Rowena was also happy to help with covering the café. Barney was trying not to mind everyone going off to have fun, but it was hard not to feel left out. It all seemed kind of underhand to him. How had Bev not known they might be going to pull a stunt like this when she first suggested the meetings? He and Nell had occasionally been involved with helping on their children's school trips if they happened to be free and those events had always seemed to take months to organise.

Barney's resentment of Rick grew a little more every time they bumped into each other. Even though the builder had finished work on the annexe, he seemed to crop up everywhere around the village and he was even at the café on Saturday helping Sam to put up a bigger fence to keep the foxes out of the bins in the yard at the rear of the place. Rick was always relentlessly cheerful, even going as far as to slap Barney on the back when they met. It was all much too matey for Barney's liking.

On Sunday morning, Barney woke up feeling restless and grumpier than usual. He muttered to himself about the prospect of being cooped up in the house with Nell and Frank. The sun was hot on his back even as he sat outside to drink his coffee at ten o'clock and there was no point in walking over to the café to plan more walks as it was closed on Sundays. He racked his brains for something useful to do instead. The annexe was ready for his dad to move into now, but Frank was taking his time in sorting out which of his many possessions he wanted to take with him, so that job had been postponed until after this pesky seaside jolly.

As he sat looking down the garden, Frank heard an evocative sound that he'd been enjoying ever since they'd moved to Willowbrook. It was the melodic peal of church bells. As he listened, something stirred in Barney's soul. Nell came outside with the rest of the coffee in a cafetiere and held the pot up with a questioning look, but Barney shook his head.

'Do you know what? I think I'm going to quickly get ready and go to church.'

'You're what?' Nell couldn't have sounded more shocked if he'd said he was going to go for a naked jog through the streets and end up with a swim in the river.

'I'm going to church.'

'But you never...'

'What's wrong with trying something different for a change? *You* do it all the time. I'm pretty sure the service starts at half past ten. Do you want to come?'

Barney was already on his way into the house to change out of his shorts when Nell said quietly, 'Yes, please.'

He turned to stare at her and was struck by how pretty she looked. His wife was wearing a long floral summer dress and white tennis shoes. Her snowy hair was in need of a trim, so she'd tied a band of matching material around her head to keep her fringe out of her eyes.

'You look... nice,' Barney said. 'Erm... had you planned to go to church already?'

'No, I just felt like looking decent today. I've been slobbing about in scruffy clothes for too long. Do you mind if I come with you?'

Barney wondered when they had become so formal and stilted with each other. They sounded like acquaintances, and not very friendly ones at that.

'Great. Of course I don't mind. I'll just have a quick change and check with Dad that he doesn't want to tag along, but I don't think that's likely. See you in five minutes max.'

It took slightly longer than five minutes to get sorted because Nell couldn't find her bag and then she decided they'd need money for the offertory, but soon they were walking down the lane together. The bells had stopped for a short while but now rang out again. Barney upped his pace, and Nell matched her strides to his as they hurried through the streets to the church. They made it inside just on the dot of half past ten and were given hymn books by a smiling elderly lady who was neat and tidy in a blue cardigan and what Lottie would have called slacks.

'Hello,' she said. 'Welcome to our church. I think I've seen you two around the village. Or maybe it was at the country park?'

Barney and Nell both nodded and smiled but neither gave any more information out. It crossed Barney's mind that all their exploring so far had been done separately and this was the first time they'd agreed to do something different together. He had almost taken hold of Nell's hand as they walked along the road, in a reflex action that would have been second nature until his illness had made Barney shrink into himself. Even the lightest touch from anyone else had turned his stomach after that point. It had been weird and very depressing. Just when he'd needed a cuddle more than ever in his life, he'd been unable to receive or show any kind of physical affection. It was as if something inside him was convinced that his cancer was catching. He felt unclean.

Nell hadn't understood this problem, although Barney had tried his best to let her know that he still loved her and really wanted to hold her tightly, especially in the night. He just couldn't do that any more though, and moving into the spare bedroom had seemed like the best option, rather than having that yawning space in between them in their king-sized bed. With hindsight, Barney could see how the cracks had appeared in their once-close marriage. At the time, he'd been preoccupied in merely trying to stay alive.

These troublesome thoughts crowded into Barney's mind as he and Nell walked into the main body of the church, but there was something about the musty, ancient scent of the place and the sound of the organ playing an old familiar hymn that calmed him.

'Do you think we need to avoid any particular seats?' Nell whispered out of the corner of her mouth. 'I'd hate to tread on anyone's toes.'

Barney glanced around and saw that only about a third of the pews had occupants, and the congregation was well spread out. 'I think we're safe,' he murmured. 'I don't reckon there's going to be a last-minute rush.' The organ music paused for a moment and there was a final, jubilant peal of bells before silence fell. A portly man wearing a voluminous cassock did some quite dramatic swinging of incense and then a much smaller individual in white robes stepped up to the lectern.

'A warm welcome to you all,' he said, beaming around at everyone. 'For any newcomers who don't know us yet, my name is Deacon Paul, and our service today will be led by the Reverend Beverly Marsh. Please stand for the first hymn, which is number 234 in your books.'

The organ music swelled again but Barney was distracted by some late arrivals who had appeared from a door in the rear of the church and were finding their seats. He nudged Nell.

'Look,' he hissed.

Nell turned her head and smiled broadly to see Sam and Rick. They nodded to her as they stood to sing the hymn, and the procession, including Bev in her flowing robes and sash, Deacon Paul and several others, made its way from a side chapel at the front of the church, down the aisle and up the middle. A large silver cross on a pole was held aloft as they made their stately way to the altar. It all looked a little dangerous to Barney as the cross-bearer turned towards the altar and swayed ominously. The choir was singing now, and the melodious noise distracted him from the fear that the pole was going to crash down on someone's head.

The service progressed in the traditional manner and Barney gradually forgot his surprise at seeing Sam and Rick here and let the comforting words and rituals flow over and around him. As a child, his mother had brought him to Sunday School every week and then when he grew old enough, he'd sometimes attended the services with her. The main reason Barney had agreed to go with Lottie was that he had a huge crush on one of the youngest members of the choir but when he'd found out that Janine was already seeing one of the bullies who hung around in the bus shelter, he'd quickly gone off the idea of church.

When the service was nearly over, Bev gave a thumbs-up to someone at the back of the church and a group of small children came forward, followed by Kate. Barney tried to suppress a jolt of pleasure when he recognised her, but he could tell that Nell had noticed.

Sam's daughter Elsie was leading the pack, and she waved to her father enthusiastically, looking around as she walked to see who else she knew. She was holding the hand of a much smaller boy who seemed to be trying not to stand on the cracks between the old stone floor tiles. There were three other children of varying sizes, and they were all clutching large colourful pictures.

Bev smiled down at them when they arrived at the front of the church. 'And here are some of the youngest members of our congregation. What have you been doing with Kate today?'

Elsie needed no further encouragement. She launched into a full explanation of the story of Noah, aided and abetted by two of the more verbose children.

'And then everyone got deaded because the floods came. They were bad people. God didn't like them much. We talked about when it rains, and everyone's carpets get soggy if they live near our river.'

'That's a bit rubbish, I s'pose, but at least they don't usually get deaded,' said a taller girl with pigtails.

'It's because they're not bad people, you see,' said one of the others. 'My aunty lives down there, and she makes good cake. Chocolate, usually. If they were horrible, they'd be deaded in a flash, I bet. Zapped. Kerpow! God doesn't like baddies, does he, Kate?'

Kate looked as if she was torn between mortification and giggles. 'Well, it's a bit more complicated than that. Let's show everyone our pictures, shall we?' she said hopefully.

The children all dutifully held up their sugar paper creations, liberally loaded with sticky strips of coloured paper and shedding glitter everywhere. The elderly lady who'd welcomed Barney and Nell at the start of the service sucked her teeth loudly and muttered about getting the hoover out as soon as this was over, but Bev didn't bat an eyelid.

'Beautiful work, everyone,' she said. 'We'll put them up on the wall in the book corner as soon as they're dry.'

After that the service was soon over and as Barney and Nell stood to sing the final hymn, he was surprised to find himself feeling more peaceful than he had been for a long time. 'Are you glad we came?' Nell said as they filed back down the aisle. 'Shall we stay for coffee? They do it in the church room, I think.'

'You can if you want to,' said Barney. 'I'm going home to check Dad's okay.'

He walked home alone, kicking himself for being so antisocial. There was no need to worry about Frank, he'd still be busy making heaps of belongings in his bedroom but the thought of having to chat politely to Rick had overridden the much more cheerful one of having extra time to talk to Kate.

'Hi, Dad, I'm back,' Barney called as he entered the cottage, but there was no answering shout. He went into the kitchen and put the kettle on, but instead of the expected sight of Frank drinking tea and eating biscuits with Anton at his feet, found the room in a state of disarray. A huge china plate lay on the floor, broken into what looked like hundreds of pieces and there was what looked alarmingly like drops of blood on the table.

22

Fear clutched at Barney's heart. He ran upstairs to check Frank's bedroom, cursing himself for having left his father alone. Horrified to find all the rooms empty, he hurried into the garden and, to his relief, spied his father right at the far end, slumped in an old camping chair under the apple tree. The nearer he came to the old man though, the less he felt reassured. Frank had a tea towel wrapped around one arm, and his face was the colour of putty.

'Whatever have you been doing? Are you okay, Dad?' Barney said as he approached the shady corner of the garden, but it was clear Frank was anything but okay. Tears were pouring down his weathered cheeks and dripping onto the large photo album open on his lap. The tea towel was stained with blood, and as he sat up straighter, Frank winced in pain. Anton lay on the grass with his nose on his master's slippers. He whimpered, but didn't get up to greet Barney as he usually would have done. His tail was still instead of wagging a welcome which was in itself a very bad sign.

Seeing his son seemed to make Frank's grief worse rather

than better and he began to sob loudly. Horrified, Barney knelt at his feet and put a hand on the bony knee nearest to him.

'What happened to the plate? Are you badly hurt?' he asked, tackling the physical rather than the mental anguish first.

'I was bringing it downstairs to wash. It was one of your mum's favourites. She used it for her lemon drizzle cake, with one of those fancy paper things on it.'

'Doily,' said Barney automatically. The memory of his mother came back sharply to him and in that moment he missed Lottie more than ever.

'I'll go and get the first-aid kit from the kitchen,' he said. 'Or do you think we need to go to A&E?'

'Oh, no need for that. It's not a bad cut, it bled a lot, but it's stopped now. I only wanted a plaster, but I couldn't remember where you kept them in this house, and I didn't know where the brush and dustpan were to clear up the mess so I came out here instead. I'd already brought the album out to look at ready for when I made a pot of tea, but I didn't do that either in the end.'

Barney got to his feet. 'Look, let's deal with the damage to you first and then I'll sort out the bits of plate and make us both some tea. Just sit tight, I won't be long.'

He was soon back with the first-aid kit which held the usual assortment of ancient, wrapped bandages, painkillers, dusty indigestion and cough medicine bottles and thankfully, a new box of plasters. Barney found a couple of antiseptic wipes, opened them up and then tentatively unwound the tea towel from his dad's much-too-thin arm.

'It's not too bad,' he said, as Frank looked away and Anton slobbered sympathetically. 'I'll just clean you up and then a large plaster should be all you need but if it starts bleeding again, we're off to the hospital, no arguments.'

Fortunately, the wound was easily sorted and before long,

Barney had swept up the debris in the kitchen and made a pot of strong tea for them both. He pulled up another garden chair and dragged a wobbly wooden table from under the apple tree. Both Frank and Anton perked up considerably when they saw the biscuit tin and soon both men had their hands around mugs of tea and Anton was munching on a chew that Barney produced from his pocket.

'What brought all this on, Dad?' Barney said huskily, as he took a furtive glance at Frank's still ravaged-looking face. The traces of the weeping storm were still there and sudden anguish at the evidence of his father's grief brought tears to his own eyes. Barney looked down at the album on Frank's lap. The plastic covering of each page was slightly yellowed now. It was still open at a collection of photographs showing his mum in various poses. They must have all been taken at around the time of the move to their large family home, just before Barney was born.

A heavily pregnant Lottie was surrounded by packing cases and boxes in some of the snapshots, and several showed her examining her treasures as she unwrapped them. Barney's eyes were drawn to the picture of Lottie holding aloft a graceful ceramic vase patterned in waves of blue and green. His mum had said it reminded her of the sea. Frank had bought it for her on their honeymoon. Lottie had loved the seaside B&B where they'd stayed and was desperate to make the move to Devon after that, apparently, but Frank's elderly parents had needed care and after they died, Frank's work always prevented them from relocating.

Frank pulled a crumpled handkerchief out of the pocket of his trousers and dried his eyes again. Barney reached out and clumsily patted his father's knee. Gestures of affection were always tricky with Frank, and he didn't want to damage the closeness between them that the impromptu tea party along with the first-aid treatment had brought about. The sound of birdsong in the branches above them was soothing, and the sun's warmth was tempered by the tree's shade. It was so peaceful in the garden that Barney had to work hard to stop his eyes from closing. A lazy bee buzzed around their heads and Frank looked up as a dragonfly flitted by, azure wings lit by a ray of sunshine.

'I definitely think we made the right decision coming here. Erm... Dad... do you wish you and Mum had gone ahead with the move to Devon when she wanted it so badly?' Barney asked.

Frank shook his head. 'No, not really. We didn't want to uproot ourselves that much. Your ma used to get the urge to live in most of the lovely places we visited on our holidays,' he said, smiling at last. 'It soon wore off. She was a homebody really. Very happy to come back to our own house. She talked the talk all right, but she wouldn't really have moved so far away from her family. There never was a more contented soul than my Lottie.'

This surprised Barney. Their home had been filled with mementos of past holidays. Prints and paintings of seaside towns all around Britain, Scotland and Wales hung on every wall. Had this been enough for his mum, or had she secretly yearned to live by the sea? He would never know for sure.

'So, enough of this maudlin stuff, it was sorting all the boxes in my room that set me off and I was stupid to try and wash that big plate. I'm sad to see it go but there's plenty more knick-knacks where that came from, and we both know it. I'm fine now. How was church? Are you going again? Have you had one of those Road to Damascus moments? Not sure if I see you as a visionary.'

Barney smiled. 'Me neither. No great revelation, but it was

interesting and I'm glad we went. It reminded me of Mum. I've been thinking about her a lot lately.'

'Oh, so have I. It felt a bit like a betrayal leaving our old home behind. As if I was deserting her, somehow. I'll feel better when I've got a few of her ornaments and pictures around my annexe.'

They both heard footsteps at the same time, and Nell came round the corner. 'I decided not to stay for coffee after all,' she said. 'It was taking forever to make because nobody had switched the urn on.' She looked at her father-in-law more closely and then at the blood-stained tea towel and first-aid kit which Barney hadn't got round to moving. 'Oh, Frank, whatever's the matter? You've been crying. And you've hurt yourself.'

Frank pulled a face. 'Not much,' he said. 'It was just a flesh wound, as the Monty Python team would say, and I'm not upset. I think I'm getting hay fever.'

He mopped his eyes and blew his nose. Nell exchanged glances with Barney. 'Did something get broken?' she asked.

'Lottie's biggest cake plate,' Frank said. 'You know, that one with the lemon patterns. It's okay, it was my fault for trying to carry too many things downstairs. I won't do it again.'

'Dad's getting itchy feet, he's ready to move into the annexe,' Barney explained. 'Shall we go for it?'

'Now?' Frank's delight was obvious. 'Have you got time?'

'I have if you both have,' said Nell. 'Let's do it. Lunch first?'

Very soon the three of them were back under the apple tree with a sandwich each, planning their next moves. Barney and Nell would set about shifting the rest of the furniture while Frank pottered backwards and forwards with small bags and boxes of his belongings.

'What a good job Rick brought the bigger stuff in,' said Nell. 'He's *so* strong, isn't he?'

'Yes, very fortunate,' said Barney, through gritted teeth. He decided not to say more. It was good to be on a better footing with Nell after their row. To rock the boat at this stage would be crazy.

By the time two hours had passed, everything that needed to be moved was more-or-less in place. Nell hung the three sets of new curtains she'd ordered online and made up the bed with fragrant linen that had been dried on the washing line near to the giant lavender bush while Barney put up a couple of lampshades before shifting cupboards and small furniture to Frank's satisfaction.

'I'm going to really like this place,' said Frank, sinking into his favourite armchair with a sigh of satisfaction. 'I've got a view of the garden, and I don't even need to trek upstairs to bed or to go to the bathroom. It's perfect. Can we put some pictures up now?'

'Only if I can open a bottle of wine to help us along,' said Nell, heading for the main house.

Barney sat down in one of the two other easy chairs earmarked for Frank's visitors. 'That's a good afternoon's work so far,' he said. 'Now, where do you want the pictures?'

When Nell returned, they all found that the chilled white wine helped a lot, and filled with renewed enthusiasm, finally finished the job by six o'clock.

'I was going to make a roast today,' said Nell rather sadly. 'But there hasn't been time. I need to bake a batch of scones for tomorrow's trip before we eat though.'

Frank launched into an explanation for Barney about why the picnic choices were important. 'We're only taking food that's made us happy for one reason or another over the years,' he said enthusiastically. 'I'm doing hard-boiled eggs with salt to dip, and

I found that bumper bag of cheese and onion crisps that you bought yesterday, Nell.'

Barney felt the familiar resentment creeping in. He'd been planning to open those crisps now and have another glass of wine in the early-evening sunshine. Suddenly he heard himself saying, 'Would you like me to rustle up my special chicken and chorizo pasta for tonight? I can make extra so you can take some with you for the picnic to eat with salad. Have we got a couple of lemons, Nell? While you've got the oven on, why don't I have a go at making Mum's lemon drizzle cake for you to take with you? I know where her recipe book is. It makes two if I use the smaller loaf tins.'

Nell didn't speak for a moment. Barney thought she was going to refuse the offer and was beginning to wish he'd never spoken when she said, 'That's a lovely thought. Thanks, Barney.'

'Thanks, lad. I've missed the taste of that cake,' was all Frank said, but his eyes were very bright.

Barney got up to go to the kitchen. For the first time since they'd moved to Willowbrook he felt as if things were falling into place. That was until Nell turned to him and said, 'Now Frank's sorted, why don't we start to give all the bedrooms a makeover? And then we can make two of them into spare rooms for when the girls and Elliot come to stay.'

The unsaid words seemed to hover in the air between them. If there were going to be two spare rooms and a study upstairs, that could only mean that Nell wanted him to move in with her. And Barney, even though he was more than relieved to be on a better footing with Nell today, found himself far from ready to take that step.

23

The weather forecast for Monday had been set to be unsettled, but Nell was very relieved to see watery sunshine after a rainy night when she opened her bedroom curtains. From her window, she could see Frank already sitting at the mosaiced bistro table that Barney had put outside his door, a large mug of tea in front of him sending wisps of steam into the morning air. It was the mug Nell had bought him, with his initial and the cricket bat. So he did like it after all.

Anton was sniffing around the garden and as she watched, Frank called his dog and bent down ready to stroke him. Anton lolloped over, ears flapping, and put both front paws on Frank's knee. The two of them looked at each other for a long moment; dog and man in complete accord. Nell felt a pang of sadness at being without a pet to love her and to love back. Their elderly cat, Ruby, had died just before the previous house had gone up for sale and it had felt irresponsible to adopt another one while it was uncertain where they would live. Ruby had always made a beeline for Nell's lap whenever she sat down for more than a minute or two. She'd been almost blind by the end, and the sight of the cat negotiating the furniture with care and making stately progress around the garden rather than scampering had made Nell want to cry.

Perhaps it was time to try again with a new pet. She resolved to talk to Barney about it. Dinner last night had been much more relaxed and friendly than of late. Barney's pasta, his only other signature dish, had been as delicious as always and they'd even had a game of Monopoly with Frank afterwards, something that hadn't happened for a long time. There was a hopeful feeling in Nell's heart as she showered quickly and went downstairs to make breakfast and pack their contribution for the picnic, but her cheeriness faded when she entered the kitchen and found Barney already standing there, face to face with Rick.

'Oh, hi, I didn't hear you ring the bell,' said Nell, looking from one to the other as she sensed frost in the air.

'He didn't,' said Barney, at the same time as Rick said, 'I let myself in, the door was open.'

'You always told me not to stand around on the step, sweetheart,' Rick continued. 'So when I knocked and nobody came, I just came in and put the kettle on. Thought I'd have a cuppa with you before we set off. I've already collected the minibus.'

Nell could see that Barney was outraged at this familiar behaviour, but she told herself firmly that there was no real reason why he should mind. Rick had been a daily visitor to their house while he was working for them so she could see why he didn't feel the need to stand on ceremony now. However, in their previous home they had never been able to leave either the front or back door unlocked because they'd lived on a busy thoroughfare where burglaries were all too common, so she and Barney had never been used to people wandering in unannounced.

Luckily Frank entered the room at this moment. He was

wearing the outfit that Nell had selected for him. It was obvious just from the way he was walking that he felt good about himself, with his much neater haircut, trimmed moustache and on his feet, a rather natty pair of casual navy slip-ons.

Rick whistled when he spied Frank. 'Woo hoo, you sure look the business, young sir,' he said, walking round the older man and admiring the new look. 'They won't know what's hit them on the east coast. I bet you'll have to watch yourself with Beryl and her gang too. Anyway, shall I make the tea?'

Barney was visibly bristling now and muttered that he'd have his breakfast later when they were all out of the way. He left the kitchen without looking at Nell, and some of her good mood drained away, but when Frank and Rick had made tea and toast for them all and the eggs had been boiled and cooled ready for the picnic, she began to look forward to the day out again. Soon, the picnic basket was packed, including one of Barney's pair of lemon drizzle cakes, and at that moment Maryam arrived carrying a basket.

'I've double wrapped the samosas, so the spicy smell doesn't get into your cakes,' she said. 'I had to make an extra-large batch because my gang looked so sad that I was taking them away. Since the boys have been back, they're eating me out of house and home. Hey, Nell – have you seen the size of the minibus? It's got to be an eighteen-seater. I'd imagined a glorified campervan.'

Nell's stomach rumbled and she wondered if anyone would notice if she ate a samosa now. Putting the idea firmly out of her mind, she called to Barney that they were leaving, and he shouted back wishing them a good day out but didn't come downstairs to say goodbye. Nell tried not to be offended. The previous evening had felt like progress for them all, with Frank so pleased about his new accommodation and she and Barney on the same wavelength for once, but now they were back to circling around each other like strangers. Even so, going to church together had been heart-warming and once this outing was done with, maybe she and Barney could settle down to giving the rest of the house a facelift and build some bridges between them.

Maryam had been right about the size of their transport. Rick had done them proud. There was plenty of room to put in all Nell's folding chairs and some rugs and beach towels. 'I think Bev's got a couple of picnic tables and more chairs,' Nell said. 'I want everyone to be comfortable.'

'Your bloke seemed a bit offish this morning. What's up?' said Rick as they drove round to the vicarage where the others had arranged to meet them.

'He's probably just tired,' said Nell, defensively. It was one thing being cross with Barney herself but quite another having someone else casting aspersions. However, when she spied the waiting group and saw Kate looking bandbox fresh in perfectly pressed linen shorts and a gingham top, Nell's spirits took a dip, and a wave of jealousy flooded over her. This was the woman who was absorbing Barney's time so effectively, and it didn't take much imagination to see why that was.

'Bang on nine o'clock, well done chaps,' said Harry Henderson. His wife was clutching his arm, pink-cheeked and smiling. 'We're looking forward to this so much, aren't we, dear? This is Penelope, for anyone who hasn't met her.'

Penelope was tiny and fragile looking but when she was helped into the minibus and her shrewd eyes met Nell's, it was as if Nell was under close scrutiny.

'I'll just jump down and help with everyone's bags, and the chairs and things,' Nell said, but Penelope put a hand on her arm.

'Don't you worry about that, there are plenty of people to

load the bus. Sit here with me and let's have a chat. I've been wanting to meet you. I was going to ask you and your husband and your father-in-law round for tea, but I've been laid low by a ridiculous summer cold. We must arrange something as soon as possible.'

By now everyone was scrambling aboard, and Penelope turned to face the driver as he got ready to set off. 'I hope there'll be a comfort stop en route, Rick,' she said. 'You know that some of us might not last until we get to Hunstanton.'

Rick laughed. 'Don't you worry. I've planned a stop for coffee halfway,' he said. 'I can't go very long without caffeine. If anybody needs a break sooner than that, just shout. Now, let's get that soundtrack playing and get on the road. We'll all be paddling in the sea before the day's out.'

'Well, *you* might be,' said Frank. 'I'm looking forward to the next stop. It's years since I was on Cromer Pier. I always had a knack with those penny-rolling games. I want to see if all the old slot machines are still there.'

The music played as the minibus ate up the miles. Beryl and Winnie were sitting together near the front and sang along lustily whenever they knew the words, and Nell sat back, observing the group more closely now she was beginning to relax. It was interesting to see where everyone had settled themselves. Bev had commandeered the front passenger seat beside Rick and was setting the satnav on her phone, although Rick was adamant he didn't need it.

Anthea had made a beeline for the seat next to Frank and seemed to already be telling him her life story. Nell wondered how long it would be before he made it clear he was bored but for the moment, he seemed to be all ears. Anthea was looking very stylish in her usual collection of draped linen garments teamed with a wide-brimmed straw hat, and her make-up was immaculate. Her lipstick was glossy, and she'd applied a delicate touch of tawny eyeshadow.

Behind Anthea and Frank sat Ingrid and Maurice. Ingrid was trying to make conversation with Maurice, but he was gazing out of the window and answering in monosyllables so after a few minutes, she gave up and turned her attention to Kate on the other side of the aisle, who had settled herself next to Maryam. They chatted about the café and Kate told everyone that her partner Milo had stepped up to the mark to help Sam for the day.

'My new part-timer's great but she was going to have to be left alone while Sam fetched Elsie from school later on,' Kate said. 'I was a bit worried because she's never been there without one of us, so as Milo works from the flat upstairs, he said he'd rearrange his hours to make today free. He's even baked us some of his chocolate brownies.'

'That one's a keeper,' Beryl called down the bus. 'He's gorgeous too. I always said so, didn't I? And remember what I told you about men with big feet?' She and Winnie nudged each other and cackled alarmingly. Kate blushed and glanced across at Nell. She rolled her eyes, and most of Nell's resentment vanished. The pride in Kate's voice when she talked about Milo was obvious. It was silly to think she'd be interested in Barney, wasn't it? It was time Nell stopped being so irritated by his new hobby. At least Kate had helped him to settle into their new surroundings quickly.

Thinking about her husband sent Nell off into a spiral of nostalgia for the simpler times when she and Barney had felt like a team. He'd always been a popular and appealing man with his substantial build and air of kindness. Barney's smiling eyes and cheeky grin had won over many a grumpy client at work, she knew that for a fact, not to mention the eclectic mix of characters he'd befriended when he'd popped into the homeless centre while Nell was volunteering. His speciality had been playing chess with a couple of the regulars, who seemed to appreciate the time he spent with them. No wonder Kate liked Barney too. It was time Nell made more of an effort to get to know her.

Bev turned up the volume on her phone's Bluetooth speaker between tracks as they whizzed down the bypass to Wisbech and everyone fell silent to see which person's song would blast out. The upbeat sound of 'Let Your Love Flow' filled the bus, and even Frank could be heard to be attempting the chorus. Nell had a moment of complete accord with the others as they sang with varying degrees of tunefulness, and her eyes met Kate's again. In that few seconds, she sensed that they could become friends if Nell could get over her prickly, possessive feelings.

When the song finished and Bev turned the sound down again, Ingrid said, 'That was my choice, and I picked it because it means a lot to Joel and me. I never know what to call him. "Boyfriend" seems a bit juvenile, and we're not quite partners.'

'People say *significant other* these days,' said Beryl knowledgably. 'I always wonder what an insignificant one must look like. Maybe a bit weedy, with not much of a chin and dressed from head to foot in beige?'

'Yes. Anyway... we made each other a Spotify playlist when we were trying to be brave enough to tell each other how we felt. He went first, and then I replied. That song was on mine.'

'How romantic,' said Nell admiringly. 'I can't imagine Barney ever doing something like that.'

'None of my husbands or boyfriends would have dreamed of it,' Anthea agreed. 'Although Conrad once bought me a Mini.'

'A mini what?' Penelope sounded confused. 'A dress to show off your legs?'

'No, a car, darling. A hideous shade of puce. Unlucky for some. It was for me, as it happened. I found out soon after that he was sleeping with my gardener.'

'You had a lady gardener? That's very unusual,' said Penelope.

'No. His name was Nigel. They're still very happy together.'

Nobody spoke for a while. Nell sneaked a sideways glance at Kate. She was gazing out of the window. Her golden-brown hair was sleek and shiny, and she looked totally relaxed, exuding a sense of calm. If Barney had been or was smitten with Kate, Nell could see why. *But he isn't*, she told herself firmly. *It's my stupid imagination. I'm just feeling raw because he still won't come back to our bed.*

Maurice was now making an effort to chat to Beryl and Winnie, and the music flowed around them as they pulled into the garden centre that Rick had chosen for their coffee break. He allowed them half an hour and then herded them back into the minibus.

'Come on, we want to get to picnic time,' he said. 'I've brought sausage rolls. I didn't make them from scratch, but I did take them from the freezer, put them in the oven and take them out again. They always remind me of kids' parties.'

'Have you got children then, Rick?' Frank asked, as he strapped himself back into his seat.

Rick didn't answer for a minute or two, busy getting out of his parking space and back onto the main road. Then he said, 'I've got two boys. They live with my ex. I only get to see them once a month because they live in Germany now. She remarried. His name's Franz. Loads of money and a big house near Munich.'

Nobody commented on these revelations, but Bev reached out a hand and patted Rick's knee. They drove on, as the playlist progressed and the memories it brought about triggered several different conversations. Harry and Penelope reminisced at length about their song and Maurice joined in with his.

'They don't write 'em like that any more, do they?' said Maurice. 'Some of the modern rubbish isn't a patch on the old stuff. No offence to you young 'uns,' he added hastily.

Beryl turned round to wink at Maurice. 'How about my song though?' she said, wiggling her shoulders as 'You Sexy Thing' began to play, altering the mood considerably. 'You've got to admit it gets you going. I've brought devilled chicken wings for the picnic. I like a bit of spice, me.'

Maurice didn't answer directly but the smile that lit up his face told Nell that he wasn't averse to Beryl's flirting.

It didn't seem long before Rick was driving through the outskirts of Hunstanton with his window wound down as they all sang along to Winnie's choice of 'One Love', with even Penelope swaying to the music.

'I can see the sea!' Bev shouted. 'Let's park up and then I'd like us to have five minutes' peace and quiet before we have the first part of our picnic. Then anyone who wants to stretch their legs can have a quick walk. After we've done all that, Rick's going to take us to a place where it's easier for you all to get down onto the sand. We can set up tables there too and maybe even have a paddle.'

Nell breathed a sigh of relief. She should have known Bev would have realised that some of the older members of the group wouldn't be wanting to scramble down steep paths or walk very far. Rick easily found a space overlooking the seafront and turned off the engine. The sound of seagulls crying took Nell straight back to her childhood, and windswept holidays on the east coast with her mum and dad.

'Right, before we set up ready for the first course, I wanted to have a quick word,' said Bev, swivelling around in the seat so that she could see everyone. 'It was good to hear all your songs a second time. I just wondered if you felt there was any sort of link between the choices?'

Nell was trying to think how to express what she felt and there were a lot of thoughtful faces around her, but Maurice spoke first. 'I reckon we were all conjuring up memories of very special times when we were either happier or...' he ran out of words and Ingrid stepped in.

'...or more secure, or with certain people, or less scared...'

'And remembering all that stuff is a bit mournful sometimes but we wouldn't have picked those tracks if they didn't make us feel good in some way,' Nell added. She waited to see what Bev's conclusion would be. She and Maryam hadn't discussed with Bev how the sessions would be evaluated, and Nell had no idea where this was going.

Bev smiled at them all. 'You're all looking at me as if I've got something profound to say, but I haven't... yet. This is only the beginning of us all exploring what makes us feel contented. We'll talk more about the music next week, but for now – food!'

24

Barney sat on the edge of his bed and looked around the room. He'd not bothered to make it more than functional since they'd moved to Willowbrook, because that would seem to be emphasising even more that this was his space, not the much larger room where Nell slept. Although to be accurate, she didn't sleep much. Barney often heard his wife pacing along the corridor to the bathroom or going downstairs to make yet another hot drink.

Night after night, his whole body had been aching to make her feel better as he lay in his single bed rolled up tightly in his duvet, with moonlight shining through a crack in the curtains. Guilt at what he was doing to Nell consumed Barney. Why couldn't he just transfer himself into the main bedroom and start again? It wasn't possible that all cancer sufferers or people who'd been ill had this much of an issue with physical closeness, or he'd have heard about it. He'd never thought to mention the problem to any of the medical staff he'd seen. There had been much more pressing questions at the time. Now it seemed a waste of a doctor's time to take up an appointment just to say *I don't know why but I can't bear to be in bed with my wife.*

Yesterday evening had been the best one that he and Nell and Frank had spent together since the move. They'd laughed and laughed as they teased each other and tussled over the tatty Monopoly board, something that hadn't happened for months. When Barney's mother was fading fast, lost in her own muddled world, Barney and Nell had realised that Frank was spending far too much time on his own after Lottie had been put to bed. They'd instigated the Monopoly challenge, and Nell had even found a small cut-glass cup with two handles that would be presented to the eventual winner.

Frank hadn't been keen to begin with, but as when Barney had been growing up and any game was suggested, he'd soon been overcome by the desire to beat his son and had enjoyed providing drinks and snacks at what he called *half time.* Both men were very competitive, and this would have led to a perfectly fair game if Frank and Nell hadn't found various ways of ganging up on Barney to stop him winning. They'd all found the battles hugely entertaining. Barney over the weeks ramped up the hurt outrage at being yet again stitched up and Nell and Frank had feigned innocence.

Last night, the old camaraderie had emerged, and the game had been fiercely fought. Barney had pretended to be a sore loser in the end but he'd been full of joy that their lives were becoming more normal again. Then Rick had turned up this morning and ruined everything. Barney couldn't get over the feeling that the man was trying to get between himself and Nell. The two of them were always joking around when the building work was going on, and Nell had sparkled when Rick was around in his cut-off jeans, flashing his six-pack and blond hair and dimples and tough-guy image and...

Barney forced himself to stop mentally chuntering. It was only making him crosser. Time to do something useful instead of brooding. There was no point in going over to the café because Kate was on the trip too, so he might as well focus on the house. What would be a good thing to do for Nell?

Downstairs, the cottage felt unnaturally quiet, and Barney switched on the radio as he prowled around trying to decide which of the outstanding jobs to tackle. He wandered from room to room, admiring the way Nell had added homely touches everywhere. The kitchen was colourful and clean with a faint smell of toast still hanging in the air, making Barney's stomach rumble, but he turned away from the bright row of copper-bottomed pans and the microwave and toaster in matching orange, focusing on clearing the small amount of washing up.

There was nothing else to do in the kitchen, so Barney went back to the living room and sat on the window seat. The radio station was now running through a string of songs from the 1980s, and Barney felt a pang of nostalgia when he recognised a Fleetwood Mac number that Nell had always loved. It was 'Little Lies', and the words were haunting. Barney had lied to Nell so many times about his reasons for sleeping alone: telling her that he didn't want to disturb her when he was restless during the worst of his treatment, that he knew he'd started snoring, that he was having bad dreams that made him wake up with a jump, and several more excuses.

What he hadn't said was that he felt dirty right down to his soul, as if the cancer had left him tainted. Of course, his logical brain knew it wasn't catching, that would be a ridiculous idea, but even so he couldn't shake off the shadow of doom that still lurked in the corners of his mind. Barney had refused counselling when his treatment was over, even though the team at the hospital had recommended it. He'd thought, wrongly as it turned out, that he could beat his demons alone. Looking round the empty room and already missing Nell with every beat of his heart, Barney had a very small taste of what his father must be feeling all the time, since losing his beloved wife.

There was only one thing for it. No amount of house-sorting would put right what was so badly wrong between himself and Nell. He was wasting time when they could be happy together again. Barney went upstairs to the study and sat down at his desk, opening his laptop. There must be places nearby where he could go to get some help. All he needed now was the courage to find them.

25

The opening part of the picnic was a great success. Rick, Nell and Bev set up the folding tables on a grassy area near the minibus while Maryam, helped by Ingrid and Kate, unpacked some of the contributions of food. Frank and Maurice erected a variety of camping chairs around the tables and got Harry and Penelope settled in the sturdiest ones. The sun was high in the sky now so even though Bev had provided flasks of tea, the Saga Louts had made an executive decision that everyone should have the option of an icy-cold drink. With this in mind, they had taken themselves off to a café across the road with a list of orders.

Soon, the whole team was seated around the tables, with paper plates and drinks in front of them. Bev held up a hand for silence.

'First, I'm going to give thanks for this wonderful spread,' she said. 'After that, before we tuck in, you're going to get a brief chance to say why you chose the food you brought. What is there about it that gives you that happy feeling? Don't worry, I said a brief chance, I know you're all ravenous.'

Bev bowed her head and most of the group followed suit, although Beryl seemed distracted by a seagull that was hovering a bit too close for comfort and Frank was similarly preoccupied by noticing he had a chair with a wobbly leg that was threatening to topple him onto the floor.

'Dear Lord – bless this food and the amazing people who have provided it today. Please be with us as we explore the different ways that we find our own contentment. Amen,' Bev said, just loudly enough for them all to hear. Three passing teenagers sniggered, and she quelled them with a look. They shuffled off, muttering to each other about bossy women.

'I don't know why they're laughing. That lot look as if they've already been on their knees for weeks. Their jeans are all ripped,' said Winnie, giving them an extra glare.

Bev smiled at her. 'Ignore them. People laugh at what they don't understand,' she said. 'Now, let's whizz around these fabulous offerings and have a word or two about each. I'll point and you speak, okay? If that seagull gets any closer, we'll set Rick on it.'

As Bev's pointing finger swiftly moved around the tables, Frank explained about his memories of picnics with hard-boiled eggs, Nell mentioned her mum's scone recipe and Barney's lemon drizzle from his mother's cookbook. Ingrid just said, 'Cheese straws. Made them in cookery class at school. Simpler times.'

Bev nodded approvingly. 'We're saving the sweet stuff for the final picnic stop on the beach later, so it's savoury first. Carry on.'

Beryl had brought naan bread, Anthea two jars of mango chutney and Winnie produced a container of her tandoori chicken pieces. 'We decided to combine our memories,' said Winnie. 'I usually cook for myself and these two girls, mostly Caribbean dishes from my childhood but always something spicy. This one's best for when we're eating away from home. Good times spent together.'

The three of them high-fived each other and looked tearful so Bev moved swiftly on. Harry and Penelope had provided two large fruit cakes for later, which had been baked by their daily help. 'They make us think of celebrations. Weddings, christenings and so on. We've got a lovely family and they always home in on Bessie's fruit cakes,' said Penelope.

Kate had contributed chocolate brownies and said they were made by her partner, Milo. 'It was the first thing he baked when we took over the café,' she said. 'He's never looked back. He's made plenty for us so you can all try them later.'

Maurice surprised everyone by indicating a large foil platter of dainty sandwiches, wrapped in cling film. 'Ham or cheese cut in triangles on very soft seeded bread with the crusts cut off,' he said. 'My mum used to make them when I had a birthday party. I bet you all thought I'd just throw in a bag of crisps.'

Rick pointed to the container of golden, crispy sausage rolls. 'I did the cocktail-sized ones but there's fifty of them so don't hold back. Kids' parties, eh? Love 'em.'

'Or not,' muttered Nell. Having Elliot and the twins close together had meant that she'd catered for many parties and attended a lot more in her time. That was one thing about parenting that she didn't miss. The noise, the need to rustle up an imaginative present for someone else's child when you'd left it till the last minute or forgotten, the mess and the eventual tears when the sugar-rush wore off. She shuddered.

Bev and Maryam exchanged glances. 'We teamed up too,' Bev said. 'I was worried I might not be able to make anything in time because I've been rushed off my feet with home visits this week, so I got Rashid to deliver the ingredients and then Maryam came round to the vicarage and gave me a lesson in making samosas. Then she made some of her own at home just in case mine were horrible.'

'That wasn't the reason,' said Maryam, laughing. 'I just love making samosas and so do my gang at home. My mum taught me how to get them spot on and her mother taught her, and so on. Food means family and continuity to me,' said Maryam. 'Now let's get stuck in. This all looks fantastic. It's the best picnic ever and we haven't even added the pudding course yet.'

Without further ado, the various plates, dishes and containers were passed around and a contented silence followed, only broken by the sound of munching and appreciative comments. The seagulls whooped and called but kept their distance thanks to Frank flapping a tea towel at them now and again, and Nell felt an overwhelming sense of peace and companionship steal over her. Her only regret was that Barney wasn't here to enjoy it. She wished she'd asked him now. Nell had almost texted Bev to see if she could invite him along this morning but then he'd looked so disgruntled when Rick arrived that she'd decided against it.

When everyone had nearly finished, and Harry and Maurice were sneaking leftover bits of pastry from the sausage rolls and samosas, Bev raised what was left of her iced coffee.

'A toast to happy memories,' she said. 'And thanks to you for sharing them. I think this session's reminded us all that food's not just for fuel. It's got semi-magical powers to take you back to your best childhood moments and lots of times since then. You can recreate those happy memories every time you eat your favourites.'

'Hang on, Bev,' said Beryl. 'You haven't told us any of your memories. You just joined in Maryam's. That's cheating, that is.'

Bev didn't say anything for a moment. Then she sighed. 'I've got a lot of favourites from when I was a kid, but they were all things that could be bought ready-made. My parents were heavily involved with church affairs. Committees, meetings and so on. I think my dad would have loved to have been a vicar himself, but I'm the first one in the family to take that step.'

'They must be very proud of you,' said Winnie. 'My ma and pa really wanted me to be a pastor in their church but I ended up getting married and having a whole bunch of kids instead. Wouldn't swap 'em, but I always felt as if I'd disappointed the folks.'

Bev shrugged. 'Yes, I think they *were* proud. Maybe a bit envious too, but my plans didn't affect them much, so they just carried on being busy. There wasn't any time left over for me to learn to cook. Food was fuel rather than something to linger over,' she said. 'After that... well, the rest of my memories of eating have kind of swamped the good ones. It's not a story for now. I'll tell you sometime, okay? The sun's shining and we've got the rest of our trip to do. Let's clear up and hit the road.'

Before long, Rick was back at the wheel and everyone was strapped into their seats. He drove out of the town and headed for the coast road. 'I'm going to cruise along and stop whenever you see a place that takes your fancy,' he said, leaning one arm on the open window next to him. 'The final bit of the picnic's going to be at a place where it's easy for everyone to get onto the beach. Then it's cake time!'

The others cheered as the minibus picked up speed. Soon, those in the party who'd been to the area before were pointing out places they'd loved, and the newcomers to Norfolk were gazing delightedly at the scenery. The sky and the sea were breathtakingly azure today and only a few tiny clouds broke up the vast expanse of blue. They caught glimpses of golden beaches, pine forests and bustling seaside towns filled with suntanned people eating ice creams. Every now and again, Rick would find a parking space and his passengers either tumbled out to enjoy the views and stretch their legs or sit contentedly in the bus gazing out of the windows, in Harry and Penelope's case.

The minibus ate up the miles once they had set off again, leaving the busy streets of Sheringham behind them and soon they were making good progress further down the coast.

'This is the most excitement we've had in ages,' said Penelope to Bev. 'Harry and I don't get out much these days, you know. Since our son Gareth passed away, we've not felt much like socialising and my old legs won't take me far, nowadays.'

There was a short, uncomfortable silence. Nell sensed that everyone was trying to think of a cheerful comment that didn't belittle the pain coming through Penelope's words.

'I could fetch you in the car anytime to come and have tea with me,' she said, before anyone else could speak.

'If you don't mind driving around in the van, I can give you lifts when I'm not working,' added Rick.

Before anyone else could chip in, Harry held a hand up. 'I know you'll all have kind offers for us, and we're grateful,' he said. 'But our daughters are very good to us, and we don't need help as a rule. This trip is a wonderful change though. We're thoroughly enjoying ourselves, aren't we, my dear?'

Penelope nodded. 'Look, we're about to go through that place where we had our honeymoon, Harry. Yes, I thought so, we're coming into Cromer. Can we stop?'

Rick obliged immediately. He seemed to have a knack of homing in on all the best parking spaces. They were in a steep little street not far from the promenade and Nell peered out of the window, wondering if Penelope would manage to get out and walk, but the old lady's eyes were shining.

'Harry, if you walk one side of me and someone else gives me an arm on the other side, I think I can get as far as the pier. Can we buy you all an ice cream?' she said.

This suggestion was met with whoops of delight, and it wasn't long before a rather noisy procession was making its way along the promenade with Penelope, flanked by Harry and Rick, leading the way. Her cheeks were pink with delight and Harry looked almost as overcome by the moment. Within ten minutes, the whole group were sitting in the sunshine on the pier clutching cornets with flakes sticking out of the top and were frantically licking to stop the drips running down.

'I haven't done this for years,' said Maurice. 'Happiness is... a melting ice cream at the seaside on a hot day. What's everyone else's secret?'

Nell looked along the row of seats to see many thoughtful faces. She decided to get the ball rolling. 'Happiness is... a steaming-hot cup of tea in bed on a winter morning. Or any morning, to be fair.' Tears prickled her eyes when she thought about Barney, still bringing her tea most mornings even though he'd long ago left their bed.

Bev grinned at her. 'It's getting to the end of delivering a passionate sermon you thought might offend the congregation and seeing lot of them nodding their heads. Winnie?'

Winnie smiled back. 'For me it's a sizzling, spicy curry served to people you love.'

Beryl gave her a thumbs-up sign. 'You can be happy in that way as often as you like, ducky,' she said. 'Mine's simple. A naked cuddle in the morning when you wake up. Mind you, it's been a while. Any offers?' She nudged Frank, who nearly choked on his cornet.

Nobody seemed tempted to follow this until Maurice piped up. 'Toast and butter with homemade jam,' he said. 'I bet you didn't know I used to make my own preserves? I can't do it now because my daughter's banned me from picking up the jam kettle. I scalded myself once. It wasn't my fault, before you say anything,' he said, glancing around at his listeners. 'The cat jumped on the worktop, and she gave me a proper fright. She's too busy to help me to do it. My Kathy, I mean, not the cat.'

Nell leaned back against the warm wooden slats of the seat. She felt contentment creep over her as she looked at the sea, sparkling and rippling away as far as the horizon. These people were here because of Bev, Maryam and herself. It had been the right thing to do. Maybe... just maybe, she was inching closer to the essence of what made her tick, and the others were joining in too. Frank's idea about Nell finding reasons to be happy might be just a dream, but his heart was in the right place and here he was, sitting beside her and leaning against her arm. Or was he just trying not to lean the other way and be closer to Beryl? She chuckled to herself as Anthea began to speak.

'I'll help with the jam anytime, Maurice,' she said. 'You should have asked before. And don't look so terrified. I'm not after marrying you. Been there, done that... too many times. Happiness is having the house to yourself and being able to eat nothing but a double portion of cauliflower cheese for dinner and not mind the consequences.'

'An intriguing recipe for bliss,' said Ingrid. 'I'd go along with that, but substitute cornflakes and ice-cold milk instead of cooking when you're tired. No drastic after-effects.'

Bev got to her feet and looked at her watch. 'There are still a few of you to chip in on that subject, but we need to get moving. Rick needs to get the bus back to his friend by six o'clock. Let's head to the beach. It's time for picnic part two.'

26

Afterwards, Nell could never remember when their perfect day began to go sour. Was it when Frank realised that he'd left his walking stick on the pier, and it was much too late to go back for it? Perhaps it was the fact that the bus ride on top of the ice cream and the hot sunshine had made Penelope too queasy to even attempt a piece of cake or a scone. Harry had been very anxious about her and had lost his enthusiasm at that point.

Also, Anthea and Maurice appeared to have had a tiff between the promenade and the minibus and refused to speak to each other for the rest of the day, and Rick had become more and more uncommunicative the longer it took to get everyone onto Walcott beach. Sand somehow got into the butter for the scones and wasps made a beeline for the cake and brownies.

All in all, Nell was mightily relieved when she was dropped off at home. Frank had been invited in for a cup of tea at Beryl's house with the Saga Louts and to Nell's surprise, he'd accepted but she was disappointed to see that Bev was still in the passenger seat when they finally stopped to let Maryam and the other four out on Fiddler's Row and headed for Hollyhocks Cottage.

'I thought you'd be getting out at the vicarage,' Nell said. 'You didn't need to see me home.'

'Oh... I thought I should see the trip through to the bitter end,' said Bev, shooting a glance at Rick, who had suddenly cheered up and was whistling along to the radio. 'It's my responsibility to make sure everyone's safely back, especially after the way things went downhill.'

'Do you want to come in for a debrief? You could walk back afterwards if Rick needs to go?'

Bev got out of the bus to open the back door for Nell. 'No, it's okay, thanks. I'm shattered. Let's talk tomorrow. Maryam's coming over in the morning to plan the next meeting. Are you free about half past ten?'

'I... guess so. See you tomorrow then. Bye, Rick.'

There was a cold feeling in her heart as Nell watched Bev and Rick drive away together. She let herself into the cottage and could feel the silence even before she called Barney and got no answering shout. Going into the kitchen, she found a note on the kitchen table.

Have taken Anton for a walk. Might call at the pub. Text me when you're back, and maybe come too? I might even buy you a pie. Xxx

This was better. Nell quickly messaged Barney to say she was on her way before running upstairs to spritz on perfume, spray deodorant and add a slick of gloss to her dry, sun-baked lips. She'd have liked a shower and change after the long day out and sticky, grumpy bus ride home but she was suddenly afraid that if she wasted time, Barney might give up on her and come home.

The church clock struck six as Nell strolled across the green towards The Fox and Fiddle. She was tempted to speed up, now that the early-evening air was cooler, but the thought of arriving at the pub red-faced and sweaty again forced her to take her time. As she stepped inside, the ancient stone floor tiles and the shadowy darkness of the bar calmed her, and the sting of feeling excluded from Bev and Rick's friendship began to fade.

'Over here, Nell,' a familiar voice called, and Nell turned to see Barney getting to his feet. Anton leaped up too and they both came to greet her. Unbearably touched by Barney's beaming smile and even by Anton's excited dribbling, Nell held out her arms to her husband, and for the first time in months, they moved into a warm, spontaneous hug.

'I missed you today,' Barney said huskily, pulling away. 'I bet you need a tall glass of very cold lager after being out in the sun for hours. Was it okay?'

'Yes, yes, yes to the beer and... erm... not sure about the other part of the question. I'll tell you about it when I've had a drink.'

It wasn't long before they were sitting beside each other in one of the pub's secluded wooden booths with Anton at their feet. Ned, the landlord, had provided a large bowl of water and in between lapping messily from it, Anton was eyeing the remains of Barney's crisps hopefully.

'I wasn't sure how much longer you'd be out or if you'd still be hungry,' Barney said, sneaking a crisp to Anton. 'Is it too hot for pie and chips?'

Nell's stomach rumbled. She'd not been able to face any of the second part of the picnic once the unsettling atmosphere and the wasps had made themselves felt. They'd packed away as quickly as they could and made tracks for home. Even the mix of favourite music hadn't helped to lift the mood. Maurice had fallen asleep with his hat over his face, Ingrid and Kate had absorbed themselves in a conversation about the desirability of living on a boat and everyone else had been silent for most of the journey.

'So, how was it?' Barney asked again. 'You look a bit... a bit...' He was clearly searching for the right words and Nell decided to save him the worry of offending her. There was an air of vulnerability about her husband this evening, and it tugged at her heart.

'Fed up?' she suggested. 'Exhausted? Boiling hot? Disappointed?'

Nell hadn't meant to add the last one, but it was true. The day had gone so well to begin with. Their musical choices had carried the group through the first part of the journey and the recipes for happiness and the ice creams on the pier had been a lovely touch, but from then on, the mood had plummeted. She began to tell Barney about the day, haltingly at first. She didn't want his comments about her involvement in the new group to be scathing, but Nell soon realised that she should have had more faith in his innate good nature.

Barney took her hand in his and encouraged her to carry on when she paused for breath. His tone was sympathetic, and his expressive green eyes were full of an emotion she couldn't read. She gazed into them, marvelling once again how any man could have such long, thick eyelashes. A hint of stubble and his newly acquired tan had given her husband a very appealing look. The one hidden dimple in his left cheek, as opposed to Rick's much more obvious two, was so subtle that it could only be noticed when he was really amused, as he was when she related Beryl's naked cuddle comment and Frank's reaction.

When Nell finally ran out of steam, Barney encouraged her to finish her beer and got to his feet again. 'You stay put and talk to Anton. I'll go and get us a chilled bottle of sauvignon blanc and order dinner.' He put a hand to his mouth. 'Oh no, I totally forgot about Dad. Is he okay?' he asked, belatedly remembering Frank.

Nell grinned. 'I'll give him a call to check, but I'm guessing he's been kidnapped by the Saga Louts, and he'll be full of nourishing food by now. They love to feed their friends, and they seem to have adopted him.'

This proved to be the case, and with the worry of their parent out of the way, Barney and Nell settled down to what would probably have been classed as a date night, if only their children could see them. The pies were baked on the premises, as the landlord told them proudly, and the triple-cooked chips were golden and crispy, with a token serving of peas and salad garnish to pay lip service to healthy eating.

'This was a brilliant idea,' said Nell, as she struggled to finish the last of her chips. 'No, don't offer to help me out, Barney, these are too good to give away.'

'I didn't know if you'd want to come over,' said Barney, looking away and busying himself with making a fuss of Anton. 'I... we haven't been getting on so well lately, have we? For a long time, really, not just lately. But I've got something to tell you.'

Nell waited, suddenly filled with a sense of panic. The expression on her husband's face was so serious that she knew... she absolutely knew that he was going to tell her that his illness was back. Instead, Barney took a deep breath and said, 'I've made an appointment to see a counsellor. I found a local one with a cancellation. I've had to go privately and pay, there were no NHS appointments for months, but it's got to be done. I need to tackle what's going on with the way I'm feeling. We can't go on like this. It's time I took action.'

For a moment, Nell was so relieved that this wasn't what she'd been expecting that she couldn't speak. In the silence that followed, Barney said, 'Of course, that means I'll have to tell this woman all sorts of stuff... personal stuff.'

'Well, yes – I guess that's the basic idea of counselling,' said Nell, regaining control of her vocal cords with difficulty.

Barney seemed to be having trouble meeting her eyes now. He fiddled with a beer mat and began to shred it. All around them, the babble of conversation and music from the ancient jukebox in the corner formed a much-needed barrier between the two of them and the rest of the customers. A group of women wandered in, laughing and chatting. They called for the cocktail menu and the new barman obliged, giving them his best patter. Nell suddenly wished she was with them, giggling about ordering a Slow Comfortable Screw and planning an evening of nothing more than gossip and fun.

'What's the problem, Barney?' she said. 'It'll be good for you to unload whatever's been bothering you since you were ill, won't it? Because I know you've been struggling. A lot. I haven't been able to help you, I didn't even know where to start.' Her eyes filled with tears, and she blinked them away, but Barney didn't seem to notice.

'Once I start talking, I might not be able to stop, and that's the danger. There are things I've never told anyone. Not even you, Nell. No, not even you.'

27

The fortnight after the seaside trip passed quickly for Nell, punctuated by the next church meeting, which was less than successful. Bev, not sure how to tackle the mindfulness session successfully, had enlisted the help of a local expert and friend. Unfortunately, although Camilla knew her subject inside out, her delivery was uninspiring in the extreme. She'd droned her way through an hour and a half of passing around lemons and onions for them to sniff, accompanied by a PowerPoint presentation so dull that Frank, Maurice, Harry and Winnie had all fallen asleep, and Frank had actually snored.

Nell's mind skittered away from the uncomfortable memories of it as the following week began. It was July now, but although she was determined to wear her summer clothes and determinedly persevered with shorts and vest tops, the weather was changeable. One day, the sun would be beating down and the gardens of the Willowbrook residents would be crying out for watering, the next, sudden torrential showers of rain lashed against the windows and the water overflowed down the side of Hollyhocks Cottage.

In desperation, Nell rang Rick to see if he would come round to unblock the gutters, and he duly turned up on one of the finer mornings, bouncing into the kitchen with only a perfunctory knock and surprising Barney so much that he dropped a plate, which smashed into smithereens on the tiled floor.

Muttering curses, Barney began to clear up the debris before making himself scarce with only a brief hello. As he left, he pointedly rolled his eyes and gave a heavy sigh. Rick and Nell were left looking at each other in dismay, until both started to laugh at the same time. When they'd gained control of themselves, Nell realised that Barney was still only just outside in the garden so was bound to have heard them giggling. Mortification flooded her, and she vowed to try and make it up to him later. They'd been getting on better since their evening in the pub but this incident wasn't going to help, and to cap it all, Barney was still refusing to tell her what he was so reluctant to divulge to his counsellor, who he'd already seen twice. In fact, he hadn't mentioned his appointments, either before they happened or afterwards. He'd merely disappeared and then presumably headed straight for the country park in relief when the soul-searching was over.

'Don't look so worried, he'll see the funny side,' said Rick, seeing Nell's eyes straying to the window into the garden, where Barney had joined Frank on the bench with Anton at their feet.

'Yeah... maybe,' Nell said. She wasn't so sure, but the close proximity of Rick in his cut-offs and vest soon distracted her and she made him a cold drink while he started work.

Soon, all the gutters were cleared and Rick and Nell, having heard Frank shout that he was taking Anton for a short walk and then to Beryl's for a cuppa, went to sit on the bench. Barney was nowhere to be seen, but Nell could hear him in his study, making a lot of noise as he led a Zoom call with his colleagues in the office. She was sure there was no need for him to be so loud, or to guffaw so often, but assumed it was for Rick's benefit, to show what an important and jolly character he was.

'So, I'm hoping tonight's meeting's gonna be better than the last one,' Rick said, draining his second pint of blackcurrant squash. Ice tinkled in his glass as he put it down on the ground and he turned to face Nell. 'That Camilla was sooo boring. I nearly joined the other guys and took a nap, but I didn't want to upset Bev. She was embarrassed, poor kid.'

Nell had never thought of Bev as any kind of kid, let alone a poor one, but she nodded. 'Don't worry, we're leading it ourselves this time. We might even meet in the garden at the vicarage if it doesn't get any cooler. Bev said something about a gazebo.'

'I know, I'm off there now to set it up. I'd better dash. See you later.'

Rick was on his feet and out of the garden before Nell could say any more. She heard the van roar into life and her spirits took a nosedive. It had been so lovely sitting under the oak tree in the dappled sunshine with Rick, listening to the hum of the bees on a nearby bush and enjoying the scent of the old-fash-ioned roses that the previous owner of the cottage had planted. She'd been just about to offer to make him a sandwich. Now, with Frank occupied along the lane and Barney still booming about data handling and spreadsheets through the open window upstairs, it was going to be lunch for one. Nell wanted to shout up to her husband that he could stop the big show of busyness because his main audience had decamped, but she resisted the temptation and decided to go along to see Maryam for a final chat about tonight's meeting.

The corner shop was empty apart from a couple browsing the treasure table and they soon departed, bearing a random assortment of goods, including a table lamp, a set of kitchen scales and a hideous orange vase patterned with green blobs that Nell knew had been donated by Maryam herself.

'Thank goodness that monstrosity's gone,' Maryam said, when the door had closed behind her customers. 'It was a present from Rashid's grandmother, and she died last year so he's finally realised we don't have to keep fetching it out in case she visits. Lovely woman, but dreadful taste in vases. Have you got time for an ice lolly? Help yourself from the freezer, it's on the house.'

Nell peered into the depths of the freezer cabinet and selected the most vibrant, stripy lolly she could find. Maybe it would lift her mood. She settled herself on the high stool next to the counter and began to eat it, wincing as the cold found a nerve.

'You look a bit glum,' said Maryam. 'What's up?'

Nell hesitated. She didn't feel as if she knew Maryam well enough yet to pour out her worries that Barney was spending way too much time with Kate or that he was still sleeping in the spare bedroom.

'I'm not sure the group's a total success so far,' she said, deciding to talk about her other preoccupation instead. 'Last week was pretty much a disaster and the trip started well but ended up not so good. I hope we can pull it back tonight or the others might stop turning up.'

Maryam frowned. 'Don't be so downhearted,' she said. 'The music session was great, and we were bound to have teething troubles somewhere. Don't forget, the whole idea is to build up a feeling of confidence as we all get to know each other. We're definitely doing that. There are new friendships developing already. Look at your Frank, for instance.'

Nell wasn't sure yet if Frank's self-imposed challenge of

teaching Beryl to play chess was a good one. He seemed to get very frustrated when she didn't take the game seriously and insisted on talking about prawns instead of pawns, but on the other hand, he wasn't giving up and it was keeping him occupied. Anton was happy with the situation too. He'd found that Beryl was now buying dog treats in case he visited, which was very satisfactory.

Maryam paused to serve a new customer who was determined to chat. Nell felt unreasonably irritated at the interruption to begin with, but Maryam was in her stride now, asking about the old lady's chihuahua which apparently had been ill. By the time she gently brought the conversation to an end and the lady left, there were smiles all round.

'You're very good at all this,' Nell said. 'I'm so glad you took the shop on.'

Maryam pulled a face. 'Rashid thinks I spend too much time talking to the customers sometimes and then a queue builds up, but I hate sending people away if they're feeling under the weather. I just tell him he should come and help me out if that happens.'

She yawned and Nell said, 'Are you okay? You look shattered.'

'I'd be fine if I didn't have Rashid snoring in my ear all night. I really need more sleep, Nell. It's ridiculous. I want him to move into Uma's room as soon as she goes back to uni, but he says that's unfriendly. The boys are sharing the other room and they're nagging me to let one of them have Uma's when she goes. It's a bedroom-based stand-off at the moment.'

Nell didn't answer. It was ironic that Maryam was longing for her own space to sleep in whereas she wanted nothing more than to move Barney back into their own room.

'We're going to be talking about the importance of sleep at

next week's group,' she said. 'We should get together with Bev as soon as possible and plan how we're going to tackle it. We might all be looking at it from different angles.'

'How do you mean?'

'Oh... just that everybody must have their own idea of a perfect night's sleep,' Nell hedged. 'Anyway, tonight's all about friendship. Bev wants to get everyone telling stories about their best moments with friends over the years. Let's hope they're all ready to spill the beans. Have you got yours ready?'

Maryam shrugged. 'I guess so. I've never found it easy to team up with a proper bestie like the other girls at school did. How about you?'

'About the same really, I guess.'

Nell thought about some of the stories from the past that she'd considered sharing. None of them seemed very inspiring if the theme of the session was to be uplifting. The idea was to follow through the concept that everyone can identify the people, places, music, food and other sensory pleasures that can bring on a feeling of contentment. Some of Nell's early experiences with friends would be less than inspiring and although she'd accumulated an assortment of people to meet up with for different activities since the children had been born, during the latter years in Sheffield she'd have been quite lonely if she hadn't had the homeless centre to go to.

'I'm off for some fresh air,' Nell said. 'I need to think back and find something useful that I can talk about later. I always think better when I'm walking. Thanks for the lolly. And... well... thanks for being here. I love coming to see you in the shop and so does everyone else around here.'

'Aw, that's sweet of you.' Maryam came round the counter to give Nell a hug. She smelt of floral fabric conditioner and exotic spices, a heady mixture. Nell leaned into the hug, suddenly reluctant to leave. It was times like this that she missed her own mum and Lottie too, although Maryam was way too young to fill those roles even if Nell had been looking for a replacement. So far, this particular new friendship was proving to be something different to anything Nell had experienced before. She felt a growing connection with Maryam and was almost afraid to acknowledge it in case it disappeared.

'See you later,' Nell said, leaving the shop just as a gaggle of ramblers appeared, boiling hot and all eager to plunder Maryam's freezer. She left the shop and instead of heading for home, set off across the green. The morning sunshine on her back as she settled herself by the stream soothed and calmed Nell's frazzled nerves. As she watched the water swirling and leaping over the stones, her fragmented thoughts strayed to a time when she'd felt so useful, back in Sheffield and attending the homeless centre most days. One person came to mind, and at last she tentatively chose a story she could share with the group tonight.

Back at Hollyhocks Cottage, Nell made a big effort to create something that wasn't merely a salad. She boiled eggs, as a nod to Frank's happy food, tossed rocket and watercress leaves with chopped cucumber and tomato in a zingy dressing and opened various tins to make it look more interesting. There was ham and salmon and a somewhat battered one of olives. Some of these had travelled with them from the previous house and reminded her of the afternoon teas she used to make for Frank and Lottie, with thinly sliced bread and butter and strawberry jam from the local WI stall on the market.

When Frank and Barney eventually joined her, Nell carried everything outside to the table in the shade and they followed her, bringing cold beer and glasses. As the garden seemed to settle down around them ready for the evening, Nell felt a wave of something akin to contentment. Barney and his father were discussing football, a safe subject that always brought them together. The various terms were familiar to Nell by now, but she wasn't really listening. It occurred to her that Barney was no better than she was at finding close friends. He had workmates, of course he did, and most of them appeared to like and respect him, and he'd had drinking buddies before they moved, but really, Frank was still his son's chief confidant and support.

What would happen to her husband when Frank was no longer around? Would he fall apart? Nell pondered on how she could help him to build a new web of friendship for himself in Willowbrook. Perhaps tonight's meeting would shed some light on this tricky problem. Nell looked across at Frank as he pontificated about some long-ago match where their team had excelled.

'Man of the match? That boy was more like man of the year. What a hat trick that was, Barney. You were there with me, do you remember? You'd only be about twelve years old. You were cheering like a good 'un.'

Barney smiled at his father. 'I'll never forget that day. I thought you were going to explode. You were waving your scarf and yelling at the top of your lungs too.'

Both men fell silent, lost in their memories, and Nell took the opportunity to jump in with the question that had been bothering her. Frank wasn't known for his skill in relating stories. He tended to dry up at the crucial moment, especially if it was a joke. 'Have you thought about what you want to talk about at the group later?' she asked her father-in-law. 'If not, maybe we can jog your memory.'

Frank smiled at Nell. 'Oh, yes, no worries on that score. I'm all sorted.' He sat back in his chair. 'I've had enough to eat, thanks,' he said. 'I'm going to have a bit of a kip now instead of at

the group, like last time. I don't think this week's session is going
to be boring at all. You should hear what Beryl's planning to say.
We're both going to make waves, I'm thinking.'

   With that, he closed his eyes and was soon snoring gently,
mouth half open. Nell and Barney exchanged glances. 'He's
really up for this thing tonight,' Barney whispered. 'What do you
think he's going to come out with?'

   'No idea. Erm... you can always tag along if you like,' Nell
said hesitantly. She wasn't sure what had prompted the spontaneous invitation because really, she was more than happy to
have these new friends to herself, and Barney would only bristle
as soon as he was in the same room as Rick. She needn't have
worried though.

   'You must be joking. Baring your souls and getting all
earnest about it? That's not my style.'

   'But counselling is?' Nell couldn't help retorting.

   Her husband glared at her. 'Are you saying you don't want
me to do it?'

   Nell sighed. *Here we go again*, she thought sadly. *Diving into
an argument when there's no need at all.* 'Of course I want you to
talk to someone,' she said. 'I just sometimes wish it was me,
that's all.'

   Barney didn't answer for a while. Nell watched a dragonfly
land on a leaf close to her head. Its gauzy, iridescent wings flut-
tered in a light breeze that made the long grass under the tree
shiver. Eventually he stood up.

   'Yes, well, I wish that too, but I can't,' he said. 'And for now,
I'm doing my best, okay?'

   Nell watched Barney walk away. She felt as if her heart was
being squeezed. The pain, triggered by a sharp sense of failure,
was so intense that for a moment she pressed a hand to her
chest. As Nell breathed deeply, willing her body to return to

normal, Barney hesitated for a moment. He didn't go back into the house but followed the path that led out into the lane. Once again, the chance to get closer to him had slipped through her fingers and Nell hadn't got the first idea what to do about it. Recovering her equilibrium gradually, she began to clear away the remnants of their meal, trying not to cry. At least tonight would provide a distraction from worrying about her marriage. She just hoped Frank and Beryl's stories weren't going to be too outrageous. Nell wasn't sure if Willowbrook was ready for this new renegade team-up.

28

Maryam called for Nell at half past six that evening and they strolled through the village to the church, pausing briefly every now and again to admire particularly lovely gardens. Willow-brook had a very active horticultural society, Maryam informed Nell.

'We've only got a back yard now and I don't think we could cope with a big plot of land as well as the shop, but I really must get some tubs of flowers organised before it's too late in the summer. I need a happy place to escape to even if it's just for five minutes at a time when the shop's empty. I've already missed the boat with the main planting but maybe if I can get Rashid to take me to the garden centre...'

'I'll take you,' said Nell. 'Our car hardly ever goes out these days. It could do with a run. We might get some herbs to make the place smell great. Parsley, sage, rosemary, thyme.'

'Careful, you're in danger of morphing into Simon and Garfunkel there. But yeah, throw in some mint and lavender, and it would be heaven when the sun warms the leaves. You wouldn't mind taking me to get them? That'd be great. I'll treat you to coffee and cake, the café there's pretty nice.'

They walked on, and Nell began to think that maybe she was actually getting the hang of this friendship lark at last. With Maryam, she felt relaxed and comfortable, and there was no pressure to try to be liked. For years, Nell had sometimes worked at friendships even after they were dead in the water and the time for that had obviously passed. Here, there was no need. Maryam was the most straightforward person she'd ever met and even though they hadn't known each other long, Nell was as sure as she could ever be that the more time they spent together, the easier it would be to feel natural around her. To be herself.

The room appeared to be empty when they arrived, but the chairs had already been arranged in a circle and the sound of voices was coming from the kitchen. Nell recognised Bev's chuckle and Rick's much louder laugh before they emerged, followed by Frank, who Rick had once again picked up in his van.

'Hey, guys, did you bring cake?' Rick asked hopefully.

Maryam produced a large tin decorated with patterns of cookies from her tote bag and Nell rummaged in her own bag for several packets of Jaffa Cakes.

'You can't eat them until we've talked about our friendship memories,' Maryam said, as Rick reached for the tin. 'I've made chocolate eclairs. I'll tell you why later. Let's get them all in the fridge before the chocolate melts.'

Soon the room began to fill up, and the chattering grew louder. Beryl, Winnie and Anthea were all wearing summer dresses, Anthea in a linen shirtwaister, a muted shade of lavender, and Winnie's caftan was floor-length and patterned with pineapples. Beryl, sporting rather a flamboyant flowered cotton number, seemed on especially good form tonight, teasing Rick with a big smile on her face. 'Have you been on them sunbeds again, ducky?' she said. 'There's no way that's a Willowbrook tan. You're the colour of my sideboard. A nice shade of teak.'

'Honest toil, Beryl. Blood, sweat and tears,' he said. 'I bet you don't see much of that around these parts. I get so hot when I'm working, I just have to take my shirt off.'

Nell felt her mouth go dry. She sneaked a look at Rick's muscular forearms only to realise Bev had noticed what she was doing. Their eyes met and both blushed. Nell cringed. Urgh. She was rapidly turning into a ridiculous schoolgirl with a crush. It must be that her life with Barney was so unsatisfactory right now. Any distraction would seem good at the moment, she told herself firmly.

Kate and Ingrid entered the room as Nell removed herself to fill the urn and switch it on. She was pleased to see that they'd collected Harry and Maurice, so that meant everyone had arrived, which was a relief after last week's debacle.

Bev clapped her hands to get the meeting underway. 'I've opened all the windows to get a draught through but shout if you're too hot. I've got a couple of fans at the vicarage. There's iced water on the kitchen counter if anybody wants some,' she said. 'Or at least, it was iced five minutes ago, it might not be now.'

'I'll wait for my cuppa,' said Beryl, turning her nose up. 'I can't be doing with water, unless it's just a splash in my brandy.'

Everyone settled into their seats and Bev smiled round at them all. 'Well, here we are again,' she said. 'And as you know, tonight we're talking about friendships and how they can help us to feel happier... or at least more contented with life. More able to cope with the ups and downs.'

Beryl nudged Frank. 'Stick with it, kid,' she said. 'I just saw your eyes closing.'

'You did not! I was just... erm... thinking.' Frank sat up straighter. 'It's different tonight. No more of that mindfulness claptrap.'

'I thought Camilla was interesting,' said Anthea. 'Poor woman needed a shot of something, that's all. Maybe if we ever have her here again, we can give her some tequila.'

'Right, well... moving swiftly on,' said Bev. 'Who wants to start the ball rolling? We're looking for times when having a friend made a positive difference to your life.'

Nell was about to volunteer to go first when Winnie stood up. 'I'm not going to go on for long,' she said. 'But these two...' She indicated Beryl and Anthea. 'These two are the best friends anybody could have. When my man died, I was in a right state for months.'

'It's true, you were a blubbering mess, love,' said Beryl. 'You couldn't even be bothered to cook. And as for having a shower or a bath...' She wafted a hand in front of her face. 'Phew. That's when we knew it was serious. Winnie normally smells as fragrant as a garden of flowers and she cooks like an angel,' she told the others.

'Why would I want to prepare food when I felt as if my heart had been ripped out of my chest and trampled on? Anyway, these girls kept me going with fruit cake and cottage pies and little outings when I couldn't be bothered to get dressed, and they *never once* uttered those bloody awful words that anyone who's lost someone dreads.'

'What words are those?' asked Bev, when Winnie paused to wipe her eyes.

'*Pull yourself together now. It's time you moved on...* that kind of thing. Not once. I love 'em to bits. They make my life better all the time. Enough of the soppy stuff. I'm done.'

Winnie sat down abruptly between her two friends, and they moved in to share a group hug.

'Now that's what I call a good start,' said Bev, beaming at Winnie. 'Who's next?'

Frank was on his feet before anyone else had a chance to get up. 'I'm not one for this kind of thing as a rule,' he said gruffly. 'But you got me thinking about my best friend in all the world. Her name was Charlotte Matilda Appledore, but I called her Lottie.'

Nell swallowed hard. She'd never heard Frank speak of his deeper feelings about his wife, and she was sure Barney hadn't either. How she wished her husband was here to listen. She should have tried harder to persuade him to join the group, although it occurred to her that Frank might not have felt so able to share his thoughts if Barney had been there too. It would have been too hard for them both.

'Anyway,' continued Frank. 'I scribbled down a bit of a poem about her when I woke up this morning. It doesn't rhyme, and it's only short. Hope you like it.'

He rummaged in his pocket and produced a crumpled piece of paper, which he smoothed out carefully.

> 'Lottie, my dear
> Sunshine of my life, you shone in my sky
> Friends till the end, we made a pact
> And I'm still keeping it. I'll love you forever
> You taught me how to live.
> I won't forget you.'

Frank subsided into his chair. Bev seemed unable to speak and none of the others attempted to comment either. After a moment he cleared his throat and began to speak again.

'I often wonder,' he said, looking anywhere but at Nell, 'why the young folk of the next generation and the one after waste so much time falling out with each other. In my humble opinion, if you find someone who makes you feel complete and you can have a laugh and a cry together, you should hang on to them for dear life. There's way too much giving up goes on in marriages these days.'

'But—' Bev began but Frank held up a hand.

'Don't get me wrong, I know sometimes things aren't possible to work out. I'm talking about the times when all a couple needs is a bit more give and take. Lottie and me never went to bed on a row. Oh, yes, we did have the odd squabble, but we didn't let a quarrel get the better of us because we knew when we were well off. Lottie was my one and only. That's all I want to say. Thank you for listening.'

Frank pulled out a handkerchief and blew his nose noisily. Nell was rooted to the spot, totally stunned by her father-in-law's contribution. To be loved like that, and for so long... forever, in fact. She wondered if Barney felt that way about her. In that instant, she knew without a doubt that she had to make things right between them, and soon. She glanced across at Rick, who was gazing at Frank in admiration. Yes, he was easy on the eye and full of chat but Barney... Barney was hers. She stood up.

'That was so beautiful, Frank,' she said. 'You made Lottie the happiest woman in the world, and hearing your poem has changed my mind about what I want to say tonight. I'd probably have come over as being a bit sorry for myself, telling you all about the homeless people I've befriended in my time but that I've never been brave enough to risk making really close friends anywhere else.'

Bev opened her mouth to speak again but then decided against it and motioned Nell to carry on.

'The thing is, hearing Frank's touching words has brought it home to me that my best friend is right here and has been for thirty years. Barney and me... we know each other well. Maybe too well. Just because a friend has always been around, doesn't mean nothing changes or that you don't have to work at it any more.'

Nell sat down again, exhausted. She wanted more than anything to leave this place and run all the way home to her husband. It was high time they talked properly about what was going wrong between them. Even more than that, Nell longed to go somewhere peaceful to have a good, hard think about their life together, and all the ways in which her husband had been the one to make her laugh, hold her tight when she cried and worked extra hard himself so that they could afford for her to stay at home and bring their children up.

'I know we're only partway through this meeting, but I reckon we need a tea-break,' said Bev, and several people cheered. She headed for the kitchen along with Rick and Maryam and Nell took the opportunity to go outside for a breath of fresh air. Almost immediately, she heard footsteps behind her, and the tap of Frank's walking stick on the worn slabs of the path.

'Well, we definitely showed them tonight, didn't we, Nellie?' he said, lowering himself onto a bench by the door and patting the seat next to him.

Nell sat down but didn't say a word. She leaned on the comforting bulk of the man who had given her away at her wedding to Barney after her own father had died the year before and had never let her down. He patted her arm. 'You're a good girl. It's all going to be fine, you mark my words,' he said quietly. 'Come on, let's go back in and see what the rest of them have got for us. I could do with a hefty tot of Beryl's best cognac, to be truthful, but we'd better do our duty to our new pals.'

They stood up together and Frank offered Nell an arm to hold. A flashback of walking down the aisle made Nell almost stumble, but she rallied as quickly as she could. Frank was right. The people inside were their friends now. Willowbrook was generously taking them to its heart, but they needed to make an effort too.

The rest of the group looked as if they'd been revived considerably by tea and cake. Nell fetched some of each for Frank and sat back down as Bev clapped her hands again.

'On we go,' she said. 'I'll wait until last for mine, in case we run out of time.'

After that, the evening whizzed by. Kate talked about the stalwart friendship of the Saga Louts and of Beryl's kindness in particular when she'd needed it badly. 'Although you have to have a strong head for prosecco if you want to be in their gang,' she said, grinning. Harry made a moving speech about how Ingrid's partner, Joel, had made a beautiful memorial bench after his son Gareth died, and the considerate way Joel had helped them to site it at the country park and be able to visit it whenever they chose.

Maryam waxed lyrical about the villagers who'd welcomed her to Willowbrook and made her feel less conspicuous. It had been a culture shock at first to be away from her family and starting again in a place where everyone knew what she was up to, but she was making new friends all the time. Maryam smiled at Nell as she said this, and Nell felt some of her anxiety about Barney melt away. She should think about talking to Maryam about her marriage when the time was right. A trusted listening ear would perhaps be just what was needed.

'And the reason I rustled up the chocolate eclairs for you

today is that my mum used to make them for me if I'd had a bad day at school, getting on the wrong side of some of the tougher girls who hung around in the toilet blocks waiting to call all of us brown girls bad names. She always said, "Friends are good, but eclairs are better." Personally, I think it's great to have both.'

Ingrid also chipped in at that point. Nell looked at her, standing tall, blonde and elegant, and thought she strongly resembled a younger version of Joanna Lumley.

'Another tick for Joel from me,' she said. 'He thought I was spiky and frosty to begin with, and I was, but he persevered. We were friends before we moved on to the next stage. He went out on a limb to show that he had no hidden agenda and that he really cares about me. It's not easy to have faith in someone new when you've had a... difficult time... but I never stop being glad I did.'

Maurice and Anthea looked at each other and got up as Ingrid sat down.

'We've decided to call a truce and be proper buddies from now on,' said Anthea. 'Maurice kept being put off by thinking I wanted to marry him.'

'Well, I am something of a catch,' said Maurice, picking an imaginary piece of fluff off his pristine white shirt.

'In your dreams, darling. But to cut a long story short, the two of us are going to make a fresh start. I won't scare him by rabbiting on about all my husbands and he'll stop making derogatory comments about my driving. I'm eighty years old and I've never once had an accident in the car.'

'That's because all the other drivers see you and get out of the way,' Maurice said. He held up a hand as Anthea bridled. 'That was the last time, honestly. I'm going to be a good friend from now on. Shake?'

They shook hands solemnly and sat down, looking relieved.

Beryl glanced around the room to make sure she had everyone's full attention. 'Obviously these two are my best mates,' she said, indicating Anthea and Winnie. 'But my niece, Sophie, should have a mention too. She does my hair, brings me treats, and sits and listens for hours while I reminisce about the family.'

'Brave girl,' muttered Anthea, but Beryl ignored her.

'They say blood's thicker than water, and sometimes it is. I know the family you choose for yourself are just as good but there was one time when our Sophie managed to stop me making a complete fool of myself. It was after my husband had his heart attack and keeled over right in front of my eyes. He never recovered.'

Beryl paused for a moment to wipe her eyes, and Bev held up a hand. 'Don't worry, you really don't need to carry on if it's too much,' she said, but Beryl shook her head.

'I'm okay, love. Well, on the evening of the funeral, I was halfway through a bottle of brandy, and getting proper maudlin. Apparently, I decided everyone in the village was talking about me and saying it wouldn't be long before I was after another bloke, like I was a right strumpet. Sophie told me afterwards that I ripped off all my posh funeral clothes and said I was going to run naked down the main street and then into the pub to give them something to really talk about. I was out in the lane before she could stop me. Luckily for the village, she got me back inside, filled me full of black coffee and put me to bed.'

'Ooh, Beryl, you never even told us two about this, did she, Anthea?' said Winnie. 'I remember the hangover you had the next day though. It took one of my biggest fry-ups to get you back on your feet. You looked peaky for at least a week afterwards.'

Beryl smiled at her. 'You two were stars that day but Sophie saved me from giving Willowbrook something to gossip about for years. Our Sophie's a diamond. I can't say the same for one or two of my extended clan, but we won't go there.'

'Oh, do let's,' said Maurice hopefully, but Beryl shook her head.

'Maybe another time. Tonight's for being a bit more glass-half-full, eh?'

'And on that note, there's only me and Bev to go,' said Rick. 'Mine's short and sweet. I wish it was as dynamic as Beryl's story but I can't top that one. I'm eight years on from a messy divorce. Bev's shown me that not all women are like my ex. That's all.'

Bev looked up at him, blinked hard and flexed her shoulders as if she was going into battle. 'My turn, I guess,' she said. 'I'm going to sit down while I tell you about my true-friend experience, because if I'm honest, thinking about that time in my life still makes my legs shake.'

There wasn't a sound in the room following this announcement. Nell was alarmed to see that Bev was very pale now, and she was twisting her fingers together.

'My worst experience ever came to a head around ten years ago,' Bev said. Her voice was quieter than usual, and several people leaned forward to hear her better. 'I was married to a man who I'd thought was my soulmate. Turned out I was more like his punchbag.'

There was a sharp intake of breath as the assembled group took this information on board. Nell was astounded. Bev had seemed to her to be one of the strongest people she'd ever met. It was unthinkable that someone like this could be a battered wife. As if reading her mind, Bev carried on.

'It's some people's view that when there's violence behind closed doors in a marriage, the victim should have more sense than to stick around. Well, it ain't that easy, folks. I was one of the luckier ones. A friend helped me in a big way when I needed her most, and I had... still have, in fact... great parents.'

Nobody moved or spoke. Their eyes were all on the vicar. She closed her eyes for a moment, then opened them wide and shook herself. 'Anyway, on with the show,' she said.

In the short silence that followed, the tea urn gave an almighty gurgle. Bev laughed. 'And normal life has resumed. The urn speaks! Now let's finish up the cake and have another cuppa. Next week will be less stressful, I promise. It's all about how getting a good night's sleep can help to make us feel more hopeful when times are tough.'

Nell got up to help Maryam in the kitchen. It was all very well for Bev to say that, but talking about her own sleeping arrangements was never going to make her feel positive. It was high time she tackled the issue head on. The best thing to do would be to make sure Frank had a lift home. First of all though, she'd text Barney to ask him to meet her at the pub later. They could find a quiet corner and Nell would pull out all the stops to find out what was at the heart of their problems. Words from Frank's poem whirled round and round in her head as she washed up the mugs and made desultory conversation with Maryam. *I'll love you forever.* All she could do was to hope Barney still felt the same.

Barney, to break the monotony of being home alone, decided to take Anton for a good long walk along the riverbank. They ambled along together, as the peace of the early evening and the dragonflies dipping and diving across the water did the work of soothing Barney's troubled soul. When he reached the mooring, he stopped to chat with a couple of the boat owners, who were barbecuing on the bank. It seemed like an ideal kind of life. Nell had told him about her friend Ingrid's narrowboat and when he left the others, he stood for a few moments admiring it, knowing Ingrid would be at the meeting so wouldn't be spooked by a strange man peering at her home.

Galadriel was everything a boat should be, Barney thought, looking at the firm, strong lines of the green and red paint. Her name was written on the side in a delicate arch of white letters, and on top of the boat were beautifully painted water cans patterned with roses, and bright tubs of red geraniums. Nell had said that Ingrid had negotiated a manageable rent for the boat while the owners were in France. He could see why she'd wanted to live here in this beautiful spot, where the trees provided a constant umbrella of shade, and the towpath meandered away towards... who knew where? Barney resolved to do more exploring. This might be a good route for one of his longer walks.

Today, however, he could see that Anton wasn't enjoying the warmth of the day. Although it was already past seven o'clock, the cool of the evening was taking its time arriving. Barney took the dog's bowl out of his backpack, filled it with water and sat down on the bank, rummaging for a can of beer for himself.

'Water for you, my friend,' he said to Anton. 'But I've earned this after all those Zoom meetings. I wish I could quit working altogether but it's not quite time yet.'

Anton lapped away happily and then flopped down beside Barney with a sigh. Ingrid's boat shifted a little as another one passed by, and Barney called a greeting to the man at the stern who was steering carefully between the moored craft and the opposite bank.

'You've got the right idea,' the man said, pointing to the beer. 'As soon as we get to the lock, I'm having one of those too.' His wife popped her head out to see who he was talking to and laughed.

'If that's a hint, I can take it,' she said. 'I'll get you a cold beer, you poor hard-done-to soul.'

The boat moved away, and Barney was overcome with envy. To be able to cruise along in that leisurely, carefree way with your partner by your side must be blissful. He tried to imagine doing the same with Nell, but the reality of being enclosed in such a small living area made all his muscles tense. Would there be more than one bedroom in a place like that?

Realising he was in danger of becoming as obsessed with their sleeping arrangements as Nell seemed to be, Barney tried hard to think about something else, but his mind kept taking him back to the same old subject. It was up to him to put things right with Nell. She didn't understand the seriousness of his problem with sharing her bed again. Could he talk to her now? The two counselling sessions had helped already, although he'd been embarrassed to find that pouring out his various anxieties and sadnesses had made him sob like a baby. It was mortifying. He hadn't even wept at his mother's funeral. The danger of losing control completely was always there. The awful thought struck him that he might not be able to discuss his innermost fears with Nell without the same thing happening.

Barney drank his beer and pondered on the way forward. He was almost ready to make a move towards home when he heard a shout.

'Daddy, it's the man who takes us for walks. Look, he's over there. Let's go and see him.'

Seconds later, Anton was on his feet, giving a welcoming bark as Elsie bounced up to them, pigtails bobbing. 'Hello... erm... man,' she said. 'I've forgotten your name. What are you doing here? We're having a walk. I didn't want to go for a smelly walk, but Daddy said we needed some fresh air because I wouldn't go to bed, it's too hot, and he was getting cabin fever. I don't know what that means, do you? Is that why you're here?'

Bemused, Barney got to his feet and saw Sam coming towards him. 'Sorry for the interruption, Barney, you looked as if you were deep in thought there,' Sam said, grabbing his daughter by the hand. 'We'll get out of your way. I only got her out of the flat by bribing her with the promise of an ice cream at the shop.'

'No problem. Come and sit down for a bit,' said Barney, delighted to have his uncomfortable musings broken into. 'I've got some apples in my bag if you'd like to have one to keep you going until the ice cream?'

Elsie considered the offer and accepted graciously. Barney rummaged in his backpack and produced an apple for Elsie and another two cans. He raised his eyebrows at Sam who nodded enthusiastically.

'You're like some sort of kind elf who waits for tired travellers, aren't you?' said Elsie. 'I was really fed up and then we saw you. Can I sit with your dog? Do you think he likes me?'

Anton was looking interested now, and Barney grinned. 'He'll love you forever if you save him your apple core. They're his favourite.'

Elsie moved a little way away from Sam and Barney, and settled herself with Anton on a fallen tree trunk. Barney could hear her singing quietly to the dog.

'She's practising her song for the school concert,' Sam said. 'They're choosing soloists for the end of term show. I hope to goodness she gets picked or my life won't be worth living.'

'You and Elsie... Kate told me you're bringing her up on your own?' Barney wasn't sure if he was speaking out of turn here but Sam didn't seem to mind.

'Yeah, her mum upped and left when Elsie was only a baby. She said she wasn't cut out for motherhood. To be fair, I didn't think I was going to win any prizes for being a dad either, but you live and learn, don't you?'

Barney thought about this question. He didn't feel as if he was learning much at the moment. This younger man appeared to have his life sorted even though it must be tough juggling work with childcare. He wondered what the secret was.

'Don't you ever get the feeling that you haven't got a clue what you're doing, Sam?' he asked.

Sam looked puzzled. 'Well, yeah. Doesn't everybody?'

'Do they?'

'I imagine so. We're all just whistling in the dark really. *You're* okay though, mate. Great new home, getting on well at the country park with the walks, and you're happily married, that's something I've never managed.'

Barney didn't reply for a moment. Then he said, 'It's not always what it seems, marriage, you know. It can be hard work.'

'No kidding?' Sam laughed.

'No, really. Haven't you ever been tempted? Would you get hitched if you found the right woman?'

'Nah. I've actually found the right boy, but he's a bit too young for marriage. He's Milo's son, Luka, and he's still at uni. I'm not sure... I mean, there are going to be temptations for him. I do get stressy about that. He's doing all that fun stuff and I'm not part of it.'

'Ah.' Light dawned and Barney felt vaguely embarrassed to have pried, but he couldn't have said why, because Sam clearly wasn't worried.

'Relationships are sometimes a minefield, aren't they?' Barney said, taking a large gulp of beer. 'But you've got Elsie and she's just great.'

'Glad you think so.'

Afraid he might say the wrong thing if they kept talking about Elsie, Barney hastily changed the subject. They chatted on for a while, with Barney diverting the conversation to the way Kate was clearly determined to bring a wider range of activities to the country park. Eventually, Sam glanced at his watch. And now... he stood up and raised his voice slightly. 'It's time for this future star to head back home, or there won't be time for an ice cream. Say goodnight to Barney and his dog.'

Elsie jumped to her feet, gave Anton a last pat and her apple core and came to stand at Sam's side. 'Sorry I forgot your name, Barney. It's a nice name. Come on then, Dad, hurry up.'

She set off at a trot, and Sam patted Barney on the shoulder and followed. 'Thanks for the beer,' he said, over his shoulder. 'See you again at the park soon, I expect.'

Barney watched them go with a strange ache in his heart. Elsie reached for Sam's hand when they reached the wider part of the path and together they marched away. If only his own life was that simple. Happiness is a large ice-cream cone with a flake in it when you're a child, he thought sadly. He wondered what it would take for him and Nell to recapture that sense of joy. He hadn't felt anything like it since... he cast his mind back... since he'd begun to have serious worries about his health. Then had come a whole string of appointments and tests and finally, when they'd known there was no other answer, the diagnosis.

Barney got to his feet, collected the empty cans to take home for recycling and called to Anton, who was still licking his lips after the apple core bonus. The air was cooler now and they made good progress, crossing the green just as a group of kids who didn't look that much older than Elsie jostled and whooped their way down the place by the stream under the willow trees that seemed to be their regular mustering place. Barney wondered how his wife's meeting was going. She'd probably be ready for a cool shower when she got home on a night like this. Maybe they'd talk, when Frank had gone off to his annexe to watch one of his old black and white films and drink Horlicks.

It was way past the time that Barney and Nell should have talked properly about what was going wrong between them, he knew that really. It was difficult to think where to begin though. Barney reached home, unlocked the cottage and opened a few windows to let the cooler air into the house. The two cans of beer he'd drunk earlier had only been small and he would have liked another one, but he was afraid he'd get even more intro-spective and maudlin.

Anton had already retreated to his bed in the kitchen, so

Barney filled a glass with ice-cold water from the fridge and went out to the garden to sit on the bench under the oak tree for a while. The distant sound of music was drifting over from a house further up the lane and he could hear laughter and snatches of a group of his neighbours and their friends singing 'Happy Birthday' in various different keys. Just as he was trying to decide what to do until the others returned, his phone buzzed in his pocket. A jolt of alarm took him back to the time when his mother was in her last days and his dad would message to give him updates before they settled for the night, but this wasn't one of Frank's texts, which were always in capital letters as if he was shouting.

> Will you meet me at the pub? Let's have a drink before bed. Your dad's walking home with Beryl! See you there? N xxx

Barney stared at the message. He and Nell hadn't been communicating in this way for a long time. She sometimes left him reminder notes around the house these days, but they never had kisses on them. Sudden anxiety made his stomach churn, but surely if Nell wanted to corner him and talk about bad stuff, she wouldn't add kisses, so what could this be in aid of? He pulled himself together with difficulty and typed a message back.

> Sure, see you soon. I'll get Ned to put a bottle of white wine in an ice bucket. You hungry?

The brief reply came back immediately.

> No, just wine, the colder the better! Xxx

More kisses. With a burst of hope, the like of which he hadn't felt for ages, Barney hurried into the house and upstairs. There, he took the quickest shower he'd ever had, splashed on some of the aftershave that Nell had bought him for Christmas last year and got dressed in clean shorts and a T-shirt. He'd have liked to wear something smarter, but it was much too hot for anything but shorts. He looked in the mirror, briefly assessing himself. At least he hadn't let himself go to seed like some of his older drinking buddies in Sheffield. All the recent walking had done him good. He'd not shaved since yesterday but the touch of stubble might be called appealing if you liked that kind of thing. His curly hair was messy but he knew Nell hated it when he tried to look too tidy. He could probably do with some new clothes though. Not the sort of body-showcasing gear that the loathsome Rick wore, maybe just something a bit more upbeat than his usual casual stuff.

Well, tonight, this look would have to do. Barney ruffled his hair into a better shape, laced his best trainers, locked the house up and made tracks across the green again, this time to The Fox and Fiddle. Whatever Nell was up to with this unexpected summons he'd do his best not to disappoint her. Somehow, this felt as if it was going to be a very important evening for them.

30

Tidying up after the meeting was taking longer than Nell had expected because only Kate and Ingrid stayed to help. Maryam had just taken an anguished call from Rashid to come back and help with the boys' maths homework because he was stuck. The older members had departed too, Maurice with Anthea, Winnie and Harry squeezed into the front seat of Rick's van. Beryl and Frank left the meeting soon after that, arm in arm and on foot. Bev had mysteriously disappeared.

Kate spotted Nell glancing at her watch. 'You can go if you like, we'll be fine. We just need to find Bev so she can lock up,' she said.

'I'm meant to be meeting Barney as soon as possible. I wanted to make sure Bev was okay though.' Nell was torn between worrying about how tonight's revelations might have affected Bev and wanting to get to Barney before she lost her nerve. Even an extra ten minutes seemed too long to wait now that she'd made the decision to face whatever was wrong between them.

'We can deal with that,' Ingrid said. 'She might need a chat after all that soul-searching so it could take a while. You go. We'll tell her you'll be in touch tomorrow to see how she's feeling, shall we? I suppose that's the danger when there's someone like Bev to lean on. We tend to forget that she's vulnerable too. What do you think, Kate?'

'You're right. I reckon if Rick hadn't been doing his taxi service, he'd have gone and found her by now. It's about team-work. We'll all do our bit to make sure she's got support. Once the Saga Louts get wind of a problem, they're always on the case too. Bev looked so fragile tonight. I reckon it gave us all a shock. Off you go, Nell.'

Relieved of any responsibility for now but still anxious about Bev, Nell set off through the village and before long was taking the narrow path across the green. The lights were shining out from the pub windows and as she approached The Fox and Fiddle, Nell picked up the sounds of raucous cries and loud applause. Puzzled, she paused and then realisation dawned. Oh, no, it was pop quiz night. How had she forgotten that vital fact? She'd heard about it from Maryam who'd really fancied taking part if it hadn't clashed with their meeting. What a ridiculous time to pick for a quiet heart-to-heart with your husband.

She entered the lounge to find it heaving with people. There was no sign of Barney, but as she scanned the room, her phone bleeped. She took it out and peered at the screen.

> Go through the door at the back next to the car park entrance, I'm in the little snug. I've asked Ned to put a closed sign on the door. I feel like a spy on a mission. B xxx

Giggling with a mixture of nerves and relief not to have to have this moment spoilt by being squashed in a corner while the landlord bellowed staccato questions about the Beatles,

Oasis and One Direction through a microphone, Nell found the door. Sure enough, there was a sign pinned to it saying the room was temporarily closed for decorating. She pushed it open and there sat Barney. He jumped to his feet and came to meet her.

'Agent Appledore, I presume,' he said, grinning. 'Shall I bolt the door?'

She nodded, suddenly overcome with shyness. For goodness' sake, this was Barney. She'd been married to him for thirty years. He looked different tonight. Rumpled but very sexy and somehow more confident... he smelled so good too. Not that he didn't usually, but this was a spicier, more lemony and altogether more alluring scent.

'The wine's already here, come and sit down and tell me why you wanted us to have this secret meeting. I'm not complaining. Your text was like a shot in the arm. I felt like a teenager getting ready for a hot date. I even had a quick shower and slapped on some of that aftershave you bought me.'

So that was the unfamiliar scent. Nell sniffed appreciatively and moved a little closer to Barney, trying to think how to broach the subject of their marriage. As she hesitated, she saw Barney's face fall. The tension that was never far away was back in his haunted expression.

'I mean, it isn't something really bad... is it?' he said.

'No, nothing bad, don't look so worried. I just thought it was time we talked, away from the house and Frank and everything. It was lovely when we had dinner here the other night but since then, I feel as if we've lost the plot again.'

'Me too. Let's have a drink and make a fresh start. How was your meeting?' Barney asked, as he poured them both a glass of chilled white wine.

She sat down and picked up the glass, grateful for its cool, comforting feel in her hand. The first sip was delicious and the second gave her the incentive to go on.

'It was a bit emotional but fine, on the whole. I'll tell you about it another time. Tonight's about you and me.'

They sat in silence for a moment, broken when Ned popped his head round the door. 'Hi guys, just to say you're okay in here for another hour or so, but don't forget our deal, mate.' He winked at Barney and closed the door again. Nell turned to look at her husband.

'What does he mean? What deal?'

Barney shrugged. 'It's nothing. I just had to strike a bit of a bargain to get the room to ourselves. No sweat.'

'Barney, what have you promised to do? Tell me before I have to go and ask Ned.'

'Oh, it was a stupid thing really. He wants someone to play the old piano in the lounge for the Christmas carols and I said you'd do it. That's okay, isn't it?'

'You said *what*? I haven't played for ages and our piano hasn't even been tuned since the move.'

Barney patted Nell's arm. 'It's only July, there's ages for us to practise yet, we'll be fine.'

'We? What do you mean *we*?' Nell's voice was squeaky with outrage now.

'Oh, well I said I'd lead the singing on the night.'

Nell gazed at Barney in amazement. 'Are you joking? It's years since you sang with the band. You don't even warble in the shower these days. We can't do this.'

Barney didn't answer for a moment. Then he said softly, 'I want us to start doing things together again, like we used to, before...'

'Before you were ill,' Nell finished, taking his hand in hers.

They sat like that for a while, drinking their wine and letting the relative quiet of the little room soothe their jangled nerves. Eventually Nell spoke. Her voice sounded croaky at first, but she persevered.

'So, let's start with when we began to lose sight of... well, of *us*, I suppose. I must have dealt with your diagnosis badly I guess, and things have never really recovered. Now we're in separate rooms, we never even cuddle and you haven't kissed me for months except the odd peck on the cheek.'

'You haven't kissed me either, but let's not nit-pick. Don't even think of saying you dealt with all that stuff badly. You were amazing all the way through. It was me who didn't cope. I know I looked as if I did, but underneath I was so scared I could hardly breathe.'

Nell thought back to the dark days, when hospital visits had been the norm and in between times when he was strong enough, Barney would insist on going back to work. She'd understood his need to keep everything as normal as possible but that had left Nell to be the main means of support for Frank as his wife became more and more confused and distressed.

'It was Lottie that broke me, I think,' she said, trying to be honest. 'You could escape to go to work, but I couldn't get away from seeing her going downhill and Frank wearing himself to a frazzle looking after her.'

Barney had tears in his eyes now, and so did Nell. Their hands were still locked together, fingers entwined, even as the accusations tumbled out. 'I tried my best, Nell,' he said. 'I hadn't got anything left to give while the chemo was going on, and then there was the radiotherapy on Monday through to Friday for weeks.'

Nell hardened her heart and carried on. All this needed to come out, but it was hard, so hard. 'Of course you tried but it was a horrible time. We all understood. It was afterwards when the problems really started. You never really came back to me. And then before we'd had chance to kind of regroup, poor Lottie died, and we needed to focus on Frank and help him to cope. You haven't had the headspace to grieve for your mum, Barney, and I somehow didn't realise how much you needed to do that too.'

'I *have* grieved. I have! You make me sound so cold.'

'Not cold at all. Just overwhelmed. And you've never let yourself cry.'

'I did the other day, with the counsellor,' he muttered. 'It was awful.'

'Really? That's great. I mean... well, you know what I mean. Did you feel better afterwards?'

Barney nodded. 'I hope she's got shares in a tissue company if that's what all her clients do. I was shattered when I came out, but I felt kind of... lighter. It's going to cost us a fortune, though. I'm not done yet, I can tell.'

'Worth every penny, if it helps. I guess once the floodgates open, everything has to come out. I wish...'

Nell couldn't go on, and Barney let go of her hand and put both arms around her. She leaned into the comforting warmth of the man who had been her strength and stay for so very long.

'You wish I'd been able to talk about it before, don't you? I just couldn't though. I was ashamed of myself for not bouncing back after the cancer was all gone. It seemed so ungrateful. Also, I was terrified of it coming back. Still am,' he admitted. 'That's not very macho, is it?'

'It's natural. I am too. Scared, I mean. But you feel okay... don't you?'

Barney said he did, but to Nell, the declaration didn't sound very convincing. She leaned away from him to get a better look at his face. 'Have you lost weight?' she asked. 'You look different.'

Barney laughed. 'That's just the benefit of all this exercise I've been having. My superhero body will be here soon and then you'll have to fight off the horde of women following me around the village.'

'Like Kate?'

The words were out before Nell had the chance to stop them, and Barney's face reddened. So, it was true. Her heart sank. He was in love with Kate, just as she'd suspected. A ferocious jealousy gripped her, and she moved out of the circle of his arms and stood up.

'It's true, isn't it? I took my eye off the ball and now you're... you're... fraternising with that woman, who's got a perfectly good partner of her own, as far as I can tell.'

A burst of laughter escaped Barney but he stopped when he saw Nell's expression. He got to his feet to face her. 'Fraternising? Where did that word come from? There's nothing between me and Kate. What about you, drooling over Rick and his giant... muscles?'

The silence in the room was oppressive now. Outside, the pub quiz must have finished because a much lower murmur of voices was all Nell could hear. She stared at Barney, face burning, and he met her gaze full on. Neither spoke for what seemed like forever. Then Barney stirred himself.

'This is turning into something I never expected,' he said quietly. 'But Nell, there was never anything between me and Kate, and that's the truth.'

'And neither is there anything going on with me and Rick.'

'Then why did you blush?'

'Why did *you*?'

Again, the oppressive silence. Nell didn't know how to go on. Exhaustion overwhelmed her. Barney was the first to crack.

'I suppose I did like her... a bit. She's very kind and sweet and

I felt lost when we first came here. But I never said anything or did anything, and now I know it was just a silly crush because I was missing us being... us.'

Barney's honesty cut right through any ideas Nell might have had about denying fancying Rick. It was time to put her cards on the table too. 'Same here, with Rick. He was there, I was feeling lost too. I didn't know how I was going to make new friends. I missed the comfort of going to the homeless centre, and Rick listened to me. Oh, yes, and you've got to admit he's very easy on the eye.'

Nell attempted a grin although her face didn't seem to want to smile. This felt like a make-or-break moment. She held her breath. Barney didn't say anything for several seconds and then he smiled too.

'We're pretty stupid, the two of us, aren't we? We've been acting like people with no clue. And if we're going to do that, we should be doing it together. Come on, it's time to leave, but I'm bringing the rest of this with us.' He took the wine bottle from the cooler and held out a hand to Nell. 'You can carry the glasses. We can bring them back next time.'

'Where are we going?'

'You'll see.'

He unbolted the door and, looking both ways, led Nell from the room and out of the back door that led to the car park. With her hand in his, Nell tried to keep in step as Barney upped his pace, heading for the path that led towards the riverbank. They moved along together, almost jog-trotting, until they reached the water's edge.

'I was here earlier with Anton,' he said. 'There's a place... oh yes, here it is.'

He led Nell along the path and under some low branches off to one side, where the trees had made what looked like a bower.

The grass was soft underfoot and Barney indicated that Nell should sit down.

'Hold out the glasses,' he said. 'It's time for a toast.'

Barney filled both glasses to the brim and took one for himself. He sat down next to Nell and clinked his glass against hers.

'What are we drinking to?' she asked, heart pounding. Barney was looking deep into her eyes. She'd forgotten how it felt to be his sole focus. A sudden longing for him to kiss her took Nell's breath away. She desperately wanted to kiss the stubble on his chin and entangle her fingers in his hair. To hold him very, very tightly.

'Here's to behaving like our kids and their mates used to before they left home,' Barney said. 'They didn't sip their drinks, they downed them in one. Go for it!'

Giggling, Nell raised her glass to her lips and did as she was told, feeling the delicious chill of the wine running down her throat, filling her with a fizzing feeling of recklessness.

Barney did the same and then put his glass down, taking Nell's too.

'What else do teenagers do?' he said.

'I can't remember.'

'Let me give you a clue then.'

Moving closer, Barney slid his arms around Nell and pulled her close. The kiss that followed made her head spin. His hands moved down her back and under her T-shirt and she felt the warmth of his fingers on her bra strap.

'Barney! What...?'

'Just seeing if I remember how to do this at speed. A teenage boy's best skill. Ah, yes...'

With a click, he released the clip and seconds later, Nell remembered how she'd felt all those years ago when Barney

Appledore had first demonstrated that trick. Her breath was coming in gasps now.

'We can't... not here... someone might come...'

'I'm definitely hoping so. And yes, we can.'

Sure enough, Nell found that they could. They really could. And so, they did.

31

The next week saw more changes in the temperature. Showers of summer rain were interspersed with hour upon hour of cloudy humidity and thunderstorms. Barney felt as if the weather was echoing the atmosphere in the house. He and Nell were having a turbulent time too. Their talk in the pub and the sizzling aftermath by the river had galvanised them both into mad activity, and not just in the bedroom.

'What's got into my lad?' Frank asked Nell as Barney hammered away at a bent nail that had been sticking out of the wall outside the kitchen and snagging everyone's clothes. 'He hasn't stopped dashing about for days. In and out. There's no holding him.'

Through the open window, Barney heard Nell giggle and was hard pressed not to laugh out loud too. It was true that his energy levels were right off the scale. Every night this week, and sometimes in the steamy heat of the afternoon too when they were both free, he and Nell had been stealing away to be under the covers or on top of them, or even... Barney's mind shied away from some of the more adventurous moments. He couldn't believe he'd avoided being in bed with his newly passionate wife for so long. But all wasn't right yet. When it was time to sleep, instead of curling up next to Nell through the nighttime, Barney was still escaping to his single bed. The pain in Nell's eyes as he left hurt him deeply, but he couldn't seem to help it. His bed was his safe place.

Nell hadn't asked him outright why this was. Barney sensed that she was afraid of the answer, and he couldn't give it, or at least, not yet. For now, he let himself luxuriate in this oasis of a second honeymoon period. There would be time for the rest later.

Barney and his counsellor, Maeve, were on a better footing too. Although it was early days in the unravelling of his troubled soul and he still cried at some point in every session, the bouts of emotion were getting easier to deal with, and Maeve was gradually teasing out of him all the years of anxiety.

'We're going to need to go back further,' she told him, at the start of the previous day's appointment. 'I want to hear about your childhood. Tell me more about your brother. Joshua, wasn't it? You only mentioned him briefly and you said you didn't see him any more. Where is he now?'

Barney didn't want to go down that long and painful road. His parents had never really discussed what happened to Josh and it was too late to talk to Lottie about the boy who had been born at the same time as Barney. His twin. His double in every way but health. He took a deep, steadying breath.

'Josh is... is dead,' he said, feeling the familiar ache in his chest that any thought of his brother triggered.

'Oh, I'm so sorry. Are you ready to tell me about this? Take your time.'

Was he ready? Barney's head screamed *no* but his heart told a different story. Even Nell didn't know what really went on with

Josh. Of course, she knew he'd lost his brother but not exactly how. She'd obviously wanted to hear the whole story when it was first mentioned, which wasn't until some years after they met when a scan had revealed that she was pregnant with twins.

He'd resisted at the time and Nell had reluctantly stepped away from the subject. Since then, he'd avoided any mention of it, although he knew Nell was naturally intensely curious. Something held her back from questioning him any more, for which he was grateful, but the time was drawing near when Barney should talk to Nell about Josh. He could make a start with Maeve. That might help to release some of the hurt.

'Josh was always delicate, as my mum put it,' Barney told Maeve, his stomach lurching already. 'He wasn't able to start school when I did because he'd had measles badly when he was four, and when he did make it through the doors of the classroom, my mum told me I had to keep a very close eye on him. I would have done that anyway, but when she said that, it was as if a heavy burden landed and made the whole thing even more serious.'

The ticking of the clock in the quiet room was the only sound as Maeve waited for Barney to continue. She looked completely relaxed; legs crossed at the ankle and hands folded in her lap. She was a comfortable-looking person, dressed in a faded summer frock patterned with daisies. Her feet were pushed into twisted leather sandals and her toenails were painted in a pale, silvery pink shade. Maeve seemed to exude an air of peace and motherliness that was immensely calming. A faint scent of lavender hung in the air. The sense of calm around Maeve gave Barney the confidence to carry on with his story.

'Sometimes, Josh was fairly well for months at a time, but when he was ill, it was crisis time. He was often in hospital for a few days while they stabilised him and I loved being alone in our bedroom at night, even though I felt guilty about it and was worried sick about my brother.'

Maeve nodded. 'It's perfectly okay to enjoy your own space. I think we all do.'

'But not when the only reason you get it is that your brother is very sick.'

There was no answer to this, and Barney hadn't expected one. He realised that he didn't want absolution from his guilt, just to get it out in the open at last.

'To get to the point, when we were twelve, Josh caught meningitis, was hospitalised and within two days, he'd died.'

The harsh words seemed to hover between them as Maeve took in their importance.

'I see. And were you able to see him in hospital?'

'No. I was on an adventure holiday with our class in the Lake District having a whale of a time. They didn't even tell me that he was ill, and by the time I got back he was too poorly to have anyone there except Mum and Dad. I was shipped off to my aunt's house, and when they finally let me come home, he'd gone. They'd cleared all his things out of our room and even moved his bed into the box room. It was as if my brother had never existed. Even the photos in frames of us together had disappeared.'

'Hmmm. I guess they thought they were protecting you from the sadness of dealing with the empty bed and seeing his face everywhere?'

'Probably. But it made me feel even worse, if that was possible. Anyway, from then on, Josh was very rarely mentioned, and then only if there was no alternative, such as if someone else brought the subject up. They wouldn't let me take a day off school to be at his funeral. Dad said it would traumatise me. Actually, I guess it traumatised me much more not to be there.'

'I see. And you found sleeping alone in the bedroom you'd shared difficult?'

'No, that was the hardest thing to bear. I slept like a log. Josh had been a very light sleeper and because of all his breathing difficulties over the years, he'd snored and kind of snorted in his sleep so I was always on alert so I could call Mum.'

'And I'm getting the impression that this is still a problem for you?'

Barney realised that there were tears in his eyes, and before he could dash them away with his hands, Maeve had passed him the tissue box which was never far from her chair. He took a few steadying breaths.

'Only fairly recently. After I was diagnosed with bowel cancer I couldn't sleep, and I was disturbing Nell, so I moved into the spare bedroom. And, Maeve, I loved it. I'm still there. I don't know how to go back. Nell doesn't know all this. I know it must seem ridiculous to have been married to someone for so long but to have so much hidden...'

'Not ridiculous at all. It's much more common than you think. And you've been dealing with a life-threatening illness too. Cut yourself some slack, Barney. There's work to be done here for you and me, but you've started to let the poison out now, and we can get on with the healing.'

Barney felt a weight begin to lift from his shoulders as he took in what she was saying. Maybe he *could* get over all this. But in his heart, he knew for sure that there was no way of recovering completely unless he gathered all his courage and talked to Nell about Josh and about the overwhelming load of guilt he'd been carrying for years. And that was never going to be easy.

32

Nell was completely taken aback when, on the day after the friendship meeting, Barney made the suggestion that they should invite the Saga Louts round for dinner. Frank was spending more and more time with them, and when Nell raised her eyebrows, Barney said he wanted to see what the dynamic was between his father and Beryl.

'He's hanging around with them all more and more and not only that, he goes to Beryl's house *on his own*.'

Barney uttered the last words in a kind of horrified whisper and Nell began to splutter with barely suppressed laughter. He glared at her. 'It's not funny, Nell. We should keep an eye on him. He's still vulnerable, you know.'

'Your dad's not a child, Barney,' Nell said. She wiped her eyes, suddenly serious again. 'Does it bother you that he's seeing someone, when it's not long after your mum... your mum...?'

'Just say it. She died. You won't upset me by using the D word. I miss her all the time, talking about it doesn't make it worse, and that must be how Dad feels. But is he actually *seeing*

Beryl? They could just be mates, keeping each other company. I'd like to know, that's all.'

'Okay, then why don't we go the whole hog and have all of the oldies here the day after tomorrow, not just those three?' Nell said, when she'd got used to the thought of having their first gathering at Hollyhocks Cottage. 'They're a great bunch. Maurice and Harry and Penelope would probably like to come too but it had better be tea rather than dinner. It might be a bit short notice, but if they do come, I bet they'd all like to eat early.'

'Fair enough. I'll make the lemon drizzle cakes, you can do the scones and we'll get Dad making dainty sandwiches instead of his usual doorsteps. Will you ask them? I can pick anybody up who needs a lift if you give me directions.'

Nell went to find the phone for the newly installed landline. She'd realised shortly after moving in that the mobile signal was unreliable in Tinderbox Lane. Although the older members of the group all had mobile phones, she knew they sometimes found texting fiddly and she was glad they'd made the decision to have what Frank called a 'proper telephone'.

Within ten minutes, Nell had collected almost the full set of acceptances for the tea party. Harry and Penelope declined because they were entertaining grandchildren, but the others all seemed delighted. Frank beamed when Nell told him of the plan and threw himself into preparations with gusto, hoovering and dusting as if his life depended on it. The weird thing was that now she had plenty to occupy her, rearranging furniture, assembling chairs, popping down to the shop for supplies and so on, the germ of an idea for a story was nudging at Nell's mind. It niggled and prodded as she, Barney and Frank prepared for their guests and refused to go away even as she lay in the bath later that evening.

When Barney came upstairs to see why she was taking so

long and to see if it was his turn for a bath, Nell wrapped herself
in her robe and padded into the study. Still only half dry, she
grabbed a notepad and pen and when she was propped up on
the bed in her dressing gown, she began to scribble. Barney
wasn't long in the bathroom, and he soon appeared in the
doorway of Nell's room wearing nothing but a towel around his
waist.

For once, Nell didn't feel very welcoming. All these months
her husband had been avoiding her like the plague at bedtime
and now, just when she'd finally got what felt like a sparkling
idea for her long-awaited book, here he was looking hopeful.
Their recent burst of passion had been a kind of awakening for
them both though and it would be a huge shame to lose the
momentum, so Nell reluctantly put her notebook on the bedside
table and turned the lights down low.

'You don't look very enthusiastic,' said Barney sadly. 'Shall I
go back to my room?'

Nell decided she'd better come clean. She was half-embar-
rassed to admit what she'd been doing after so long procrastinating but as she warmed to her theme, Barney's eyes lit up and
she was surprised to see he'd abandoned all thoughts of leaping
into bed and ravishing her.

'Look, Nell, press pause for a minute. I'll go and get us both
a glass of wine and some crisps and you can tell me more,' he
said. 'I thought this'd never happen. My dad's kept telling me I
should be chivvying you to start writing. You'd better get some
words down before they slip away. I know this is what you
need.'

Touched, and if she was honest, surprised that Barney
understood how she felt about this so readily, Nell plumped up
the pillows and settled herself more comfortably. He was back
within five minutes in his dressing gown with a tray containing

two brimming wine glasses, a bowl of crisps and another of olives.

'Right, away you go,' Barney said, when they were organised. 'Give me the outline.'

He took a huge slug of wine and sat back expectantly while Nell tried to get her rambling thoughts in order. After a moment or two of listening to some largely incoherent babbling, Barney took pity on her.

'I tell you what,' he said. 'Why don't you give me the notebook and I'll do it. You give me the gist and I'll break it down into bullet points. How would that be?'

The prospect of someone else taking charge of a rough plan was tempting because that was the part she'd been dreading but Nell wasn't sure if there was enough of a story to go that far. However, once she began to talk, the bubbling excitement that she'd felt while she was soaking in the bath came back in force. Before long, Barney's neat bullet-pointed list had filled three pages of the book, and the end was in sight.

'So, in a nutshell, your story's about a woman searching for the key to happiness. She's been in exile in the far north of Scotland for years, hundreds of miles from her hometown but when she turns sixty, she decides to travel around the UK visiting all the most significant places from her past and reconnecting with old friends and lovers. Yes?'

'That's the main theme. I'm not sure exactly how to finish it though,' Nell said. 'Does that matter, do you think?'

'I guess not, so long as you know roughly what's going to happen.' Barney peered into his empty glass and raised his eyebrows. 'Will she find happiness?'

'Does it actually exist?' asked Nell, frowning. 'That's what our meetings have all been about. I think she'll learn a lot about herself and reach a kind of contentment, especially when she starts to be more honest about what happened in her past.'

Barney was looking at her oddly now. 'Sounds like a great idea to me,' he said slowly. 'All you need to do is write it. But not tonight, that's enough for one go. More wine... or...?'

Nell looked across at her husband and her heart melted. He grinned at her rather shyly and she had a sudden flashback to how he'd looked when he first asked her out all those years ago. His kind eyes had lately regained something of their old sparkle and the expression in them made her want to reach and touch his face. She put a hand against his cheek and Barney covered it with his own. They sat for a moment in complete silence, then an owl hooting very close to the window made them both jump.

'Is that a real bird, or could it be a secret signal? Maybe it's your dad calling to Beryl to tell her the coast's clear to come round,' said Nell, laughing at Barney's expression.

He didn't bother to answer but instead pulled her close. Her notebook and pen fell to the floor as Barney reminded her exactly why she married him. The years melted away as they kissed for what seemed like an eternity.

'Oh, Nell, I've missed this so much,' Barney breathed as they came up for air.

'Do you remember how you used to spend ages saying good-night to me on the doorstep? It was only when my mum leaned out of the bedroom window and flung a glass of water over us one night that we toned it down.'

'Yes, she was always a bit... forceful, your mum. I thought she might stand up and object in the church when there was that awful pause, but afterwards she hugged me and said I was going to be her favourite son-in-law.'

'Well, that's because you were her only son-in-law, and always would be,' Nell said. 'But you did grow on her, to be fair.'

'And on you? Are you still glad we got together?'

Nell leaned away from Barney to get a better look at him. His voice sounded unbearably sad. 'Why are you asking me that?'

'Well, you know... with me being in the other room... and everything.'

Nell settled back into Barney's arms. Exhaustion at the thought of a deep discussion about Barney's disappearance from their bedroom and a sudden need to blot out all their previous worries made her reaction instinctive. As she kissed him again, she felt him respond, slowly at first and then with the sort of overwhelming passion she'd not seen for a long time. It was better than the night on the riverbank. Better than the few sizzling times since.

'Light on or off?' she murmured, reaching for the switch. Barney knew she'd always been reluctant to parade her post-babies body even in front of him.

'Leave it on,' he said huskily. 'I don't want to miss a thing.'

Much later, as they sleepily argued about who was going to make tea and fetch biscuits, Nell wondered if tonight, Barney would actually stay with her until morning. Her senses were still reeling and she was tingling all over. She could hardly bear the thought of him going away again, back to his single bed. But when they finally kissed goodnight, Barney slid out of her arms and made for the door.

'See you tomorrow, love,' he said.

Nell didn't answer. Somehow or other, this had to stop.

33

The day of the tea party dawned mistily and there was a dampness in the air all morning, but the sun warmed the atmosphere when it finally came out and the grass was soon drying nicely. Barney set out as many garden chairs as he could find around the old wooden bench under the spreading branches of the oak tree but decided that the food should be served inside when he narrowly avoiding being stung by a wasp.

'We can give them a cold drink out here to start with, and then herd them all indoors,' he said, when Nell looked disappointed. 'Otherwise, we'll spend the whole afternoon swatting flies and batting away more of these wasps. It's too risky. Someone's bound to be allergic to stings, and anyway, picnics are no fun when you're juggling cups of tea and plates.'

Frank wandered out at this point. 'You could have a couple of blankets on the ground for the younger ones if there aren't enough chairs,' he suggested.

'Younger ones? You mean me and Barney?' Nell said, rolling her eyes heavenwards.

'Oh, didn't I tell you, Nellie? I saw that nice chap from the café when I went along to the shop this morning and I invited him and his little girl to come along after she finished school for the day. They'll liven us up no end.'

'Sam and Elsie are coming? That's fine, but are there any more guests you haven't told us about?'

Frank shrugged. 'Well, the vicar was in there, so I mentioned it to her. Oh, and Maurice can't make it. He's had an attack of the collywobbles. He thinks he ate too many of Beryl's pickled onions. They're her speciality, apparently. He rang a few minutes ago.'

Barney was beginning to feel this party was getting confusing. 'So, hang on a minute, that's Beryl, Winnie and Anthea, Sam and Elsie, Bev and us three. Is that right?'

Frank counted on his fingers. 'Yep, that's it. Nine. A bit female-heavy in my opinion. Should we ask that nice builder fellow to balance it?'

Barney could see that Nell was considering this awful idea. 'Maybe not,' he said hastily. 'Otherwise we'll need to invite all the rest of your group.'

'Hmm. That's true, we'd have to include Maryam and Ingrid and Kate or they'd feel left out,' Nell said. 'Anyway, we need to get moving. Sandwiches, Frank. Dainty ones, like that selection Maurice brought to the picnic. Barney – you can dig out those nice plastic tumblers we used to take camping for the cold drinks. I'm going to iron the biggest tablecloth, the one your mum embroidered. Go, troops.'

By four o'clock everything was ready, and as Winnie was getting a lift with Anthea and the others were making their way round on foot, Barney had no need to get the car out. He was tempted to open a cold beer but restrained himself, not wanting to look like someone who couldn't make it through a hot afternoon without a drink in his hand. Instead, he began to decant a variety of soft drinks from the fridge and put them into a bucket full of water and ice. As he added the last can, there was a shout from the garden, and he heard Frank welcoming the Saga Louts.

'Come in, come in, ladies,' his father boomed, taking Barney right back to the days when Frank and Lottie had been the best party hosts in town. That was before... but his mind shied away from the darker thoughts, and he hurried out to add his greetings.

The three ladies had pulled out all the stops, dressed in their best summer finery. Beryl's flowery summer dress flowed around her as she reached up to kiss Frank's cheek. Barney stared. On kissing terms already? His attention turned to Winnie, in a purple and jade-green geometric-patterned robe and headwrap. Anthea was positively low key in comparison, her floaty layers of linen a cool ice-blue and cream. To his relief, the other two ladies also kissed his father fondly. So Beryl wasn't the favourite? Somehow this show of general affection seemed less of a threat to his mum's memory. Barney cursed himself for his touchiness. Surely Frank was entitled to female friends? But even so, a niggling sense of outrage dogged him even as he got the gang of three settled in the shade and offered them a selection of drinks to choose from.

'I'll have a tonic water with ice, thanks,' said Anthea. 'I'd rather have a large gin, but I've got to get Winnie back safely and she moans enough about my driving when I'm on the soft drinks, let alone if I was tipsy.'

'I'm gagging for a cold lager,' Beryl said. 'I've only got to walk around the corner, so it doesn't matter if I wobble. I've brought prosecco to have with our sandwiches.' She handed two bottles to Barney. 'Stick them in the fridge, would you, love? I hate warm fizz.'

All thoughts of a genteel afternoon sipping tea and chatting quietly about village affairs began to slip away as Barney went into the kitchen to fetch the drinks. Winnie had opted for a large vodka and fresh orange juice 'with lots of ice and lemon please, dear, that's at least two of my five-a-day', and as he passed his wife in the doorway, they exchanged grins.

'Oh, here's Bev, and she's got Sam and Elsie with her,' said Nell. 'At least Elsie and Anthea will be sober at the end of the afternoon. I'm tempted to go for a beer too, how about you?'

'I'll get them,' said Barney, once again filled with yearning for a long, cold drink.

Through the open window and doorway, he could hear Nell admiring Elsie's rainbow-striped tutu and silver Dr Marten boots, but Sam was already heading for the kitchen.

'Beer...' he muttered. 'And soon.'

'Bad day?' Barney handed him the bottle he'd just opened for himself and reached into the fridge for another.

'You could say that. The drinks machine at the café blew up and spat wet coffee grounds all over the place, then a customer complained that there was a fly in her sandwich.'

Barney thought the second part was probably the worst. 'And was there?'

'No, it was a tiny currant from the scones I'd been making but by that time she was hysterical and two other people walked out in disgust. Then I forgot to take Elsie a change of clothes to school ready for coming to yours, so we had to go all the way back to the flat and that's why I'm hot and she's cross.'

'Just a regular day then,' said Barney, raising his own bottle to clink with Sam's. 'Well, you're here now. And by the sound of it, Elsie's already entertaining the rest of the guests.'

Sam helped Barney to load his drinks tray, and they went out into the garden to find Elsie doing handstands in front of the Saga Louts and Frank, who were applauding enthusiastically.

'I wish I could still do that,' said Beryl. 'When I was at junior school the boys used to give me their sweets to do it. I didn't realise they just wanted to sneak a peek at my knickers.'

Barney saw Frank open his mouth to speak and quelled him with a look. His father appeared suitably chastened, but Barney could see that he was still looking across at Beryl admiringly.

Soon, the level in the glasses and bottles was going down and the chatter was getting louder. Elsie moved on to cartwheels along the lawn, ending with a stylish, Olympic-gymnast-style finish.

'Do you want to have a go now, Dad?' she asked Sam. 'He can do four cartwheels in a row and then a forward roll,' she told her audience. 'But he usually only does it when we go to the beach.'

Sam shook his head. 'I think these good people would fear for their lives if I did a stunt like that out here,' he said, clearly trying hard to sound regretful. 'Maybe Bev would like a go. Don't I remember you once saying you used to be in a gymnastics club, Vicar?'

Barney, distracted by the need to shoo away a sleepy wasp for a moment, didn't realise that Bev hadn't replied until Nell started to fill the pause with inconsequential babbling about falling off a climbing frame as a child. He craned his neck to look at the vicar, who was sitting on a rickety deckchair slightly away from the main group. Her face was very pale, and she looked close to tears. He began to collect empty glasses in readiness for the move indoors and as he passed Bev, said out of the corner of his mouth, 'Are you okay?'

She didn't meet his eyes, but muttered, 'Yes, fine, thanks.' Barney took his tray inside and then came back out, sitting down cross-legged next to Bev's chair as Nell began the long-winded task of herding her older guests into the living room.

'Want to talk?' he asked Bev. 'I'm always available if you need a listening ear.' He wasn't sure what had prompted him to make this offer, not usually being the kind of person that invited soul-searching conversations, but something about the veiled misery in her eyes touched his heart.

'I suppose I would like to, but this isn't the time or the place, is it? We need to go inside to eat.'

Barney nodded and held out a hand to pull Bev out of the saggy deckchair. 'Why don't you say you want to help us to clear up and stay behind when the others go?' he said. 'I've got a decent bottle of claret that I've been saving for a special occasion. We can open it out here when it's all quiet. Frank'll probably go round to Beryl's for a game of cards and Nell's deep into writing the second chapter of her book at last, so she'll be glad of the excuse to head for the study.'

Bev stood up and stretched. 'Okay,' she said, rather unenthusiastically, Barney thought.

'Come on, let's join the party or the posh crisps will all be gone,' he said. 'We only buy them when we have guests.'

They went indoors, and Barney couldn't help being intrigued by what Bev's troubled look was all about. Would she tell him later? It occurred to him that he was at last starting to feel as if he belonged in Willowbrook, and not just at the country park and café. It was a small world but all the better for it. Barney's curiosity grew as he watched Bev switching on the charm as she interacted with the others, all worries shelved. It was her job, of course. But what sort of strain had put that haunted look in her eyes? He would just have to be patient. Later on, in the warm summer garden with the delicate aroma of night-scented stock in the air and the bats beginning to wheel above the trees, there would be time for confidences. Plenty of time.

34

The party was a riotous success, apart from a couple of minor incidents. The first happened when Elsie and Frank both reached for the last sausage roll at the same moment and banged their heads together painfully.

'You can have it, dear,' Frank said graciously, rubbing his forehead, but Elsie was inconsolable.

'My head hurts, Daddy!' she wailed. 'I think I've got percussion. I'll have to go to the hospital right now. I'll probably die.'

Sam pulled Elsie onto his lap and cuddled her as she sobbed. Barney thought this show of emotion was way out of proportion for the size of the injury, which turned out to be a small red mark on her temple, but Bev pulled him to one side when he opened his mouth to speak.

'Elsie's got a few separation issues. The situation with her mum's complicated. We need to follow Sam's lead,' she murmured. 'He knows how to deal with it.'

It was true that the sobbing had almost stopped now. Sam was talking to Elsie in a low voice. 'You're fine, my little bird,' he

said. 'You just need to ask Bev to kiss it better now,' he said.
'She's got powerful magic.'

'Is it true?' Elsie said, gazing up at Bev wide-eyed. 'Is that
because you're friends with Jesus?'

'Might be that,' said Bev, grinning. 'Or maybe I'm just a
magical kind of person. Shall we try?'

She opened her arms wide and Elsie, after a moment's hesitation, ran into them and was enfolded in a huge hug. Bev gently
pushed Elsie's auburn curls back and kissed the offending mark.
Her eyes met Barney's over the top of the little girl's head, and he
saw that Bev's were shining with tears.

'How's that?' Bev asked. 'I think you're all better now. You'll
need the final cure though.'

'What's that?' Elsie reached up to pat Bev's spiky hair.

'The last sausage roll. Then your head will be totally better.'

Frank passed the somewhat-squashed sausage roll over and
Elsie ate it in two bites. 'I'm fine now, Dad,' she said, spraying
everyone nearby with flakes of pastry. 'Is it time for the cakes?'

The second problem arose after tea when it became clear
that Beryl was more than a little tiddly. She wobbled over to
Frank as he lounged in an easy chair and flopped onto his
knee. To give him his due, he took it well but when Beryl
began to list aloud his sterling qualities, his face told another
story.

'You're quite a guy, Frank Applecore... I mean Apple... erm...
pie? Or are you more of an apple turnover?' Beryl said, with only
a slight slur in her voice. 'You're tall and quite strong and still
very good-looking with those bushy eyebrows and lovely wavy
hair. I like a man with blue eyes, I do, and a well-trimmed beard
and moustache are always nice. I bet you've got all your own
teeth too. You're probably pretty good in—'

'Right, time we were off, I think,' said Winnie loudly,

glancing at Elsie in alarm. 'Anthea, shall we give Beryl a lift home?'

'I think we'd better,' said Anthea. 'Before she completely lets the side down. Come on, you old strumpet, let's go.'

'What's a strumpet?' asked Elsie, but by this time Barney had helped to get a protesting Beryl on her feet, to Frank's obvious relief.

The three ladies, with Beryl in the middle being strong-armed towards the door, eventually made it to Anthea's car as Sam and Bev distracted Elsie with a football she'd found in the undergrowth earlier. 'You misherable shpoilsports,' Beryl mumbled. 'I wanted to ask Frank back to mine for a game or two.'

'That's what I'm worried about,' said Winnie, exchanging glances with Anthea. 'A game of what?'

'Chess. It's just chess we play, there's no harm in it,' said Frank, red in the face and avoiding looking at Barney, who was trying not to look at Nell. He could see her shoulders shaking. They'd always had a tendency to make each other laugh at the wrong moments.

Winnie shoe-horned Beryl into the car and Anthea turned to face her hosts. 'I do apologise,' she said. 'Beryl can usually hold her fizz, in fact it's unusual for her not to be able to drink us all under the table. I don't know what's gone wrong today.'

Winnie straightened up after clipping Beryl into her seatbelt with difficulty. 'It's the new medication,' she said. 'I don't think it reacts well with the booze. She'll be right as ninepence in the morning. Thank you for a lovely tea, we really enjoyed it.'

'What medication?' Frank was bending down to speak to Beryl who had managed to wind the window down. 'Are you poorly? Why didn't you say anything?'

'I'm fine, lovely Frank Applecore, my little cutie-pie,' Beryl said, as Anthea and Winnie got themselves sorted in the front of the car. She hiccupped and put a hand over her mouth. 'Don't you worry about me.'

Anthea released the handbrake, and the car slid majestically out of the drive. Nell, Frank and Barney waved, turning as Sam appeared with Elsie.

'Oh, they've gone,' Elsie said sadly. 'Did Beryl go all tired? She was a bit green in the face and sweaty-looking. That happens to me sometimes and Dad has to put me to bed before I throw up. Is Beryl going to throw up?'

'I hope not, for Anthea and Winnie's sake, but we do need to get you home to bed,' said Sam. He turned to Barney and Nell. 'Do you mind if I leave you all the clearing up? I think we should probably quit while we're ahead.'

'Quit what?' Barney heard Elsie saying as they went off hand in hand. 'You told me when I wanted to give up on those stupid homework sums last week that we should never quit.'

Barney didn't hear Sam's reply. He was too busy pacifying Frank who wanted to follow the car down the road to make sure Beryl wasn't ill.

'Leave her to have a good sleep, Dad,' he said. 'If you want to do something useful, you can collapse the garden chairs and stack them by the shed. Then go and put your feet up. You look shattered. And Nell, pour yourself a drink and go and write some sparkling words. You did most of the food prep and Bev's offered to help me clear up.'

Nell and Frank both seemed worried at the thought of abandoning the other two, but Barney soon managed to shoo them away and finally made it to the kitchen with Bev, who looked even more exhausted than Frank. He switched on the radio and gestured to a chair by the table.

'Sit down, and I'll open that bottle. No, you can't help just yet because I'm going to load the dishwasher first, and as anybody knows, ladies can't do that job properly,' he said.

Bev pulled a face at him but accepted a glass of red wine. She watched as Barney methodically stacked plates and dishes. 'That's about the only thing I miss my husband for,' she said eventually, as he finished his task and closed the door.

'Like I said, you can talk to me, if you want to. I'm a safe pair of hands... or ears...' he corrected himself, wondering inconsequentially what safe ears might look like. He began to do a general tidy up. 'Stay where you are, I'll only have to tell you where everything goes so it's easier if you just watch.'

Bev sighed but obeyed the instruction. She sipped her wine appreciatively. 'This is very good,' she said. 'Shouldn't you be saving it to share with Nell?'

'She only drinks white,' said Barney. 'She wouldn't thank me for it. So come on, spill the beans. What have you been bottling up?'

'Not bottling, exactly. More burying. I'm not supposed to do envy in my job, but I'm really jealous of your great marriage, Barney. You and Nell always look so happy together.'

'Do we?' This was a new one on Barney. If he'd given any thought to the image he and Nell projected as a couple, he'd probably have imagined outsiders saw them as two people who were used to each other's ways and jogged along quite well together, but happy? Not so much.

'Of course you do. You complement each other. You share jokes. There's a lot of love there. Anyone can see that.'

'But we don't sleep together.' The damning words were out before Barney could stop them.

He paused in his rather rudimentary wiping of all the kitchen surfaces and Bev looked up at him in alarm. 'You mean...?'

'Oh, well, we do... we have... you know... or at least it's happening again now... but...'

Bev looked even more disconcerted than before and Barney cursed himself for blurting out the damning confession. It was one thing talking to Maeve about what he saw as his shortcomings as a husband, but now he'd gone and dropped this bombshell into a conversation that was supposed to be about Bev's own problems. Barney reached for another glass and poured himself some wine before sitting down opposite the vicar.

'Look, this wasn't meant to be about me and Nell,' he said. 'Can we just move on? I'm really glad we seem happy and I'm sure if Nell wants you to know anything about our relationship, she'll tell you herself. Let's cut to the chase and talk about you.'

To Barney's dismay, Bev's face crumpled and she began to sob. Barney stood up and went around the table to give her a hug. 'Don't tell me about it if it's too difficult,' he said, cursing his own clumsiness. He must have read the situation completely wrongly. Bev had seemed to want to talk to him about something important. After a few moments, Bev reached into her pocket for a tissue and gradually began to regain her usual composure.

'I'm sorry,' she said after a while. 'I didn't mean to let myself down like that but it turns out my relationship disaster isn't something I feel as if I can go into right now. Maybe another time. It's just that I don't always think people realise how lucky they are to be in a stable marriage with a person they love.'

Bev's voice faltered and she looked away from Barney. He felt a sudden conviction that she'd noticed his and Nell's marriage was going through a sticky patch for all her talk about him being happy. Was this her way of making him realise he was lucky, and telling him not to mess things up any further?

'So, what's brought all this emotional wobbling to the surface is that I heard from my ex, Michael, out of the blue today,' Bev said. She swallowed hard and carried on. 'He's getting married again. We divorced after... after what happened between us. I worked my way towards getting accepted onto a theological degree course and eventually completed my training and Michael... well, he sort of reinvented himself. You won't believe this, Barney, but he actually wants me to marry him! And, not only that, but in the church where my parents are still members.'

Barney was totally confused now. 'But... I... but you said he was marrying someone else,' he stuttered.

'No, I mean *marry* him. As in, perform the service? He says it's my Christian duty to forgive him for... stuff...'

The long pause that followed this gave them both time to drink more wine. Barney's head was beginning to spin.

'What are you going to do?' Barney asked, when his thoughts had begun to settle into some semblance of order. 'Are you asking my opinion? Because if you are, I'd say straight out that you'd be mad to have anything to do with this crazy idea.'

'But... the forgiveness aspect? Surely I should be able to...?'

Barney held up a hand. 'Stop right there. Do you think this Michael character is truly sorry for what went wrong between you? I've got no clue as to what happened but I'm assuming the break-up was his fault, because it's hard to imagine *you* damaging your relationship in any way. It must have meant a lot to you to make your marriage vows. It did to me too.' Barney's shoulders sagged. The weight of his own problems suddenly seemed too much to deal with.

Bev bit her lip. 'No,' she said. 'Michael's not really regretting anything he did, as far as I can see. He just wants to get back into everyone's good books at the church so he can stop feeling guilty.'

'And forgiveness is for people who are sorry, isn't it?'

She nodded, light dawning.

'You know, for a clever, kind, sparky woman, you can some-times be a bit dim, can't you?'

For a moment Barney thought he'd gone too far. Then Bev smiled. 'I guess I can. I should tell Michael to sod right off, shouldn't I?'

'You definitely should. And what's more, you should carry on with the amazing job you're doing here. The sessions in the church about happiness... well, I wish I'd joined in at the start, but I can tell they're helping Nell, and they must be doing the same for the others. You're not going to let one sadistic, self-centred guy bring you down, are you?'

Bev's eyes were sparkling now. 'Too right I'm not. He's history, and I'll tell him so. But Barney... should I try and contact his fiancée? What if she has no idea about his past? She needs to be warned.'

'I think unless you give me a bit more background on what he actually did, I can't answer that.'

'I... I don't want to say any more about it... not tonight. I'm too tired.'

Barney frowned. 'In that case, I can only give you a general answer to that question. Would she listen if you contacted her and told her what you're not telling me? She'd probably just think you were stirring up trouble out of sour grapes or some-thing. I get your point though. Do any of the congregation at your parents' church know all about this proposed wedding?'

'Some do. The Parochial Church Council will definitely know. They don't miss a trick.'

'Okay, so get one of *them* to tell her if you think she should be alerted to something about his history with you. Then if she ignores the warning, you've done your bit, and it won't look biased.'

Bev clapped her hands together. 'That's the best idea ever. I've been stewing over this all day, and you've just waved your magic wand and sorted it.' She raised her glass to Barney. 'Cheers, oh wise one.'

Barney lifted his glass in response, and they clinked them together. He smiled at Bev, although his mind was in turmoil. Her story had affected him deeply and the bravery of her fight back to normality after the grim ending of her marriage was touching and deserved celebrating. But wise? The last thing he felt was that. To find enough wisdom to get over the mountain in his own relationship would take more than a couple of glasses of wine and a chat. It was going to necessitate delving into the past. And much as his subconscious shied away from the thought even as it reared its head, Barney knew this could only mean an urgent heart-to-heart with his father.

35

The penultimate meeting of what Nell and the others had come to refer to as the Happiness Gang fell on the rainiest night of the summer so far, which didn't exactly bode well. There had been no sign of Bev since the tea party, and most unusually, the vicar wasn't answering her WhatsApp messages. Nell had gone along to the Sunday service just to see if Bev was okay, because she'd sensed something odd about her friend while they were having the party and she knew Barney had been chatting to her while she was writing, but he didn't seem to want to discuss their conversation afterwards. However, it turned out that a relief priest was taking the service and Winnie, resplendent in peacock blue and fuchsia that day, said Bev had gone to visit her parents.

Nell's confidence, still shaky when it came to being sure of her husband's affection, even though he was spending more time in their bed now, took another dip. She'd thought he was interested in Kate and now here was Bev taking his attention. At least Kate was safely in a relationship with Milo, but Bev was another matter. Was she a danger? Nell couldn't imagine a vicar would be interested in someone else's husband. Surely not. It wasn't in the job description. But she and Barney had looked kind of furtive when Nell had finally emerged from her writing sprint and suggested coffee.

There was also the matter of Beryl's tipsy shenanigans to negotiate. Nell knew Frank had been embarrassed by the whole thing and she fervently hoped he'd get back on track with his friend at the meeting. As Nell got ready to go out, donning her most all-encompassing raincoat, she heard a loud pipping at the gate and peered out of the window to see Rick once again in the minibus waving to her from the driver's window, which he wound down as she emerged.

'Come on, babe,' he shouted. 'It's a filthy night so I'm picking everyone up. Is Frank ready?'

Soon they were trundling around the area, stopping every now and again to collect members of the group. Maryam was already sitting in the passenger seat looking very pleased with herself. 'We used to have a people-carrier when the kids were younger,' she said. 'But I always ended up sitting in the back with one of them, usually mopping up sick if we were going further than a mile or two. They were a very vomity lot, my kids. It's great being up front, even if it is pouring with rain.'

Gradually the minibus filled up, with everyone in dripping raincoats and wielding wet umbrellas. Beryl was the next to be collected after Nell, Frank and Maryam. She climbed into the back and plonked herself next to Nell. She was wearing a fluorescent pink mackintosh and a clear plastic rain hood in the style of the one that Nell's mum used to keep in her handbag for such emergencies. She took it off and shook the raindrops onto the floor.

'Hello, all,' she said breezily. 'I think I've got an apology to make to you and Frank, Nell. Anthea says I was in a right old state at yours. It was those pills. I told the doctor they didn't agree with me last time I had them, but would he listen? No, he would not. Anyway, I'm very sorry. I flushed them down the loo the next day. Blooming medics.'

'What's all this about?' asked Rick. 'Have you been experimenting with drugs, Beryl?'

She grinned at Frank, and he beamed back, clearly charmed by Beryl's apology. 'Let's draw a veil, eh?' she continued. 'I'd have got better all on my own if I hadn't listened to Winnie and gone to the surgery. Rookie error,' she said. 'Right, who's looking forward to tonight? I've brought some of my rock buns and Anthea's made flapjacks. I hope they're better than the last lot. I nearly broke my top set of dentures. Anthea's cakes are always a gamble, but she will keep on trying.'

'Beryl, why did you need to take tablets in the first place? What was the problem?' Frank asked, his bushy brows furrowed. But she didn't answer and struck up an animated conversation with Maryam about the fact that the shop was now stocking her favourite shortbread biscuits.

The minibus trundled around Rick's carefully planned route, gradually collecting all the group. Harry elected to join them but said that although Penelope had specifically asked if she could come along to the meeting this time, she was 'suffering with her chest'. He sat down next to Kate and took off his trilby. 'It's delicate, you see, Penelope's chest,' he told them all.

'Not like mine. It's very robust, you might say,' said Beryl, winking at Frank who blushed and looked out of the window at nothing in particular. The rain was still pouring down but by the time they reached the church it had eased enough for them to scuttle inside without getting too much wetter. A jagged flash of lightning lit up the sky and the rumble of thunder that followed hard on its heels had everyone rushing for the safety of the church room.

Nell was relieved to see that Bev was already there and had organised the furniture and switched the urn on. 'I know it's the middle of summer,' she said as they all divested themselves of their wet coats. 'But I think we all need a hot drink before we begin tonight.'

Studying Bev out of the corner of her eye as they made tea and coffee, Nell could see that although there were dark shadows under her friend's eyes, she looked relatively compos mentis.

'Are you okay?' she risked, as they loaded mugs onto trays and added plates of cake.

'Why wouldn't I be?'

'I just wondered... with you going away suddenly... and everything.'

Bev turned and glared at Nell. 'Has Barney been talking?' she said. 'Only I assumed what I said to him was in confidence.'

'Oh no, he hasn't said a thing. I was worried about you, that's all. There's no need to snap.'

Nell picked up a tray, trying not to look hurt, but Bev put a hand on her arm. 'I'm so sorry, Nell,' she said. 'I'm a bit touchy. It's been quite a week. I'll fill everyone in later, okay?'

They went back into the meeting room and distributed the drinks and cakes. The level of chatter had risen while they'd been out of the room and there was a comforting feeling of togetherness about the group, Nell thought. She had mixed feelings about tonight's subject, it being the value of good sleep. Barney was still no nearer staying with her all night, and she wasn't sure if it was something she could bring herself to discuss. It was very personal, but on the other hand, someone might have an idea about fixing what felt like a huge issue.

Bev had put their soundtrack on, and it was playing quietly in the background but as the room fell silent waiting for Bev to speak, the sound of 'Let Your Love Flow' filled the room.

'I think that's a significant song to start us off,' said Bev, turning the music off as the words faded away. 'I've been doing a lot of thinking this week, and it seems to me that you've all been doing exactly that thing recently. Letting the love flow, that is. I don't want to sound cringy but there's a lot of love in this room, and when we're talking about finding happiness, that must be significant.'

Nobody spoke for a few moments. Frank was concentrating on drinking his tea and not meeting anyone's eyes and Maurice was suddenly very preoccupied with a rock bun, but the others all looked at Bev expectantly. She grinned at them.

'Don't all look so solemn, you're not at the dentist. We're going to talk about the importance of a good night's sleep when it comes to our general wellbeing and ability to be happy... or contented... or at one with ourselves, whichever we choose to focus on. But first, I've got something to say on the subject. It's about my marriage.'

Nobody spoke, but Bev seemed to feel the warm support flowing from the group. She began to speak, quietly at first but then gaining momentum.

'Michael, my ex, was a popular guy. He was captain of the local rugby team, darts champ at the pub, even leader of the litter-picking team in the neighbourhood. Big, tough, kind-hearted. Everybody loved him. Except me. I did to begin with, of course I did, but when the mental cruelty started, the love dwindled away. Jibes and taunts, gaslighting too.'

Beryl nodded. 'We know about that, don't we, ladies? We watched an old film. The absolute...' Words failed her, and she rubbed her eyes.

Bev tried for a reassuring smile, but it didn't really come off. She carried on talking. 'And then it got physical too. He was always careful not to leave marks. I couldn't leave, though. Or so I thought.'

Rick stood up abruptly and went to the kitchen, coming back with a glass of water. He handed it to Bev, and she drank from it in several large gulps.

'So, to cut a very long story short, the friend who saved me and gave me the strength to walk out was called Fliss. She lived just up the road, and she eventually rumbled what was going on. It took her a while, but she persuaded me to move back in with Mum and Dad, and she made absolutely sure that word got round Michael's friends to say why I was there. Some of the guys didn't believe her, but funnily enough quite a few of their wives and girlfriends did, and eventually plenty of them got the message. His name was mud around town after that.'

'Where is he now?' Nell asked tentatively. It was as if the spectre of this big thug of a man was in the room with them, still managing to browbeat Bev into a shadow of herself.

'Oh, he moved away. He couldn't stand people talking about him, so he sold up and decamped with the landlady of the pub, Veronica, who'd had her eye on him for ages. I almost felt sorry for her at the time. She had no idea what he was really like. He could turn on the charm when it suited him. I heard they split up not long afterwards. I guess Veronica was a tougher nut than me. She wouldn't put up with that kind of treatment. He wasn't on his own for long after she left him though. And that's quite another story.'

The others seemed lost for words. Eventually Kate spoke.

'And... then you decided to train to be a vicar?' she asked, her eyes wide with sympathy.

'It took a few months to get my courage up. I was battered

emotionally as well as physically. But yes, I applied to go to theological college. I'd stopped going to church for a while before I
left Michael, because I didn't want to face all my parents' friends
in the congregation. I felt such a coward. Afterwards, I went back
and threw myself into every part of it. And now, here I am. Fliss
and my lovely mum and dad saved me. Friends and family can
sometimes be a life raft. I try and pay it back by helping at a
women's refuge in town, but I'll never be out of their debt.'

Anthea stood up rather shakily and moved over to Bev. She
put a hand on the other woman's shoulder. 'Well, darling, I must
say I've been married to some rare specimens in my time, but
your man takes the biscuit. I wish you could have unburdened
yourself to someone sooner though. Anyone.'

'I wanted to, but I felt... I don't know... scared, embarrassed...
ashamed. I couldn't bring myself to tell anyone how he acted
behind closed doors. He was... cruel.'

The single word at the end of the sentence had more effect
than a whole host of them might have done. It wasn't a
complaint, just a statement of fact. Winnie and Beryl looked
close to tears and the others had varying expressions of horror
and sympathy on their faces. Anthea gave Bev's shoulder one
last pat and went to sit down. Rick's eyes were blazing with fury,
but he had the sense to let Bev continue. Nell had the feeling
that any interruptions would have stopped her in her tracks. Bev
squared her shoulders and took a swig from her glass of water
before continuing.

'Anyway, back to the subject in hand; sleep... or lack of it.
Our marriage didn't last long. We stayed together for almost a
year. I hardly slept for the last part. I didn't dare. There's no need
to go into detail about what he did... or threatened to do... or
both... but in the end I was one of the lucky ones. I escaped.
That's why I value peaceful sleep so very much. It took a long

time to shake off the shadows and the fear but when I turn out the light these days, I know the only things that might disturb me are the owls in the trees behind the vicarage and the spectre of my unfinished sermons. My story isn't complete, I'm not going to burden you with any more of it, but it just illustrates an extreme case of how necessary sleep can be. Now it's over to you, tell me why a great night's sleep, or the missing out on it, can affect our happiness.'

Nell glanced around the room. The rest of the group appeared to be in a state of stunned silence. She knew that if she was going to contribute to this session properly, she would have to bring her own marriage into the conversation. Was it fair to talk about Barney when he wasn't here to add his side of the story? She didn't even know what that was, fully. While Nell was pondering, Ingrid raised a hand.

'I totally agree with how important sleep is, but for me it's more about *where* I sleep rather than for how long. I loved living over the corner shop during the months when I was selling my treasures... and tat... and the log cabin was fairly relaxing but now that I'm on the boat I've found a whole new peacefulness. Lying in my bed, feeling the movement of the water and listening to the ducks settling down for the night is the best thing ever. It doesn't matter if I doze off or not, it's just so restful.'

Beryl snorted. 'That's all right for you, lovey, but if that was me, I'd be losing my dinner before I could fall asleep. Do you remember that mini cruise we went on, girls?'

Winnie and Anthea exchanged grimaces. 'She spent most of the time in the loo,' said Winnie. 'I was glad it was Anthea sharing with her and not me. I'm with Ingrid, a life on the ocean wave, or the canal in her case, is great for getting more sleep but I have to say I love my bedroom at home more. I'd never share it again, even if that Daniel Whatshisname came along.'

'Craig?' said Anthea helpfully.

'No, his name's definitely Daniel,' Winnie said, frowning.

To Nell's relief, Bev looked as if she had her emotions under control again, now the discussion was properly underway. Nell cleared her throat. 'I hope you don't mind me asking, but do those of you who regularly have a room to yourselves prefer it that way?' she said, feeling her cheeks getting warm and her heart beating faster. 'I know it's not from choice in some cases.'

This question sparked off a babble of responses. Beryl and Winnie said that they'd missed their husbands terribly when they were first widowed but had now got used to the solitary space. Maurice, a lifelong bachelor, shuddered at the thought of sharing and wondered if any woman would put up with his nighttime habit of watching TV and eating hot buttered toast in bed and Kate said that the arrangement that she had with Milo where they kept their own homes worked perfectly.

'We get to choose if we sleep in the same place,' she said. 'It works for us.'

Anthea rolled her eyes at this point. 'That idea might have saved some of my marriages,' she said. 'I've got a very low tolerance level for husbandly behaviour.'

'Such as?' Bev sounded intrigued.

'Oh, don't get me started. Burping and breaking wind loudly in bed, eating biscuits and leaving crumbs, constant noisy trips to the bathroom, hogging the covers... and snoring... that was the worst.'

Everyone was laughing now but Maryam was the first to add to Anthea's comments. 'Yes, snoring. Rashid might look like a quiet kind of bloke to you but boy, can he raise the roof when he starts to snore. I've at last persuaded him to move into Uma's room for a while now she's back at uni. It's absolute bliss. We both sleep better, and the bonus is that we don't argue any more.' She grinned. 'Well, not about the sleep thing, anyway. He's still got a problem with me ordering things online when I wake up in the middle of the night and then realising they're a complete waste of money.'

Harry had been looking puzzled and now shook his head. 'I see your point but can't agree with the separate sleeping theme,' he said. 'Penelope and I like a chat in the night when we can't sleep. And a cuddle,' he added with a chuckle, flushing pink when he realised everyone was smiling at him fondly. 'I mean, I'm in my eighties... it's just a cuddle these days... usually...'

'That comes under the heading of too much information,' Bev said, giggling. 'Who's next, before we break for cake?' Nell was pleased to see the vicar had regained something of her equilibrium and the tight set of her shoulders had relaxed at last. She wished she could let go of her own tension, but that wasn't going to happen yet. It would be Nell's turn to speak soon, and she still hadn't decided exactly how much to reveal.

36

The only members of the group who hadn't contributed to the sleep discussion so far were Frank, Rick and Nell herself. She waited to see if the other two were up for joining in, still unsure of how much to reveal about the lack of bedroom-sharing with Barney. Frank looked uncomfortable too, but he spoke up at last.

'I miss my Lottie most of all in the night,' he said. 'I hate sleeping alone.'

'Well, we'll have to see what we can do about that situation then,' said Beryl, then covered her mouth with a hand. 'Good heavens, did I say that out loud?'

Winnie gasped and nudged her friend. 'Ooh, Beryl, you've really let yourself down now. Ignore her, Frank. She's just an old blabbermouth. Never knows when to zip it. And she's just told everyone how much she likes her own space, too. What a hypocrite.'

Frank raised his eyebrows but said nothing. Nell noticed that his eyes were twinkling. Rick was still silent, his gaze fixed on Bev. She turned to face him. 'Do you want to say anything?' she asked. 'It doesn't matter if you don't, it's fine.'

Rick shrugged. 'Nothing much to add really,' he said. 'I live on my own these days. I miss my kids but not my wife. She was... unpredictable. Fiery. I used to like going into the boys' bedrooms at night to make sure they were safe and tucked in. I don't sleep so well without them.'

The mood in the room had dipped now. Bev looked at Nell. 'Anything from you?' she asked.

Nell took a deep breath and decided that if everyone else had been prepared to share their private thoughts on the matter, she ought to join them. It was hopefully a confidential place to talk and really, she'd bottled up her worries for far too many months.

'I'd love to sleep in the same room as Barney,' she said. 'I expect most of you don't know that he had cancer not so long ago. He's been given the all-clear to get on with life, but his treatment pretty much disrupted our sleep pattern, and he said he needed to be on his own for the time being, so he didn't disturb me any more than necessary. I didn't mind being disturbed at all, to be honest, but I understood. And now...'

Nell's voice tailed away, and she swallowed hard, but it was no use. Her eyes were stinging, and she rubbed them angrily. 'I'm sorry, I didn't mean to get upset. And I probably shouldn't have said anything. It's a bit personal.'

Frank was the first to react, but Nell could hear sympathetic murmuring from the others as he got to his feet. He came over to Nell's chair and Kate, who'd been sitting next to her, got up to make space for him. Nell felt her father-in-law's arms go around her and picked up his familiar comforting smell, a mixture of Imperial Leather soap and mint humbugs. It was a long time since he'd hugged her, it wasn't really his style. Nell leaned against Frank and let the tears flow as he patted her back and made soothing noises.

'You don't need to worry about spilling the beans to us,' Nell heard Beryl say. 'We're all friends here and you know what that old advert for the phone company used to say. *It's good to talk.*'

'You'd have been a good poster girl for them, in that case,' said Anthea. 'You never stop. She's right though, Nell. You can tell us anything. What happens in the church room stays in the church room, okay, gang?'

There were cries of agreement from all sides of the room, and Nell heard Maryam and Bev say it was time everyone had another nice cup of tea. Frank reached into his pocket for his handkerchief and gently dried Nell's eyes. 'Don't worry, it's a clean one,' he said very quietly. 'And also, don't fret about our Barney. Worse things happen at sea, and he'll be back in there with you before long, you mark my words. He'd be mad not to. I think you need to ask him straight out what the problem is. Get it sorted once and for all. Do it tonight. I'll keep well out of the way.'

After that, everyone got up and began to mill around. The Saga Louts all headed for the cloakroom at speed and Frank got to his feet, holding out a hand to Nell. 'Come on, you need a good hot cuppa,' he said. 'If we learn nothing else from these meetings, at least we know how much we rely on tea to make life better.'

When everyone had settled back down with their drinks, Bev clapped her hands for silence. 'I think we've all said enough on the subject of sleep for one session,' she said. 'Just to sum up, it's clear from all your contributions... and thanks for being so open about this, it's a delicate subject... it's clear that we're all vastly different in how much sleep we get and where we choose to get it. I think it's useful to realise that being peaceful and restful when you turn in for the night is just as valuable as being out for the count for hours.'

'Too right,' said Maurice. 'And if old episodes of *Morse* and

Antiques Roadshow float your boat, then who's to say it's wrong? We've found out that we're all different.'

Bev smiled at him, but her eyes were still troubled. 'I've got to be honest, I never intended to pitch in with my own murky past,' she said. 'The group was meant to bring all of *you* together and give you the chance to get closer to finding your own personal happiness. And that brings me to my next point. We've only got one more meeting left to come.'

There were groans from all sides. 'I'll miss this group,' said Maryam. 'It's been a great way to get to know all of you. Thanks for hosting this for us, Bev.'

'I'm glad you feel that way. Next time we'll sum up what we've discovered over the weeks and talk about why precious memories are so important. Bring your thoughts, but there's no need to provide anything else. If the weather's fine, I'll lay on fizz and other cold drinks and nibbles in the vicarage garden as a grand finale.'

It wasn't long before Nell was walking home, having elected to get some fresh air rather than have a lift with Rick, who seemed more than happy to seize the chance to stay and help Bev to put chairs away. It was good to have Frank holding her arm protectively and Maryam following close behind. The rain had stopped at last, and the evening air was cool and fresh. A light breeze had blown most of the clouds away and stars were starting to be visible here and there.

'Good luck with... everything,' Maryam said, as she waved goodbye at the end of the lane leading to Nell's house.

'Oh, Frank, I've really gone and done it now,' said Nell as they walked the final stretch, avoiding puddles as they went. 'Barney's always said I over-share. He'll hate it if people start gossiping about us.'

'They won't,' said Frank firmly. 'And you needed to get all

that off your chest. Now the next step is to strike while the iron's hot.'

Nell smiled. Lottie had often had a favourite saying for every occasion and now Frank was taking over the habit. Her expression changed when their cottage came into view. Talking about all this wasn't too hard once you got going. Doing something about it was entirely another matter.

With Frank off to bed and the kitchen lit by one small spotlight in the corner, Nell flicked the kettle on and went to search for her husband. She found him in the study, frowning over a complicated-looking spreadsheet. Her own computer had been left on, and for a moment or two, Nell debated with herself. She could join him and carry on writing. There was no need to do any soul-searching tonight when she was still feeling unsettled from all the talk at the meeting. Or... she could take this opportunity to clear the air once and for all. Before Nell could decide, Barney looked up at her and smiled.

'Thank goodness you're home,' he said. 'I was looking for an excuse to abandon this for the night. Shall we go downstairs and have a cup of tea?'

More hot drinks for comfort. Relieved to have the matter taken out of her hands, although rather awash with tea after the meeting, Nell nodded and led the way to the kitchen. Barney started his familiar comforting routine of warming the teapot, measuring out his favourite leaf tea with a scoop kept specially for the purpose in the old tin caddy, and getting out their favourite china mugs. Nell sat down at the table and watched him, her heart full of love for this man who she knew so well, and yet sometimes didn't understand at all.

Eventually, settled with a mug each and a packet of chocolate digestives on the table between them, Barney smiled at Nell.

'Was it a good get-together tonight?' he asked. 'You said it was the one about how important it is to sleep...'

His voice tailed away, and he looked down at the biscuit he'd been about to dunk in his tea. He put it down on the table instead, brushing crumbs from his fingers. Nell reached out and took his hand.

'It's not just the sleeping that's important,' she said. 'It's who you share your space with when you go to bed. I think that was the main message that came across.'

'Tell me more.'

'Well, no names because it was a confidential chat, but some people said they'd had to get used to sleeping alone, even if it wasn't by choice. One or two preferred it. What came out of it was that the actual sleep isn't as important as feeling peaceful in the nighttime.'

'And what did you say?' Barney's eyes were full of anxiety now. He held her hand more tightly.

Nell bit her lip and wondered how much to divulge. In the end she decided to simplify. 'I said I'd rather spend the night with you than on my own,' she said.

There was an uncomfortably long silence as Barney digested this answer, only broken by the sound of a light knock on the door between the kitchen and the annexe. They looked at each other in surprise. Frank had never before announced his arrival like this.

'Come in, Dad,' Barney called. They waited, eyes still on each other. The door opened slowly, and Frank peered in.

'I won't ask if I'm disturbing anything, because I can see that I am, but I think this is one of those times when I should... get in the way, I mean,' he said.

Nell stood up to greet Frank, unsure if this was a good development or a distraction from her and Barney's long delayed Big Talk. He smiled at her, but his expression soon reverted to sombre. 'I want to say something and also to give you this, Barney,' he said, holding out a carrier bag that Nell hadn't noticed before.

Barney took the bag and gestured for his father to join them at the table. Nell went to pour Frank a mug of tea, but he shook his head. 'Maybe after we've spoken,' he said. 'I need to get this off my chest first. Open the bag, son.'

It took less than a minute for Barney to extract a slim photograph album and set it on the table in front of him, but he didn't seem keen to open it. Nell was alarmed at the way his face had paled. Barney's eyes were wide with what looked almost like horror.

'Josh?' he said, quietly.

'Yes. And you should have had this book a long time ago but your mum and I... well, we both wanted to protect you. I don't want to make excuses for never talking to you about your brother, but please believe me, we meant well, honestly we did.'

Barney didn't reply at first. He reached out and touched the cover of the album and then withdrew his hand as if he'd been burned. 'Why now?' he said. 'After all these years, why now, Dad?'

Frank sighed. 'It was the meeting tonight. I'm not going to talk about what was said but I got the feeling that you might have... I don't know what the proper term is... unresolved issues?'

Now Barney's gaze turned to Nell and the look of disappointment in his eyes wrenched at her heart. 'You told them about us?' he asked huskily. 'Nell, that stuff's private. How could you?'

Before either Nell or Frank could stop him, Barney leaped out of his chair so suddenly that it fell backwards with a crash. He turned to leave and then at the last moment grabbed the photograph album. 'You're both one big let-down,' he shouted. 'Skulking about, keeping secrets of your own then blabbing mine to all and sundry. I'm going to bed.'

There was a scrabbling and whining at the door and Anton burst in from the annexe. He skittered across the tiled floor and hurled himself against Barney's legs. Barney bent to stroke him. 'At least someone cares,' he said. 'See you in the morning. Or maybe not.'

Nell and Frank watched Barney go. From bitter experience, Nell knew that there was no point in following him. It would be complete shut-down now until such time as her husband decided he'd sulked for long enough. Sudden fury filled her soul.

'He always walks away from problems,' she said.

'Always has. But that doesn't mean he always will,' said Frank. 'I think we've reached something of a watershed tonight. Let him be for now. I'm to blame, Nell. We kept too much from him, and he was only twelve years old when Josh... when Josh passed away. Do you mind if I tell you about it?'

'Please do,' said Nell. 'I've held back from asking for details because both you and Lottie didn't seem able to talk about Barney's brother, but I really want to know all about him, and about what happened, if you can bear it.'

'I need to tell you a few things,' said Frank. 'And when my lad's ready to listen, I'll talk to him too. Properly. Now, are you going to make more tea? Should we have a nip of whisky with it? This might take a while.'

By the time Frank had finished talking, they had drained the teapot and had two large drams of Frank's best single malt each. Nell's head was spinning. No wonder Barney was so mixed up and sad. It was one thing understanding her husband's grief and regrets about his brother's death, but it would be quite another knowing how to help him to deal with it. She said goodnight to Frank, and their hug lasted even longer than the one they'd shared at the meeting. At least they were in this together, both loving the same mixed-up man. But where to go next? Nell took herself slowly to bed on leaden feet. She had a feeling that sleep wouldn't come easily tonight.

37

Barney awoke the next morning with a start. He'd been dreaming of a long-ago time when his parents had taken Josh to the clinic in Scotland for some kind of revolutionary treatment that was meant to give him a better chance of surviving childhood.

At the time, Barney hadn't realised the significance of their trip. His mother's much older sister Avril had come to stay to look after him, and she and Barney had had a whale of a time. Luckily, the summer holidays had begun so there was no school to get in the way. They'd spent the week jumping on and off buses with Avril gaily waving her bus pass and telling all and sundry that the world was their oyster, and they were going 'to kick our heels up, oh yes we are!'

Every evening, the two of them would make a picnic of all the delicious items that were usually kept for treats in Barney's world and take them outside to the garden. Avril rigged up a kind of Bedouin tent using all Lottie's best bedspreads and throws, and she and Barney toasted each other in brilliantly red cherry pop before devouring every scrap of food. Then they would spread a blanket on the grass and wait for the stars to come out. Of course, this meant that Barney's bedtime was much later than usual, and he revelled in that fact, but he also delighted in the silence of his bedroom when he finally tumbled into bed, grubby and sticky-fingered, because Avril's view of the holidays was that if a boy didn't want to have a bath or a shower until just before his parents came home, that was absolutely fine.

The bedroom without Josh in it felt strange to begin with. His brother's bed was smooth, without the usual chaos of tangled sheets caused by Josh's wakefulness. There was no need for Barney to sleep with one ear open, alert for any unusual breathing. He could even listen to his transistor radio under the covers or read into the small hours. Most nights he was too sleepy to do either of these forbidden things, but he knew that he could if he wanted to, which was a joy in itself.

Deep in the dream, Barney's alarm clock was an unwelcome jolt back to reality. He pressed the snooze button and lay back on his pillows. He had a Zoom call booked for ten o'clock and it was nearly nine thirty already. He'd deliberately timed the alarm for much later than usual on a working day in the hope that gentle Morpheus would blot out his feelings of grief and remorse from last night.

His throat was aching and there were tears on Barney's cheeks. He realised that he must have been crying in his sleep. The image of Josh was very strong – a paler, more fragile version of himself with the widest grin ever and green eyes just like Barney's and their mother's that sparkled with mischief... except when he was feeling at his worst. The guilty pleasure of those long, sunlit days and starry nights with Avril but without his brother glowed in Barney's memory, jewels in a sea of pebbles.

When the family returned, it was immediately clear that the

trip had been useless. From then on, Josh's decline had been punctuated with episodes of manic activity and then bouts of exhaustion. Gradually, the tiredness took over and Barney's nights were filled with sudden wakings and trips along the corridor to fetch whichever of his parents looked most alert. At last, Frank overruled Josh's wishes and set up a baby alarm by his bed.

'But I've got Barney,' Josh had wailed, when he thought Barney was out of earshot one morning. 'He listens out for me. He won't let anything bad happen.'

'This is too much for your brother now,' Frank answered gruffly. 'I've had the school on the phone twice this week already. Barney's falling asleep at his lessons. He can't do this. It's either you have the alarm, or we move your bed into our room, son. I'm sorry, but we need to keep you both safe and well.'

Barney remembered with an awful pang of guilt how he'd wished and wished that Josh would choose the second option. He hadn't. The two of them had always slept in the same room. They'd shared one big cot as babies, and since then had never been apart for long. The unsuccessful Scottish mission had been a reprieve for Barney, but he'd stoically settled back into his role as part-time carer for his brother. What else could he do?

Now, as the dream receded, Barney reached for the photograph album that his father had given him the night before. He knew in his heart that he'd behaved unreasonably, storming out like that, but he'd not been able to stand Nell's and Frank's sympathetic eyes on him for a second longer. With the book in his hands, Barney shuddered. Could he do it? He took a deep breath and opened the album at the first page.

Here, smiling up at him, were two small boys, hand in hand in their sandpit, dressed in identical outfits of blue shorts and tops with pictures of dinosaurs on the front. Neither of the twins had been particularly fond of prehistoric creatures but Barney remembered that they had hated it if their clothes didn't match. On that day, Josh had spilt blackcurrant squash all over his tractor-patterned T-shirt, so Barney had done the same, which meant their mum had to change them both. Satisfied, they'd run out to the garden to celebrate with a few sandcastles and Lottie had taken the opportunity to take the picture while they were still relatively clean.

Barney began to turn the pages, nostalgia tugging at his heart with every page. The photographs were stuck in at random, with no effort at all to add them chronologically. Pictures of cute babies in romper suits or sometimes stark naked were interspersed with the first day at nursery school, a rare visit to a safari park when Josh was feeling strong enough for a long drive, the Christmas tree being decorated with a mishmash of traditional and homemade baubles and finally, Josh and Barney's last school photograph, aged twelve years and two months. Josh had been sick that morning, and would normally have been kept at home but Lottie had insisted they took him in, even if it was just for the morning.

Josh died three weeks after that picture was taken, Barney recalled with a sinking feeling. He closed the book and placed it carefully on his bedside table, pushing back his single duvet ready to head for the shower. Enough for now. Just as he was walking along the corridor, keeping a wary eye out for Nell in case she was still angry with him, he heard a cry from the garden.

'Nell, Barney, come quickly!' Frank shouted at the top of his lungs. 'It's Beryl. I left my stupid phone at home and there's nobody in at either of the nearest neighbours. She's on the floor and I can't get into her house. Help me... and make it quick!'

38

Horrified, Nell hurtled from the kitchen at the sound of Frank's voice, stumbling over Anton as she ran. Barney was running down the stairs dressed only in a pair of boxer shorts patterned with pictures of Bart Simpson.

'Have you tried Kate next door to Beryl? She's got a key,' Nell said, already heading for the lane, heart thumping.

'Yes, of course I did, I told you. I banged on Kate's door, but she wasn't there. What are we going to do?' asked Frank.

'Come on, we're wasting time, we'll think of something. Maybe Barney can go and find Kate at the flat over the café if she's still not there.'

'I'll ring for an ambulance and then follow you to see what's happening. Don't worry, I'll put some more clothes on first,' Barney added, seeing his father's horrified expression.

Nell and Frank set off towards Fiddler's Row at a speed slightly faster than Frank's normal walking pace. He was still gasping from his earlier panicked dash. 'You go on ahead,' he panted. 'You're so much faster than me.'

Nell took him at his word and continued at a trot, reaching Beryl's cottage just as Kate was entering the one next door. 'Thank goodness you're home,' Nell gasped. 'Frank came round to see Beryl and the door was locked. He says she's lying on the floor. He must have gone round the back and looked through the window.'

Kate wasted no time talking, but quickly let herself into her own house and came out seconds later brandishing a bunch of keys. 'I've got half the street's door keys here,' she said. 'Just let me find... ah, yes, this is it.'

They were soon inside the tiny hall, and now Frank was with them too, panting alarmingly. Barney was close behind, thankfully now clad in his usual shorts and T-shirt. He was holding his phone to his ear. 'The switchboard lady's still on the line,' he said, as they jostled their way through to the kitchen. 'We need to answer some questions once I've seen Beryl, but the ambulance is on its way already.'

Everyone froze as they saw what Frank had glimpsed through the back window. Beryl was spreadeagled on the kitchen floor, her face hidden from view by her hair. A trickle of blood had formed on the tiles and her left ankle looked to be at a very strange angle. Nell got down on her knees and automatically felt for a pulse. Her time at the homeless centre had included several intensive first-aid courses which she'd needed on a couple of occasions, but never in a case where she'd been so terrified of the outcome.

'Her pulse is a bit erratic but she's breathing,' Nell said, smoothing back Beryl's hair which was as usual stiff with lacquer and refused to cooperate. A slight moan escaped Beryl's pale lips, and she tried to stir.

Barney was relaying all this to the person on the phone.

'Beryl needs to stay as still as possible for now,' he said. 'Could one of you find a blanket to keep her warm until the ambulance comes?'

Kate took the stairs two at a time and returned with a fluffy throw. She tucked it gently around Beryl. 'Stay put, darling, help's on its way,' she said quietly, her face close to the old lady's. She patted Beryl gently on the shoulder and turned an agonised face to the others. 'I can see that she tried to ring me earlier, but I wasn't here. I had my phone on silent because I stayed over at the flat with Milo and it wakes our dog up if it bleeps in the night. Sorry, I'm babbling. I wish that ambulance would hurry up.'

At that moment, the sound of the wailing siren filled the air, getting closer all the time. Before long, the small kitchen seemed much too full of people.

'Could you give us some space, guys?' the younger paramedic of the two said, shooing them all out into the living room. 'We'll let you know as soon as we've assessed the patient.'

Frank looked as if he was about to argue but Barney ushered him gently through the door as the second paramedic knelt on the floor and began to talk gently to Beryl, who moved an arm and groaned.

'Is she going to die?' Frank asked Nell, clutching her arm. He seemed childlike all of a sudden, his usual gruff composure a thing of the past.

'It's not likely. I'm guessing she possibly felt dizzy and fell, banging her head on the way. Let's leave it to the experts now. I'd make tea but we can't really get to the kettle,' said Nell, falling back on the old failsafe cure yet again even though tea was the last thing she wanted right now.

'Leave that to me. I'll go next door and sort hot drinks out,'

Kate said. 'If they take Beryl to hospital, I can't go in the ambulance with her because I've got to go back and take over from
Milo in the café in ten minutes. Saturdays are always crazy. That
is, unless I can get Sam to step in,' she added, frowning. 'Yes, I'll
phone him.'

'No, I'll go with her,' said Nell, Frank and Barney in unison.
They looked at each other doubtfully as Kate disappeared to
make tea.

'Let's wait and see what the paramedics are going to do,' Nell
said. 'We'll just have to be patient.'

That was easier said than done. There was no word from the
kitchen and the door had been firmly closed behind them so no
clues could be picked up as to how Beryl was faring in there.
Kate returned with a tray of mugs.

'It seems wrong to have a kind of tea party while poor Beryl's
lying there on the floor but what else can we do?' said Kate.

'Well, we should probably ring someone to let them know,
shouldn't we? Anthea or Winnie… or what about Beryl's niece?
She talks about her now and again, her name's Sophie and Beryl
obviously thinks a lot of her,' said Frank.

'I know Sophie well. I can get in touch with her, no problem.
Shall I do it now?' said Kate.

Barney shook his head. 'We'll just panic all of them if we
haven't got anything definite to report. Let's wait until we know
what's happening.'

They sat drinking their tea in silence in a semi-circle on
Beryl's very comfortable easy chairs and sofa. Nell's stomach
was churning. Beryl had looked such an awful colour. It took
her back to Lottie's final days when her mother-in-law had
been so pale her skin had almost looked translucent. Frank's
face was twisted with anxiety. She wondered if it was the same
memories haunting him or if he'd become fonder of Beryl in

the last few weeks than they'd realised. Probably a bit of both, Nell decided.

Finally, when everyone's nerves were stretched to twanging point, the kitchen door opened, and the younger paramedic poked her head out. 'Hi, I'm Jan. Are any of you Beryl's next of kin?' she asked.

The words clearly struck horror in the group, and she held up a hand. 'That sounded worse than it was meant to,' Jan said. 'Beryl's responding well but we don't know yet whether she fell or collapsed, because she can't remember, and her ankle looks as if it needs an X-ray. I was asking the question because I wondered if anyone wanted to come with her to hospital. Just one person, I'm afraid,' she added quickly when three hands went up.

Nell turned to Frank and Barney who were sitting together on the sofa. 'I think it'd better be me,' she said. 'Not that Beryl wouldn't love your company but if she needs any... kind of... personal care... the toilet and so on...'

The two men exchanged horrified glances and nodded. 'Fair point,' said Barney. 'I'll run home and fetch your bag. Have you had breakfast?'

Nell smiled at him gratefully, although she thought it must seem odd to the others for a married couple not to know if the other had eaten. 'I had cereal earlier, but I will need my bag, my phone and its charger, thanks, Barney. Could you put my Kindle in too in case it's a long wait?'

Barney was soon back, just as Beryl was being loaded carefully onto a stretcher and transferred to the waiting ambulance. Her eyes were closed and although she winced slightly, she didn't attempt to speak. Nell hugged the others in turn, feeling as if they'd been through a major ordeal together, and climbed into the back, strapping herself in as instructed.

'I'll keep you all posted,' she called, as the doors were closed. 'I'll ring the others from the hospital, and update you, Kate, so you can contact Sophie. Try not to worry.'

As they drove away, Nell reflected on the foolishness of those last words. Barney, Frank and Kate stood waving the ambulance off as if they were sending Nell and Beryl on a day trip. Their faces told a different story.

39

The next three hours felt like some of the longest of Nell's life. Waiting in a series of waiting rooms and corridors with the only similarity being the uncomfortable plastic chairs, she blessed the overworked NHS for their patience and calm. Snippets of painful flashbacks to previous illnesses and deaths in the family haunted her. Nurses and doctors hurried back and forth, intent on getting as much done in the day as was humanly possible. Tea trolleys were wheeled around too but Beryl was still not able to sit up and needed a full set of test results back before she could take nourishment, so Nell didn't feel that she could sit and drink coffee or munch chocolate bars in front of her friend.

By now, Beryl was much more alert and getting hungry. 'This is tiresome, Nell,' she said. 'I was going to cook a nice bit of pork for my tea today and have it with cabbage and mash. When are we going home? I'm perfectly well now. It was just a funny turn. Everyone gets them at my age.'

The nurse who was at that moment taking Beryl's blood pressure shook her head. 'Not just yet, sweetheart,' she said. 'You won't be leaving here until the doctors are absolutely sure why you ended up face-planting your kitchen floor. You were lucky to get away with just a dressing on your head and no stitches. You don't want that happening again, do you? And that ankle needs attention too.'

Beryl moved position in the bed as the nurse spoke and let out a yelp of pain. 'It's probably just a sprain,' she said, when the twinge had passed. 'I was always twisting my left ankle as a girl. It's been my weak spot ever since.'

'Probably all those handstands,' said Nell. 'It sounds as if you were an adventurous child.'

'And I've been an adventurous adult,' said Beryl with a cackle. 'I'm not done yet. But I just want to go home.'

Luckily, the doctor on call in A&E appeared at this point and the nurse stood back to give him more space in the small cubicle. He was one of the older ones, with twinkling eyes and a fine white beard. 'Well, my dear, I have your test results here. Is this lady okay to stay with you while I tell you the news?' He gestured to Nell and raised his eyebrows.

Beryl nodded impatiently. 'Yes, yes... I've got no secrets from Nell. Well... no relevant ones anyway. Carry on, Doctor. I'm dying to get home. At least, I'm not actually dying... am I...?'

The doctor laughed. 'Far from it, I hope you'll have plenty more happy years yet. Your problem is low blood pressure, for which I gather you've been prescribed a course of tablets?'

He left the question hanging, and Beryl had the grace to look abashed. 'Yes, well, they didn't suit me,' she mumbled. 'I felt dreadful when I was taking them. Tablets are meant to make you feel better, aren't they?'

The doctor pulled up a chair and sat down. 'You can leave us to it, Pat,' he said to the nurse, who hurried away with one backward, sympathetic glance at Nell. 'Now, Beryl, if I may call you that?'

Beryl gestured for him to continue but she didn't meet his eyes and avoided looking at Nell.

'The problem is that without the pills to regulate your blood pressure, when it dips suddenly, you will either feel very dizzy or black out completely. That's what happened this morning, and you were lucky, in a way, that you were at home. It could occur anywhere at any time. I can prescribe a different course of tablets which should work just as well and shouldn't make you feel poorly. How about that?'

'Oh... well, it's worth a try, I suppose. But can I still drink prosecco? Life's too short to give up all my pleasures.'

He smiled. 'In moderation, yes, you can. But you must continue with the course of medication and then see your GP when you're near the end of the packs. And as for your ankle, you've been fortunate again. There are no bones broken but it's quite a nasty sprain so we'll strap it up and if you treat it gently for a week or two, you should be perfectly fine to carry on with your normal activities.'

'Does that mean I can go back to Zumba tomorrow?'

The look of amazement on the doctor's face caused Beryl to splutter with laughter. 'Only kidding, chair yoga's more my thing these days. I'll be sensible, I promise. Everything in moderation.'

She winked at Nell, who stifled a giggle. 'When will Beryl be able to come home?' she asked.

'I'd like to keep her in for a couple of days for observation, and then she'll be free to go.'

Beryl groaned but didn't argue. Nell could see the old lady was exhausted and would probably need a very long nap soon.

'I've asked them to find you a bed on a ward as soon as possible,' the doctor said. 'In the meantime, we'll organise some lunch for you and maybe this kind friend will arrange for your nightclothes and so on to be brought in.'

'Of course I will.' Nell reached into her bag for the notebook and pen she always carried. She anticipated there would be quite a list, and she was right. The doctor took his leave, shaking Beryl's hand and giving a courtly bow.

'Good to meet you, my dear,' he said. 'But let's hope we don't see each other here again, eh? Moderation and medication are your two watchwords from now on.'

Beryl beamed at him but didn't reply. When he was safely out of earshot she whispered to Nell, 'I'll try the new tablets but I'm not giving up my prosecco nights with the girls. That's what makes life worth living. All this talking we've been doing about looking for happiness has made me do some serious thinking. I've got everything I need here in Willowbrook but the best part of it is the friendship of Anthea and Winnie, and our holidays together and so on. I love those two. We have a right laugh. And the rest of you aren't so bad either.'

She settled herself on her pillows as comfortably as possible. 'It's time you went home for some lunch, Nell. Mine should be here soon. I hope it's not mince. I can't be doing with sloppy grey food. Someone can bring my bits and bobs later if that's okay. I'm lost without my dressing gown and slippers and a good book.'

As Beryl said this, Nell's phone pinged. She picked it up and found a message from Barney.

> Any news yet, love? How's Beryl? We're both missing you here. Do you need a lift home or are you staying longer?

A sudden warmth filled Nell's heart. Was this happiness?

Someone to care about you and miss you when you were away? It certainly felt like it.

To give Barney time to drive here, Nell texted back:

> Ready in fifteen minutes

She began to tidy the cubicle, collecting her own belongings and straightening the rumpled bedclothes. Eventually, Beryl reached out a hand as Nell turned to leave.

'Thank you, dear,' she said huskily. 'I do appreciate this. If our Sophie was here she'd be helping me out straight away but she's off on her travels in Spain for at least a fortnight. You're a true friend, and so are Barney and good old Frank. I'm lucky to have all of you around me.'

Nell wasn't sure how Frank would feel about the 'good old' tag, but the sentiment was genuine, as was everything about Beryl, she reflected. Moderation, though? The concept didn't seem to fit this lady, somehow. She said a fond goodbye and walked down the long corridor that led to the exit. Barney had made good time and was just pulling into the car park. Nell waved, relief to be escaping the confines of the hospital with all its latent atmosphere of worry and grief making her feel guilty for a moment.

Barney had all the windows open in the car. He slowed to a halt and jumped out to give Nell an enormous hug. 'Don't say anything for a minute, you can update me as we drive. The others all know what's going on now, as far as I could tell them. There's a cool bag on the back seat with some cans of that orange fizzy stuff you like, have a drink before you dehydrate completely. It's so hot today.'

The ice-cold drink went a long way to reviving Nell as they wound their way home. She sent brief texts to update Kate,

Sophie, Winnie and Anthea to follow on from her earlier, less reassuring calls and then sat back in her seat, sighing with relief. 'I think Beryl's going to be okay,' she said. 'Low blood pressure and a sprained ankle. She's just got to take the tablets and practise moderation in all things.'

'As if.' Barney looked across at Nell and they both started to laugh.

40

Sunday morning saw Barney awake before the birds. He'd had a restless night, and finally gave up on sleep at half past three. The image of Beryl lying bleeding on her kitchen floor still burned in his mind and brought back bad memories. Frank had only ever called him out once in that kind of situation, towards the end when Lottie had slipped in the bathroom and got herself wedged between the sink and the bath. That had been a long night. Confusion had set in, and Lottie was convinced Barney was trying to strangle her, for some reason. She fought back fiercely as he and Frank tried to get her on her feet. They'd managed it eventually but not without tears on all sides.

Slipping on his towelling robe, Barney made his way downstairs barefoot as silently as possible, brewed a pot of tea and took a mug of it outside. He sat down on the bench under the oak tree and tried to relax. The morning was already warm even at this early hour and gradually, one by one, the resident songbirds in the garden began their daily warm-up for the dawn chorus. The sound was magical. Barney closed his eyes to appreciate it better, sipping his tea and wriggling his toes in the grass.

Gradually, a much warmer memory took the place of the distressing ones, and he opened his mind to it willingly.

He was standing at the front of a church racked with nerves – not the one in the village with Bev presiding over the service but a smaller, less ornamented building. It was the Methodist chapel near Nell's childhood home in Sheffield. The pews were full of people dressed in their best and there was tense excitement in the air as the organist paused in his gentle medley of popular hymns and then launched into a stirring rendition of the Bridal March. The congregation got to their feet and turned to face the rear of the chapel. Coming towards him, walking slowly up the aisle, was Nell on the arm of his father, who was beaming down at her proudly. Nell was wearing an uncharacteristically floaty dress decorated with many sequins. The flimsy fabric wafted around her in a sparkling cloud as she made her way towards him. As the two of them reached Barney and his best man, they stopped and Frank, in a move that hadn't been included in the wedding rehearsal, bent to hug Nell, almost dislodging her veil in the process. 'Oops,' he said loudly, treading on her train as he turned to go to his seat.

Nell giggled and set her headdress straight before turning to Barney. 'Going well so far,' she whispered, and he remembered the wave of pure joy he'd felt looking down at her, so beautiful in the dress that somehow managed to cling to her figure and still flow around her.

After that, Barney's memories became muddled. A lovely service, hymns chosen so that everyone knew them and could sing with gusto, which they did. 'Love Divine, All Loves Excelling'. The words and music of that one could still make Barney's eyes fill with happy tears. And then the invitation to kiss his bride. Maybe he'd accepted the offer a bit too enthusias-tically, because that was when Nell's veil lost the plot completely and slid to the floor. But there was nothing of the Bridezilla about Barney's new wife. She'd merely laughed, gathered up the gauzy folds of net and passed the whole lot to her waiting chief bridesmaid who'd rolled her eyes at Barney and muttered that she wished he'd give her boyfriend a few tips.

As he reminisced, Barney heard the sound of his father's footsteps. There was no accompanying clunk of the walking stick, and Barney realised that on some occasions lately Frank had been moving around much more easily. He opened his eyes.

'You're sounding very sprightly these days, Dad,' he said. 'Is it the new tablets you're trying or has Willowbrook put a spring in your step?'

'Never mind that, have you heard how Beryl is today?' Frank said, sitting down beside his son on the bench and half-turning to glare at him. 'I've barely slept, you know. That poor woman, stranded on the cold floor for hours...'

'I think she'd only been there for a few minutes, to be fair,' said Barney soothingly. 'And nowhere's cold at the moment. It's already warm out here and it's only...' He squinted at his watch. '...only six o'clock.'

'Yes, yes, that's as may be, but do you know how she is?'

Barney sighed and abandoned the last vestiges of the blissful daydream. 'It's much too early to ring the ward yet but we'd have heard if there was any problem. Nell left the staff her phone number because Beryl's niece is on holiday. I'll take you to visit her later if they give us the okay. Although you'd better get in the queue, Winnie and Anthea are bound to want to be first in line.'

'Harrumph.'

This multi-purpose sound was one of Frank's trademarks, used when he was cross, disgusted, confused or even, on occasion, sad. Barney reached out and patted his father's arm. 'Try not to worry. We'll get more updates later, I'm sure. In the meantime, what do you say to scrambled eggs on toast, some strong coffee and a visit to church?'

Frank peered at his son dubiously. 'I like the sound of the first two suggestions, but church? What's all that about? You don't do religion as a rule.'

Barney thought about this. It had been a spontaneous idea, no doubt brought on by the happy recollections of his wedding day and the fact that he'd enjoyed their previous visit, but it wasn't a bad idea. It would be good to be peaceful and to have some time to think, and a service might keep Frank from brooding about Beryl's welfare for a while.

'I just think it'd be... nice,' he said lamely.

'Nice? Organised religion isn't usually described as nice, Barney. Thought-provoking, controversial, stimulating, annoying... but not *nice*.'

Barney stood up and tied the belt of his robe tighter. 'Well, I'm going to the morning service anyway,' he said. 'Come along too, if you'd like. Let's eat, I've been awake for hours.'

Muttering, Frank followed his son into the kitchen. There was no sound from Nell's bedroom and Barney didn't want to wake her if she'd finally managed to get some decent sleep, so the two of them ate the creamy, buttery scrambled eggs that were on the shortlist of Barney's signature dishes and then went their separate ways to shower. Barney had taken Nell a mug of tea as usual, but she declined his invitation to come with him, saying she wanted to stay at home in case the hospital rang. Barney strongly suspected she also wanted to do some writing while he and Frank were out of the way, which was all to the good.

'I'll put my phone on silent but you can message me anytime,' Barney said, bending to kiss the top of Nell's sleep-rumpled head. At the last minute she turned her face up to his and their lips met. Nell's arms seemed to wrap themselves around Barney's neck of their own accord and he was just about to throw himself into the action completely, his mind still full of the picture of his new wife in her stunning wedding dress, when his father's voice broke into the tingling moment.

'Oi! Barney! Are you coming to church, or what?' Frank bellowed, startling a couple of pigeons who were having their own special moment on the shed roof.

Nell laughed as Barney pulled away. 'Maybe later?' she said.

'I'll hold you to that.'

Barney rubbed his hands over his face and tried to get his thoughts back onto a less steamy level as he went to meet Frank, who was pacing up and down outside the kitchen door.

'Come on, I hate being late,' he said, setting off at a faster pace than usual.

Barney followed, relieved that his dad was slowing down as they reached the centre of the village. The last thing he needed was another collapsed OAP to resuscitate. They entered the church and the atmosphere inside immediately calmed them both. The organist was playing a very similar kind of medley to the one Barney remembered from his pre-wedding jitters and as they looked around for a seat, Barney realised the church was unusually busy. He and Frank settled themselves near the back and waited for the procession of clergy and outriders to emerge from the vestry and do their circuit of the building, complete with staffs, candles and snowy-white robes.

Bev was looking reasonably perky this morning, Barney thought, as the congregation got to its feet with much shuffling and a few coughs. She sailed up the aisle with her attendants and took her place in the pulpit as everyone raised their voices to sing the opening hymn, which was clearly one that Frank knew because he raised his voice enthusiastically.

'I'll have that at my funeral. Make a note of it, lad,' he said as the last notes died away. '"How Great Thou Art", it's called. I'd have liked it at Lottie's do, but my mind went blank when the funeral chaps asked me about music, and you were no help at all.'

Barney was about to reply forcefully to this jibe when he noticed several people in the rows in front turning round and one particularly ferocious female saying *shhhh* very pointedly. He held his fire but resolved to have words about the accusation later.

Light dawned when Bev began her welcome speech. There was to be a christening this morning, which explained the higher number of attendees, some of whom were behaving as if they'd never been inside a church before. The christening party were all seated at the front, with the more regular congregation spaced out around Barney and Frank. One of the visitors had already sloped off down the aisle, reaching for his vape and mouthing apologies with his phone pressed to his ear. Bev was trying hard to rise above the low-level chatting emanating from the front pews.

The service wore on and the parents and godparents moved to the back of the church to assemble around the ancient stone font. The baby being baptised was very smiley, round and rosy cheeked. She was squeezed into a shiny, befrilled christening robe. The rest of the congregation either gathered around the main party or stood up in their places and turned to face the font. Barney and Frank looked at each other and joined those on their feet.

The baby, who it turned out was going to start life with the grand name of Pandora Melissa Belinda Wildsmith, was passed to Bev, and this was the moment when things could have gone horribly wrong. As Bev took the little girl in her arms, Pandora wriggled and squirmed so hard that the slippery fabric of the white robe caused her to slither downwards so fast that it was only the quick reflexes of another member of the congregation that saved the day. A man leaped forward and caught the baby just as she was about to hit the stone floor. A loud gasp rang out and the watchers surged towards the infant who was now being held aloft in strong hands.

'That bloody Rick, he gets everywhere,' muttered Barney, glaring at the hero of the day who was passing the baby carefully back to Bev and being slapped on the back by all and sundry. Bev was now bright red in the face and apologising profusely, but Barney couldn't see how the problem could have been avoided unless the offending gown had been fitted with grip handles. He could still remember the nightmare of the twins' baptism service. They'd both been hard enough for the vicar to handle even dressed in sensible woolly outfits. The hubbub gave Frank the chance to speak again.

'Good job he *is* everywhere, under the circumstances,' said his dad, grinning. 'Imagine the damage if that poor kid had made it to the floor. Rick did a fine job there. You know, you've got absolutely no need to be jealous of that bloke, son. Your wife might have looked him up and down a bit for a while but there was never anything going on. I'd have noticed.'

'I'm not jealous!' The outrage in Barney's voice made Frank smile even more.

'Of course you're not. But... let's just say, if you were, there'd be no need, right?'

The christening service was now underway again and progressed with no more hiccups. Barney's desire to come into the church for quiet contemplation had definitely gone by the board and he felt distinctly ruffled by the thought of his father watching Nell watching Rick. It was tacky. But as the next hymn rolled out and the congregation's singing drowned even the twittering of the baptism party, an unexpected sense of peace stole over Barney. He was here in a church with Frank, an event that never usually happened. They were doing something together, and it felt good.

He wondered what else he could suggest for them to try. Maybe Frank would like to go to a big cricket match with him in the local town. Frank had already wandered down to the green a couple of times to watch the locals playing and had wanted Barney to go with him but planning the walks at the country park had tempted him away. It was time Barney spent more time thinking about what Frank needed... and also Nell. Shame flooded over him as he realised how fixated he'd become with organising his own new life in Willowbrook. What about Nell and her dreams of being a published author? And when was she ever going to get back to enjoying playing the piano again if he never gave her any encouragement?

By the time everyone was filing out of the church, Barney had formulated two plans. He told Frank to go ahead without him and saw his father make a beeline for Rick, who was chatting to some other villagers in the churchyard. When the pews were all empty, he approached the man who was just finishing playing a rousing march on the organ. He waited for silence and then clapped enthusiastically. The man turned on his wooden bench and smiled. He was small and dapper, wearing a linen suit that had seen better days but looked comfortable and stylish in an old-school way.

'Why, thank you,' he said, holding out a hand for Barney to shake. 'Everybody's usually made a dash for the sunshine or to the pub before I get to this bit. I don't think we've met before. I'm Winston Clarke. And you are?'

'Barney Appledore. We moved here fairly recently... my wife

Nell, my father Frank and me, that is... we live in Hollyhocks Cottage on...'

'Tinderbox Lane. Yes, I know the place well. The previous owner was a friend of mine. I do miss the old chap. And are you settling in well?'

'Yes, we are, we love the village, but I realised as I was listening to you making such great music earlier that I still haven't made enquiries about getting someone to tune our ancient piano. I don't think it liked the move much. It would be great if you knew a local person who might do the job? I'd love it if Nell could get back to playing again.'

Winston thought for a moment and then he nodded. 'I'll do it for you, if you like. I've not taken on any tuning for a while because my mother was very ill and needed me to be at home most of the time, but now...'

His voice faded away and he pulled out a blue-checked handkerchief and blew his nose noisily. 'Anyway, now I've got more time on my hands, so I'd be happy to come along and sort the piano out for you, providing it's not too much of an antique to fix. It would be good to see what you've done to Edwin's place too.'

Barney was delighted. He fixed a time for Winston to come round and turned just in time to see Bev emerging from the vestry. She looked harried, and for a moment he hesitated, not wanting to burden her with any more issues, but if he didn't seize the moment there was no saying when he'd catch her alone again.

'Hang on, Bev,' he called, gesturing to Winston that he had to run. 'Have you got a minute?'

Bev stopped in her tracks and turned to face him. She looked unutterably weary, and Barney's heart went out to her. 'Is everything okay?' she asked. 'You haven't heard anything new about Beryl, have you?'

Barney reassured her that there was no bad news to impart. 'I just wanted a quick word. I won't keep you long, I guess you're busy,' he said.

'I've got to go and show my face at the christening do, even if it's only for half an hour,' she said. 'It's going to be at the pub, and it'll go on for hours, but I'm popping into the hospital to check how Beryl's doing straight afterwards so that's my get-out excuse. I'm postponing tomorrow's happiness meeting in the hope that she'll be out and well enough to be there next week. It doesn't seem right to get the gang together without Beryl. What did you want me for?'

Barney tried to make the idea that had just come to him as brief as possible. 'I don't know if she's told you, but Nell's writing a book,' he said. 'It's not going very quickly because I think she gets distracted when she's working at home. I wondered if there was any chance that she could come and write at the vicarage. I'm sure she wouldn't get in your way.'

Bev looked relieved, and Barney wondered what she'd thought he was going to say. This was obviously a better option, whatever her imagination had conjured up.

'Of course she can. Does Nell know you've asked me?'

'No, I've only just thought of it.'

'I'll ring her when I get back from the hospital to update her about Beryl and suggest it at the same time. Now I've really got to run, Barney. It's lovely that you're thinking of Nell. It must be great to have a person looking out for you like that.'

Before Barney could think of a suitable answer, Bev had left him and was almost sprinting down the aisle. Barney followed her more slowly. It was all well and good having these ideas to improve Nell's day-to-day life, but he was well aware that there was one more thing he needed to do before his wife would be truly happy. It was time to square up to the elephant in the room.

Barney turned to face the altar, in the quietness that had descended now Bev and Winston had both left the church. He moved forward to stand in front of the ornate table. The candles were now extinguished but the evocative scent of melted wax and incense still hung in the air. As a little boy, Barney's mother had taught him a simple prayer to say at bedtime, but he'd thought it had been lost in the mists of childhood memories. Now a few words from it came back to him, and he said it aloud.

'God is our refuge and our strength.'

In the deep quietness of the beautiful old building, Barney willed himself not to feel ridiculous. He couldn't see why any prayer of his should be answered after ignoring the deity for so many years. It seemed rude to even be saying these words. But strength was what Barney needed right now and also a refuge from his unhappy thoughts of Josh. He heard the distant sound of Frank's voice from the churchyard calling his name. It was time to go. What happened next with Nell was up to him. The future of their marriage was entirely in his hands.

41

Nell wasn't surprised to get a call from Bev later that day because she knew the vicar was planning to visit Beryl and would want to give her a proper update as soon as possible. Once this had been covered, with the report that Beryl was doing very well and would be home the next day but that this week's meeting would be postponed until the following Monday to give her time to recover, Bev hesitated.

'Is that all? Are you sure you're telling me everything?' Nell asked, suddenly apprehensive.

'Oh yes, at least, there's nothing else to do with Beryl. It's just that I was talking to Barney when he and Frank came to church earlier and he suggested an idea.'

Nell listened, astonished, as Bev outlined a plan that Nell should have a back door key to the vicarage, free use of the kitchen and anywhere else but especially the best spare bedroom which had an enormous old desk situated right under the window. It had recently been inherited from Bev's uncle, but she already had her grandfather's desk in her study and was very fond of it.

'Barney thinks you need a place to get this book written where there are no distractions,' Bev finished. 'I promise I won't keep popping in to talk to you. What do you think?'

'I... I'm... I don't know what to say,' Nell stammered. 'He planned this without telling me. Is that sweet, or a bit controlling?'

'Nell, it's obvious to me that your man adores you,' said Bev firmly. 'He wants to help. Just say thank you and be grateful you're with someone thoughtful who really cares.'

That's told me, thought Nell, ashamed of her churlishness. 'Sorry, Bev,' she said quickly. 'Of course I'm chuffed to bits at the idea. Can we start tomorrow? I'll come round whenever you're free.'

They arranged a time the next morning and Bev rang off, still with a touch of frost in her voice. Nell decided to buy her some flowers and a bottle of wine before she called for the key. She was mortified that she'd offended her friend, but it had been such a random idea to begin with, and completely out of the blue. Now, she could see the benefits. Barney could have the study all to himself and make as many noisy Zoom calls as necessary, and she could have blissful peace and quiet, only a short walk away. It was the perfect solution.

Nell had intended to talk to Barney about his plans for her writing, but before she had the chance to go and find him there was a knock at the back door and she heard her husband greeting someone whose voice wasn't familiar. Sunday evening wasn't the usual time for a caller, but Barney sounded delighted to see whoever it was so Nell went to find out who the visitor could be. In the living room, a dapper older gentleman stood, clutching a large case which he was in the process of opening.

'Nell, I don't think you've met Winston Clarke, the church organist. He's very kindly offered to tune our piano for us,' said

Barney. His eyes met hers, eyebrows slightly raised as if to say *wasn't expecting this* as the man busied himself getting out the tools of his trade before straightening up to shake Nell by the hand.

'I'm sorry to drop in on you like this with no warning, but I didn't want to make you wait ages for me to do the job. Immediately after I saw this young man in church, I had a telephone call from my sister in Cornwall asking me to go and house-sit for her. She's having to go away quite unexpectedly tomorrow evening, and it seems as if the situation might take a while to sort out. A family crisis. I won't bore you with the details, but Irene has three rather demanding poodles that need caring for. I couldn't say no, so here I am. I hope it's not too inconvenient.'

By this time Winston was all ready to start work so Nell sent Barney to make him the green tea he'd chosen and cleared all the detritus off the top of the piano. 'I haven't played it properly since we landed here,' she said. 'It sounds pretty awful, but Barney's very kindly volunteered my services to accompany the Christmas singing at the pub this year, so I need to get my act together and practise.'

Winston was humming to himself as he began his task and Nell could tell he wanted her out of the way, so she went into the kitchen to finish off the clearing up after their large Sunday lunch, which Frank insisted on eating at one o'clock, as had always been his custom. Barney had delivered a mug of tea to Winston and was already up in the study finishing off some work, having loaded the dishwasher to his satisfaction. She found her father-in-law sitting at the kitchen table wading through the Sunday papers.

'Are you two speaking now?' he whispered, so loudly that if Barney wasn't safely out of the way upstairs he'd have bound to have heard.

'I guess so,' Nell said. 'He's organised for me to have a writing space at the vicarage for some peace and quiet.'

'He told me on the way back from church. I was worried it was me that was disturbing you. I didn't mean to get under your feet when we all moved in together.'

'Oh, Frank, you'd never stop me writing,' Nell said, her heart going out to him. He looked so dejected sitting there. 'I'm just really good at procrastinating. It makes me happy having you with us. I love you being here.'

Frank beamed at her. 'Well, if you're sure. And talking of happiness, I gather we're putting off tomorrow's group session so Beryl can hopefully join us next week. What should we all be doing to get her house ready for her coming home? Is it going to be soon, do you think?'

Nell bit her lip as strange twangs and plink plonk sounds emanated from the living room. She'd been so busy thinking about her own affairs that she hadn't given a thought to the practicalities of Beryl's return. 'I'll go and give Kate a ring now to see if we can all sort something together,' she said.

Frank seemed to catch the rather dubious expression on Nell's face when she mentioned Kate's name. 'I hope you're not being silly about that nice lady. I've been in the café when my lad's been there, and I reckon he enjoys being needed, as we all do. She's a lovely person, mind. But just remember, love, no marriage is completely safe.'

'Really?' Nell stared at Frank. 'Are you saying you and Lottie... I mean...?'

He smiled. 'We're all human, Nellie. For a while, Lottie was convinced I was making sheep's eyes at her sister Avril, even though she was quite a bit older than us and determinedly single. She was probably gay, now I come to think of it, but in denial. Then later I had my suspicions about a young neighbour called Oliver who used to pop round to the house when I was at work and help Lottie in the garden.'

'But... but there was never anything in it, was there?' Nell was still gazing at Frank, surprised beyond measure and somewhat ruffled. Surely not. Her in-laws had been well-known for their long and blissful marriage. She waited. Frank still hadn't answered. He shrugged his shoulders.

'Not on my part with Avril, as I said, but I'm afraid to say there was something in the other suspicions. It was a kind of Lady Chatterley and Mellors thing, I think. I found them in the potting shed when I came home early one day. That gamekeeper's name was Oliver too, funnily enough.'

Nell's voice came out as a croak. 'What did you do?' How had she never known this? But why would she? It wasn't the sort of topic you discussed over tea and scones with your mum-in-law.

'I did what any self-respecting chap would do and punched him on the nose. Then I grabbed him by the scruff of the neck and threw him out. He never came back. The garden never looked as good after that,' Frank said regretfully. 'Oh, it was only kissing. It might not have been just that if I hadn't interrupted them though. Lottie had her head turned by all those rippling muscles on show. Temptation can strike at any time, can't it?'

Nell blushed scarlet as Frank gave her a beady look. 'So how did you get past it and move on?' she asked. 'Weren't you eaten up with jealousy?'

'I must admit I was, for a while at least,' he said. 'I wanted to make her feel as guilty as possible. But then I reasoned that she wouldn't have been tempted to stray if we'd have been completely fine. I upped the ante, as they say. Booked a holiday, took Lottie out for a couple of slap-up meals and generally started to help more around the house. Oh, I'm not saying it was easy, but I loved her so much, Nell. She was a splendid woman. We got over it.'

Nell reached for the kitchen towel and tore off a couple of sheets, passing them to Frank. He was soon in control of his emotions again.

'So, the reason I told you this was obviously a kind of gypsy's warning,' he said. 'Don't let anything come between you two. All things pass and you've got a great relationship.'

'Have we?'

'Of course you have, don't be silly. Now, moving on. Let's sort out a right royal welcome for Beryl when she comes home. That's another splendid woman. She'll no doubt say she doesn't need any help. We'll ignore her, of course.'

Nell nodded and headed off to find her phone to ring Kate. There was a whole lot to think about here, but for now, Beryl must come first. She deserved the very best welcome home.

42

The next week whizzed by. Try as she might, Nell was finding it hard to pin Barney down to have a proper chat. There was so much happening one way or another. He'd been asked by Kate to run a series of walks in the forthcoming school holidays, which would need a lot of preparation. Also, Beryl was turning out to need a lot more help than the old lady had expected or wanted. Between the group and other friends, a rota had been created to make sure she had plenty of home-cooked food to eat, and Maryam and Rashid had organised deliveries of milk, bread and other useful items. Keeping Beryl company was also important because she wasn't used to being housebound and was finding it immensely frustrating.

'I just want to get on with my life,' she complained, as Nell sorted out the several vases of flowers that were fading at varying rates. 'I need to be properly fit for my next holiday with the girls. We've booked a coach trip to the Yorkshire Dales for September. It's Saturday already and I bet you lot will try and say I'm not going to be able to come to the group on Monday. Spoilsports, all of you.'

Nell had already talked to Bev about this, when she'd tracked her down to the vicarage garden after a particularly long writing stint the day before.

'Beryl's going to be better staying put at her house, at least until she's had her check-up,' Bev said. 'It's a shame, but we can always postpone for another week.'

'Or we could take the group to her?' Nell had been pondering the problem and had checked out Beryl's garden the day before to see if there was room. 'The weather's set to stay fine and we can ask Rick to collect all the garden chairs and some tables and parasols in his van. How about it?'

Bev didn't seem enthusiastic, and Nell realised that the vicar was looking totally exhausted. 'Are you okay?' she asked. 'If you're busy, I don't mind organising it all. Maryam and Kate and Ingrid will help. Have you seen Rick lately? I haven't noticed him around the village since he fetched Beryl home.'

'I... erm... no, he's not been here,' said Bev. 'You could ring him though. Do you mind getting things moving if Beryl's agreeable?'

Now, with Beryl waiting for an answer, Nell outlined the plan. It had all been surprisingly easy to organise. Everyone was willing to help. 'So you wouldn't need to leave your house. We'd all come to you on Monday, and it'll be just like that old Cliff Richard film. Was it *Summer Holiday*? When someone said, "Let's do the show right here?"'

Beryl clapped her hands together, eyes sparkling. 'Oh, you treasure. You'd do all that for me?'

'For sure we will. We can't have a meeting without our star performer. So, it's a yes?'

'It's a great big *yes*. Thank you so much, Nell. Come here and give me a hug.'

They embraced warmly. Nell was wrapped in Beryl's strong

arms and picked up the delicate scent of her perfume. She recognised it as one of Lottie's favourites. 'L'air du Temps'. It would always remind her of her gentle mother-in-law, but her retrospective view of Lottie had shifted since Frank's revelations. Their marriage had survived upheavals. That was what she wanted for herself. She was strongly tempted to spill all her marital preoccupations out to Beryl, but in the instant before she formulated where to begin, she heard the 'Yoo hoo' of Winnie and Anthea's arrival and the moment passed.

The next morning, Barney went to church alone because Nell was giving Beryl's house a once-over before the visitors landed. He came back looking worried.

'Bev wasn't doing the service today,' he told Nell. 'There was another vicar there instead. Someone said he was an intern, whatever that means. I waited till everyone had gone and asked him where Bev was, but he seemed very vague about it. He just said she'd been called away. Have you heard anything?'

Nell checked her phone but there were no texts and when she rang Bev's number there was just a recorded message. She left a voicemail and put the phone down. 'I wonder what's happened,' she said. 'We've got the group at Beryl's tomorrow night, and Bev's the one with all the notes for it. It's the final session. I'd better get in touch with Maryam and make a contingency plan if Bev doesn't reply soon.'

By seven o'clock neither Nell nor Maryam had been able to contact Bev, so Nell left Barney to have a game of cards with Frank and hurried up the lane and along Fiddler's Row to the shop. Rashid greeted her with a wave and pointed to the stairs as he served a customer, so Nell made her way up to the flat, still mulling over what could have happened to Bev.

Maryam made coffee and soothing noises as Nell explained how worried she was. 'Bev's not been herself for the last week.

I've been round there most mornings to do some writing, and she's seemed kind of withdrawn. Preoccupied. Where do you think she's gone?'

'I don't know, but we'll have to make a quick plan B. All we need to do is recap on the sessions, get feedback from the group and then have a drink and some nibbles,' said Maryam. 'Why don't I run through each week's themes to begin with, as a reminder for everyone and then you... I don't know... sort of summarise? Get people to say what they've learned about what makes them feel contented and what happiness really is? Bev wanted us to talk about precious memories that make us happy when we think of them, didn't she? We need to finish on a positive note. How does that sound?'

'I guess we can do it between us. If Bev does turn up at the last minute, we can hand over to her, and if she doesn't... well, she can always do another final session later if she wants to. I can't help thinking this has got something to do with her digging up all that stuff about her ex-husband. It's stirred up bad memories. Rick's been keeping out of her way too this week. What's all that about?'

'No idea, but let's get some bullet points down and just hope for the best, okay?'

Maryam got out her notebook and they sat at the table. The Habeeb boys could be heard playing a very noisy computer game in their bedroom and Rashid was singing along to the radio down in the shop. It all felt very cosy and friendly. Nell began to relax. Wherever Bev was, she'd be bound to be in touch soon. Vicars didn't just disappear. She might have left to see her family like the last time she'd gone away suddenly. In any case, that was Bev's business. It was up to Nell and Maryam to hold the fort and make sure their new friends weren't left high and dry. The series of meetings was about to come to a close. Nell was determined not to let anyone down.

'Which memory will you talk about, Nell?' said Maryam, as she began to organise their ideas for the meeting. 'I'm going to tell them about Uma being born. We didn't know if we were having a girl or a boy, but secretly I was longing for a daughter. Of course, I would have loved a boy just as much,' she added hastily. 'And I did, when they both came along. But looking down at her little face, I felt complete. Then she screamed for what seemed like the next month and I couldn't manage to feed her myself, so we swapped to formula and got on with it. That early part was tough on the whole but the first few moments were magical.'

Nell pondered. 'I think my wedding day stands out more than most memories as a happy one,' she said. 'Elliot was a month premature and was quite small, so it was an anxious few weeks after he was born and by the time the twins arrived less than two years later, I was totally mind-boggled.'

Maryam nodded. 'But Bev hasn't done the parent thing, and she can't have many, if any happy memories of her marriage. I wonder what she'll say. That is if she turns up at all.'

Nell wondered the same thing. It was a depressing thought. Suddenly, she wanted nothing more than being safely back at the cottage with Barney and Frank. 'Let's get all this sorted as fast as we can,' she said. 'I need to go home.'

43

The final meeting didn't go to plan in any way, shape or form. For one thing, Bev still hadn't returned, and neither was there any sign of Rick, so Barney offered to come along to Beryl's to help Frank to set up the chairs and tables. Nell was very glad to have him there, because all the others were unfashionably early. By the time the last guests, Maurice and Harry, arrived by taxi, Beryl had already thrown moderation to the wind and was getting stuck into the first bottle of prosecco.

'Do we need to substitute something non-alcoholic for her?' Ingrid whispered to Nell as they filled more champagne flutes. 'There's some of that Nosecco in the fridge. Would she notice?'

'Don't even think about it,' said Anthea, who had overheard the question as she was tipping twiglets into a bowl. 'Beryl never drinks the stuff. I'll keep topping her up with water every now and again, but she needs something to soak up the booze now. Have we got anything more substantial than crisps? And is your Barney staying for the meeting? I hope he is. What a handsome chap.'

Nell watched Anthea bustle away and thought about what

she'd said. She looked across at her husband, who was currently easing Beryl into a garden chair and simultaneously removing the plastic champagne flute from her hand. He did look particularly enticing tonight, in a white T-shirt and cargo shorts with his curls all ruffled and the small dimple in his left cheek on show as he laughed with Beryl. Surely his arms were more muscular than they used to be, and his long legs were brown and strong. *I wonder what I'd think of Barney if I met him for the first time today,* Nell wondered. She saw how well he interacted with this random group of villagers, making sure everyone was comfortable and had a drink in hand, and her heart swelled with pride.

'Are you staying for the main event, lad?' she heard Maurice ask Barney. Her husband looked across at her for guidance, raising his eyebrows.

'Am I?' he asked. 'I don't want to butt in.'

'Don't be silly,' Anthea said, giving Barney one of her best femme fatale smiles. 'You'll always be welcome with us, won't he, folks?'

The others all made noises of agreement, and Anthea passed Barney a brimming glass of prosecco.

'Where's Rick?' asked Beryl suddenly. 'I've just noticed he's not here yet. Is he running late?'

'No idea,' said Nell. 'I haven't heard from him. I was kind of expecting him to just appear at the last minute. Has anyone else had a message?'

No one had, it seemed, so Maryam declared the meeting open. As everyone settled themselves, Barney worked his way around to where Nell was standing. 'Is this okay?' he said. 'Do you mind if I hang around? You'll need me to help with the clearing up anyway, so...'

Nell looked up at him, surprised to see how unsure of

himself he looked. A moment ago, Barney had been full of confidence as he organised the small area to fit everyone in.

'Yes, please stay,' she said, giving him an impulsive hug. 'I don't just want you here for your muscles, you know. It's nice when we do things together.'

Barney kissed Nell quickly on the cheek and then pulled up a chair for her before going over to sit in the only vacant space, which fortunately was next to Beryl, giving him the chance to pass her a glass of water. She looked at it rather dubiously but took a sip, pulling a face.

'Waste of time, this drinking a load of water lark,' she said. 'It only makes you wee more.'

'You're flushing out your system. It's good for us oldies,' said Harry. 'Also, have you discovered the benefits of bran? Penelope swears by it on our porridge. It helps to—'

'Right, well, let's make a start and hope that Bev and Rick join us at some point,' said Maryam, reaching for the clipboard that contained her fresh sheet of notes. 'I'm just going to give us all a quick recap of the meetings we've had already to remind us of how far we've come, because to be honest, it feels like a long time since the first one.'

There were murmurs of agreement as Maryam cleared her throat and began speaking. She wasted no words but ran through their previous topics clearly and with a brief comment on each one. It made an impressive list. *We did it, we actually did it*, Nell thought, beaming at Maryam.

'Now it's over to you,' Maryam said eventually. 'Bev initially wanted us to use this meeting to share precious memories of times when we've been particularly happy, but Nell and I aren't sure if that's the best way to wind up these sessions. What do you all think? Do you want to talk about past times or focus on the present and the future?'

Nobody spoke for a few moments, and then Ingrid raised a hand. 'Can I make a suggestion?' she asked. 'I've loved these meetings, and I guess they've stirred up a lot of memories for us all, but why don't we use this last one to talk about what we've each found out about happiness?'

Nell glanced around the circle and found that everyone was looking towards her for a decision. 'That sounds good to me. What do you say, Maryam? I'm sure Bev won't mind.'

'No, she absolutely won't.'

Bev's voice startled them as she emerged from the back door. She grinned at them all.

'I'm so sorry, you all look as if you've seen a ghost. I didn't think I'd be able to join you tonight, but I made better time than I expected. I had a few things to sort back at the place where I used to live. Thanks.' This last remark was directed at Barney who had jumped to his feet and offered Bev his chair, but Nell had the feeling she was thanking him for more than just finding her somewhere to sit. Barney settled himself cross-legged on the grass in front of Nell and she couldn't resist reaching out to touch his shoulder.

'Carry on,' Bev said. 'You're doing a great job between you. I've been on courses that tell you to work on enabling people to do their own thing, but you lot have done it all on your own. Go for it.'

Nell smiled at Bev, relieved that she wasn't offended at their unavoidable take-over manoeuvre. 'Okay, maybe you can start, Ingrid, as it was your suggestion to change tack?' she said.

Ingrid bit her lip and then nodded. 'Right. Well, I've learned to value my own space even more than I did before. My privacy and peace make me happy and being with all of you has been fun too.'

Nell was about to suggest that Maryam went next to keep the

ball rolling and give the group time to reflect on what information they wanted to share but it was soon clear that everyone had plenty to say. One by one, they voiced their opinions. Winnie talked about the joy of making new memories through adventures with friends, Harry's love of his wife and family got a glowing mention, Kate said how much she was appreciating being able to be part of the Willowbrook community through the café and the group, and Maryam echoed Kate's views, adding how much she was enjoying running the shop with Rashid.

Bev's eyes shone as she listened to all this and Nell smiled at her. 'Has it all turned out as you hoped it would? The quest for happiness, I mean?' Nell said.

'It's been everything I was aiming for and more,' said Bev. 'I don't mind telling you all something that I wasn't expecting to be saying at this point, but some of you might have already guessed anyway. I've come to realise that although I wanted to help other people to discover the secret of being contented, I needed to find that out for myself just as much.'

'And have you, darling?' said Anthea.

'I'm well on the way to it now, I think. It's a work in progress but thanks to the Happiness Gang, I'm on the right track. Anyway, this isn't all about me. Carry on, folks.'

Anthea and Beryl's turns came next and they both said that they were looking forward to having platonic friendships with men even though they'd been married in the past. Frank looked immensely gratified when Beryl made it obvious that he was her chosen friend and said that like the others, living in Willowbrook was giving him new hope for the future. Maurice, however, seemed a little nervous when Anthea made him the focus of her comment.

'All this talking has made me take stock of my life,' he said. 'It's made me realise I've still got choices.'

'Good luck with that one,' muttered Barney, so quietly that only Nell heard him. She spluttered with laughter and then stopped when she realised everyone was waiting for her to take a turn.

'Oh... erm... well...' Nell took a deep breath. 'I guess like all of you, I've done a lot of thinking over the last few weeks. Barney and Frank and I made a big life change coming here and it's been good for us all in different ways, but what I've learned is that we can't sit back and take relationships for granted. To be happy, or better still be long-term contented with our lot, we have to work to let the important people in our lives know how we feel about them. Not just now and again, but as a matter of course.'

'Bravo,' cried Harry, and led a spontaneous burst of applause. Barney leant back against Nell's legs. He didn't say anything, but she could feel his warmth. She put a hand on his shoulder and felt the strength of him, both mental and physical. Tonight, she'd tackle the last of the barriers between them, she resolved. It was time.

Bev was the only one left to have her say. She stood up. 'Rick has asked me to give his apologies for tonight,' she said. 'He's had to go to Munich to be with his family because his ex-wife's new partner has left her. He felt as if he should support her and the boys.'

Silence greeted this announcement, then Beryl jumped in with her usual lack of tact, saying what most of the others were probably thinking. 'So how will that affect you, love?' she asked Bev. 'I thought you and Rick were getting to be something of an item?'

Bev exchanged glances with Nell and rolled her eyes. 'The trouble with you lot is that you add two and two together and make five, as my gran always used to say,' she said. 'Rick and I are just friends. I'm not up for a relationship. Not now, maybe never. So, to add to your thoughts about happiness, I've come to realise that being in exactly the right place at last is what floats my boat. And for me, that's enough.'

It was getting late, and the midges were starting to make their presence felt even though Maryam had previously lit some of her special garden candles that promised to deter all biting bugs. 'Let's call it a day,' said Bev. 'And if anyone wants to discuss carrying on our meet-ups now and again, perhaps on a less formal basis, you've all got my email address, please feel free to drop me a line.'

'It'd be a shame to lose touch,' said Harry tentatively. 'I've loved being with you all. It's meant such a lot to me.'

There was a chorus of agreement as Barney began to tidy up the chairs and tables, helped and sometimes hindered by the others. Eventually all was tidy, Beryl was safely inside with Bev, Anthea and Winnie, protesting all the way that there was still prosecco in one of the bottles, and Maurice, Ingrid and Harry decided to share a taxi.

Kate, satisfied there was nothing else for her to do, departed for her house next door and Maryam and Frank walked through the village arm in arm, closely followed by Nell and Barney. When they reached the turning for Tinderbox Lane, Maryam kissed the other three on both cheeks and set off home while Frank made tracks for his own rooms as soon as they reached the cottage. That left Nell and Barney facing each other across the kitchen table.

'Glass of wine in bed?' Barney suggested, when the silence became uncomfortable. 'Shall I open a bottle?'

Nell turned to head upstairs. 'Yes, but on one condition,' she said. 'You need to talk to me. Really talk, Barney. No holds barred, okay?'

It was more than an hour later when Barney finally got to the end of his outpouring of grief, guilt and regret, and both he and Nell were exhausted. He lay back on the pillows and heaved a huge sigh. 'So, after all that sadness and the cancer and everything, do you think we've got a chance of being happy now?' he said, turning to face her. 'Really, steadily, happy together?'

'We both want it to happen more than anything in the world,' said Nell. 'And so between us we'll make sure it does. But is there any way you can go a step further towards remembering your brother without feeling guilty?'

'How do you mean? I won't forget Josh. I couldn't.'

Nell wasn't sure what she was trying to say. She just had a strong feeling that something else was needed so that Barney could move on with his life. While she was pondering this problem, he jumped to his feet and grabbed both Nell's hands in his.

'I've got it! Why don't I commission a beautiful bench with a plaque like the ones in the country park? Then I'd have somewhere to go when I want to think about Josh. He didn't have a grave. Mum and Dad couldn't handle it. They just scattered his ashes in our garden when I was at school one day. I didn't find out until much later. And now we don't live there any more. I've always had a sense of abandoning my brother. But a bench... that'd feel so right.'

'It's a perfect idea. We can find out who made the ones round the lake and contact them. I've got a feeling someone said it was Ingrid's partner. I'll ring her in the morning.'

Nell reached out her arms to Barney and they clung together. Their faces were streaked with tears, but Nell felt lighter than she had for months. 'Yes, we've definitely got a big chance to make a go of being together for the rest of our lives, and it'll be a very good life, whatever it means to be happy,' she said. 'Not blissfully happy all the time, nobody ever is. It might be an elusive kind of feeling that comes and goes, at least for now, but I know it'd be easier for me to be contented and peaceful if you stayed with me until morning. We can be each other's happiness. You can always escape partway through the night if it's too much, but please don't keep leaving me when I'm just getting used to you being...'

Nell didn't get to finish her sentence because Barney's mouth was on hers, hot and passionate. That night he didn't head for his own room. In fact, truth be told, he never did again.

* * *

MORE FROM CELIA ANDERSON

Another book from Celia Anderson, *Dancing Under the Moon*, is available to order now here:

    https://mybook.to/DancingMoonBackAD

ACKNOWLEDGEMENTS

Here we are again in Willowbrook, still with some of the usual suspects, and I've just realised to my shame that I haven't thanked the wonderful couple who gave me the title for the Saga Louts' gang. Their names are Wendy and Denis Barratt and they have their own group of this name, who are all now of a certain age. They meet up as often as they can but don't get through the prosecco in the quantities that Beryl, Winnie and Anthea do. Or so they say...

I'm also very conscious how crucial my clerical character, Rev Bev is to this story. She definitely isn't modelled on anyone in particular but I have several vicar/minister friends who always give friendship and support when it's most needed, so a shout out to Rev Moira Biggins, Rev Liz Chamberlain, Rev Lynda Coates, Rev Fiona De Boltz and Rev Andrea Sims; all stars in their own right and great fun too!

Some of Living the Good Life was written in France, in one of my all-time favourite places, Chez Castillon, where the words flow like magic along with the wine, and the wonderful hosts, Janie and Mickey, make every day a new writing adventure. Fabulous food, great company and a venue like no other. My fellow author Anne Booth also helped a lot while I was here last time on a retreat. Now I'm back again being tutored by the wonderful Jo Thomas, and it's just as good as before.

Special thanks go to my very good friend Kay Holman, who

for this book has stepped up as chief advisor on how to get the best night's sleep ever. She used to concentrate on going for plot walks with me but even though we now live 200 miles apart, Kay still manages to be available for virtual support and ridiculously funny texting. Also big thanks to Liz, Sonja and Lynda, who, with Kay are shaping up well to be the next Saga Louts along with my cousin team, led by Rosemary. We will be formidable when we've finished our training! There are too many other friends to mention, but I'm sending love to you all, with thanks for all the cheery messages and helpful comments along the way. There will definitely be plenty of room on the bus for you too. We'll take some of Rosemary's cake and Kay's energy bar with us. What could possibly go wrong?

My wonderful agent Laura Macdougall always gets a huge thank you, as does my fabulous editor Francesca Best. (She really is. The best, I mean.) Francesca's sound structural edits are a joy to work with and she never fails to understand when the turbulence of real life gets in the way of the writing for a little while. Also sending thanks to the great team at Boldwood led so enthusiastically by Amanda Ridout. This includes copyeditor Cecily Blench, proofreader Candida Bradford and cover designer Rachel Lawson, all so very much appreciated.

Like Nell and Barney, I've been finding my way around an unfamiliar kind of life in a different place recently. I've discovered excellent places to eat, new friends, cocktail bars, the local theatre, many beautiful churches, a friendly yoga class, a brilliant choir and so much more but the love and support of my family here has been and continues to be my shining light. My playdoh/glue/glitter/paint/cheese string expenditure has risen considerably lately but there's nothing I'd rather be investing in, and the slightly older members of the family even provide delicious food parcels along with their hugs. As inspirations for writing, they are absolutely unmatched. Thank you so much, all of you. Here's to lots more books (and dinners. Let's not forget the dinners).

ABOUT THE AUTHOR

Celia Anderson is a top ten bestselling author of women's fiction. She writes uplifting golden years fiction for Boldwood.

Sign up to Celia Anderson's newsletter and get a FREE short story!

Follow Celia on social media:

f facebook.com/CeliaAndersonAuthor

◎ instagram.com/cejanderson

X x.com/CeliaAnderson1

g goodreads.com/CeliaAnderson

ALSO BY CELIA ANDERSON

Life Begins at 50!

A New Lease of Life

Dancing Under the Moon

Living the Good Life

BECOME A MEMBER OF

THE SHELF CARE CLUB

The home of Boldwood's book club reads.

Find uplifting reads, sunny escapes, cosy romances, family dramas and more!

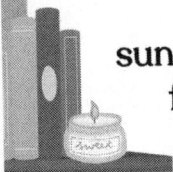

Sign up to the newsletter
https://bit.ly/theshelfcareclub

Boldw**oo**d

Printed in Dunstable, United Kingdom